Jackson
In the Kush

◇

by

Robert R. Peecher Jr.

Robert R. Peecher Jr. grew up in Watkinsville, Georgia, and graduated from Oconee County High School. He has spent his career working as a journalist at a number of different daily and weekly newspapers in Georgia. He is a graduate of Georgia College & State University. He is married and has three sons and lives with his family in Bishop, Georgia.

Jackson Speed In the Rush

For information the author may be contacted at

PO Box 967; Watkinsville GA; 30677

This is a work of historical fiction. While some characters represented in this book are actual people and some of the events represented took place, these are fictionalized accounts of those people and those events.

ISBN-13: 978-1546956785
ISBN-10: 1546956786

Copyright © 2017 Robert R. Peecher Jr.

ALL RIGHTS RESERVED

The Jackson Speed Memoirs

Volume VI

1847 - 1851

Edited & Arranged by

Robert R. Peecher Jr.

Dedication

Always, for Jean,
my first reader,
who cries at all the right spots.

EDITOR'S INTRODUCTION

The present volume of the Jackson Speed Memoirs begins where the first volume left off. Readers familiar with the timeline of Jackson Speed's life know that he left the Mexican-American War in the summer if 1847, determined to return to his new bride and life in Georgia. In this volume, Speed recounts the events that led to his finding gold in the California Gold Rush of 1849.

Readers of the Jackson Speed Memoirs will already know that Speed was among the fortunate few who actually struck it rich in the Gold Rush, but this volume is less about the Gold Rush and more about Speed's journey from Mexico to California. As was typically the case with Jackson Speed, it was a wayward journey that led him to a marriage in Indian Territory (present day Oklahoma) and an overland trip to California. Along the way, Speed encountered some of the most famous names of his day, including Stand Watie, Jesse Chisholm, the youngest son of the pioneer Daniel Boone, and William T. Sherman.

Though he is little more than a footnote in American history now, Speed was well known among his contemporaries, and he had a knack for being involved in some of the biggest historical moments of the 1800s. He fought for both the Union and the Confederacy in the Civil War. He likewise knew both Abraham Lincoln and Jefferson Davis, Ulysses S. Grant and Robert E. Lee, he acted as an agent for the Pinkerton Private Detective Agency and rode with the Regulators and the Texas Rangers.

Speed's memoirs, unpublished in his life, only came to light in 2011. As editor of The Jackson Speed Memoirs, I have sought to clarify the historical context of the memoirs through footnotes and provide the reader with some reference where necessary.

I am editing and published the memoirs in the order in which they are provided to me by Speed's descendants, and so the memoirs do not typically flow in a chronological order.

As editor, I make no judgement upon the man other than to note that his own written recollections tend to shatter the image of the man built during his life.

In his life, Speed was toasted by Theodore Roosevelt for bravery; honored by Robert E. Lee for "invaluable service" to the Confederacy; brevetted by Jefferson Davis with a battlefield promotion; and distinguished by Abraham Lincoln with the Medal of Honor for his exploits at the Battle of Gettysburg.

But his memoirs paint the picture of a scoundrel, a cowardly rascal whose only motivations were saving himself and bedding any woman who was so unfortunate as to catch his eye.

Nevertheless, it continues to be a pleasure to serve as the editor of Jackson Speed's Memoirs, and I remain grateful for the opportunity.

Robert Peecher
Editor

CHAPTER 1

Back in the '70s and '80s – even into the '90s – whenever I visited my California mines to see how much my foremen were stealing from me, the old miners still talked about Joaquin Murrieta. They employed his legend to scare small children and coerce pretty girls to sit up close to them in the wagons. I've even heard that there are writers penning poetry about him, and that Joaquin Murrieta has become a folk hero for some Californians.

Well, Yellowbird's mythology not withstanding, I can tell ye Joaquin Murrieta was full to the brim with evil, and I don't know what poor bastard donated his head to Harry Love's jar of alcohol, but it weren't the real Murrieta. Yellowbird, who was my cousin by marriage, never met the real Joaquin Murrieta. [1]

I've no doubt that a dozen or more banditos invoked the name of the hated Joaquin in the early days of the Gold Rush. Back in '49, miners all up and down the South Fork feared that name more than they feared any other thing, for Joaquin had made a general nuisance of hisself, causing all sorts of trouble and murder.

For a time, miners and shop keepers and virgin maidens – what few there were – were safe in their camps, shops and beds, for Joaquin Murrieta no longer marauded.

But in the early '50s he showed back up, holding up stores, killing miners, robbing Forty-Niners of the measly quantities of dust and the tiny nuggets they worked months to accumulate, and forcing himself upon helpless womenfolk. But that Joaquin – or, perhaps more appropriately, those Joaquins, were never the real one. Why, if the tales could be believed, Joaquin Murrieta was holding up a store in San Francisco in the morning and by midday he was up in the Sierra Nevada raiding mining camps, and by dark he was below Los Angeles raping ranchers' daughters. Not even Joaquin Murrieta was capable of such daily journeys, but a dozen or so banditos looking to hide their own identity and at the same time paralyze their victims with fear, well, they might be expected to steal the man's name in order to also borrow the man's legend.

But having known a fair few number of California banditos, maybe even some of whom took on the name Joaquin Murrieta, I can say with absolute certainty, when it came to pure cold-blooded evil, not a man among 'em could stand in the same company as the real Joaquin Murrieta. It's a fact that I've known murders who would cut your throat for no reason other than they had not yet killed a man all week and it was already Tuesday. I rode for a bit with Billy the Kid. I've been hunted by the entirety of the Third Corps of the Army of the Potomac, sent to do me in by none less than Devil Dan Sickles, but I've never known a man so filled with joy by doing evil as Joaquin Murrieta. If he knew that they'd made him a romantic robber, he'd cut off the fingers of the poor fools who penned such nonsense and laugh with glee as he force-fed those fingers to the poets. There can be no truth in these fables that Joaquin's bloodlust was the result of cruel treatment to him and the murder of the girl he loved, for Joaquin Murrieta was evil from the word go, and he never had it in him to love another thing. It weren't revenge the man sought, but only vicious murder.

No, by 1850, the real Joaquin Murrieta was in a river at the bottom of a canyon where I'd left him with three of the fingers of one of his henchmen, and good riddance to him and them.

Perhaps it was the only time in my entire life when danger bared its vicious fangs, and rather than flee or hide, I wheeled my horse and rode back into the thick of it. And I'll say this, too: – Of all the things I've done in my life, fair and foul, there's not much I'm more proud about in my old age than putting two balls of lead in that bastard's gut and one in his eye.

It's a good story, but to explain it fully, I have to start on a lonely river in what is now Oklahoma but was then Indian Territory. [2] I came to the Indian Territory in the early fall of 1847, having fled the war in Mexico. I was out of my way, taking the long way home to Georgia, because a strange wanderlust had erupted in me. But if I had returned home as I had initially planned, the course of my life would have been forever altered. And while I've had many an opportunity to regret my decisions, as I look back now on the totality of the thing, I can't say that I'm too sorry for the way it all went. The truth is, the wanderlust that set my compass north rather than east is what made me a rich man, so I'll be damned if it was all bad.

It's impossible to understand a young man's mind, even when once you were that young man, and so I'll make no effort to explain my meanderings. I left Mexico in the summer of '47, bent on never returning again to that hellish country nor to the horrors of war. Having come closer than I cared to being dragged to death by a couple of Mexican marauders and killed by a jealous husband, I was so adamantly opposed to violence that were it not for the threat of encountering banditos or Injuns or rattlers, I'd have probably abandoned my weaponry. As it was, fear of the many unknown and known perils that could menace a traveler kept me armed.

My first intention, upon leaving Mexico, was to travel back east to my home in Georgia, reunite with my lovely bride with whom I'd spent only a few months of wedded bliss, and then spend the remainder of my life enjoying the fruits of our marriage bed. I supposed that I would run her grandfather's dry goods store where Old Man Brooks had made a decent living. I knew at the store I could also make a decent go of it. And I suspect it would have been a decent enough life, and I might have avoided a fair bit of trouble along the way had I chosen that path, but that was some other man's life, not mine. I was bound for bigger adventures, whether I wanted them or not.

What led me to that lonely river in Indian Territory was a chance encounter a month before in the middle of Texas. I'd been in the saddle for a couple of weeks or more, riding up the Preston Trail from San

Antonio. I had with me my spotted mustang, Courage, who was the best damned horse to ever crisscross these United States, and a spare mount I never bothered to name. I alternated horses along my trip so that neither one would be over-burdened.

Along my journey, I came upon a little settlement at the ford of the Trinity River. You'll know the place, though today it's unrecognizable as the settlement I encountered in the summer of '47. It's called Dallas. [3]

In those days, Dallas was not much more than a few log cabin homes, a tavern and traveler's rest, a grist mill and a dry goods store built up around what started as just a trading post. It was an enterprising little settlement, though, and a smart man could have seen that it was going to grow through the industrious nature of its people. As I rode into the settlement, there were men in shirts and trousers sawing timber, and there were livestock roaming the hillsides, and other men out working fields. I even saw some men downstream surveying the river as if they were making plans to construct another mill.

It was late morning when my horses and I forded the Trinity River and sauntered into the settlement. A quick look about revealed to me the local tavern, and it was there that I led my horses. I tied them both to the post outside and walked across the little clapboard porch to enter the tavern.

The place was dark as night on the inside, with the only light coming from the open doorways and a couple of lanterns on tables. These early settlement cabins were all constructed for shelter, and not comfort, and there were no windows in them. I noticed on one of the tables an open Bible perched in the light cast from one of the open doors.

I've never been one to spend money on whores, as I've found their wares could often be obtained at a smaller price with a well-timed wink and perfectly placed pinch, but I was just a teenager back in '47, and the truth of it is that after days on the trail with only horses to keep me company, I was desperate for some comfort when I walked into that tavern. I'd have been willing to pay a fair price for it, too. But I sized up Dallas pretty quick as the sort of settlement where my tastes were unlikely to be satiated.

As I crossed the threshold, I was aware that I was alone in the tavern. Not only was there no bartender, but neither was there a bar. I stood for a minute wondering what I should do, when eventually a pretty young woman in a long skirt and bonnet came in through a back door.

"Oh!" she exclaimed. "You startled me!"

And no doubt that I did. I'd been on the trail for days, and I was covered in dust. I was wearing a pair of trousers and a blue shirt, a linen duster jacket and a wide brimmed straw hat – all clothes that had belonged to the late husband of the glorious Marcilina de la Garza, whose bosom I was sore missing now. But the clothes were filthy with dirt from the trail, I was unshaven – though that didn't mean much back in those days of my youth – and I'd not smelled soapy water in more than two weeks.

"Sorry 'bout that," I said. "I was just hoping to get some breakfast and a drink."

The woman stepped into the room a bit closer to me. "You traveling?" she asked.

"Yes ma'am. Come up from Mexico."

"Are you in the war?" she asked.

"I was. I was with the Mississippi Rifles for a bit, and then the Texas Rangers. But my enlistment has expired, and now I'm headin' home."

"Where's home?" she asked. I wasn't sure if she was being friendly or scouting me out to see if I was trouble, but I sure wanted her to get on with reading me the menu.

"Georgia," I said.

"So you're heading east?"

"I plan to. Been riding north, so far."

"What's your name?" she asked.

"Jackson Speed, ma'am," I said, and tipped my hat to her.

"Well, Mr. Speed, you're too late for breakfast and too early for supper. I might be able to cook you up some sausage and some biscuits, but you'll have to wait for it."

I gave her the Ol' Speedy grin that had won over my wife and Marcilina, both. "There gravy with them biscuits?" I asked her.

She must have decided I wasn't trouble, for she gave me back a pretty good grin of her own.

"I could mix you up some gravy, I suppose," she said.

"I'd be obliged," I said.

She fetched me a bottle of beer and then went out back to the cook house to make me up some breakfast, and with nothing else to do, I followed her. Outside, in the sunlight, she took a better look at me.

"Why, you're just a boy," she said. I've always been a big man, taller than most and a good bit stronger, too, and only seeing me with the sun at my back in that poorly lit tavern, she must have thought I was older. "It's hard to look at that face of yours and imagine that you've returned from a war at your age."

I rolled up my shirtsleeve and showed her the scar from where a Mexican bullet gouged me at Monterrey. "I got this to remember the war by," I said. I'll say this about war wounds – hard as they are to come by, I've always found them useful when wooing women. A scar from the war, and women will at once size you up as the brave sort who can care for and protect 'em and at the same time they'll have a mothering sympathy for you that leads them to want to hold and comfort ye. And at that point, they're as good as undressed.

6

I reckoned she was about thirty years old, maybe not that much, but she was a pretty enough woman with pink cheeks and long dark hair braided and tied in a knot under her bonnet.

She reached out and felt the scar on my arm, and her fingertips against my skin gave me chills. It had been too long since I'd left Marcilina.

"I didn't catch your name, ma'am," I said to the woman.

"I didn't tell you my name, Mr. Speed," she said, turning to her work at the stove.

Having just escaped the clutches of one cuckolded husband and not interested in having to flee the rage of another, I asked her the most pertinent question on my mind. "Do you and your husband own this tavern?"

With her back to me, she gave me a bit of a giggle, and I thought, "Speed, old son, this one's interested."

"I am not married, Mr. Speed."

"Well now, what's a pretty young woman like you doing unmarried in a hard worn town like this?" I asked her, and I took a step closer so that if the opportunity seemed appropriate I might give her backside a playful pinch.

"I'm not that pretty," she said.

Honestly, she was a bit homely, but not so much that she couldn't find a man, especially in a place like this where the men were likely too drunk to see straight most of the time and woman flesh was hard to come by. The homeliest woman in a little river town out on the frontier could still expect to have her pick of men.

"I moved here from Virginia with my family about three years ago," she said.

"It's not much of a place to move to," I said. "Just a few log cabins set in rows. Do ye like it here?"

She stood up and turned around and gave me a very sincere look. "It's not much, now, Mr. Speed, but one day this little settlement will be a bustling city and the pride of Texas. I have dreams of it."

I looked out across the settlement at the log cabins and the men working and the children going about in their bare feet, and I gave her enthusiasm a laugh. "Not likely," I said.

"Oh, Mr. Speed, you see what is, but I'm talking about what can be. What will be. One day."

She was as sincere as she could be, and I couldn't help but wonder if she wasn't a bit touched in the head and maybe that's why she was unmarried. But by then the sausage was starting to smell pretty decent, and what with my hunger and everything else, I wasn't much interested in whether or not the woman was dim-witted. Instead, I was interested in those comforts that had brought me here in the first place.

I was just about to reach out and take a fist full of what she was poking at me as she bent over the fire, but then I heard clanging spurs and the footfalls of heavy boots approaching from behind us, and I drew back my hand.

A man's voice from behind me said, "Food smells pretty good. You making that up for me?"

Now she laughed a pretty laugh, and without turning around she answered, "I'm making it up for Mr. Speed, here, but I can make enough for two if you're staying."

"Speed?" the man said, and the question in his voice made me turn around.

"By God! Jack Speed! Tarnation, son, what in God's green earth has brought you to Dallas?"

There before me was Alex Cockrell, with whom I'd served in the

Texas Rangers under Ben McCulloch. Like me, Alex had been a courier for McCulloch, and I'd ridden the Camargo Road with him more than a couple of times.

What I knew of him was that he'd lived among the Injuns for a bit and chased runaway slaves before becoming a Texas Ranger. I was fairly sure he'd been among the Texas Rangers that had scaled the cliffs leading up to the back side of Fort Libertad while I was with the Mississippi Rifles storming Fort Teneria. The Rangers called him Cherokee Cock because of his time living among the Indians. It had been so many months since I'd had any contact with the Rangers that I did not know that he was now out of the army. [4]

"Cherokee Cock," I said, grinning all over at seeing a familiar face after having been alone for so long, and Alex grabbed me by my paw and shook me like the devil – old friends from the war meeting in a frontier village, don't ye know.

"Sarah, darlin', this 'ere's young Jack Speed! He is the Hero of Fort Teneria! When General Taylor stormed Monterrey, it was Jack Speed who led the charge up and over the fortifications. You know, I told you about McCulloch riding through Santa Anna's camp at Encarnacion? Well, Speedy here was one of them Rangers who did it! What were there, Speed? Half a dozen of you that rode into Santa Anna's camp, Patersons blazing and Mexicans running scared?"

"Sixteen of us, Cock," I said. "There was sixteen. I remember clear as day that McCulloch told me he was only taking sixteen on the scout, and thinking to myself that surely he wouldn't pick me to be among 'em."

Cherokee Cock slapped me on the back and gave me a hearty laugh. "B'God I bet you're glad now that he picked you! In all the history of warfare, I can't imagine any more daring mission than you and Ben McCulloch riding hell for leather through Santa Anna's camp!"

Alex Cockrell was like pretty much every other man who rode with

McCulloch – a big, brawling son of a bitch who made me feel small even though in truth I was a hair taller and maybe even a bit bigger built than him. But those Texas Rangers carried themselves with large personalities that always made them seem bigger than they were.

Cockrell, still hanging onto my fist, must have decided a good shaking of the hands wasn't enough, because now he jerked me to him and picked me up in a great bear hug. "My goodness, Speedy, but I am glad to see you. Are you done with the fightin'?"

"I am," I told him. "I got dragged by a couple of rancheros and beat all to hell by an angry husband, and after getting back my strength I decided the only thing left for me was to go on back home."

"Dragged by rancheros?" Cockrell asked. "You're lucky to have survived it."

"Weren't much luck in it, Cock," I said. "A lovely little senorita I took up with saved me. Shot one them bastards dead and the other took off running."

I said it off handed, but there was a sob stuck in my throat as I thought of Marcilina de la Garza. I've known hundreds of women in my time, some for a night and some for a month and some for many, many years. Some flitted out of my life as quick as they came never to be heard from again, and others came and went, staying as long as they pleased or until I began to worry that Eliza might know what was what. And with only a few exceptions, I never gave a whit for any of them.

But Marcilina de la Garza was different. She was a beauty to top them all, dark and lovely, soft and light, and when she danced at a fandango, spinning and twirling in a dress full of color, she floated. My lord, as an old man sitting here today remembering that lovely Spanish woman, I am brought to tears.

Cherokee Cock seemed to guess that I was having some memories, so he gave me a moment. Then he said, "Who was that fella you rode with? Big Jim Willcox, right? Big Jim still Rangerin'?"

"Naw," I said. "Big Jim's done being a Texas Ranger." I shook my head and gave Cherokee Cock to understand that Jim was killed, and Cock did not mention him again.

War veteran though I was, I was not much more than a boy, really, and the pain of loss stung in a way then that it would not later. It's a fact of the war with Mexico that more United States soldiers died from disease than ever departed this earth from a Mexican bullet. If you had ten good pals in Mexico, you might expect to lose one or maybe two, and one or both of those most likely was killed by accident or disease. So even a veteran of that war was never too accustomed to loss. But look ahead a dozen years, and you find that in the War of Yankee Aggression, if you had ten pals, you needed to find yourself ten new ones pretty quick because seven or eight of the original ten would be dead and gone before Antietam was over, and the other two or three would be dead by Chickamauga. I learned as I got older to overcome the grief of loss pretty quick. It was an easy enough trick. Just imagine yourself in the place of the ones killed and maimed, and in a hurry you can quit your mourning over another man's misfortune. But in the summer of '47 those cuts were still raw, and it hurt in my heart to think of Big Jim Willcox and Marcilina de la Garza.

And, truth be told, it wasn't just the pain of loss. But thinking on Marcilina, I was quick to remember that I'd not been belly-to-belly with a woman since leaving Marcilina's hacienda, and my trousers were starting to get damned uncomfortable.

Cock was a good ten years or more older than me, and I suppose like the rest of those Texas Rangers, he looked on me with the kindness an older brother has for a younger brother, and I think he read in my face that we'd ventured into a territory where I didn't care to tread. He cast about for some change in the topic of conversation.

"Now as I came into the cookhouse here, it looked to me like you were poised to molest this fair peach," Cherokee Cock said. "Is that a fact?"

Sarah, as he called her, turned a bright red and Cherokee had a good laugh, and I folded my hands behind my back. "Not sure what you're talking about, there, Cock. I was just brushing away a fly."

Cock laughed and slapped his thigh. "Speedy, son, lemme introduce to you Sarah Horton, soon to be Sarah Cockrell. She'll appreciate it if you'll keep you paws off her backside."

Sarah, who was stirring sawmill gravy in a heavy skillet, gave me a little nod. "I will assume that Mr. Speed is forgiving of your sense of humor, Alexander, and I'll not apologize on your behalf."

"Darling, me and Speed have told a thousand jokes to each other up and down the Camargo Road. I don't suspect I'll say much today that'll need apologizing for. So, Speedy, tell us now, what's what that you're riding through this little town of ours?"

There were some rough cut tables and benches out back by the cook house, which was really just a pavilion with a big adobe brick oven built on one end. While we waited for the biscuits to be ready, Cock and I had a seat at one of those tables, and I gave him some version of how I found myself to be in the middle of Texas.

I told him that my intention was to head east to return to Georgia, but that I was feeling compelled to ride around a bit. I confessed to him that I wasn't too sure what I was looking for or where I thought I would find it.

"Feeling a little lost after the war?" he asked me.

"A bit, maybe," I said.

"I can understand that, Speedy. When I came home, I found that driving cattle was about the only thing I could take any pleasure in. I needed some time under a starry sky to get my head right again. I imagine you're feeling a little bit the same."

"A bit, maybe," I said.

Cock leaned toward me from across the table, and he became very serious.

"You should ride north into Indian Territory," he said. "Go and live among the Cherokee for a while. Maybe spend the winter with them. Go and find John Ross. He was like a father to me when no one else was, and he taught me things that are worth knowing. The Cherokee have one foot in the white man's world and one foot in the Indian world, and they have a way of helping you to cleanse your mind. Go and tell John Ross that you have been sent to him by Alexander Cockrell. He will know how to help you."

"Hell, Cock," I said. "I just want to get home. I've got a wife back in Georgia whom I've not seen in more than a year. I'm just a bit homesick."

Cock shrugged and leaned back away from the table. "You must follow your own path, Speedy, and I won't blame you none for going the way you think is best for you. But you've got a lost spirit, and the Cherokee people can help you find your spirit again."

Sarah Horton now brought us a couple of plates loaded with sausage and biscuits drowning in gravy, and I can tell you my spirit was immediately lifted as she set one of those plates down in front of me and the other in front of her betrothed.

I ate heartily.

I spent a few days there with Cherokee Cock. Cockrell had a tent south of town where he was living, and Sarah was living with her family in town. But Cock and I went into town every day where I joined him in his work splitting logs. I even spent a couple of days working for the town's blacksmith. My uncle, the one who raised me in Scull Shoals, had been the town's smithy, and he'd taught me a fair amount about his craft. In that way, I was able to earn a little money and make myself useful while I imposed on Cockrell's hospitality.

He tried to convince me to stay through the wedding in September,

13

but I decided that no matter where my travels were going to take me, I needed to get on with the traveling and not be caught when winter came. Cockrell worked on me the whole time I was there, though, encouraging me to go and find his friend John Ross in Indian Territory.

When I finally decided to leave, Cock saw me to the edge of the town.

"Follow the Preston Trail north," he told me. "When you get to the Red River, you can turn east and follow the Red River all the way to the Mississippi River. You'll be able to cross the Mississippi at Fort Adams. From there go north a bit to Natchez, and you can pick up a trail that will take you straight to the Old Federal Road. The Federal Road will take you on home to Georgia.

"Or, when you get to the Red River, keep going north. You'll get into Indian Territory there. Head northeast toward Missouri, and when you reach the Spavinaw Creek you'll be able to find people who will get you to John Ross."

After days of listening to Cockrell tell me how necessary it was for me to go and visit his Cherokee friends, I was starting to believe him. Cherokee Cock talked to me of feeling a peace in my soul and a fullness in my heart, and at that time, these things he spoke about appealed to me. But I was hesitant on one account.

"The Indian Territory," I said. "For a man traveling alone, how dangerous will it be?"

Alexander Cockrell laughed at that and slapped Courage's hindquarter. The horse started, and we were again headed up the Preston Trail.

"It won't be nothing an old Texas Ranger can't handle, Speedy!" Cockrell called after me. "Good fortune to you, son! I hope we'll see each other again one day!"

Well, that was the last I'd see of Alexander Cherokee Cockrell.

Rather than pay him the $200 he owed, a city marshal decided it would be less expensive to shoot old Cherokee Cock in the back. But I would make my way to Dallas again, and see that his widow's dreams of a bustling city had all come true, largely through her own doing. And in those days still to come, Sarah Cockrell would remember me and offer me shelter in a hellacious storm, God bless her. [5]

CHAPTER 2

By mid-September, with cooler weather settling in, I found myself well north of the Red River, up on the banks of the Spavinaw Creek, in search of John Ross.

A more pastoral and pleasant location than the Spavinaw Creek I cannot imagine. The Spavinaw is a wide but fairly shallow creek of water so clear you can see down to the rocky bottom. While I was spending time on the banks of the Spavinaw, we did not lack for rain, and it was a quick running body of water. If ye've seen pictures or heard stories and imagine Oklahoma as a dry and dusty flatland with outcroppings of rock or wide open prairies where an eye can see for a thousand miles, ye'd have it about right. But that was out in west Oklahoma, where cavalrymen met their death from lack of water. But east of the Arkansas River, over close to the Ozarks and Arkansas and Missouri, the Indian Territory was a rich land with rolling hills and freshwater and a canopy of hardwoods, and in September of '47 it had erupted into a glorious canvas of autumn golds and oranges and browns and greens.

The Cherokee settled here from their homes in northern Georgia, and for the life of me I could not think that they would know the difference from one place to the next. Cherokee lands in Indian Territory felt like home to me, they so resembled the places I'd known growing up.

When I came upon the Spavinaw, I was not even sure it was the right creek. Since stopping at a trading post along the trail, I'd not seen another human being for three days. But the creek was running pretty fast and the water was clear, and so I left the trail and looked for a spot where I could walk the horses down to water them and fill my canteen without having to trod too much through the cold water.

The muddy banks were spotted with large boulders, but I eventually found a spot where a sandbar took me down to the water, and I hopped off the back of my spare mount and walked both horses down to get a drink.

It was peaceful as could be up in those hills, with only the wind rustling the leaves and the running water to keep me company, and I felt that I was beginning to understand what Alexander Cockrell had in mind in sending me here. Solitude and natural beauty have a way of putting a man's mind at rest, and as I drank the cool water from my canteen I was beginning to feel refreshed. It came as a surprise to me when I realized that the terrors of war were not so stark in my mind's eye. For months, visions of dead and dying men suffering from horrific wounds – made more horrific by my imagination – had haunted me. Every time I closed my eyes or my mind stopped thinking, I was bedeviled by a flash of a lasso coming round me and pinning my arms to my body, the violent jerk as I was sent flying through the air and then dragged across the terrain. Or I would think on that awful moment when I saw my pal Big Jim Willcox shot from his saddle by that vile bastard Uriah Franks. Or I saw that big Bowie knife plunging into the backs of fleeing Mexican soldiers at Fort Teneria, and with horror I would realize the hand wielding that knife was mine own.

It was all a ghastly business, haunting my mind day and night, and to rid myself of those visions I would force myself to think of Marcilina and those dark nipples sitting atop those round teats, or I would cast my memory back to the softness of the insides of Eliza's thighs, how smooth her white skin was in that place. I would think of the taste of her, and how her ribs felt under my fingers as I pulled her body to me. And my mind would be clear, for a while, of those terrible visions.

If I'd had any idea what was to come, I'd have embraced the horrors of war in Mexico and kept them with me as a good friend, for Mexico was nothing compared to what I would later encounter in Virginia, Tennessee, Pennsylvania and Georgia. But for a teenager who wanted no part in any of it anyhow, Mexico was bad enough.

But now, after all these days of riding in loneliness and talking only to my horses, I found myself perched over this idyllic stream of cool, clean water and there were no visions of death and destruction. When I thought of Big Jim, I only saw his bearded face guffawing at some dumb joke.

I wondered if this was why Cherokee Cock sent me here.

I dipped my canteen down into the water one more time to fill it, and as I rose to get back on my way, downstream a ways I caught sight of a man standing knee-deep in the river, casting a line from his pole. He had his back to me, and so he did not see me.

I'll tell you, along my ride through Indian Territory, I was wary of strangers. I'd encountered no problems, but I'd grown up with stories of Injuns taking scalps, and I was intent on keeping my hair. I didn't know it then, because I was unfamiliar with the tribes and their locations, but I'd ridden up through Choctaw territory and into Cherokee territory, and those tribes were both mostly friendly to strangers. I'd had nothing to fear, whether I realized it or not.

Now, I watched the man for a bit. His pants legs were rolled up above his knees to keep them dry. He was wearing a small, straw basket strapped over his shoulder and hanging down at his thigh. He was wearing sleeves and his britches were held up by suspenders, and he had a neat little felt hat perched atop his head. He had a mane of flowing black hair down to his shoulders. He was short, but powerfully built, and from a distance he looked to be middle-aged.

Though my horses were both stepping around and neighing, he never appeared to hear us. I assumed the sound of the river coming past him must have drowned out the noise the horses were making. He seemed intent upon his fishing.

I watched as he hooked a fish, and there was animated joy as he brought the thing in. He took it off his hook, examined it and spiked its brain. He then dropped the fish into his straw basket.

The man's demeanor out in the middle of the river in no way gave me to worry about my safety, so I decided that I would take the horses back up onto the bank and go along the bank in his direction and hope to talk with him and find out where I was. I thought perhaps he could even point me in the direction of Cherokee Cock's friend John Ross. So I led the two horses up into the woods and started to follow the contour of the river, but I'd not gone far when I could see that on the trail ahead there were three horses, all saddled and hitched to trees.

I don't know what compelled me to investigate farther. A smart man would have turned around then. I'd seen one man, but I now saw three horses. It all looked wrong, and the old fears should have warned me not to proceed. Whatever was happening was none of my business.

But like a damned fool, I lashed my horses to a tree, drew out one of my Patersons, and began walking quietly along the trail.

When I came to a break in the trees, I could see downstream that the fisherman was still at his work, his back turned from the bank where I was. So, too, could I see that there were three men, all younger, sneaking up on the fisherman. One of the three had a long rifle in his hand, and it was evident to me that these men intended murder.

My natural cowardice prevents me from getting involved in such things. None of this was my business. I did not know the assassins nor their victim, and I did not care who was right or wrong. The best thing for me to do would have been to turn and flee before the killing started. But I lingered, maybe to see what would happen. Intervening was certainly not in my mind.

But paying too much attention to the action in front of me, and not looking at where my feet were, I stepped too far, lost my footing and tumbled head over ass down the embankment and came to rest half in the water and half on a sandbar. Pure instinct had made me keep the hand holding the Paterson in the air to keep it dry.

I came down with such commotion that the assassin Injuns on the bank all jumped and looked at me. The Injun fishing in the river, too, heard me and turned around. He quickly ascertained what was happening. Faster than you would think a man his age could move, the Indian in the water splashed across toward the opposite bank.

The assassin with the rifle tried to salvage their mission, getting off a single shot at the fisherman. The other two decided that I was a problem and they drew their knives and started splashing through the creek to come deal with me.

Well, b'God, I didn't survive Mexico to be stabbed to death by a couple of Injuns.

I stood up big and straight and fired off a ball from the Paterson that smacked one of them in the chest and dropped him dead, right there in the Spavinaw. I cocked the big revolver and the cylinder moved to the next chamber. The second Indian coming at me, he quickened his step, but he was coming through the water and he couldn't move fast enough to beat the cylinder. I could see in his face he was trying to decide if he should turn and flee or keep on coming, and I gave him that moment to decide. But the poor bastard was caught out – too close to get away and too far to get at me. So he kept coming, and I shot him, too.

The third man was still standing on the sandbar, and he was loading his rifle to get off another shot, and I presumed this one would be aimed at me. I cocked the Paterson and started walking toward him through the shallow water. The bottom was rocky as hell and it was hard to keep my balance, but I walked deliberately, watching him try to hurry to get the powder and ball down the barrel. I wanted to get close so that there would be no chance of missing him. I had plenty of time, high stepping through the creek, and when I was within ten yards of him, the Indian threw the rifle into the sand and reached for the knife on his belt.

I let loose one more time with the Paterson, and the big ball smashed into the man's chest, lifting him off the ground and depositing him on the sandbar where he choked a few times and then passed on. I've always been a decent shot with pistol and rifle, and my aim was made all the truer if I found myself in mortal danger. Even so, it wasn't a bad bit of gun work. I've never enjoyed killing a man – well, not many times – but I've found over the years that it never troubled my conscience much if the choice was between me or t'other. A man coming at me with a Bowie knife in his fist can expect to be shot dead if I can get at a pistol. I'll credit my time with the Texas Rangers in Mexico for making me good with a revolver, for in the times when we were not actively engaged in one duty or another, we sent a fair few balls down range simply for sport. A man couldn't last long among them Texians if he lacked the ability to shoot a bottle at twenty yards.

"Marvelous!" some man called from across the river. "That was some spectacular shooting, my friend!"

I looked to see that the fisherman was now back in the river, a great big grin spread across his Injun face and his arms raised in congratulations for my work. I was shaking like a bastard, and it wasn't because my clothes were soaked through with freezing cold water.

He marched across the river, going in up to his waist to get across to me, and his rolled up pants were soaked through by the time he reached me.

I kept my Paterson in my fist. But he was grinning like a daft fool, and I could see he didn't mean me any harm.

"You have a strange style of ambush, friend – coming through the limbs and leaves and landing on your back in the water – but it is very effective, and I am most impressed."

"I weren't trying to ambush nobody," I said.

"Do I know you?" he asked me, looking quizzically into my face.

"You do not," I said.

"So then what is the name of this stranger whom God has sent to

21

spare me from assassins?"

Having just killed three men in Indian Territory, and not really sure how much trouble I might be facing, I decided to give 'im my official credentials. "My name's Lieutenant Jackson Speed of the United States Army. I served under Colonel Davis in the Mississippi Rifles and under Ol' Ben McCulloch of the Texas Rangers."

The Indian laughed at me. "You are in Indian Territory here, friend. You may not want to announce that you are with the United States Army. A fair few men along the Spavinaw Creek would gladly cut your throat for the company you keep."

I swallowed hard and looked over my shoulder, but we appeared to be alone in the river. I was worried that where there were three assassins there could be more and they might have heard the reports from the Paterson and be on their way to investigate.

"Jackson Speed, it is a sad day when a man cannot fish walleye from a stream without fearing attack," he said wistfully. "I am grateful that you came to my aid. I am only armed with a knife, and surely these men would have killed me if you had not ambushed them."

He looked around the river.

"I have lost my pole and my basket and my supper, but I have been spared my life through the grace of God and the kindness of Jackson Speed of Georgia. I would say that I have come out better than I might have hoped for. I am a blessed man this day."

"How do you know I'm from Georgia?" I asked.

He smiled and clapped me on the shoulder. "Because I, too, am from Georgia, and I recognize you by the way you talk. I am Degataga Uwatie of the Cherokee Nation. Standhope Watie. My friends, of whom you are now one, call me by Stand Watie." [6]

"Did you say this is the Spavinaw?" I asked.

"I did say that," he responded.

"I'm looking for a man here on the Spavinaw. A friend of mine sent me here to meet him. His name is John Ross."

Stand's smile fell from his face and he shook his head sadly. "I am sorry to say, but I do not think that John Ross will want to see you, at least not on friendly terms."

Watie pointed to one of the dead Indians in the river, who had floated down river some and gotten hung up on a deadfall.

"That is John Ross's kinsman. If you are seeking John Ross, you would have been better to let these men kill me. Though they quite probably would have killed you, too, as a witness to the affair. No, I am afraid that you are now as much an enemy of John Ross as I am." And then he put the smile back on his face and his tone changed completely. "No, Jackson Speed, you do not want to find John Ross now. But come with me back to my home. You are soaking wet and shivering fiercely, and you need a fire and dry clothes. We'll see if my wife Sallie cannot also scare you up some warm supper."

I was transfixed to the spot, as if the cold water had frozen me. I was stunned, I suppose, having just been reflecting on the wonders of peaceful living and then suddenly and unexpectedly encountering violence. It wasn't that I had any qualms about shooting them Injuns. Instead, what worried me was that I might have just thrust myself into the middle of some trouble I did not want to be in. As you'll see, my concerns were not misplaced. Stand Watie was encouraging me to follow him across the river by tugging at my sleeve. "Come along," he said. "We should not linger in this place."

"My horses," I said. "I have horses in the woods here." I pointed back over my shoulder with the Paterson.

"Then we will ride," Stand said, and he scurried up the bank from which I and the assassins had come. I holstered the Paterson and I followed him up the side of the bank.

In the woods, Stand Watie spotted the horses that belonged to his assailants. "We shall take these," he said. He mounted one of the horses and took the leads of the others.

I was not sure that I wanted to tag along with this Injun, but I was certain sure I didn't want to hang around with the corpses of the three I'd just done in. I was too afraid that their friends might come looking for them. So I got on Courage's back, took my spare mount's lead, and I followed Standhope Watie. We rode first to a river crossing where we forded the Spavinaw River, and then we followed a creek I learned later was Brush Creek north a few miles before we came to Watie's home.

I suppose what I expected to find was a log cabin similar to those I'd seen in Dallas and other little settlements along the trail, but I was shocked when I first came upon Stand Watie's home not far from the Spavinaw. It rivaled the estates of some of the planters in Georgia, and Stand Watie even had negro slaves working his livestock, which consisted mostly of cattle but also pigs and chickens.

It was a big house painted white with four brick chimneys and a second floor balcony looking out over the grounds and a grand entrance with a pebble walkway leading up to it. There were fences for keeping the livestock on the estate, and barns and outbuildings of all manner, even a rock building built over a small stream used to store food and keep it cool. The smokehouse was as large as a home. There were pretty trees dotting the pasture, and I had a hard time reconciling this grand estate to the Injun with his rolled-up pants legs standing in the middle of the river.

"This is your place?" I asked him.

"It is," Stand said. "I moved to the Territory more than a decade ago, before the enforced movement, and I settled along the creek with the Old Settlers. I've built up a pretty nice homestead, don't you think? I like it."

"Pretty nice" was putting it mildly. I'd been to the cotton plantation

Eliza's father owned, and I can tell you that other than a few more acres of cleared land and a few more slaves, the Brooks' place weren't a bit better than Stand's spread. Other than his skin, he in every way resembled the wealthiest of cotton men in Georgia.

The Yankees burned it, ye'll know, but in its day, before the war, Stand Watie's home place was just about as fine as you could find west of the Mississippi. And because it was so similar in construction and in every other way to the plantations I knew back home, it only reinforced my sense that Oklahoma was quite a bit like Georgia. And in that way, too, it made me start to feel a bit homesick.

Stand Watie's place wasn't alone, either. I'll get to it later, but I came to live with the Cherokee for a number of months, and I can tell ye that many of them Injuns in the Cherokee Nation were living as well as he was.

A couple of negro servants met us on that pebble pathway leading up to the grand entrance of the house and took the horses from us, leading them out to a stable. Stand told the slaves to wash my mounts, clean and oil the saddles and hide the other three horses.

"It will not be much to rebrand those horses and sell them in Fort Smith," Stand Watie told me.

The house had large windows in the front and back, and even though the weather was cooling, all the windows and the doors stood open on the house. At the end of a hot summer, I always liked to allow the first few days of chilly weather to sweep in and cool things off in the house, myself. Or I did at that time when I was younger. Anymore, I find I like to have a blanket for my knees even in July.

"I would like to show you around my farm, here. You being from Georgia, you will appreciate how I have built up my property here. But before we do that, we need to get you dry and warm."

"Look here," I said as the negro walked off with my horses, "I appreciate your hospitality, Mr. Watie, I sure do. But I just put three men in the grave, and I think I'd better be on my way afore the law or their kinsmen start looking for me. I'd take some dry clothes, if ye can spare 'em, and I'd be grateful for a decent meal, but I really do think I should be on my way as quick as can be."

Old Stand Watie just laughed at my speech, and he clapped me on the shoulder like we were good chums. "Young man, I am the law in these hills and valleys, and you'll have nothing to fear from the kinsmen of those men you have killed."

Well, it turned out that that was not entirely true.

"I can vouchsafe for your safety as long as you are with me and my people. Do not concern yourself with fear of the law or revenge, for these things will not touch you."

Oh, aye, fine for him to say, but within that very hour, hadn't I nearly witnessed the Watie being shot by assassins?

Stand Watie led me up into his home, and he'd not skimped on the inside, either. The entry opened on a wide hall lined with portraits of Injuns dressed like white men and pretty furniture. There was a sitting room, a dining room and a women's parlor on one side of the hallway, and on the other side Stand Watie had a pretty decent library, considering that we were in Indian Territory where, at the time, I'd have not expected to find a single book, much less an entire library.

My preconceptions were colored by my upbringing. The Indians I knew down along the banks of the Oconee at Scull Shoals were mostly a rough bunch of wildmen who lived in the woods and still hunted with Osage bows. When Stand Watie moved to Oklahoma, I was just five years old, and when John Ross and the rest were forcibly removed, I was just eight years old. I'd not seen nor heard of Indians living like white men. Growing up, all I ever heard about Indians was that in the old days they'd been dangerous as hell and now they were being obstinate about moving out of North Georgia so that civilized men could get at the gold in the streams.

26

That was most of what I knew about the red man, other than the traders who sometimes came into the village and the couple who lived in Scull Shoals and worked at the mill, but they were half-breeds and were expected to act like white men if they were going to live among us.

So my introduction to Indian life was a surprise to me because it was so much like regular life. But this was Cherokee Nation, and they were one of the civilized tribes. In later years, I spent time among the Apache and the Comanche out on the plains, and I'll suffice to say they lived in quite a different style from the Cherokee.

Behind Stand Watie's house was a large, single story building that I thought at first served as a servants' quarters, but I learned it was a spare house built for the numerous visitors who came to see Watie and also for the many nieces and nephews and cousins who resided with him for long stretches. He was an important chief among his people even back then, and as such, he often had guests and kin who would live with him for months at a time. The feud that erupted between Watie's family and John Ross had taken Watie's father, uncle, brother and cousin, along with others from his family, and so he had a lot of orphans in his family who came to him to live for years.

A whole crew of his house slaves now led me back to this addition to the house. A couple of them were toting buckets of warm water that they poured into a tub, and another one had towels and a razor and another had a stack of clothes. An older man who walked with a limp, he must have been the head house slave, for he now gave me my orders.

"Mars Stand says fer you to get warshed up and put on these here clothes and get yoursel' warmed up," the servant told me, handing me a stack of clothes. "Says these ain't gone be long enough fer ya, but they'll do fer now. You leave them dirty clothes in that basket on the floor, and we'll come git yer things and git 'em all warshed fer ye."

I soaked myself in the bath tub and got cleaned up pretty well. The clothes were decent enough, though the britches were too wide in the waist and too short at the ankle, and the coat was a bit short, but it was nice to put on clean clothes after so much time on the trail.

When I came out of the guest house, there was a good bit of activity across a garden over at the cookhouse. Slave women were bustling about, I suppose preparing supper, and I couldn't help but cast an appraising eye over them. It had been a while since I'd seen a proper woman, and being cleaned up and shaved, I was wondering if there might be a slave girl I'd like to meet at my room later in the evening. But as I cast my eyes about, I spotted Sallie Watie, and I immediately picked her out as Stand's wife because of the way she was directing the slave women about the cookhouse. She was a squat and plump Indian woman, and older by far than anything I cared for. But as I watched the goings on, my eyes landed on an Indian girl who was standing nearby.

She was roughly my own age, and I was struck immediately by her beauty. She wore her coal-black hair parted in the middle with two long braids on either side, and though she wore a dark cotton skirt, her top was deer skin with a painted zig-zag design. She wore a beaded necklace around her neck. Her skin was a soft brown color and flawless. Her lips were full and her eyes were darker than her hair, like the openings of two frightening black caves that might hold within them treasures or horrors. Her face was impassive, and I caught myself saying out loud the only word that came to my mind, "Magnificent."

I found myself standing too long staring across the garden at her. She looked up and saw me watching her. She stared back at me, her face expressionless, so that I felt compelled to look away. There was strength in her savage beauty, and I was immediately infatuated. It didn't hurt, neither, that I'd not had my hands on a woman in several months.

Presently, Stand Watie found me on the back patio and led me off on a tour of the grounds.

He was proud of his place, and I couldn't blame him for being so.

The carriage house and barn were each larger than my little cottage back in Milledgeville. There was a store house built over the Brush Creek running through the property, and that was intended to keep the perishables cool. He had a smokehouse full of meat and a smithy with a cold fire. The grounds were kept pretty neat, too, with rose bushes lining the pebble driveway and shrubs and an apple orchard planted in the front of the house. I marveled to see such a place out here in Indian Territory. I will note that John Ross – the man Cherokee Cock had sent me to find and Watie's nemesis – lived in even grander style.

Watie's fields were planted with corn and potatoes and wheat and whatever else. He had constructed his own mill on the place, and I understood that some of the other local farmers used his mill. He had a large amount of livestock, as well, and it was clear to me as he showed me around the place that Stand Watie was well pleased with what he had built. Stand's son, Saladin, was about two years old at the time, but he could always be found walking in his father's shadow. And so it was that he tagged along with us during the grand tour.

I suppose Watie had more than forty slaves working the place, and he remarked to me that the slave who had worked as his blacksmith had run off north just a week before.

When I first rode up to Watie's place with him, I was intending on making it a short visit. I was concerned about the repercussions of having committed murder. I was disappointed that my peaceful reverie had been interrupted by unwelcome violence, and I was also disappointed that somehow I had come to the Spavinaw River in search of John Ross and blundered my way into killing his kinsmen.

But I also knew that winter was coming on. If I'd needed reminding, the chilly river and the cool breeze in the afternoon were plenty to put the coming winter back on my mind.

"I'm pretty handy as a blacksmith," I told Watie as he lamented his runaway slave. "I'll not work for slave wages, but for a fair wage and a room to sleep in, I might be convinced of staying on through the winter.

At least 'til you can get your slave back."

Standhope Watie was known to be a brave man, but it's a fact that his bravery was matched by his generosity. He clapped me and hugged me and shook my fist, grinning like a red devil, and told me, "Jackson Speed, you are welcome in my home as long as you could possibly wish to stay here! Because of you, I am today again saved from assassins, and you are now my brother!"

"Eh?" I asked him. "Did you say, 'again'? How many times have you been saved from assassins?"

"Today marks the third time that John Ross has failed to kill Stand Watie," he said with a grin.

"Oh, aye, ye've had assassins come after you twice before, eh?" I didn't give it more than a moment's consideration. "Maybe I'll just have supper and be on my way."

CHAPTER 3

The men and women all ate supper together at an enormous oak table.

"This table was made by my father's father when my people were in the mountains," Stand Watie told me. "My father brought it with him to Echota in Georgia when he moved to the territory there, and I brought it with me to this place. Where will my son be when he eats from this table?" I would learn that this was the sort of nonsense Indians were given to spouting all the time.

There were so many of us gathering for supper that the slaves brought in extra chairs and the place settings were nearly on top of each other. In addition to Stand and his wife Sallie, the toddler Saladin ate at the table, a cousin of some sort named Timothy, another cousin named Frank and Frank's wife, a couple of other men who I do not remember, and one of them had a wife with him, too. Watie's nephew John Rollin Ridge sat next to me. John Rollin Ridge was a year or two older than me, and was then newly married to Elizabeth. They all called him John Rollin, but he introduced hisself to me as Yellowbird, and I've always thought of him as such ever since.

Yellowbird was fascinated by his race and proud of his heritage, and so he adopted his Cherokee name even though most all of the Cherokee around him used Christian names. As he got older, Yellowbird eventually accepted that everyone wanted to call him John Rollin, but you'll note that when they put a name on his book about Joaquin Murrieta, Yellowbird was the name he gave 'em.

I liked Yellowbird pretty well. He had a mischievous streak, and though older than me and married, he was more a boy than I was, what with me being a veteran and having killed men in battle. In the coming weeks Yellowbird and I would form a pretty decent friendship.

Across the table from me, though, seated next to Yellowbird's wife, was the individual in whom I was most interested. She was the lovely girl I'd seen in the cookhouse earlier in the day. Stand told me her name was Mary, but the girl corrected him. "My Christian name is Mary, but I choose to be called by my Cherokee name of Weenonaw."

"That there's a beautiful name," I told her. "Wee-no-naw," I said, drawing out the syllables. "I like that pretty well."

It did not matter none to me what she wanted to be called – I was captured by this native woman's stunning beauty. I'll admit it, I was smitten from the moment I'd seen her at the cookhouse, and it was my good fortune that Stand Watie had seen fit to place her across the table from me at supper.

Yellowbird had no lack of interest in the war, and asked me all sorts of questions about what it was like fighting in Mexico. So prompted by his questions, I started to relate to them some of my more exciting experiences from Mexico. It was my first real experience of being back among civilized society – if you can call Indian Territory civilized, and I suppose you can since they lived just like proper white folks and even had negro slaves waiting on them. It was here, sitting at Stand Watie's table, that I first realized I had an ability to spin a yarn and keep 'em interested. I was still young and a bit raw with my storytelling talents, and I would get better as the years came on and I had more stories to tell, but even then I told a pretty good tale in a dramatic fashion, and I kept them Injuns on the edge of their seats.

More importantly, it was the first time I realized that war stories could be employed to great effect in wooing women. I held back the gruesome details, but Weenonaw was the most attentive member of my audience, gasping and exclaiming at all the good parts. I realized it didn't take much to cast myself as a hero and get those dark eyes to light on me full of lust. With a bath and some clean clothes on me and a plate of decent food on the table in front of me, I found myself feeling more like myself than I had in some time, and so lust was just exactly what I wanted to find in those dark eyes.

I first told Yellowbird about storming the works at Fort Teneria, and I didn't make much of it. But that's when I realized Weenonaw was paying close attention, and then I saw that Standhope Watie hisself had stopped his conversation and was now part of my audience, and by the time I got to the part about Jeff Davis and me chopping our way through the walls and rooftops of them Monterrey homes, everyone at the table was engrossed in my war stories.

"After I left the Mississippi Rifles in Monterrey, I joined up with the Texas Rangers," I said. "Riding with them Rangers was a bit more like what you folks would be familiar with, what with your braves and all. The Rangers didn't have much of what you might call 'army discipline.' It was mostly just a big hunt, just a ride through them Mexican mountains, only difference from a hunt bein' that periodically we'd come up in front of some Mexican soldiers who wanted to shoot at us."

Stand Watie got a big kick out of that, slapping his knee and laughing, and his reaction only encouraged me in my storytelling.

"So one day, General Taylor, he comes to me and Ben McCulloch – Ben bein' the war chief for the Rangers – and he tells us that he's worried about Mexicans down south at this place called Encarnacion."

Stand Watie interrupted me here. "General Taylor addressed you directly?" Watie asked, in awe of my recent stature in the United States army. "You're just a boy!"

Well, General Taylor never did address me, but there was no sense in telling these Injuns the strict truth, was there? Weren't they more interested in hearing a few embellishments so as to believe their dinner guest was a man of some importance?

"Oh, sure," I said. "Them Rangers didn't worry with rank and seniority and other things. We pretty much addressed each other common, and so whenever the general came into our camp he talked to whomsoever among us was available.

"So, General Taylor, he's worried about them Mexicans down at this place called Encarnacion, and he wants the Rangers to scout down there and see what's what. Ben didn't want to take a big group, so he picked just a dozen or so of us to ride down there, and on an important scout like that, he of course wanted me along."

I could tell it brave now that it was all behind me, but there'd been no courage in me at the time.

"We rode all through the day and late into the night, and we stayed on the road since none of us really knew where to find this hacienda we was hunting. With the chaparral on either side of us and only the moonlight showing us the way, we spotted something on the road ahead of us – someone in our group whispered it was a fence. But it weren't no fence."

I paused for dramatic effect, leaving them waiting to find out what it was that had been mistook for a fence. It was all great entertainment for these Injuns, and they repaid me by holding their breath while I looked around the table at them.

"Blam!" I shouted slapping my hands on the table, and all them Cherokees jumped. Weenonaw's eyes went wide with excitement.

"It was a row of mounted Mexicans, and they let loose with their muskets, firing a volley right into us!"

"What did you do?" Yellowbird asked, his hands cupped at his mouth and a look of genuine worry across his face.

"Well, Ben McCulloch ain't never been shot at that he didn't know how to respond," I told them. "'Charge!' Ol' Ben yelled, and we Texas Rangers drew our pistols and rode right into that band of Mexican cavalry. We shot them bastards up pretty good at close quarters. They didn't have time to reload their muskets, and our Patersons were making a bloody mess of them. So they wheeled their horses south and ran like a bunch of damned cowards."

I was well into my story now, and the truth of the night had conveniently escaped my memory. I did not then recall the way my gut rumbled with fear or the way I farted my way through the charge. I didn't remember that the whole time them Texians were coming to grips with the Mexicans, Ol' Speedy was dragging at Courage's reins in an effort to get that horse to turn north so I could run in the other direction.

"When I saw them Mexicans running, I was worried they'd get to Santa Anna's army and warn them that the Texas Rangers were nearby, so I gave chase and the other Texians followed me up," I lied. Truth was, Courage saw the mounted Mexicans running south, and he thought it was a great game and he wanted to run with 'em.

"We were charging at a full gallop, and I didn't even have time to think when we came into a great clearing full of campfires. Them damned cavalrymen had fled back into Santa Anna's encampment, and we'd chased right into the camp behind them."

"You didn't!" Stand Watie exclaimed, and he slapped his knee and guffawed all the more now.

"Oh, aye, sure as I'm sitting here in Injun Country, we absolutely did," I said, grinning like a devil. "The entire Mexican army – tents and campfires and stacked guns – all stretched out in front of us, and we were riding like a band of white devils, all through them, shooting off our Patersons, hollering like banshees, riding through tents and jumping fires and causing all forms of commotion and confusion among them Mexicans."

"What did you do?" Weenonaw gasped.

I gave her a long, careful look. She was a stunning beauty. And not just a stunning beauty for an Injun. There weren't many white women could've compared favorable to Weenonaw. And though I was still just a pup, I knew I'd captured her imagination. Here I was, the handsome young stranger who'd saved her uncle's life and ridden right into Santa Anna's camp with the Texas Rangers – well, most any young woman would've been charmed right out of her dress. As exceptional as Weenonaw was, she shared the same weakness for a dashing young soldier that was soon to be the ruin of the rest of her gender.

I looked right into Weenonaw's black eyes and with a grin on my lips, I lied straight to her face. "I counted campfires," I said.

This left my audience confounded and speechless, but Stand Watie knew right off what I was talking about, and he supplied the explanation.

"General Taylor sent the Texian Rangers to find out Santa Anna's strength," Watie said. "And so our young guest here, riding through the enemy encampment, had the presence of mind and composure in the fierce fighting to count the campfires so that he could give an accurate accounting to General Taylor of Santa Anna's numbers."

"That's right," I said, nodding admiration at my host. "We figured about a dozen men to each campfire. My count may have been a bit off, but it was close enough to give General Taylor the information he needed, and you'll know that we licked 'em at Buena Vista." [8]

Standhope was full of admiration hisself, and it was probably that boastful misconstruction of the truth that convinced him I was good enough for his niece. There was no truth in it. Riding through Santa Anna's camp, I hugged Courage's neck and pleaded to God Almighty that he only take the other Texians but allow me to get out with my skin intact. Ben McCulloch, though, he sure enough did count campfires. He was a madman, don't ye know? He warn't born with the sense God gave the dumbest of beasts. Even an old mutt would know to high tail it out of the enemy army's encampment, but not Ben McCulloch. He and those other Texians, they all thought dashing through that camp with their Patersons spitting hellfire was fine entertainment. [7]

Stand Watie thought the retelling of it was fine entertainment, and for someone who was very nearly the victim of a trio of assassins, he was in a surprisingly pleasant mood as we finished up our supper. We sent the ladies off to the other parlor, and the menfolk lit up hand rolled cigars. And it was then Stand Watie's turn to entertain his guests, and he did so by recounting for us the troubles that brought assassins to him at the river that day. I suppose the other gathered assembly knew the story well enough, but the only thing them Cherokee liked better than telling a story was retelling it. Of course, storytelling is how they passed their histories from one generation to the next, so I suppose Watie's tales were as much for the benefit of later generations as they were for me.

Back when the tribe was still in Georgia, white men wanted to move into the Cherokee lands in the mountains because they'd found gold in the rivers up there, Stand explained. Believing that the best way to retain rights for the Cherokee in the United States, Watie's uncle John Ridge – Yellowbird's father – and others of Watie's relations signed a treaty to give the Cherokee lands out in Indian Territory. Some among the Cherokee – the Old Settlers – had already moved out here to this corner of land north of Texas and west of Arkansas and Missouri. The Ridge clan gave up the Cherokee lands in the foothills of the Appalachians in exchange for this property, and without the necessity of army intervention, they moved out west.

But John Ross, the principal chief of the Cherokee Nation, was opposed to the treaty. It was his intention to stay in Georgia. Well, you know as well as I do how it all turned out – President Jackson sent in the army and marched all them Cherokee out to Oklahoma. And when they got there, angry and humiliated the way they were, they decided to take out their frustrations on those Cherokee who signed the treaty – Ridge and Watie's father and whoever else they could find.

As Watie told the story, John Ross sent assassins after all of Watie's relations, and he sent assassins after Watie, too.

Stand told me how he jumped into a gulley to avoid about fifty assassins once, and there were other attempts against him. He gave as good as he got, killing one of the men who killed his brother, and the feud went on for a number of years.

"I had hoped it was behind us," Watie said, wistfully, "but today's events suggest that John Ross has not yet decided to bury the hatchet. I have always endeavored to be honest and fair in my dealings with my people and with other people, and yet I am forever judged harshly by other men who do not know the intent of my heart. Tomorrow we will resume this wearisome path down which I have tread too long, and the feud with John Ross will go on." [9]

We smoked our cigars and listened to Stand Watie talk about his favorite fish to pull out of the Spavinaw River and the sizes of some of the more memorable ones, and then one of the negro slaves answered a bell and was instructed to take me to a bedroom so that I could get sleep.

I didn't have much in the way of luggage – just what was in my saddlebags – so there was naught to unpack. I stripped my borrowed clothes off and left them in a pile on the floor and collapsed onto the soft, stuffed mattress. Having been on the road for months now, I felt a wave of exhaustion pushing me to a fast sleep. Even so, I can still recall that nagging feeling tugging at my conscience like a warning: "Speed, old son," it was trying to say to me, "let's not forget that today ye've murdered three men. Somewhere those men are going to have fathers, brothers or cousins who would probably like to have a talk about how ye did them in."

But another part of my mind answered this nagging warning in typical fashion, "Weenonaw."

CHAPTER 4

When I woke the next morning, the sun was forcing its way through and around the curtains, but I pulled the blankets back up over me and fought pretty hard against the waking. Overnight, the weather outside had gone from cool to cold. The stuffed mattress that had lulled me so quickly to sleep was just as comfortable as the night before, and every bit of my body was stiff from weeks of riding. So I ignored the sun and consciousness and shut my eyes and pretended to myself that I was not awake.

Eventually, though, there came a knocking on my door, followed by a call from a sweet and soft voice.

"Lieutenant Speed," the woman said through the door. "My uncle has asked me to see if you would care to join us for breakfast."

"Oh, aye," I called back at the door. "Just give me a moment to throw my britches on, and ye can lead the way."

There's not much like a fine filly at my door to raise me, even on a chilly morning. I jumped from my bed and dressed in a hurry, and when I flung open the door I found Weenonaw patiently waiting for me in the hallway.

"I hope you slept well," she said, pleasantly smiling at me.

"Aye, not bad at all," I said. "Truth is, I've spent most of the nights through the summer sleeping in the dirt beside a trail, and the mattress was a likeable change. Of course, it got a might bit chilly through the night, didn't it?"

"It did," Weenonaw said, as she led me down the hallway. "We should have provided you with an extra blanket."

"Oh, I had blankets enough," I said. "But there's better ways than a blanket to keep one's self warm at night."

Weenonaw gave me a sideways glance, and I caught a knowing grin spread across her face. Oh, aye, she was mine if I wanted her, and I did want her. I gave her back a grin of my own, and decided to try my luck.

I stepped in front of her and cut her off, and I grabbed her by the waist and pulled her tight up against me so that her face was very near to mine. She smelled like rain, and I was fully infatuated. It had been too damn long since I'd had a woman in my arms.

"Lieutenant Speed!" she gasped, playing it pretty coy. She pushed against my chest with her arms as if she were trying to get away. But she didn't push all that hard, and her eyes told the truth. Wild, dark eyes suddenly full of excitement as she looked into my face. So I held her tight, our bellies pressed against each other.

"Aye, you'd keep me plenty warm, I think," I told her.

Now she blushed and looked away, but there was no argument in her.

"Lieutenant Speed, we should not keep my uncle waiting. And you should know, I am a Christian woman!"

"Oh, well it's all fine, then," I told her. "I'm a Presbyterian, meself."

She laughed and shook her head, and now she did push herself free of me. She was a strong woman. "We will get to know one another, Lieutenant Speed," Weenonaw said. "And when we have gotten to know each other, if I like you well enough, and when we have stood before a preacher, then we can see about keeping you warm at night."

"Ah, you're the marrying sort of Christian," I said, feeling grateful that I'd not let it slip to any of 'em that I was already married. "Well, that's fine by me, too, but I do hope you ain't too complicated."

She frowned at me. "What do you mean 'complicated'?"

"Oh, well, it's just that if we're to get to know each other before we get the wedding bells ringing, I hope you ain't too complicated to get to know. If ye are, it could be a long, cold winter."

Her eyes flashed, and there was a hint of redness below her pretty brown cheeks. I was not sure if she was angry or embarrassed, but then she gave me that delightful smile. A gift. "I am not complicated, Lieutenant. I expect we'll manage to get through the winter just fine."

"I am relieved to hear it," I said. "I ain't complicated neither. About the only thing I can think of that you might need to know about me is that I ain't never seen a woman as pretty as you, Weenonaw. And if marrying you is what it's going to take to see the rest of you, then I'm ready to get on with it as soon as you are."

She blushed again and grinned like the devil at me, but she started walking down the hallway again, and – disappointed but undeterred – I followed along behind her where I could watch the way her body moved under her skirt and sweater.

I didn't give much thought at the moment to the fact that I was already married to a pretty redhead back in Georgia. Nor did it concern me much that to bed this pretty squaw I'd have to commit bigamy [10] – if it actually came to such a thing. Even though I wasn't much more than a boy in the autumn of '47, I'd already come to realize that when it came to the constraints of marital vows, I didn't have much use for them. Perhaps the blame was with Ashley Franks, the married woman who first seduced me, or maybe the blame was all on my inability to control my sinful lusts. But whatever was at fault, I wasn't going to let a promise I'd made to Eliza Brooks Speed back in Georgia prevent me from getting into this lovely girl here in Injun country. Why, for all I knew, the laws of Georgia didn't even apply here.

Neither was I going to let my natural fear of assassins prevent me from hanging around long enough to get belly to belly with Weenonaw. It wasn't much of a lie I told when I said she was as pretty a girl as I'd laid eyes on. As a man who has a good bit of experience in these

41

matters – I suppose in my life I've gotten belly to belly with hundreds of women – I can say that I always found the prettiest woman ye've ever known is the one in front of you at any particular moment. And a walk down a cold hallway with this beautiful Injun girl was enough to erase all my fears. So when Stand Watie offered over breakfast to let me stay on through the winter if I'd work as his blacksmith, I seized immediately upon the offer. I suppose it was all down to me saving his life, but in addition to the room and my meals, he was offering me a pretty decent wage.

I spent the next several days in Stand Watie's smithy heating and hammering metal. Since his blacksmith slave had run off, Watie had amassed quite the collection of broken tools that needed repairing. I realized how much I had forgotten about forging since I'd left my boyhood home of Scull Shoals. There, I had been raised by my aunt and her husband, who was the town blacksmith. When I was young my uncle taught me his craft, because my aunt was barren and he had no sons of his own to help him in his shop. I became quite good at it, and had events not sent my life in a different direction, I might well have become a smithy myself. But when I fled Scull Shoals just three steps in front of Ashley Franks' enraged and cuckolded husband, my future as a blacksmith was abandoned. And now I found that I'd been too long out of practice, spending the last couple of years shop keeping for my wife's grandfather and then soldiering in Mexico, and I'd become rusty at the metal work. I'd done a big of smithing in Dallas when I stopped with Cherokee Cock, but the town smithy was there to clean up my messes and I never did much of the precise work, so I had not realized how badly out of practice I was.

Here, my circles all looked like eggs and my nails were all too long or too short, and I had a terrible time keeping my fire hot enough. I'd forgotten, too, just how heavy the hammer was. I went to bed at night with my muscles stiff and sore so that I could not roll over in bed without discomfort.

But eventually I caught the hang of it again. The slave blacksmith had a better set of tools than my uncle ever had, and I was soon again proficient at hammering out plow blades and door knobs and hay hooks and horse shoes and whatever else Stand Watie could find for me to do. When I had the knack of it again, I spent half a day hammering out a toy rocking horse. My uncle used to make them for the children in the village, and it was the first thing I learned how to make on an anvil. The horse was not much bigger than my hand, and it could be set down on its rocker and, if made well, with a gentle nudge would rock back and forth for a bit. It was a small thing, but I borrowed a bit of red ribbon from Sallie Watie to tie a bow on the iron horse's neck and stuck it in my leather satchel for safe keeping. I intended to give it to Weenonaw as a gift.

In addition to my work in the smithy, I also spent a fair bit of time chopping wood in expectation of the coming winter. Already it was well cool outside, and the fires were burning in the house each evening so that Watie was fretting over whether or not he had enough stacked and dry wood for the winter.

Between hammering metal and chopping wood, my hands were raw and blistered within my first few days in Indian Territory. But I didn't much mind the hard work. I spent a fair amount of time alone with my contemplations, and I found myself well enjoying the tranquility of a life of hard work without any Mexicans or cuckolded husbands attempting my murder.

In the evenings, while there was still light, Stand Watie would walk with me around his farm and into the woods, and he would teach me some of his Indian wisdom. He would point out things in nature that hitherto had escaped my notice. He showed me how to listen to the calls of birds as a warning of danger. When I pointed out to him that he'd misunderstood their calls the day we met on the Spavinaw, Watie laughed and told me that the rushing water sometimes made the birds difficult to hear.

He showed me, too, about tracking animals, how to read their prints and their droppings, how to look for sign on the leaves or in the grass. He showed me the difference between dog tracks and cat tracks. He showed me how to follow the contours of the earth to know where to find game and how to stay downwind when hunting.

Most everything he showed me were things my uncle had taught me hunting on the banks of the Oconee River and in the woods around Scull Shoals when I was a boy, so I don't know that any of it was really Injun wisdom so much as the observances of any woodsman. But Stand enjoyed these walks through the woods around his farm, and I didn't mind them at all. More often than not, Yellowbird and Saladin would join us on our walks.

Often, Weenonaw would come to visit me in the smithy or bring me fresh spring water to drink while I cut the timber, and whenever she did I would be sure to remove my shirt so she could get a good look at my chest and arms. I was uncommon strong when I was young, big and well-built, and when combined with my natural ability to charm, I was pert near irresistible to any women who crossed my path.

After just a few days, it was well understood among everyone around the Watie household that I was courting Weenonaw, and I believe old Standhope Watie was well pleased with this turn of events. I'd saved his life and so he liked me well enough, and a marriage betwixt me and his niece would give him one less dependent about the place. So the poor squaw was getting encouragement from every angle, and combined with her own desires, it was just a matter of time before I was able to successfully sue to get her into my bed.

It was one of these late mornings, me un-shirted and her with a pail of spring water, when the opportunity came up for me to press my case.

"My aunt Sallie has asked me to go into town to fetch some salt and other supplies before the winter sets in. It's a two hour trip to town and a two hour trip back, and I'm getting a late start. I'm worried I won't be back from town before dark. It would be pleasant to have someone accompany me on the journey. Aunt Sallie suggested I see if you'd like to make the trip with me. She said Uncle Stand will not be angry if you take the afternoon off."

"Well that sounds like a fine diversion," I told her, grabbing up my shirt and coat so that I would be dressed for town. "And before we go, I made something for you that I'd like to give you."

I had the little iron rocking horse with its red ribbon bow tucked inside a little leather haversack I was toting around at the time. I fetched out the rocking horse and handed it to Weenonaw. Her lovely brown face split into a smile, her almond eyes lighting up as she looked at it.

"You made this?" she asked.

"I did," I said. "My uncle taught me to make them when I was a boy."

"It's very nice," she said. She set the thing down on a split log and tapped it so that it rocked back and forth. "It even rocks! Oh, Lieutenant, it's simply a wonderful gift!"

"Aye," I said. "I thought it would be a little trinket which might remind you of me."

She took my hand and brushed her lips against my cheek to give me just the slightest of kisses to show her appreciation, but I felt that she should be a good bit more appreciative of that. As her lips left my cheek she still had hold of my hand, so I pulled loose and then grabbed her by the wrist, twisting her arm around behind her back and pulling her tight up against me, and I pressed my lips hard onto hers. Then I reached up with my other hand and took her by the back of the head and held her mouth against mine as she struggled to free herself.

It's a fact if a woman is interested but won't readily get belly-to-belly with ye, the best way to get what ye're after is manhandle her a bit. Oh, aye, she'll struggle and protest to put on a good show of protecting her chastity or dignity or what have you, but as long as ye don't surrender and keep pressing the issue, soon enough she'll be spreading a blanket out across the ground and hitching up her skirt.

When I let her up for air, Weenonaw gave me a sharp slap across the face and pushed me away. You'd have thought, from the look of fire in her eyes, that she was set to scalp me. But then I caught on that it wasn't a fire fanned by anger, but a fire fueled by lust, for her mouth was pursed to hold back a grin I knew too well. So I gave her back my own lustful grin and a wink to boot, and the next thing I knew Weenonaw had burst into laughter until there were tears streaming from her eyes. I was as ready to come to grips with that tantalizing beauty as I'd ever been to get belly to belly with a woman, but with her laughing, I could not help but laugh myself.

"Lieutenant Speed," she said at length, "please put on your shirt and come along with me to town."

The slaves had the wagon hitched to a couple of horses when we got to the barn, and I took up the reins as Weenonaw seated herself beside me, and in a moment we were off and headed down the road.

Weenonaw was a pleasant traveling companion, pointing out birds and squirrel in the trees or deer in the woods as we traveled the road. She chatted pleasantly about nothing and teased me that I had become something of a hero to Yellowbird.

"He is your new shadow," she said.

"Is he, now?" I asked.

"Do not pretend you've not noticed how he follows you around and hangs on your every word, Lieutenant."

"He does seem to be around a good bit," I acknowledged. It was true, too. Often when I was chopping wood, Yellowbird would turn up with a pencil and notebook, and he would write poetry while I chopped wood. I could count on him to stack logs at the end of the day when I was too tuckered to keep going. He was always on hand to run and fetch me water when I was working in the smithy, and from time to time I'd even show him how to do parts of the work.

"He's even told Uncle Stand that he wants to go to Texas to become a Texas Ranger."

"Aye, he'd probably make a good one," I said.

"Except that he is supposed to return to his studies in Fayetteville to become a lawyer. I believe Uncle Stand would rather he be a lawyer than a soldier," Weenonaw said.

"Yellowbird's no lawyer," I assured her. "He's got a streak of wild in him."

She went suddenly silent, and I looked over at her to see why. I was surprised to see that she'd gone angry and was shooting daggers at me with her eyes.

"What?" I asked.

"Is that what he is to you?" she asked. "A wild redman? Just a savage Indian? Do you think we are all savages?"

She bit off the word "savages," and I could see I'd offended her by calling the boy "wild," but it honestly was not what I'd intended.

"Oh. No. That ain't what I'm saying a'tall. I'm just saying Yellowbird ain't the sort to sit behind a desk in an office. He's got a spirit that needs to wander."

Weenonaw eyed me suspiciously, and I could tell she was deciding if she was still angry.

"Look 'ere, now, Weenonaw," I said. "I've already told ye that I'd like to be married to ye. Do ye think I'd marry a woman I thought of as a savage? I've been living with y'all long enough now that you should know me better than to accuse me of thinking poorly of ye just because you're an Injun."

47

Well, her stern look softened a bit at that, and I gave the reins a snap to speed up the horses a bit.

"So what about it, Weenonaw?" I said. "We've gotten to know each other pretty well. Are you ready to be my wife?"

She took a long look at me as we bounced over the rough cut road, and I could tell she was imagining a life with me. Truth was, other than watching me chop wood and hearing my stories of Mexico, Weenonaw still knew nothing of me. We'd not once talked about what it might mean to be married. Would we live there in Injun Territory? Would we return to Georgia? I knew, of course, that going to Georgia would never happen, but she had no idea that by marrying her I'd become a bigamist and – even if I chose to stay with her and abandon Eliza back in Milledgeville – we'd not soon return to the place of my roots. If I had any ambitions in life, any plans beyond working in Standhope Watie's smithy, we'd never discussed it. I suppose, perhaps, Weenonaw simply believed we'd stay on there forever.

As for myself, I can't say exactly what I intended to do. I'd been a long time away from Georgia and a long time away from my lovely redheaded bride. I found that when I closed my eyes at night, I couldn't exactly imagine Eliza's face any longer. Marcilina de la Garza was a clearer memory to me than the woman I married.

And with Eliza a distant thought and Weenonaw a present temptation, I suppose I was easily imagining a future of myself working in Standhope Watie's smithy and making a slew of papooses with Weenonaw. I'd not had a letter from Eliza, nor had I sent one, in so many months, she might already have deduced that I was in a Mexican grave. I didn't worry that she wouldn't be able to find herself a substitute for her missing husband soon enough, and at times I even convinced myself that she probably already had.

I'd also not entirely determined that I would not eventually abandon Weenonaw, even if she did agree to become my Injun bride. There was no doubt that running Eliza's grandfather's store in

Milledgeville was a good bit easier an occupation than pounding metal and chopping timber for Stand Watie, and the truth of my present situation was I didn't see staying on Watie's plantation beyond the spring anyhow. So maybe I'd marry Weenonaw, get what I was after – which was a warm and pleasant winter – and come spring I'd find a way to ride on back east without another thought of any of my Injun in-laws.

Having relieved my conscience of any guilt, I was ready to get on with the marriage and get that beautiful squaw out of all them layerings of clothes, and so on our wagon ride I pressed the issue.

"Have you asked my uncle if he would consent to such a thing?" Weenonaw asked.

"I've not, yet," I said. "But I believe the man likes me well enough, and I suspect we'll be married with his blessing."

"And that is what you want? To be married to me?"

"You know that it is," I said, flashing her a grin and giving her a wink. "Why, from the moment I saw you, I've been head over heels in love with you, Weenonaw. Why, I've been from Georgia to Mexico, all through Texas and Injun Territory, and what I know for sure is that nary a woman can compete with ye for beauty or charm. And I'm so eager to get to know your charms more intimately that I am fit to burst."

It was true, too. It had been so long since I'd known any woman's intimate charms that even old Sallie Watie was beginning to give me the stirs every time she walked past.

"Then I accept your proposal," Weenonaw declared, throwing her arms around my neck and kissing me on the cheek. "You must first seek permission from Uncle Stand, but if he will consent to our marriage, then I will be glad to be your wife."

And now I was wondering if we couldn't arrange for a ceremony that afternoon. I said so, and tried to give her left teat a squeeze, but she turned wild squaw on me and slapped my hand away.

"You'll wait for that!" she said, and then she laughed at my consternation.

My overwhelming joy at knowing my suffering would soon be at an end was short lived.

When we arrived at the small town where Weenonaw intended to get her essentials, I found it was not much more than a trading post at a crossroads. There were a few dozen houses scattered around the town, a small traveler's rest that had four upstairs rooms, one dedicated to the owner, and a small saloon on the ground floor where a person could find a meal if they didn't care too much about the quality of the food. There was a livery and a saw mill, and not far from the center of the town there was a grist mill, and there was the one dry goods store that was overrun with people looking to stock up for the winter.

We left the wagon on the street near the store and went in there to fetch the items Sallie had sent us there to get. Weenonaw had a list prepared that she gave to the clerk, and he took a wooden pushcart and started loading it up.

I picked some candies out of a jar to give to Saladin, some candles for Sallie and some pipe tobacco for Stand. I found a nice knife that I bought for Yellowbird. Watie's wages were generous – the perks of having saved the life of your employer, I suppose – and I was feeling pretty flush. So while we were in the store, I told Weenonaw to pick out a pretty jeweled necklace to wear at our wedding.

"Isn't that a bit presumptive?" she asked. "You've not yet secured permission from my uncle."

"Go ahead and get the necklace," I said. "I reckon there'll be a wedding before we come back to town."

While Weenonaw was engaged in finding herself a pretty necklace, and having already paid for my other gifts, I wandered back outside to the wagon to wait for the clerk with the pushcart. But when I got to the wagon, I saw two Injuns in white man's clothes examining the horses.

One of them was about my age, give or take, and the other was a good bit older than me by twenty years or more. The older one was a grizzled, hard-looking man. Neither of them looked much like an Injun, except they were both just dark enough that they weren't white men, either. I figured they were just a couple of friends of Stand Watie who'd recognized his horses and were wondering if he was about.

"How are y'all?" I asked them.

They looked up in surprise.

"Are these your horses?" the older one asked me.

"They belong to my employer," I said.

I looked at the horses, and in an instant I recognized that one of them was one of the horses we'd taken off the Spavinaw River assassins. Watie had said he'd sell those horses, but he'd not yet done it, and one of his damn fool slaves had hitched a dead man's horse to the wagon.

"Who's your employer?" the older one asked.

I'd already figured these were a couple of John Ross's men – the older one might be Ross hisself – and that damned horse had at one time belonged to his kinsman that I'd murdered. Now my mind was racing as I felt my gut clench. Would they dare gun me down here in the middle of town? And where was my Paterson? The damned thing was safely tucked in my satchel under the seat of the wagon. God forbid, if it came to it, I couldn't even defend myself.

A lie was needed here, but for the life of me I could not construe one. So I stood like a mute, dumb before their question.

"I asked who's your employer," the older Injun said again.

They were standing in the street, the other side of the horses. I was standing on the rough timber boardwalk in front of the store. I could not see their waists to know if they were toting pistols, but I reckoned it was a good bet they were.

I took a step up to the wagon and set down my sack with the knife, the sweets, the candles, and the tobacco. I reached to grab my satchel, but the older man took a step away from behind the horses and pulled his coat back to reveal a revolver on his hip.

"I asked you a question," he said to me. "Before you reach for that satchel, you answer my question. This here horse is stolen from my stable, and I'd like to know the name of the man who claims ownership of it."

Well, I wasn't going to be hung in Injun Territory as a horse thief, but neither was I going to be shot for reaching for my satchel. If it meant creating trouble for Watie to save myself, I had no qualms about doing it.

"That there horse belongs to my employer, Mr. Standhope Watie," says I, putting on an act of being brave and bold. I thought maybe if I took a stance of righteous indignation I could back 'em down a bit. "If you think ye've got some claim on that horse, you can take it up with him."

The older Injun dropped his hand from his coat to the grip of his revolver.

"I'm taking it up with you," he said. "More important to me than that horse is the recent disappearance of the man who rode it. He was my cousin, and no one has seen him in weeks. The last time he was seen, he was astride that very horse. What do you have to say about him?"

Now my knees were knocking like a drum.

I glanced over my shoulder to the alley that ran between the dry goods store and the saloon. In my mind I was measuring the distance and wondering if I could be around that corner before these two shot me. Maybe this older one, with aged eyesight, would have a tough time hitting me. And maybe the younger one, not being any older than I was, didn't have enough experience with a gun to make a good shot of it. But I was fairly certain they could both get off at least a couple of shots, maybe even three a piece, before I was safely behind the corner of the building. The odds of not getting hit by six bullets weren't good enough to make me feel any better about my situation.

And then what? Even if I got around the corner, the hilly land immediately around the town was well cleared. There were no woods to quickly disappear into. I could run, but I did not know to where.

So I stalled 'em a bit longer. "I've already told ye. My employer, Stand Watie, these horses are his. If you want to know more about it than that, ye'll have to ask the man hisself."

The one Injun with his hand on the grip of his pistol was ready to say something else, but none of us had seen Weenonaw approaching. She must have overheard me, for she did not hesitate. She stomped her feet as she marched right up to the man who'd been addressing me.

"Koo-wees-gu-wee!" [11] Weenonaw stormed. "You are a devil if God ever created one! You've no business with these horses, and you've no business with my fiancé! If you want to keep your horses, and your kinsmen, you'll leave my uncle be. Do you hear me? Are you such a coward that you send three assassins to kill an unarmed man fishing in a river?"

The old man was caught off guard, and he and the young buck with him both turned their eyes on Weenonaw, and that gave me the chance I needed to reach into my satchel and withdraw my Paterson.

I was making a gamble. I believed that these Injuns had no desire to shoot me on this street, or I'd have been running for the alleyway the moment they took their eyes off me. My gamble was that with the Paterson in my hand and resting on the footboard of the wagon, the old man and the buck would think twice about reaching for their own revolvers. And if it came to it, I'd always trust my cowardice in a gun fight. Some men might become petrified from fear – and I've known that fear, too – but just as I had on the Spavinaw River, I knew that if shooting meant the difference between killing or getting killed, I'd be quicker to shoot. And in my life, many a man found out too late for them how quick a coward can pull a trigger, and how true his shaking hand could aim.

To be on the safe side, though, I cocked the hammer of the Paterson back with my thumb so that I could get that first shot off even quicker.

"I sent no assassins," the old man said coolly. "But now that you mention it, the body of one of my men was pulled from the Spavinaw River not far from your uncle's homestead. I want to know how my man came to be dead. And where are the other two who were with him?"

"They snuck up on my uncle intending to murder him," Weenonaw said. "But my fiancé was there to rescue my uncle."

Now the old man and the young buck both turned their attention back to me, and the blood in my veins turned to ice water. Just like that, Weenonaw declared me the murderer of this man's kin, and she put a bounty upon me. I watched the old man's eyes drop to my Paterson as he realized for the first time I'd armed myself. He let go of his own revolver and stuck out a restraining hand to the buck who had now reached for his gun under his coat.

"Not here, Silas," the old man said to him.

I kept a stone countenance, trying to give them the impression that shooting them wouldn't trouble me a bit. But inside, everything was churning fear. I'd been foolish to stay on Watie's plantation. My first instinct had been the right one – grab some dinner, maybe spend the night and be gone by morning. But I'd stayed weeks now, all in an effort to bed a woman.

It's the folly of youth. As an old man, I now know that it's foolhardy to risk yourself for a woman when there are a dozen more on the horizon who'd gladly take her place. But at the time, a pretty face and ample teats were enough to make me hang about even when every instinct I had was commanding me to run. And now I found myself with my insides turning to jelly and two rough looking half-breed Injuns glaring murder at me.

"That's right, 'not here, Silas'" Weenonaw mimicked him. "This is a Texas Ranger, a veteran of Mexico! Do you think he fears you?"

"Ah, now," says I. "There's no need –" but the old man cut me off.

"A soldier of the United States government?" he asked, and there was venom dripping from the words. "The same government that stole the homes of my people?"

"Well, it warn't like that," says I, sheepishly. "I was in the militia, not a government soldier, exactly. The Georgia militia. The Mississippi militia. And, as Weenonaw says, the Texas militia."

But none of them were paying me any heed. Weenonaw's blood was boiling, and she was letting the old man and the one called Silas know what she thought of them sending assassins after her uncle. We were beginning to draw the attention of others on the street. I could tell some of them Injuns in town for their final supplies for the winter were eager to see this white man gunned down, and I was worried if I didn't do something to settle Weenonaw they were going to get what they were hoping for.

Keeping the Paterson in my fist, I walked to the post where the horses were hitched and untied the reins. "If we don't get moving now, it'll be dark before we get back to your uncle's farm," I said to Weenonaw.

"You'd be wise to end this feud, John Ross," Weenonaw said to the old man. "Too many have died already, but if it continues, you'll find the dead on your side will mount quickly."

Ross took Silas by the arm, and the two of them walked to the saloon.

The store clerk, who was remarkably disinterested in all these goings-on, had been steady busy loading our purchases from his cart into the wagon. I now paid him for the necklace Weenonaw had picked out, and with our supplies loaded into the wagon, we climbed onto the seat of the wagon.

But I handed the reins to Weenonaw and kept the Paterson in my hand.

"You drive the horses," I said. "I'd like to keep my shooting hand free in case those two decide to follow us."

"There's no fear of that," Weenonaw said. "John Ross will not stain his own hands. He'll send men to do his work for him."

"Right," says I. "And I suppose now the chances are good that he'll send men for me."

Weenonaw scoffed. "He only has fools and boys, like those three you dealt with on the river. This feud was supposed to have ended. There was supposed to be peace between my uncle and John Ross. But Ross will not let it die. Dozens have been killed. My father among them. All because Ross will not let go of his grudge against my uncle."

"Right," says I. "But you say all Ross has to send are fools and boys, but they've been successful a fair number of times, haven't they?"

Weenonaw snapped the reins, and I could see that she was full of anger.

"Why would John Ross be this far north anyway?" she asked, mostly to herself. "Rose Cottage is all the way down in Park Hill, and there's no call for him to be this far north, unless he is looking for trouble." [12]

"Maybe he's looking for those three men I gunned down," I suggested.

But Weenonaw didn't hear a thing from me. She was working out the details for herself.

"He must have come to find out what happened to his men, those assassins he sent," she said. "We must hurry back to the farm and let my uncle know that we have seen John Ross."

Weenonaw kept the horses moving at a pretty good pace down the road leading back to her uncle's plantation, and I kept a watch behind us for any signs of riders. The knots into which my stomach had twisted had not yet undone themselves, and my mind was racing full of fearful thoughts.

What misery I was suddenly in, and what a wagon ride it was now compared to the ride into town. Going into town I was contemplating marriage, and getting belly-to-belly with this fine squaw, but now I was a marked man! And worse, my bride to be with her fiery tongue had done the marking.

"That was John Ross, was it?" I asked when we were far enough from town that I could again find my voice.

"It was. John Ross, the Principle Chief of the Cherokee Nation," she said. "And his son Silas."

The road we traveled was a mixture of cleared farmland and wooded forest, and I can tell you that I was quaking with fear throughout. I kept myself turned in the seat, having Weenonaw control the horses, so that I could keep a watchful eye behind us. When we came to open clearings at farmhouses, I would keep a sharp watch for any dust on the road behind us that might indicate Ross and his son had decided to pursue us. As we rode under the dark canopy of the woods, every bend in the road left me with terrible dread that at any moment I might see riders appear through the trees. As the sun sank lower in the sky, the woods got darker and darker, and I knew that the closer we got to Watie's plantation we would go at least a couple of miles through dark woods.

I was still young then, of course, and I didn't know as much as I would later learn about ambushing and the strategy of killing, but I'd already had enough military experience to know that the shelter of the woods could offer a man plenty of protection if he wanted to establish an ambush. What I did not count on was that there were other roads, or trails, leading from town through the woods – paths not wide enough for a wagon, but well suited to a couple of mounted men who wanted to out-pace a wagon. And with all my attention focused behind us, I never gave a thought to the threat that might be ahead of us.

So it was that my back was turned to the horses, my eyes keenly watching through the trees we'd already passed, when an almighty crack broke the monotony of the hoof falls and the turning wheels rolling along the worn roadway.

I dropped as low as I could behind the seat of the wagon, still searching behind us. "Go fast!" I screamed at Weenonaw, but she didn't need to be told. Already she was snapping the reins. Another shot echoed among the trees and splinters flew from the seat, and I realized now that our assailants were somewhere in the woods ahead of us.

I remained crouched, but turned awkwardly in time to see the faces of John and Silas Ross as we passed by them. They were dismounted, just a few paces off the roadway. The horses were moving at a quick gallop, and though father and son Ross were just a blur as we passed them by, they seemed to be suspended in the air – hanging there like a couple of haints – and the time it took to pass them was interminable. I saw their sneering faces as they looked down the barrels of their pistols, and I could even see the flash of the muzzle and the smoke billow as John Ross fired another shot.

The bullet embedded itself in the handrail of the seat, not four inches from where my face was. I fell back into Weenonaw as the handrail split in two and a large chunk fell away behind us.

"B'God faster!" I screamed, trying to right myself. The speed of the wagon made it bounce over the road, and I was off balance leaning against Weenonaw's legs and I couldn't find anything to grasp with my free hand to right myself, but I stuck out the fist still clutching my Paterson and I jerked my finger to send a wild bullet in the general direction of those Injun bastards.

We rounded a bend in the road and I leaned more heavily into Weenonaw. She was snapping reins like the devil and yelling at the horses. I heard another shot fire from behind us.

"They're chasing us!" she yelled to me. "For Heaven's sake, get up and shoot back!"

Down at the footboard, leaning against Weenonaw the way I was, there was a certain safety. The seat back and the back of the wagon were offering protection I could not find if I got up from my perch. But I knew, too, that the Injuns would easily catch us up and overtake us. And when they were upon us, I had no desire to find myself holding an empty revolver.

At the time, the Paterson was as fine a gun as a man could want. It was one of the only guns manufactured that gave a man five shots before he had to reload, but it warn't like later revolvers with cased bullets that were simple to slide into the chambers of the revolver. You had to pack powder and ball and grease the chambers and slip on the percussion caps – a chore that could take a full minute for the men who were good at it, or several minutes for the men who weren't. I was stuck somewhere in the middle so that I knew it would take me more than a full minute to get the thing completely reloaded, and reloading a Paterson was not a thing you wanted to be doing with two Injun assassins riding down on you.

I knew there was slim chance I could hit them if I tried to shoot back while the wagon was racing along the road. My only hope of defending us was if I got a chance to shoot at them when they were close up on us and holding still.

My old captain from the Texas Rangers, Ben McCulloch, would

have told Weenonaw to pull back on those reins and let the bastards come right up to us. He'd have not run from two men. But I warn't Ben McCulloch, and ye'll not that I've lived to be quite a bit older than he did.

"Faster!" I yelled at Weenonaw, still down at the footboard.

The shots from our pursuers had stopped – apparently they had no more desire to reload their revolvers than I had to reload mine. Without letting go of the Paterson, I grabbed hold to the back of the seat and hoisted myself back up. I could see them closing the distance behind us. They were, perhaps, thirty yards and gaining. I glanced ahead and saw that we were coming to a bend in the road. Both men were riding as hard as their horses would go, and I didn't think we had much time before they would be upon us.

"How far to your uncle's farm?" I asked over the din of the wagon.

"We can't be more than a mile now," Weenonaw said, her eyes locked on the road ahead and her whole body leaning forward in the perfect picture of concentration as she maintained control of the horses.

We rounded the bend with our pursuers still thirty yards or so behind us, and they briefly disappeared from view, but as the road straightened back out, they quickly reappeared, now closer to twenty yards behind.

A boy seeing his father fall in battle would be full of rage and vengeance, and he would maintain his pursuit for the sake of revenge. But a father seeing his son fall might well cease pursuit to care for his wounded progeny. There would still be vengeance in his heart, but he would know there would be later opportunity to get his revenge.

So I determined that if I was to spend another of my four remaining bullets, it would be better spent on young Silas.

I watched as they closed the distance, and then I steadied my arm against the back of the seat. I hunched down so that I could look right down the barrel and get a good aim, and I grasped my right hand with my left to try to steady the Paterson with both hands. With my left eye shut and my right eye squinting down the barrel, I tried my damnedest to hold young Silas in my line of sight.

The damned wagon bounced and shook, though, and I couldn't keep Silas at the end of my revolver.

But they came on closer, and when they weren't but ten yards or so from the back of the wagon, I pulled the trigger.

Well, I missed Silas by two feet, but I did the next best thing. The bullet buried into the chest of his horse, and the thing let loose a terrible scream; it's legs went from under it, and in a terrible commotion of dust and rider and horse and legs and bodies, Silas and his mount went to the ground.

I cocked back the hammer on the Paterson and fired another shot at the mass of body and dirt, but whether it found a mark in all that rubbish I had no idea. My first shot had done the trick. Old John Ross reined in his horse to care for his fallen son, and now the distance between us and them Injun bastards grew by the second. We'd left them behind.

"Keep this damned wagon going!" I yelled at Weenonaw.

Several minutes passed with me still watching behind us and Weenonaw snapping reins and calling to the horses, when at last she called out, "There it is Jack! We're nearly home!"

I turned in my seat to see the woods disintegrating before us, opening up to the wide expanse of Stand Watie's plantation.

His manicured yard was fenced off from the road, and so we had to ride a hundred yards to the drive up to the house, but we were no longer facing pursuit. I spun in the wagon seat to look ahead, and I saw Watie, Yellowbird, and a couple of slaves running down the drive with muskets in hand.

Weenonaw reined in the horses as we got up to Stand Watie.

"We heard shots," he said, concern etched all over his leathery face.

"John Ross and his son Silas followed us from town!" Weenonaw said. "They must have taken the Spavinaw path and got ahead of us, because they tried to ambush us where the path meets the road."

I climbed down from the wagon, and found that fear and the rough ride had combined to make my legs useless. I tripped and fell to the ground, and one of the damned slaves had to pull me up to my feet.

"Damnation!" I cussed at him, looking for some target to vent my fears. "Take your hands off of me!" I gave him a stiff punch to the shoulder and he backed away, looking disgust at me.

"I shot the boy's horse," I said. "That stopped them, but they're not far down the road. Get up some men and go after them!"

Stand was looking down the road for any sign that our pursuers were still coming, but at my suggestion that they get after our attackers, he looked up into the sky.

"It will be dark soon," he said. "John Ross is no fool. He will know that you have arrived here, he will have suspected that we heard the shots, and he will already be escaping. It would do no good to try to go after them, and it would expose us to unnecessary risk. All the same, we will stand a guard at the houses tonight to keep watch." He gave instructions to one of the slaves to take the wagon, unload it and put up the horses. He told Yellowbird to have his cousins and other hands around the farm to get their muskets and be prepared to keep a watch through the night.

As the slave mounted the wagon, Weenonaw called out. "Wait!" And then she fetched from the back the necklace I'd bought her.

"Uncle Stand!" she said, taking it from its sack. "Look at what Jack has bought me! And he's asked that I marry him!"

There is no sense in a woman. I've bedded hundreds of them – sweet girls full of innocence and hope and dreams, whores who chewed tobacco and could out-shoot Bill Hickok on his best day, squaws and negro women, white women with dainty hands and batting eyelids, fat women with teats the size of watermelons. I've known women who were spies, women who were thieves, women who were killers, and women who were spies and thieves and killers. I've known women in all kinds of shapes and sizes and colors, and I've not yet found one that I didn't enjoy seeing naked. But as wonderful as they are to look at and put hands upon, I've never yet known a woman who had a lick of sense.

We'd just been chased by two murderers bent on doing us in, and here's this damned crazy squaw flaunting her necklace and talking engagement! Can you find reason in such a thing? My heart was still pounding like a war drum, and all I could think of was getting out of Injun Territory as fast as possible, preferably with an armed escort of about a dozen of Stand Watie's men, and here's this daft Injun woman making wedding plans.

But if there's no sense in a woman, there's no sense in an Injun, neither. Stand Watie's face broke into a smile and he squeezed Weenonaw into a great big hug. "I am so happy for you, daughter," he said, even though she was a niece or cousin or something. "I have prayed the two of you would find happiness with each other!"

"Should we go inside or something?" I asked. "What if John Ross is still coming?"

Stand looked down the road. "He will not come now," he said. "I believe he will go home to Rose Cottage now, and he will look to his revenge at a later date. But if he comes today he will wait for night when he thinks he can sneak up on us. But I do not believe he will come tonight."

CHAPTER 5

Old Stand was right on both counts. John Ross didn't come that night, but he would come eventually.

Though I was relieved from standing watch because I'd endured the chase, I spent a fretful night awake on the sofa in Stand's front room. Just in case John Ross did attack the house, Stand wanted everyone close and available. So instead of sleeping in my bed, I slept in the front parlor of the main house. I had terrible visions all through the night of John Ross rallying up a war party and attacking the house at dawn.

Apparently Stand had concerns of his own, because he kept a watch running at the plantation for the next several days.

My fears abated as the days passed without attack from Ross and a regiment of braves, but while I continued my employment in the smithy I kept my Paterson on my hip or within my reach all the time. I also started taking a musket with powder and ball out to the smithy to have handy if I needed it.

After a few days following the event, Stand Watie began sending some of his men out in parties to search for signs that John Ross was still in the area. Eventually, they were able to confirm that Ross had returned to his home near Tahlequah, the Cherokee capital. None of his men had been seen in the area either, and so after several days Watie called for an end to the night watches and spread the word around the countryside that any sighting of a Ross loyal in the area should be reported to him.

All the while, Weenonaw and Sallie Watie were making plans for the wedding day, and as my fears of John Ross's revenge dissipated, my eagerness for the wedding grew. It had been months since I'd properly pressed up against a woman, and those autumn nights in Oklahoma were growing colder by the day.

I urged Weenonaw to plan for a quick wedding, thinking the ceremony could be had in a few days at the most, but Sallie Watie insisted that the thing be a big affair. They set a date for the middle of November, and Yellowbird was constantly engaged in delivering invitations. Nearly every Injun for 20 miles was invited to the thing, and a shocking number of them showed up.

The second time I got married the weather was superb. It was a chilly morning as we loaded up in half a dozen wagons and rode to the church, but the sky was a beautiful, clear blue and the sun shone bright the whole day. There were still plenty of colorful leaves to be found on the trees, so that everything was bright and colorful in the sunshine.

The church was not large enough to house all the guests to the wedding, and so out in the church yard there must have been another two hundred or more Injuns loitering about, in addition to maybe as many as another two hundred who squeezed into the church. Of course, they were not there to see me or to see Weenonaw, but were there instead to see Stand Watie and curry favor with him.

Weenonaw was a stunning bride. She wore her long black hair tied in braids that fell on either side of her face. She wore a red dress with white patterns woven into it, and beaded bracelets on her wrists. She wore the necklace I'd bought for her – a beaded necklace with a golden medallion of some sort.

According to the customs of her people, Sallie Watie and Yellowbird stood with Weenonaw to symbolize that we were joining her maternal clan, and Yellowbird was there to show that he would teach our children the ways of the Cherokee.

By Weenonaw's choice, the wedding was a combination of Christian and Cherokee, so that the preacher blessed us and read some of the common phrases from the Bible, but then some of the women attending the ceremony placed blue blankets over both me and Weenonaw. Then the preacher blessed us again, this time speaking in Cherokee, and after that they removed the blue blankets and placed one white blanket over both of us.

With the blanket covering us, I took a moment to grab Weenonaw by the back of the head and pull her lips to mine. She laughed and pulled away from me, but I could see in her eyes that she was as ready to get on with things as I was.

When the preacher was finished with his talking, they took off the white blanket, and that was the deed done.

I'm sure there was some meaning and tradition to the ceremony and the blankets and everything else, but I had no idea then, nor do I know now, what any of it was supposed to signify.

With the rituals all done, we now went out to the grounds of the church where a great picnic was prepared, and all them hundreds of Injuns came by to congratulate Stand that he'd gotten shed of a dependent, and then they all commenced to eating the food like they'd not had a bite in a week. Between 'em, Stand and Weenonaw had to introduce me to every Injun present at the wedding, and as a result I didn't get more than a piece of cold fried chicken to eat.

But I didn't much care. After all, I was not there for the food.

I spent the whole of what remained of the morning and the early afternoon shaking fists of Injuns whose names I couldn't begin to remember, but among the wedding guests was an older Injun whose skin had all turned to leather and his dark hair was already peppered with gray. Like most of the other Cherokee, he bore a white man's name, and I understand his father was Scotch, so he wasn't a full blooded Cherokee anyhow. His name meant nothing to me then, though I could tell he was a man of some importance by the way Stand Watie greeted him, but in the years after the War, his name would be repeated a thousand times by every cattle driver from Texas to Kansas.

"This is my good friend Jesse Chisholm," Watie said, introducing the man to me. "You'll find him a fascinating fellow. He's spent a fair amount of time in the plains speaking with the western Indians – the Comanche and the Kiowa. These are the buffalo hunters, and truly wild. Jesse has represented the interests of the government in negotiations with these tribes." [13]

Like so many of them Injuns, Jesse Chisholm – even though he was half Scotch – wore the leathered look of a man who'd spent his life never out of the sun. He was an interesting character, and I spent much of the morning and early afternoon of my wedding day engaged in conversation with him. It spared me of having to spend too much of the day listening to them Injuns flatter old Stand Watie in the hopes that he might do some thing or another on their behalf.

Chisholm entertained me with stories of the Plains Indians, the wild bastard savages whose idea of a fun bit of sport involved kidnapping, torture, scalping and murder. Back in those days, before the Gold Rush and before the War and before the Iron Horse connected one coast to t'other, no white man east of the Mississippi knew much of the Pach or the Comanch, and I'd wager most had never even heard of them. I suppose we always knew, or suspected, that out West there were terrible savage Injuns full of murder, but they weren't talked about in decent society because they only ever bothered each other.

Chisholm's descriptions of the brutes was my first real introduction to the Apache and the Comanche and the Kiowa. I suppose in Mexico some of them Texians talked of them from time to time, having had some experience with them, but I had never encountered them, never intended to, and paid little heed to their descriptions.

Other than the rumors of savagery I'd encountered back east or from the Texas Rangers, Chisholm's impressions, then, were the first I knew of the Plains Indians, and while he had respect for them, he mostly looked on them as ruckus children who sometimes got into too much drink.

"They love a sport," Chisholm told me. "Their favorite game is buffalo hunting from horseback, and anytime two tribes meet on the open plain, you can rest assured they will be competing to see who can shoot the most buffalo from atop a horse."

"Are they dangerous?" I asked.

"Dangerous," he repeated. Old Jesse Chisholm thought on this for several moments. "They respect me because I speak their language, and I've seldom had cause to be concerned for my safety," Jesse said.

It's a fact that you can look up in the history books that Jesse Chisholm spoke more than a dozen languages.

"The Plains tribes have been known to raid the haciendas of Mexican rancheros and kill the adults," he said. "They abduct the children. I have rescued many kidnapped children from the Plains tribes. When I cannot find family to return them to, I adopt them as my own children." [14]

"Oh, aye? And if you don't rescue the children?" I asked, and I suppose I figured the answer would be that the white children would be scalped and the Injuns would turn to cannibalism. Back in those days, the Plains Tribes were as wild and fearsome a creature to folks living back east as a Chinaman. Of course, when I actually had the opportunity to encounter the Apache and Comanche, I'd learn they were much more horrific than your typical cannibal. "What becomes of 'em then?"

"They are used as slaves, but when they reach adulthood, most of them are taken into the tribe and live as a member of the tribe," Jesse said.

"So, I'll ask ye again," I said, "are they dangerous?"

Jesse nodded his head thoughtfully. "They are fearless warriors. If they do not feel threatened or provoked, I believe they are peaceful enough. The trouble is, they are easily provoked. If a man builds a ranch on land they consider their hunting ground, they will raid his ranch and steal his horses. If he stays, they will come back and take something else – maybe his women or maybe his scalp."

I suppose it was around that time during our interview that Stand Watie came over with some cigars that we lit, and the three of us for some time smoked cigars, and Chisholm continued to tell me stories of kidnapped Mexican children and the Plains Injuns he rescued them from.

Most of what he talked about was their love of sport. As an ambassador, for the Republic of Texas, for the United States and for the Cherokee Nation, Jesse Chisholm had attended any number of councils with the Plains tribes, and he recalled that nearly every one got started with a competitive hunt or a wrestling match. He looked me up and down.

"You're a big man," he said. "Strongly built and tall. The Plains tribes would want to test your strength right away. If you could best a brave, either hunting buffalo or wrestling or in some other game of courage, you would earn their respect."

It's funny the way life turns. It was a chance encounter with an old timer who knew the Pach Injuns better, probably, than any other white or half-white man in the country – but those words of his would one day come back to me when I desperately needed them and save my life. But that was years later, after the war. As it turned out, my brief friendship with Jesse Chisholm at my wedding would save my life sooner than that.

Not many folks alive today can say that Jesse Chisholm attended their wedding and smoked cigars with them. Of course, Jesse Chisholm warn't famous at the time, and really wouldn't be until after his death. Though in life he'd had some fine and interesting adventures, it would be in death, when the cowboys started using his trading trail to run their cattle, that the name Chisholm Trail would make old Jesse a household name.

I suppose it's the sort of thing I could dine out on today, spinning yarns about how Jesse Chisholm of the famous cattle trail smoked cigars with me and my uncle-in-law at my wedding, but then I'd be forced into explaining to Eliza which wedding I'm referring to, as she'd be quite certain that no half-breed Injun was on the guest list of our wedding, and so rather than getting a free meal out of it, Chisholm's presence at my wedding to Stand Watie's niece is something about which I don't often talk.

At long last, enough Injuns had pumped my fist and – more importantly – made certain sure that Stand Watie knew they'd attended the wedding of his niece, and the picnic following the ceremony broke up.

It could come none too soon for me. My wedding day with my second wife was one of the prettiest autumn days I can recall, with a soft breeze blowing through the hills, and the trees full of gold and red, yellow and orange, the sky clear as a bell and the afternoon filled with laughter and the sounds of children playing. But as pleasant as the wedding day had been, I was so eager for the wedding night that I was beginning to lose my patience with the fist pumping Injuns.

Weenonaw and I rode together in a buggy back to Watie's plantation. Well away from the big house, Stand Watie had a small log cabin on the farm that had been his first home in Injun Territory before the big house was fully constructed. It was a quaint little cabin that sat high up on a bluff with a spectacular view of the Spavinaw down below it. The bright autumn leaves of the hardwoods presented a gorgeous portrait for as far into the distance as we could see, and after eating a supper at Watie's home with just family around us, Weenonaw and I walked together along a path through the woods to the cabin.

As simple a place as it was, the slaves had been sent up a couple of days previous to clean it of dust and cobwebs and dress it up with a fresh straw mattress and some candles and plenty of firewood – most of which I'd cut. It was Stand's intention that Weenonaw and I would permanently move into the log cabin, and she seemed well pleased with the idea. I was indifferent. The log cabin lacked some of the niceties of living in the plantation house, but the one comfort I was most seeking was the one who was gushing enthusiasm about us moving into the cabin.

"Oh, Jack, it will be the perfect home for us to start our life together," Weenonaw said as we approached the cabin. She was walking alongside me with her arms wrapped around my left arm and her head resting against my shoulder. "This is all too perfect to be real," she said.

"If we don't get too much sleep this night, that should be perfect," I said, but Weenonaw missed my point.

"Oh, it's a fresh mattress," says she. "We should sleep just fine."

I built us a fire and we opened a bottle of wine, and I took my time in getting her in the mood. Though I was an old hand at having wedding nights, it was a fresh experience for Weenonaw and I wanted it to be a memorable one for her. So rather than tear her clothes off and get belly to belly with her right away – an instinct honed to a fine point during weeks of eager anticipation – I started in on her with soft kisses, and I took my time getting her out of that wedding dress.

Her body was nothing to disappoint, either.

She was lean and strong, but soft in the right places. She had big, dark nipples sitting on top of nearly perfect teats that fit just right in my cupped hands. I rolled those nipples between finger and thumb until she squealed, and it was almost more than I could stand to not get at her with a passion.

For a woman who was saving herself for marriage, I'll say that Weenonaw took to the experience like a trained artist, proving to me that some among the fairer sex are born with a knack for the thing. It had been months since I'd last had my arms around a naked woman – a lapse I intended to never allow again – and at some point earlier in the proceedings than I would have preferred, I found that my eagerness could no longer be contained. But being a young man and newly married, I was soon back at it again. And Weenonaw, having discovered with me a new talent she'd never before imagined, was more than happy to get in some more practice.

In the end, we made rough use of the fresh mattress without getting much sleep at all.

Late at night, spent and exhausted and with her cheek pressed against my chest and her fingers softly stroking me, Weenonaw gave me a new name.

"You know that for me, my people's history is important," she said idly. "I use my Cherokee name because I do not want to lose the tether I have with my ancestors. Yellowbird is the same. And if I am to be married to a white man, it is important to me that he take a name from my language. Is this something you would do for me?"

At that point in my life, I'd have done damned near anything she asked. And I told her so. "Of course, Weenonaw, I'll do damn near anything you ask," I said.

"Then I believe I will call you Unega Galagina," she said. [15]

"And what does that mean?" I asked her.

"It means that you are my White Buck."

"That's good enough for me," I said, and I snatched her up – spent and exhausted though I may have been – and gave her another good bucking.

And so we lazed around in bed most of the next day, rising only to open the windows when it got warmer and to eat when we were hungry, and we continued this behavior for a day or two more. When I married Eliza, the next day I was up early and off to work in her grandfather's dry goods store. But I much preferred the Cherokee way of marrying, where the husband and wife were left alone from in-laws and chores for a few days.

As I have noted, it never troubled me that I was now a bigamist, nor did I give much thought to what my future might look like. I was well content to spend my time with Weenonaw, at least for now, and if I considered at the time leaving her to return to Milledgeville and Eliza, I do not now remember it.

But as always, I would soon learn that whatever time a man might spend making plans for hisself is all wasted time, for he can never know what plans others are making that will interfere with his own.

CHAPTER 6

Among my concerns that had me eager for the wedding with Weenonaw was my suspicion that the nights there in the foothills of the Ozarks in Injun Territory would get to be fairly cold, and so I was eager to have a warm body to nuzzle up to when the wind started to blow. We were married just a few days before my concerns were made real.

I'd been down at the smithy all day making hooks for meat that Stand Watie intended to hang in the smokehouse in the next couple of days, and so in there with the furnace I'd not realized how much the temperature had dropped during the course of the morning and afternoon. The sun was already well low on the horizon when I came out of the smithy to walk back up to the cabin where I was living with Weenonaw, and I realized that my duster was going to be a poor substitute for a proper coat. I pulled it tight around me and pushed my hat down in the hopes of staving off the wind, and before I got to the trail through the woods leading up to the cabin, it began to snow.

Having grown up in Georgia, snow was a rare sight, and I'll admit to being a bit excited to see it. I ran the path in the woods to the cabin where I found Weenonaw at the hearth cooking up a stew of beefsteak, potatoes, carrots and onions.

"It's snowing!" I said, bursting into the cabin, full of excitement like a fool child.

"Is it?" she asked. "I'm not surprised. The birds were very active this morning, and the clouds today have looked like snow."

She didn't seem to care too much. "I hardly ever seen a snow," I told her. "I can't remember more than a time or two, and it was just ice."

"Well, the snow can mean a tough few months ahead of us," Weenonaw said. "It can mean swollen rivers and difficult traveling. Uncle Stand has plenty of supplies, but we have not given much thought to ourselves."

"I'm sure he'll be glad to share all he has," I said. "There ain't no way he'll get through all the wood I've chopped for him."

"Yes, but if we get bad ice and snow and we can't even get down to the big house, we might find a few uncomfortable weeks up in this cabin. I had to go down to the house today just to get what I needed for tonight's supper. As much as I love you, Jackson, we'll not get through a bad winter with just love making."

"Bah!" I shouted at her in mock anger. "Bite your tongue ye little Cherokee lass! Making love with you is all I need to get me through any season, cold or hot."

Weenonaw gave me a good laugh at that, and she left her pot at the hearth and came across the room to put her arms around me and kiss me.

She was a fine filly, no doubt, and I'd have had her then and there if we'd not been interrupted by a knock on the door.

"Oh! That will be Yellowbird and Elizabeth," Weenonaw said, prying herself loose from me and going to the cabin door. "I told them when I was at the house today to come and see us for supper. I've hardly seen them at all since the wedding. Living out here in our cabin, I feel so far removed from the rest of the family."

"It's snowing!" Yellowbird said, coming into the cabin and shaking the few bits of snow off his hat. Elizabeth also came in, and she was wearing a shawl over her head that she shook off.

"It's more ice than snow, really, but it's coming down pretty hard," Elizabeth said.

I grabbed my duster and my hat and I walked outside to get a look at it. Already icicles were forming at the ends of branches, and small pellets of ice were to be found everywhere on the ground.

In the years since, I've nearly froze to death in snowstorms. I remember a blizzard in Richmond in the winter of '63 where each step sank my boots so deep in the snow that a fresh batch would fall in over the tops of my boots. I've suffered bitter cold nights in snow covered tents where all I wanted to do was cry but my very tears themselves were frozen icicles. Life has taught me to hate snow with a fury, and in my old age I dread the coming of winter when enough coats and blankets cannot be found to keep me warm.

But on this day, even though it was just a poor storm of little ice pellets, I thought it was a wondrous winter vista piling up outside our cabin, and I opened my mouth and stuck my face toward the sky to try to catch some of the little bits of cold water on my tongue.

Weenonaw laughed at me and came out and put her arms around me. "Unega Galagina, it is not even a good snow," she said.

"How long will it last?" I asked.

"We should hope not long. This is all just ice. It will build up on the trees and bring down branches or whole tree tops. And it will make the paths slippery and difficult to walk upon. Although with the sun going down, it will get colder, and perhaps it will turn to snow. Then it won't be so bad."

We went into the cabin and had supper with Yellowbird and Elizabeth.

Through Weenonaw, I had learned some of Yellowbird's story, and he began to make more sense to me then. He was studying law in those days, and had been east, Connecticut or Massachusetts or somewhere in New England, where he'd attended school, met and not long ago married Elizabeth. They'd returned to Injun Territory earlier in the year and in the spring he would be going to study law over in Fayetteville, Arkansas.

What drew him to me, I believe, was the way in which I had dispatched those assassins what had come for his Uncle Stand.

Yellowbird never spoke of it to me, but Weenonaw had confided that when he was just a boy of twelve years, Yellowbird had been present when a gang of John Ross's men dragged John Ridge — Yellowbird's father — out of his home and murdered him. The boy had witnessed the entire thing.

"Uncle Watie fears that Yellowbird's desire to come back here is not to study law but to seek revenge now that he is a man," she had told me. "Elizabeth has said as much to me. She knows that Yellowbird burns with a desire for retribution. She says that he has murder in his heart."

He was drawn to me, I believed then and now, because he saw in me a man who could help him become the hand of revenge he sought to be. What Yellowbird knew was that I'd been a mighty warrior in Mexico and had slain three assassins who'd come after his uncle — men sent by John Ross, who also sent the assassins who killed his father. I would not doubt that Yellowbird imagined a time when the two of us would seek out his father's killers and together we would pay them back.

So you see, for all the time he spent hanging about, Yellowbird never understood who I was at all. Which was my own doing — I'd told all these stories of my own bravery in Mexico, and he had no reason to doubt me.

We ate stew for supper, and I made up stories about the Texas Rangers to entertain Yellowbird and Elizabeth. Before we were finished with our supper, both of them had joined Weenonaw in calling me Unega Galagina, and they thought it was a great joke that I was now known among them as White Buck.

By the light of an oil lantern we played cards for a bit, and Yellowbird read to us some poetry he'd written. I only recall one of the poems, and what I remember of it is that it was a love poem, dripping with sweetness, and that he referred in it to what I presumed was Elizabeth's bosom, white and pillow-like so that he'd like to lay his head against it. She was buttoned up against the cold so that I couldn't get much of a look, but she didn't strike me as having pillows worthy of setting pen to paper and writing a poem over, but maybe so.

Finally, Yellowbird stretched and yawned and I gave Weenonaw a wink, but when we showed him and Elizabeth to the door, the ground outside was thick with white stuff.

In the three hours or so since our guests arrived at the cabin, the snow had piled up pretty heavy on the ground and was still coming down at a fearsome rate.

"You can't go back to the house in this weather," Weenonaw said, testing the snow at the bottom of the porch steps and finding a thick layer of slick ice beneath it. "You'll just have to spend the night here with us."

Regardless of the slick ice, the four of us went outside the cabin for a bit and threw snowballs at each other and chased each other through the snow. The snow continued to fall, and it was cold as all hell running about like that and getting hit with snowballs. But we was having fun and didn't care much about the cold.

Yellowbird decided he was a Texas Ranger, and every time he hit me with a snowball he would yell, "Yee-haw!" and "Remember the Alamo!"

It was fine fun, but it wasn't long before my shirt was soaked through and my teeth were chattering, and Weenonaw and Elizabeth – who'd both been spared the worst of the snowballs by Yellowbird and me – decided it was time for us to go inside before we caught colds.

Before we turned in, I built the fire up pretty good so that it might last through the night. Yellowbird and Elizabeth slept on the rug in front of the fireplace, and Weenonaw and I slept in the loft. The warmth of the fire did pretty well to keep the loft warm, and I found that Weenonaw and a couple of blankets were sufficient to beat back whatever cold drifted in between the boards of the cabin walls.

Sometime during the night the snow stopped. There was plenty of it on the ground all the next day, but a couple of days after that it was all gone but a few patches in the woods where the sun didn't reach. There'd been enough of it, though, that everything was mud and wet, and the rivers and creeks were swollen so that some were impassible. Winter had settled in but good.

By Christmas, the walks through the woods to the smithy were bitter, and our cabin proved to be full of opportunities for the cold wind to get inside. Even so, our visits to the big house were rare. We put our mattress on the floor of the cabin near the fire, and we spent our nights under blankets with our bodies offering each other warmth, and I can say that in the nights I never felt so much as a chill. Weenonaw was the perfect woman for snuggling with through a cold winter.

Many nights we kept a lamp burning late into the evening as we read books to each other or talked late about nothing. Weenonaw loved to talk about the children we would have. She had decided there would be three boys and a girl, and I would teach the boys to be brave warriors and she would teach the girl to be a strong woman who would shun advances of any man not fit for her.

"Is that what you did?" I teased. "Did you shun advances until ye found one fit enough for ye?"

"That is what I did," Weenonaw told me. "That first night that you appeared at the big house, after having saved Uncle Stand, I knew you were the man who was fit to have me."

She was a fine filly, and she knew better than most how to make a man feel good about hisself. And I don't mean with pretty words or compliments. A look, a touch, a stroke of the hand, a brush of the lips. She had a talent, that girl.

When the snow came heavy and the path was frozen with a sheet of ice, we spent days at a time together in the cabin. And when the sun came out to give the slightest hint of warmth, we'd venture down to the big house for supplies or a meal with the family, or I would chop some wood to be sure we had plenty at the cabin.

It was not uncommon, neither, for Stand Watie to come up to the cabin when the sun was out to go for a walk through the woods and along the bluffs overlooking the Spavinaw Creek. We sometimes hunted for deer together, but I only remember ever killing one doe for all the mornings we spent sitting at the foot of a tree and watching in the bottoms below for signs of deer. Had it been a little warmer with less snow, I'd have been reminded of hunts from my childhood with my own uncle.

Mostly, it was a leisurely life in those winter days at the end of 1847 and the beginning of 1848. We were near enough to the plantation house where there were plenty of supplies so that we never had a moment of concern, but it was rustic enough in that cabin that, Weenonaw and me, we formed the sort of closeness a couple finds in times of want when the only comfort that can be found is in each other.

Throughout the winter, too, Stand Watie had big dances at the house or in the barn. At Christmas and New Year, you've never seen so many Injuns dressed in their finest and dancing to the music you'd have expected to hear at a planter's ball back home in Georgia. All my preconceptions of Injuns were shattered during that winter of living among the Cherokee to see how they lived just like any other white folks back home.

Of course, the Cherokee and some of them eastern tribes were all pretty well civilized. The western tribes – the 'Pache and the Comanche, the Blackfoot and the Lakota – of whom I would one day experience too much, there warn't no civilization in them, nor would there ever be.

As the days wore to weeks and the weeks wore to months, it was a pleasurable life I found myself living in the foothills of the Ozarks there in Injun Territory, and I came often to think of Cherokee Cock, my fellow Texas Ranger who sent me north when I was bound to the east. Cherokee Cock understood that my soul was soured by the violence I'd experienced in Mexico, and he knew these Injuns had some secret medicine for the soul. Of course, the medicine I needed I found in my new wife, whether that's what Cherokee Cock had in mind or not.

I now found myself married to two different women, both from better families than my own, and I had double options of a better life than I might have once thought possible. I expected I could live here in Injun Territory as the nephew-in-law of a prominent chief with a big plantation and do all right for myself. Or I could return home to Georgia and inherit the store of a wealthy merchantman. Either way, it seemed my future was bright enough. If I was leaning toward one future more than the other, my intentions probably were to stay with my new wife. It was nothing against Eliza or how I felt about her, but Eliza was five hundred miles away and I'd not seen her for many, many months. Weenonaw, though, was here in front of me, and all I ever had to do was give her a wink, and I could get to grips with her right away.

CHAPTER 7

Come spring, Yellowbird and Elizabeth intended to return to Fayetteville where he would resume his law studies, and in late winter Yellowbird asked Standhope if I could escort him into Arkansas. The fear that Yellowbird would fall victim to the feud with John Ross was a present concern, and Watie was opposed to him making the journey without some sort of escort.

Yellowbird did not announce to me his intentions to seek permission for me to accompany him to Fayetteville. Had he asked, I'd have invented some good reason for me not to join him. Though my encounter with John Ross had been a few months prior, I'd not forgotten it, and I was in no hurry to leave the safety of the Spavinaw plantation. And I certainly had no interest to travel as the armed escort serving as protection against Ross or his surrogates. I'd seen how them Injuns at my wedding had cottoned up to Stand Watie, and I felt certain that along the road to Fayetteville there would be plenty of Injuns who'd be glad to likewise get in the good graces of John Ross who, at that time, was the primary chief of the Cherokee nation. And what better way to impress an Injun Chief than to bring to him the scalp of a hated enemy?

No, if asked, I'd have put an end to all that talk of me riding protection for Yellowbird. But no one asked me.

Instead, the first I learned of Yellowbird's interference was from Weenonaw, and she was thrilled with the prospect.

"I have a surprise for you," she said one afternoon when I returned from working in the smithy. Though the sun was brighter and warmer than it had been for months, the late afternoon still got chilly as spring was not fully on us.

I shook out of my coat and hung it on a peg beside the door. I pulled off my gloves and put them on a table below the peg. I rubbed my hands together to warm up my fingers, for the leather gloves were really just work gloves and did little to keep off the cold, and then I rubbed my hands against my face.

"I hope it's some of that stew I smell," I told her. The stew was steaming hot coming out of a large pot hanging in the fireplace.

Weenonaw took a piece of bread and put it on a plate, and then she spooned some of the stew atop the bread.

"I have stew for you, but that's not the surprise," she said.

I took the plate and a fork and started into the stew even before I sat myself at the table. Potatoes and carrots and cabbage with chunks of beef and all sorts of seasonings made up a good stew on a cold day. Some fresh bread below it was enough to fill a belly. Weenonaw slid a chair out for me and then she sat beside me.

"Yellowbird and Elizabeth are leaving tomorrow," she said. "Yellowbird is returning to Fayetteville to study law. The roads are good, and with a wagon, the trip will take a few days. Uncle Stand needs someone to go along with them, you know, just to keep an eye on Yellowbird. There is probably no danger, but Uncle Stand does not want Yellowbird and Elizabeth to travel alone. And, of course, someone must bring home the wagon and mule team."

"I'll be sorry to see them go," I said, my mouth full of potato, carrot, beef and bread. My mind wasn't quite operating, so focused on the food as I was, and I did not immediately realize that I was being invited into danger. "Yellowbird has been like a shadow to me all these months, and I'm sure I'll miss his company."

"Yes," Weenonaw agreed. "That's right. And like a true shadow,

Yellowbird has asked Uncle Stand if you might accompany them to Fayetteville. You could stay a few days and help Yellowbird and Elizabeth settle in, and then come back."

I nearly spit beef stew all over my bride. "What?" I asked. "But, why?" I raged. Immediately my mind was full of John Ross's hired assassins filling the hills of Injun Territory and northwest Arkansas. Through the winter John Ross and his vendetta against me was a distant concern, but now that it was beginning to warm up and the snow was melted and the roads passable, I'd had more than passing worries that I might yet find myself part of this feud between Watie and Ross.

"Yellowbird likes you so much, and I think he wants a last opportunity to hear of your adventures in Mexico so that he has plenty of Texas Ranger stories to think about when he's supposed to be studying the law. Uncle Stand was intending to send a couple of men and a slave or two along with Yellowbird, but he knows sending you would be worth sending half a dozen men, and so he has acquiesced to Yellowbird's requests."

It was my own doing, having bragged for so long to all these damned Injuns about my imaginary exploits in Mexico, and now they thought I was some sort of heroic gunslinger who could ride protection for a schoolboy poet and his wife.

I searched about in my mind for some excuse that would get me out of this mess. Down at the smithy there were two dozen finished horseshoes in a pile, so my excuse could hardly be the barefooted horses. There was neither need for hinges nor hooks, and no child on the plantation – including the slave chillen – was without a wrought iron rocking horse. I couldn't imagine Stand Watie would need firewood even for the next two winters after all the lumber I'd cut back in the fall.

"I can't be expected to bring back a team of mules and a wagon by myself," I said.

"Oh, Uncle Stand will still send a couple of slaves along to help you bring back the wagon," Weenonaw said.

I cast about in my mind for some other excuse that would prevent me from being able to accompany Yellowbird through John Ross's back yard, and looking at the pretty, glowing face of Weenonaw seated at the table across from me, I found my reason.

"It's hardly fair," says I, "to ask a man newly married to leave the bosom of his wife to travel through the mountains when it's not yet hardly springtime."

Weenonaw smiled, believing my sincere regret would be in leaving her and not in leaving the safety of the plantation.

"I don't know if we can still say we're newly married, but I had a similar thought. I said so to Uncle Stand, and he agreed with me," she said to my great relief. I was glad these damned Injuns had been swayed by common sense and sound argument.

"Well, then that's that settled. We'll be up early to see off Yellowbird and Elizabeth and to wish him luck in his studies."

"No, Unega," Weenonaw said. "I told Uncle Stand it was not fair to send you off when we would miss each other terribly. He agreed, and so he's going to let me go with you!"

"But, what if Ross, now that it's spring, has sent assassins to watch the plantation?" I asked. Though my concern was completely for myself, I said to her, "It cannot be safe for you to go!"

Weenonaw laughed, and her laugh was very pretty, very melodious. She was a like a song when she laughed.

"Oh, Unega, there will be no assassins. John Ross has forgotten you over the winter. But it will be a fine trip for us to spend a few days away. Uncle Stand wants us to stay one night with one of my cousins who makes pottery. We'll only be gone for a few days, three weeks, or four, at the most, and it will be a fun little journey for us to make together."

Weenonaw in Cherokee means "pretty face" or something, but it might just as well have meant "mule," for my bride was as stubborn as a pack animal. I made weak arguments against leaving the comfort and warmth of our cabin, whether it was wise to travel with the possibility that there might come up another late snow, and finally whined a bit about my desire to have privacy with her. But Weenonaw heard none of what I said and instead insisted it was going to be a wonderful time, and she could hardly sleep that night for her excitement.

In spite of my nerves, I found a way in which we could take advantage of her restlessness, and that did a good bit to take my mind off my fears of assassins lurking in the hills and forests. In my marriage to Weenonaw I will say this, she was as eager to come to grips as ever I was, and the good woman never once told me no or pushed me away. I spent my life with Eliza, and the longevity of our marriage gives me a certain loyalty to her, but I don't have any qualms in saying that of all the women I found myself married to over the years, Weenonaw is far and away my second favorite wife. And of all of 'em I bedded, I suppose only Kate Cherry ever out-ranked my Cherokee bride for being more eager to mess up the bedsheets.

Back in those days nobody'd ever heard of such a thing as a honeymoon. I suppose it's possible it was the sort of thing that wealthy New England Yankees might've engaged in, but the notion would have been as foreign in Injun Territory as a Chinaman. But that was sure enough what we did – Weenonaw and me, with Yellowbird and Elizabeth and a couple of worthless slaves tagging along, went on a honeymoon to Fayetteville, Arkansas.

In the morning we set off. Two slaves were driving a team of mules pulling the covered wagon, loaded down with furniture, books and no doubt reams of paper on which Yellowbird intended to write poetry. We had a couple of spare mounts lashed to the wagon. Elizabeth and Weenonaw rode in a four-wheeled buggy drawn by a single horse, and both women were wrapped in blankets all around them. I was riding Courage, and Yellowbird was on his own stallion. I was layered in long johns and britches, shirts and a heavy coat, and I had a wool scarf wrapped around my face to keep the wind from freezing my snot. There was still a wintry bite to the air, and I wasn't convinced that if a rain came up in the late afternoon it wouldn't turn to snow after dark.

I had a long gun already loaded with ball and powder in a scabbard on my saddle and my Paterson on my hip, but my intention was to never have to use either. I'd already made up my mind if John Ross's assassins attacked, I was hightailing it in the other direction. I'd run until I was back home in Georgia, and to hell with my Injun wife and in-laws.

I'll say that after a few miles, I found that I didn't mind being out there. With enough clothes it wasn't terrible cold, even galloping on Courage's back, and after the long winter months it felt good to be riding along the road toward Arkansas. I'd spent so much time on Courage's back – first in Mexico riding escort to supply wagons or toting messages north and south, and then riding up through Texas to find the Spavinaw – that I had come to enjoy the traveling. And now that I was back out on a trail for a long ride, I realized how much I had missed it while spending the winter cooped up in the cabin.

I suspected, too, that Weenonaw was feeling her own bit of cabin fever, and that must have been why she was so eager to go on this trip.

The heavy snows through the winter had turned everything to muck for weeks on end, but the last snowfall had been back in February, and the sun had shone through the past couple of weeks. The result was that the road wasn't terrible now. It was dry enough that we had no issues with the wheels getting stuck, and Courage seemed to relish the times that I'd give him free rein and he'd gallop on up ahead of the caravan. We had no big rivers to cross, and the few streams we went over, while a little swollen, were easy enough to ford.

Other travelers were rare up there through Injun Territory, which suited me fine. When we did pass by another wagon or a rider, I'd keep my hand on the grip of my pistol. Weenonaw was driving the buggy, and Elizabeth kept a loaded musket across her lap. Yellowbird was armed with a pistol that he kept his grip on most all of the time, whether there were other travelers in sight or not, but the farther we got from the Spavinaw the more I grew at ease. I reasoned if there were to be any assassins about, they'd have probably been watching Watie's place and would likely have attacked us not long after leaving there. But we'd traveled at a good pace all morning, and now miles from Watie's plantation, I felt comfortable that we would see no assassins.

Even so, all through the day I'd ride up ahead of the group and then double back, all to be sure that there were none of John Ross's men lying in wait ahead of us or following behind. I was fully convinced that we were not being followed and that there was no danger ahead.

So I relaxed my fears, though I should not have.

In addition to seeing Yellowbird and Elizabeth to Fayetteville, Stand Watie asked that along the way we make a stop at the home of a relation – a cousin to Weenonaw – who made clay pots, vases, and pitchers. Watie used the clay pieces at the plantation, but he also sold them at a spring market. Watie asked that we bring back with us as many of the vessels as we could get into the wagon for selling at the market.

This cousin of Weenonaw's lived in Arkansas in a tiny little village called Lee Town. It's not there now, having been abandoned not long after the war, and it was the location of a rough fight. If you were wearing gray there in 1862, ye'd have known the place as Pea Ridge, and if you were in blue, ye'd have known it as Elkhorn Tavern. The Elkhorn Tavern was there in '48 when Yellowbird, Elizabeth, Weenonaw and I came through, but it was still just a home at that point. [16]

Of course I did not know it at the time, but I was at the place where my old captain from Mexico would meet his end as a general for the Confederacy. Ben McCulloch, still leading his men from the front like a damned fool, would be shot dead on the edge of a hay field not 200 yards from the road we traveled that evening. And, of course, Stand Watie would be leading an army of Cherokee braves at the same battle, also fighting on behalf of the Confederacy. But all that was well in the future, and I mention it only as an aside to show how small the world was back then.

The cousin was an older woman, a widow, with eight children of varying ages running about the place. She was thrilled to see us, and not least because we brought with us a fair amount of cash from Watie with which to purchase as many of her clay pots as we could fit in or tie on the wagon.

The woman, whose name I've managed to forget over the years, didn't have much of a spread to put out for us, but she sent some of her children to run and fetch up other relatives who lived nearby, and in a couple of hours we were overrun with relations, most of whom Weenonaw did not recognize and could not remember having ever met. As they had at the wedding, these Injuns lined up pretty quick to make certain sure they were seen, not because they cared anything for Weenonaw and certainly not for me, but because they wanted to be sure Standhope got word that they'd been to see his niece and nephew and their spouses.

Weenonaw found it amusing to no end to introduce me to all her kinfolk as Unega Galagina, the Cherokee name she'd given me, and they all took to calling me Unega without question. Yellowbird and Elizabeth both also found sincere joy in it, and I couldn't help but wonder if there wasn't some joke I was missing.

I don't know if it was the hint of spring in the air, the first bit of moving about we'd tasted since the fall, or quite what it was that got into me, but I was feeling a bit sprightly after supper, and I was desperate to get Weenonaw off to a place where we might find some privacy.

We were in the crowded parlor of her cousin's home, a room not big enough for ten adults and now teeming with a dozen children and twenty adults all making conversation and having a big time at the occasion of our visit. Weenonaw was talking with some distant kinsman that I doubted she even knew. I pushed my way past a couple of them Injuns and came up behind her. From that vantage, I slid my hand down Weenonaw's back until I had in my palm the roundness of her backside. I ran my hand over it without any of them Injuns seeing what I was doing, and then with both hands I wrapped up her waist and pulled her back toward me so that I was pressed hard against her.

"Maybe there's a room where we can retire for a bit?" I whispered into the back of her head, and I could see her cheeks raise in a smile.

"Oh, certainly Unega," she said loudly for the sake of the other Injuns. "Unega would like to see where you make your pots," Weenonaw said to her pottery making cousin. "Would you mind if I showed him your workshop?"

"No, no, dear," the cousin said. "Please, take him out and show him."

It was damned chilly outside that night, but it felt spectacular. The house, with fires lit in both the fireplaces and all them Injuns standing around so tight, was getting uncomfortably stuffy, and the fresh, cold air was like a baptism.

Weenonaw shivered, and I put an arm around her.

"There must be a hundred children in that house," she said, laughing her musical laugh. "Too many bodies in too tight a space. It was getting so I couldn't breathe!"

"Oh, aye," says I. "I was having a bit of trouble breathing, meself, but it warn't the children running about that were giving me trouble."

"Is that right?" Weenonaw asked suspiciously. "And so why was it hard for you to breathe, Unega Galagina?"

"You, my dear, were taking my breath away," I said. It was foolish sentimentality, but she glowed at that because she knew it was true.

We came up to a small log cabin. "In here," Weenonaw said to me, and her voice was heavy. "I will steal your breath in here."

The workshop was a single room with a couple of tables, some shelves, tubs full of wet clay, a stool and a wheel, and fired pots were stacked everywhere.

I'd barely gotten the door closed behind me before Weenonaw turned on me, her mouth reaching up to mine and her hands pulling my shirt tails from my britches. Her fingers were sliding up under my shirt, kneading into my muscles. I held her tight in the small of her back with my right hand and slid my left hand up along her ribs, feeling the curve of her teat through her blouse. Now there was a pillow on which I'd lay my head.

"Damned if I can get enough of you," I said with her lips pressing against mine own.

I pulled up her buckskin skirt and lifted her up to the table that was in the center of the room, and we rocked that table pretty hard to see if it would stay together, and she clawed at my sides with those strong fingers of hers, sometimes reaching up to pull my face down to her face so that we could bruise each other's lips with kisses.

We were coming to grips pretty rough, and I took a step to get a bit more leverage, and that's when I stuck my foot into a low, wide clay basin with freezing cold water in it. The freezing water made me jump and yelp, and I stumbled headlong into a stack of clay pots that must have been six feet high.

The pots came crashing down, with me in tow, and before I realized what had happened, I was sprawled on the floor of that dark cabin with broken pottery shards all around me and Weenonaw, spread awkwardly on the table, laughing her damned fool head off.

"This is funny to you?" I asked.

"It is so funny to me!" she said, and with the moonlight coming through the windows and shining silver against her brown skin, white teeth, and black hair, I swear I've seldom seen a prettier sight.

With my arm, I swept the pottery shards out of the way so that we had some room to operate. "Come down here and ride your white buck," I said, and Weenonaw obliged me. She was a fine filly.

When we'd done our bit, Weenonaw and I swept up all the broken pottery onto a flat clay tray, and I walked the tray to a creek running beside the cabin and tossed the broken bits into the stream in the hopes that our frolicking might go undiscovered. There were so many stacks of pots in the cabin, that I couldn't hardly see how one stack more or less could make any difference. For the next few days, anytime I was feeling frisky and wanted to see my beautiful squaw blush, I'd ask her if she wanted to break pottery with me.

All these years later I can say it's a fact that I never did a piece of pottery break that I didn't think immediately of getting belly to belly with my beautiful Cherokee wife.

When we woke the next morning, half the Injuns who'd been at supper had spent the night, on a sofa or a rug on the floor, so that breakfast was an ordeal of screaming young'uns and fist pumping Injuns insistent that I remember them to Standhope. Old Stand Watie was a powerful man in the tribe.

CHAPTER 8

In 1848, Fayetteville, Arkansas, was exactly the sort of lawless place ye'd expect to find near the border with Injun Territory. Murders were common enough that they had a hill specifically designated as Gallows Hill, and there were periodic feuds that blew up into small battles from time to time. There were at least two colleges and a female seminary in town, and a recently constructed woolery, and they were in the process of building a church while we were there, and so there was no doubt that Fayetteville would soon be abandoning its wild, border town ways for a gentler lifestyle with less shooting and fewer hangings.

Yellowbird and Elizabeth rented a house in town from the Tebbett family. [17] Weenonaw and I spent a few carefree days helping Elizabeth set up the home to her liking. While we were in Fayetteville, Elizabeth confided to Weenonaw that she was a couple of months pregnant, and she asked Weenonaw to share the news with the family when we returned to the Spavinaw plantation.

Yellowbird and Elizabeth had met and married in Fayetteville, so this was a homecoming for them. Yellowbird's widowed mother was still living in Fayetteville, as were Elizabeth's parents. Their visit to Watie's plantation had always been just an extended stay, and their intention all along was to return here. As such, Yellowbird had already arranged by letter to secure a position at the local newspaper, and so he started work while Weenonaw and I were still there.

What with the knowledge that Elizabeth was pregnant and the fact that Yellowbird was away at work through most of the day, Weenonaw and I decided to stay only a few days before making the return trip to the Spavinaw plantation. Yellowbird was, of course, disappointed, and encouraged me to consider coming to Fayetteville to live, promising that he could help me find work there. Before we left, I told him I would give it some serious thought and said I would write and let him know what I had decided.

For our return, Weenonaw recommended that we travel west back into Injun Territory and then north toward Spavinaw. This would have us making a big circle, for our initial trip had been east to Lee Town and then south to Fayetteville. She and Yellowbird had some heated conversations about it, but at the time I did not understand why. Weenonaw insisted that the roads that way would be better than the roads we'd traveled to get to Fayetteville, and Yellowbird repeatedly told her it was unwise to go that way.

Ignorant of the difference, I offered no opinion either way, but I was greatly concerned at how adamant Yellowbird was that we should avoid the route Weenonaw had selected. When I asked her about it, she brushed it off as Yellowbird being overly cautious, but she did not say what it was he was being cautious about.

On the morning of our departure, the slaves with the wagon and the clay pots left out before Weenonaw and me. As I mounted on Courage, Yellowbird climbed upon his Stallion and rode with us to the edge of town. It was a good bit warmer, having come into mid-March by then, and I'd shed a layer or two of the clothes by that point.

We were leaving the buggy for Yellowbird and Elizabeth, so Weenonaw was riding in a saddle now and skipping along up ahead of us. Yellowbird stopped me as we left Fayetteville proper to have a word.

"When you get back to Indian Territory, you'll be well south of Uncle Watie's plantation," Yellowbird said. "You'll be riding right through the part of the territory controlled by John Ross and his faction. Keep a careful watch, Unega. Weenonaw is too careless of these things. I have seen for myself how dangerous John Ross and his people are."

I put on a brave face as I shook Yellowbird's hand, bid him farewell and rode off to catch up to Weenonaw, but I can tell you his warning had turned my guts to a squirming, rumbling mess.

I knew nothing at the time about the lay of the land, but if ye were to look at a map of eastern Oklahoma, what was then just Injun Territory, you would see the foolishness of our return trip. Fayetteville was almost directly east of Tahlequah, which was the capital of the Cherokee nation. Tahlequah was where John Ross made his home. Our return trip would take us straight west from Fayetteville, almost on a line with Tahlequah. We wouldn't go quite that deep into Injun Territory before turning north, but all that part of the Territory was controlled by Ross and his people.

With both of us on horseback, it did not take long for us to overtake the slaves in the wagon. Neither of us gave any thought to riding along with them. Both of them were older men with families back at the plantation, and they were unlikely to make some attempt to runaway – there was nothing life could offer them any better than what they had on the Spavinaw with Stand Watie. And so we rode along at our own pace.

By then, much of the chill had left the air and we could feel some of the spring warmth, and it was truly a pleasant trip out through the countryside. The road was good and we made quick work of getting through Arkansas and into Injun Territory.

Without betraying my own fears, I decided to try to weigh how much danger we were riding into. I rode up alongside Weenonaw and said to her, "Yellowbird says we're riding into territory controlled by John Ross."

Weenonaw smiled at me. "We'll be safe," she said. "Ross and his people will not bother us. We are in Cherokee territory, not John Ross territory. He does not own the Cherokee people, and we have as many friends here as we have at home. And besides, we both know who gets the worst of it when you come up against John Ross and his men."

I found no comfort that our salvation might be determined by Weenonaw's faith in me.

We traveled leisurely through most of the afternoon, but before evening we stopped at a tavern to spend the night. The tavern keeper was a white man, which gave me some comfort that he likely wouldn't be a John Ross loyalist, but I don't mind admitting I was nervous as hell. The tavern was at the intersection of the east-west road from Fayetteville through Tahlequah and the north-south road that would take us back up toward Watie's Spavinaw plantation. This was as close to Tahlequah as we would get, and my gut was knotted up like a black walnut tree.

The tavern warn't much. A dining room with a couple of tables and a few rooms with rope beds and flat mattresses, but it was a place to stay for the night. The front porch of the tavern had a few comfortable rocking chairs. We made arrangements with the tavern keeper for the slaves with the wagon to spend the night in the barn, so Weenonaw and I sat the front porch for an hour or so waiting for the slaves to come along in the wagon, and then we directed them along to the barn.

The supper at the tavern was decent enough, but my guess would be that the slaves had a better night's sleep. Weenonaw and I slept in different rooms – the women travelers being appointed to one room, and the men travelers sent to another. Thankfully, there were not so many men staying the night that I was forced to share my bed with another man as was common in crowded taverns back in those days.

At some point in the night, not long after I'd turned in, I was aware of a knocking on the front door of the tavern, and from the noises below I realized some number of men had come late to the tavern and had taken at least a couple of the empty beds in the back of the ground floor, but I thought nothing of it.

I woke early the next morning, realizing this was the first time I'd spent a night separated from my wife since our wedding day, and I found myself in a state where I was missing her terribly. So I quietly dressed myself and tiptoed past the other men sleeping in my room, and I walked down the hall to the room where the women were housed.

"Weenonaw," I whispered at the door. "Come, let's go for a walk."

The sun was just creeping up, and only a soft blue light was coming around the curtains covering the windows at the end of the hallway.

I whispered at the door again, and was about to give up when I heard from within the women's room a stirring of noises, and as I'd hoped, a moment later Weenonaw was smiling at me through the crack in the door.

"Unega, what are you in the hall whispering about?" she asked, but she knew well enough what was in my mind.

"Let's go for a walk," says I, with a wink. "Surely there's some pottery about here that needs breaking."

She smiled and nodded, and opened the door a bit more so that she could slip through it, and together we walked quietly down to the bottom floor and out the front door of the tavern.

"I was missing you," Weenonaw said. "I woke up and I was so lonely not having you there with me. This is the first night we've spent apart since we were married."

"Well, you know what I was thinking about," says I.

Weenonaw laughed as I wrapped an arm around her waist and pulled her up tight against me. "I do know what you were thinking about," she said, and a sly smile went across her face.

We walked together, my arm around her and Weenonaw leaning into me. It wasn't particularly cold, but it was still early enough in spring that there was some chill to the air. We went out past the barn behind the tavern. There were other outbuildings around the barn, and I pulled on the doors and found them all barred. But eventually we came to a door in the stables that was unlocked, and then we found an empty stable that was cleaned out.

"In here?" I asked.

Weenonaw walked into the stable ahead of me and found a blanket that she spread out onto the floor of the stable, and then we set about undressing each other. Weenonaw's brown complexion was the loveliest I've ever seen, without blemish or flaw of any kind, and I would know for I had surveyed every inch of her glorious body. Her hips were rounded like a stone statue, and her black nipples stood out like a couple of elderberries pointing to the sky, perfect for biting and pinching. Oh! She was a marvelous beauty, and if I close my eyes now and think back hard enough, I can feel the softness of her perfect skin as she moved and writhed beneath me.

She was an outstanding woman, that Weenonaw, and I am glad that for a while she was mine.

Later when we were finished and were laying on that musty old horse blanket on the floor of the stable, Weenonaw started laughing, and when I looked at her, she had tears coming from the corners of her eyes.

"Are ye daft?" I asked her. "Laughing and crying? What is wrong with you, girl?"

She just looked at me for a bit and then she said, "You make me very happy Unega Galagina. I did not know it was possible to be happy like this. To be at peace in my soul like this. I never thought it would be possible to have my heart so full and my mind so still."

She took a deep breath and let it out slowly, and I could feel her peace.

"I am glad you're happy Weenonaw," I said.

"I do not know why," she continued, "but I have a sick feeling in my stomach that it cannot last."

Without cause, I thought of Eliza, that red-headed beauty back in Georgia, and for some reason I felt Weenonaw was probably right. In a flash, I felt certain that this beautiful native girl was just a spell, but forever was waiting for me in Milledgeville.

We dressed and walked back to the tavern where the wife of the tavern keeper was already starting to fix breakfasts for the guests. It was ham, eggs, potatoes, and red eye gravy, I remember.

CHAPTER 9

We were the first of the travelers at the tavern to get our breakfast, and we both ate with an appetite heightened by our exertions in the stable. In fact, when Weenonaw was done with breakfast, I was just getting a second helping. Weenonaw went to pack her bag so that we could get back on the road. As she left the dining room, three other lodgers came down the stairs. I noted that one of them, in particular, took notice of her and watched her as she walked past them up the stairs. But I paid no more attention to it. Weenonaw was a beautiful woman, and it would have been a damned odd man who didn't give her a second look if she walked past.

There were only two tables in the dining room, but they were both long tables. I was seated alone at the end of one table, and the three men took a seat at the same table, but down at the other end. They paid no attention to me, and I paid no attention to them other than to note that they were all three Injuns and looked to be Cherokee. Nevertheless, their conversation drifted along the length of the table, and I could not help but overhear them as they tucked into their breakfast.

One of the men leaned forward to the other two and said, "I'll swear that was Stand Watie's niece."

"You know, you may be right," one of the others said. He looked at the third man and said, "Weenonaw. That's the one John Ross said was marrying the man who killed your brother."

In a moment, I felt my breakfast rush at the gallop into my throat, followed not far behind by my stomach.

One of these men was a brother to one of the would-be assassins I'd killed in the Spavinaw River. They had recognized Weenonaw and had heard that the man she was marrying – me! – had killed the would-be assassins.

These Injuns were too slow to put one and one together, and it had not yet occurred to them that the only other man breakfasting in the tavern was with Weenonaw. I tried to think of what to do. A headlong sprint for the door, a race to the barn to get Courage saddled, and I could gallop halfway to Georgia before these Injuns came to two. But if I ran, I would be abandoning my bride to whatever fate these men devised for her.

I reached to my hip for the Paterson. I could gun these men down while they were still adding one and one. Cowardly it might be, but damn cowardice when it means survival.

But my revolver was carelessly left upstairs in my room.

My heart was pounding and my guts were twisted. I could feel perspiration beading up all over me. B'God would I even make it to the door before one of these damned Injuns realized I must be Weenonaw's husband?

What would happen when Weenonaw came back down the stairs? I anticipated all sorts of horrors. Would these three Injuns stand up and draw on her? Would she acknowledge me and alert them to my presence? Would they finally finish their arithmetic, draw on me, and gun me down? Would they abduct us and take us to John Ross so that he could put some sort of terrible Indian torture on us? Would he burn us or scalp us, force us to run the gauntlet or treat us to some other sort of horror?

Before I was even done calculating all of the possible terrible deaths that awaited us, I could hear Weenonaw softly humming to herself as she came walking back down the stairs. Any moment she would reenter the dining room, and at that point I would get the answer to what fate had in store.

I was paralyzed with fear.

But before Weenonaw came back in, one of the men stood up, motioning to the other two who followed his lead, and the three of them left the dining room, walking out the front door of the tavern.

I was not fool enough to think we were suddenly and mysteriously spared, and so I did not waste time. I stood from the table and walked briskly out the side door of the tavern and into the kitchen house. There I found the proprietor of the establishment in a rocking chair smoking on a pipe. His wife was at the cook stove stirring the skillet.

"I'll need my horses saddled right away," I told him. "Tell my slaves out in the barn to get that wagon hitched up and be on their way home. But I'm going on ahead, just as soon as ye've got them horses saddled."

"All right, then," he said. "I'll have my boy take care of it."

I stood for a moment and waited for him to get up to fetch the boy, and he realized I was in a rush.

"Right now," he said. He stood up from his rocking chair and walked back toward the barn where the horses, mules and wagon were.

I turned back toward the door, but I only opened it a crack – just wide enough to look into the dining room. Weenonaw was seated at the table where I'd been. She had her saddle bags with her, and she was alone in the room. I hurriedly walked inside and knelt at the table beside her.

"We have trouble," I whispered, keeping my eye on the door where them Injuns had disappeared. "Those three men who came in when you were leaving, they recognized you. I heard one of them say he was the brother of one of the assassins I killed down on the Spavinaw."

Weenonaw's eyes lit with fear. She immediately understood the danger.

"What will we do?" she asked.

"Not stay here," I said. "I've got to get my saddle bags. The damned Paterson is in my room. I ain't even heeled. I've told the landlord to get our horses saddled, and we'll ride like hell away from here."

Just as I said it, we could hear footfalls on the boards of the front porch of the tavern. I snatched Weenonaw by the wrist, she caught up her saddlebags that were setting on the table, and I all but dragged her up the stairs to my room.

I pulled on my duster and tucked my Paterson into my belt, and then I took a look through the window of my room. I was fortunately in a room that overlooked the front of the tavern, and the roof over the front porch, sloped though it was, was just a step outside my window.

"We can go out the window," I said. "When the proprietor brings the horses around, we'll just drop off the roof, mount up and go. With a bit of luck, we'll be five miles up the road before they know we're gone."

My fear was that Weenonaw would demand I face the men, gun them down in a fair fight, but she did not argue. She seemed genuinely afraid, and only nodded agreement to my plan.

I slid open the window over the porch and listened for a moment to be sure there were no voices that would indicate them Injuns were still outside the tavern. I guessed they were inside, either in the dining room or the hallway behind the stairs, plotting murder. I nodded to Weenonaw and quiet as a mouse she slipped through the window and onto the roof of the porch. As I handed her my saddle bags and then her bags, I saw the landlord's son come around from the back of the tavern leading Courage and Weenonaw's horse.

It seemed that my plan was going to work.

"Drop yourself over the side, quick. I'll drop the saddle bags down to ye!"

Weenonaw inched along the steep roof, and when she reached the edge she lowered herself and dropped. I listened for a moment to make sure she didn't drop down into an ambush, and then I stuck a leg through the window to follow her.

That's when the door to my room crashed open, and I found myself staring into the three most awful brutish faces ye've ever seen. B'God they were ugly sonsofbitches, made no prettier by the fact that every one of them had a revolver in his hand.

I tugged at the Paterson, but bent double and straddling the window the way I was, I couldn't free the damned thing from my belt.

"Kill him!" I heard one of the Injuns say, and I saw all three of them raising their fat fists and pushing on each other to be the first one through the doorway to get a clean shot. I jerked at the Paterson with such violence that I tumbled out of the window and nearly rolled right off the damned roof. I came to rest at the lip of the roof, sprawled on my back with my head and right shoulder hanging in midair.

Now the Paterson came free, and without thought I aimed it at the window I'd just fallen through and fired off a shot that shattered glass. Both saddlebags were on the roof by my right foot, so I kicked them down to the ground where Weenonaw could get them, and then I rolled one more time, sending myself flailing from the roof to the ground below.

I hit the ground hard and knocked the breath out of myself.

Weenonaw was already mounted, having tossed her saddlebags and mine over our horses. "Unega!" she yelled. "You must come now!"

The shock to my body had not yet subsided. I could not breathe, nor did I have strength to stand, but the desperation in her voice triggered my own natural fear, and through fright alone I was able to push meself off the ground.

"Now, Unega!" Weenonaw yelled at me. "They're coming down the stairs!"

I hoisted myself onto the saddle, and as I did, Weenonaw dug in her heels and galloped away. Courage, a damned good horse if there ever was one, didn't need telling, and before my feet found the stirrups he was galloping to overtake Weenonaw in a dash.

I heard the report of the pistols behind us, but it would have taken a better marksmen than them Injuns to hit us at full gallop as we distanced ourselves from them.

As I caught up to her, I realized that my Cherokee bride was laughing her fool head off. She thought it was the best sport, getting away from them Injuns like that.

We rode like hell for a mile or more when we came to a fork in the roadway, and Weenonaw reined in. Courage came to a halt without any prompting from me.

"This is the road north back to home," she said to me, her horse dancing in circles. "They might try to cut us off and ambush us on this road. I don't know them, but I am sure there must be trails that would allow them to get in front of us."

I pointed along the other road. "And this way?"

"That will take us west, very near to Tahlequah and John Ross's plantation. We could ride west and then cut back northeast toward home," Weenonaw said. "Or we could ride north from here and not know if an ambush is ahead of us."

I tried to think of what was best. What I knew for sure was we didn't have long to make up our minds. If we rode north, they might be waiting for us around every bend, unless we got ahead of them quickly. If we went west, we could be riding directly toward worse danger. Deep in my gut I felt a weight on the decision, as if I had an intuition that whatever way I chose now would alter the course of my life, and that premonition scared me as much as the real danger that I knew was chasing me from behind.

"If we ride west, there is little chance they will catch us," I said, reasoning it out loud so that Weenonaw could help me make up my mind. "There is some possibility that we could ride into John Ross or more of his people and create for ourselves a new danger. But if we turn north, we can be sure that them Injuns what was chasing us will – at the very least – still be chasing us. If they come to this fork in the road, they'll turn north without thinking about it. And there's the possibility that they know some trail that could put them on this road ahead of us. Ahead of us and waiting to fight us on ground they choose."

Our situation was grave, and for the first time Weenonaw seemed to understand just how desperate a spot we were in.

"Forgive me, Unega, for doing this to us. We should not have come this way, and I should have known better."

It caught me aback as I realized that tears were flowing freely from her eyes. She'd gone in a short span from laughing at our situation to crying over it, and the fear she showed compounded my own rumbling belly.

"I wanted to live a long life with you, to carry your children, to grow old with you in the happiness I have felt these past few months. I fear I have forsaken that life, Unega. And it is my deep regret."

"There ain't no reason for crying," I insisted. "We've just got to get a move on. You think they'll ambush us if we go north?"

"I do," she said.

"Then let's go west."

I turned Courage west, and we raced against fate.

Weenonaw's tears, and her terrible prediction, were like a hundred pound weight in my gut. I've always known that Injuns have mystical insight, and I feared she'd had a premonition of my murder. As such, I was terrified, and found that it was difficult as hell to keep my wits about me. I knew not to race west as hard as the mounts would go. We might put distance between us and them Injuns behind us, but if we ran into trouble up ahead, we didn't want to be on horses that were exhausted and could go no farther. So we kept them at a trot, understanding that our pursuers behind us might not be so careful with their own mounts. My hope was that the men from the tavern had taken a trail and were planning an ambush for us on the road north and we would never encounter them again. If they were coming up behind us and caught up to us, we would be able to turn our horses loose on a fast dash and their exhausted mounts would allow us to escape.

And so I spent a fair time in the saddle looking over my shoulder for any sign that riders were coming up behind us.

Before long we began passing farms, first one, then another, spread out along the road. "We'll be to Tahlequah soon," Weenonaw told me. "When we pass through town, we must be careful about being seen. Most everyone here is a John Ross supporter, and many people will recognize me."

We slowed our pace as we could see the town on the road below us. We neither wanted to linger nor draw suspicion by hurrying through town. Tahlequah was the Cherokee capital, and it was as decent a city in those days as you'd find back home. Maybe not quite up to par with Milledgeville, but there were numerous brick buildings, schools and churches, shops and the great brick meeting house for the Cherokee government.

Our road west brought us to the central road leading through town, and there were many buildings facing the street on both sides. The road was still muddy from spring rains and heavy traffic, and the women walking across the road lifted their skirts to keep the hems from the filth.

The town was crowded with people. Men at the supply stores and dry goods stores, collecting gossip and news and the things they would need for spring planting. It was obvious the town was still just coming alive after the winter.

I took a drink from my canteen as Courage walked me through the town, and as I bent to stash the canteen back in the saddle, I caught sight of a rider coming down the road behind us at a full gallop.

He was a lone rider, and I could not be sure he was one of the Injuns we'd seen back at the tavern. But I had a bad feeling as he raced down the road.

"We may have trouble riding in behind us," I said to Weenonaw.

She glanced back and saw the rider.

"Is he one of the men we saw at the tavern?" I asked her.

"I cannot be sure," she said.

He was coming fast. "He'll overtake us in a moment," I said. I'd tucked my Paterson into the saddle, and I now reached down and took the grip in my fist. Weenonaw and I both came to a stop, and I turned Courage in the road so that I could keep an eye on the man riding toward us.

I was watching for any sign of recognition from him – a second glance or a sudden start – anything that might suggest he recognized us. I saw nothing, even as he was nearly on top of us. There was a lot of traffic in the road – people walking, buggies and wagons, horses and oxen – and the man was riding hard. His focus was on avoiding obstacles as he galloped through the town, not on who those obstacles might be. And so he passed us by without any sign of recognition. But I recognized him as he rode by us. He was one of the three men seated down the table from me at the tavern. I could see him in my mind as he tried to push his way through the door of my room at the tavern, revolver in hand.

I watched him as he passed us. He rode to a cross street and cut down to the south.

"That was one of them," I said to Weenonaw.

"He is riding toward John Ross's home south of town," she said.

"He didn't seem to recognize us."

"Where are the other two?" Weenonaw asked.

"Let's not wait around long enough to find out," I proposed, and we both wheeled our horses back west and kept moving.

Tahlequah was nearly the western border of the Ozark foothills. West of the town, the terrain began to slowly change. It was flatter and more expansive, and from the crest of a hill we could see for some distance. The road was not more than a dirt trail now, and huge swaths of land had given over to the tallgrass that twenty or thirty miles west of us would completely dominate the landscape.

I'll never know for sure what was happening as Weenonaw and I put Tahlequah behind us, but I can probably put the pieces together pretty well. As Weenonaw suspected, them Injuns back at the tavern knew some trail to take. Two of them took a trail to cut us off and ambush us. I would suppose they did not lay in wait, but instead rode back south down the road where they expected us to be. But they never encountered us, and so they turned west toward Tahlequah. Meanwhile, they sent the third on to Tahlequah to find John Ross and raise up a posse.

Maybe as they roused up a posse someone spoke up and said they'd seen us ride through town. Maybe the other two, the ones who'd tried to ambush us and never found us, rode fast to Tahlequah and stopped the posse from going the wrong direction.

Whatever it was, Weenonaw and I were only a few miles out of Tahlequah when, stopped on a high ridge, I saw behind us a mass of riders. There must have been twenty or more of them, and they were closing the gap between us at a frightening pace.

"Can they possibly be coming for us?" I asked.

"I fear they must be," Weenonaw said.

And now my strategy of sparing the horses for the hard chase paid off. We gave the horses rein to run and tore quickly across the dirt path. At the crest of each hill, I would look back over my shoulder for any sign that the posse was continuing to close the gap, but instead I had lost sight of them.

After an hour of mostly hard riding we stopped by a creek to rest the horses. Courage could have gone on, I knew, but I wasn't sure how long Weenonaw's horse could keep up the race. As the horses grazed and rested, Weenonaw and I sipped from our canteens.

"There is an army fort south of here," she said. "We could ride there and seek protection. It is at the confluence of the Arkansas River and the Neosho River. When we reach the Neosho, which must be not far ahead of us, we can follow it south and come directly to the fort. If we turn north at the Neosho it will take us to the Spavinaw, and there we will be back among friends."

"I could not see them from the last few hills we topped," I said. "Maybe they called off the chase?"

"I cannot believe they would have," Weenonaw said. "They might simply have been below the horizon and out of sight. We cannot trust that they abandoned their effort to catch us."

"Can we cross the Neosho?" I asked. "If there are good options for safety to the north and south, it may be that they have split up and are going to try to cut us off in both directions. Our best opportunity for safety may lie west across the river."

"The Neosho is usually high in the spring, and we've had plenty of rain," Weenonaw said. "There is a ferry at the fort to the south. If I remember right, and it's been many years since I have been here, this trail will take us directly to a ford, but I cannot say if we will be able to cross there. If we can cross, we must be careful of the sand. It will be wet after the winter, and the horses will easily sink into it."

What I'd learned traveling through Texas and into Indian Country the previous summer was that most well-worn trails led directly to a ford. I was convinced that I had not seen the posse because it had split up to cut off our escape north and south. Surely John Ross and his people would expect us to ride south or north when we reached the Neosho River, and rather than chase us to a place where we could find protection, they would attempt to stop us from getting there by getting there ahead of us.

"We should try to ford the river," I decided. "They will expect us to flee south to the fort or to the north to find people friendly to your uncle. They will not expect us to run west."

Weenonaw's face was taut with concern.

"Do you disagree?" I asked her.

She kissed me on the cheek and wrapped her arms around me. "I will run with you, Unega Galagina, in whatever direction you choose. But we will not outrun our pursuers this day."

"Damnation, woman. Do not say things like that," I said, a cold chill running down my spine. I put my arms around her, feeling the curve at the base of her back and pressing my hands into it so that she was pressed tight against me. "That's no way to talk," I whispered into her hair. "We'll get away. This will turn out fine. I promise you."

As pleasant as she was to hold, I did not linger there. "Mount up and let's keep moving," I said.

As we crested a hill and I could still see no sign of our pursuers, I did not know what was worse — seeing the posse as a small cloud of dust on the trail behind us and knowing they were still chasing, or not seeing them and having no idea where they might be.

When we stopped to rest the horses we were closer to the river than either of us realized. The trail slowly descended through a long stand of hardwoods, and it was not long before we came to the Neosho River. The river reminded me of the Oconee River back home at Scull Shoals, not much wider or deeper. The flow was moving along at a good rate, but it was not rushing water. We could swim it without trouble if we had to, but it was shallow enough across a rocky shoal that I believed we could move bank to bank without getting any deeper than our ankles.

We dismounted to walk the horses across the ford.

"You go first and pick the way across," Weenonaw told me. "I will follow you."

I found a long tree limb on the ground near the river and broke the twigs off of it until I had a nice, long pole that I could use to test rocks to make certain they would not shift under the horses' weight. Taking Courage's lead in my hand, I slowly and cautiously stepped out on the rocky shoal. The first break in the shoal allowed the river to rush through the gap in a foamy flow and it made a tremendous roar so that I could not even hear Weenonaw behind me. The gap was not more than five or six feet wide, but too big to step or leap across.

I led Courage out across the rock ledge and we were fine until we reached that first big gap. There I prodded the rocks up stream with my stick and found them to be solid enough. I stepped off the rocky ledge into the water, placing my feet carefully on the rocks I had tested. I made my way upstream a few feet to avoid the rush of the water coming into the gap, and I was knee-deep as I made an arc upstream of the gap in the shoal. Courage carefully followed me, trusting me to find the safe way.

Having cleared the gap in the shoal where the water rushed through, I turned back downstream to the shoal. The rocks here were looser and I had to be careful about my steps, and when I was back on the shoal, I used the stick to point Courage where to put his hooves. In a moment, he leapt out of the deep water and back onto the dry shoal with me. Weenonaw was leading her horse upstream of the gap now, and I yelled at her over the roar of the water. "Here!" I said, pointing to the rocks where Courage and I had walked. "Lead your horse here, these rocks are stable enough."

Weenonaw nodded to me but kept her eyes on the rocks along her path, carefully placing her feet as she braced herself with her horse's lead.

The next gap in the shoal would be easier. It was only a big step across and wouldn't require us to get wet, but the water passed through the narrow gap with even more force. When Weenonaw and her horse were both secure on the shoal, I continued along the ford, taking the big step and leading Courage across behind me. This rock led to a wide sandbar, and then we would be back on the trail.

"Be careful on the sand!" Weenonaw called to me. "It is loose and you can sink deep."

At the edge of the rock I pressed my stick into the sand and was shocked to see how deep it slid. I tested the sand all around, but it was all loose. There was nothing for it but to just step into it and force my way through. With the first step my boots filled with wet sand, and I sank in almost up to my knees. It was miserable trying to force my way through, and Courage was none too pleased to be walking through the deep sand, either.

It was just a few feet of it, though, before the sand gave way to solid ground and I was able to more easily make my way up the bank.

Weenonaw was now stepping through the sand. I let Courage walk up the bank while I waited at the edge of the sand so that I could give Weenonaw a hand.

The roar of the rushing water masked any noise the men on the opposite bank made, and they had come down the bank in the shelter of the trees so that I never even noticed them. Our exertions to ford the river had kept our attention, and that gave them plenty of time to set up their attack.

I reached down and offered Weenonaw my hand, and as I did, she looked up at me and smiled.

"Unega Galagina, this is not an easy thing to do," she said.

Even over the rushing of the water, I heard the crack of the gun on the opposite bank, but I did not immediately understand the noise. Weenonaw suddenly convulsed, her arm went stiff for just a moment, and then I felt her hand go limp in mine. Even as she looked into my face with her big, dark eyes, her smile seemed to slide away, and her brow furrowed into a look of confusion.

"Unega, not easy," she said, but there did not seem to be any meaning behind the words.

I felt a sick swelling in my gut and my heart dropped, but I still had not comprehended what was happening. I just knew instinctively that something terrible was wrong.

Weenonaw slipped forward, still up to her knees in sand, and when she fell forward I could see the back of her head had opened up with a terrible wound and blood was pouring from the hole. Only then did I look up at the opposite bank where I saw a dozen men. Three of them were pointing muskets at me, and a fourth – standing behind a puff of smoke, was peering down the barrel of a musket examining the damage he'd wrought. Before I could think, one of the muskets spit out a cloud of smoke, and a ball crashed into the earth near me.

I grabbed hold of Weenonaw under both arms and dragged as hard as I could to pull her out of the sand. Her horse crashed past me just in time to get hit in the shoulder by another musket ball. The wounded beast, struggling out of the sand, reared and I thought it would bash in my skull with its flailing hooves. I wrenched Weenonaw free of the sand and rolled with her away from the wounded horse.

A third crack came from the far bank, and a ball whipped through the leaves above us.

I scrambled, dragging Weenonaw with me, into the tree line where I might find some safety.

When we were behind some trees, I bent over her and pushed her hair out of her face. Blood was coming from her nostrils and mouth, and her eyes were vacant. Her hair was all matted with blood, and my hands were covered red. My beautiful Cherokee bride was killed on the bank of the Neosho River, and the men who had murdered her were reloading their muskets to do the same to me.

I had just a moment's hesitation. I felt as long as I held Weenonaw's limp body in my arms that perhaps there was some chance that she would spring back to life, that I had misunderstood how bad the wound was, that she would get to her feet and dash with me up the bank, and I believed that if I let go of her that she would be lost to me forever. And tears like the river rushing through the gaps in the shoal were suddenly pouring hot from my eyes, and my heart was in my throat so that I could neither swallow nor breathe, and rage and hate were flaming up in my chest, and every instinct I had was telling me to run, but I did not want to let Weenonaw go.

And then I saw that some of the men were moving off the bank, moving down onto the shoal to come after me, and fear overtook me and I turned loose of my Cherokee wife.

Her horse, crazed and dying, was crashing through the trees along the bank, moving downstream and well away. Courage, spooked by the other horse, had dashed up the hill along the road, and now I gave chase to catch Courage. As I did, the men still on the opposite bank let loose a volley, and balls smashed through the leaves above me again.

I ran as hard as I could up the hill leading away from the river, and when I reached the crest of the hill I could see Courage galloping away to the west.

I tried to catch my breath, and I shouted as loud as I could. "Courage! Damn you! Come back and get me!"

I resumed my run toward the horse, but Courage, because he was damned good horse, had wheeled and was coming back for me.

I'd never reloaded the one chamber in the Paterson from that morning when I'd fired a shot and broken a window at the tavern. But I still had four shots left. When Courage got to me, I pulled the revolver out of the saddle and walked back to the crest of the hill. The men were making their way across the river, slowly. Five of them were caught out in the middle of the shoal. They were paying attention to their business of fording the river and assumed I was still running. Their friends on the opposite bank were still reloading.

With the hammer cocked back, I took careful aim. I'd always been a good shot, and I handled that Paterson pretty well. I wanted revenge. I wanted to kill all of them, though there weren't shots for that.

The lead man took a step off the rocky shoal to go upstream and make the arc around the first gap where the water rushed through. I held the Paterson in my right hand and steadied it with my left, and I squinted down the barrel, looking right at the man's torso. I pulled the trigger and the Paterson erupted, spitting smoke and fire, and sending its bullet spinning down at my target.

I suppose I must have hit him right in the chest, for the man's body jerked as he went sprawling into the river. His body was carried by the current into the rocks, and then he slipped through the gap in the shoal and washed down river. I cocked back the hammer and aimed the Paterson a second time. The men on the shoal were scrambling back toward the other bank now, but they had created a huddle of human flesh and I knew I could get off one more shot and bring down a second one. I aimed into the mass of men and fired another shot.

One of the men hollered and grabbed at the back of his thigh, falling onto the rock. The men were all shoving each other now, trying to get to the far bank.

I looked down through the trees on the bank where I was standing to the place where I knew rested my wife's body, but mercifully I was spared one last look at her. Courage was behind me, so I quickly mounted my horse, and now we charged out west at a full gallop.

CHAPTER 10

I rode in a daze, heartbroken and scared as hell.

I was sure those men wouldn't stop just because they'd killed Weenonaw, particularly not after I'd killed one of them and shot another.

Beyond the Neosho River, Injun Territory turns entirely into tallgrass prairie, with expansive vistas broken only by small clusters of trees, herds of buffalo, and low, rolling hills. The trail we'd followed went from dirt track to nothing more distinguishable than a wide buffalo path through the prairie grass.

Courage galloped until he could go no farther at a run, and then he walked. At night he refused to go farther, and despair and exhaustion had so overwhelmed me that I simply collapsed off the horse's back and fell into a fitful sleep there in the grass.

I dreamed of mad Injuns with grotesque and distorted faces chasing me through an endless hallway in a tavern, and Weenonaw was calling to me. "Unega Galagina, you must run faster!" And then Weenonaw's calls became more urgent, and there was desperation in her voice. "Unega! You must run!" I could not see her, but she was licking my cheek, and then awareness came to me and I realized Courage was nuzzling my face.

I sat up with a start. It was still dark, but there was a blue light in the sky that let me know sunrise was not far off.

Courage was still standing over me, blanket and saddle still on him. I did not need a moment to reflect on where I was, why I was here, or what devastation had transpired the previous day. I knew immediately that my wife Weenonaw was dead.

"We need to keep moving," I said to the horse. "I promise when we stop for the night I'll take that saddle off of you. But we've got to go now, Courage."

Because it was still dark and I was stiff from sleeping on the ground, I chose to walk Courage for a while. I loosened the straps on the saddle to give him some relief as we walked along. We were not long before we came to a river. It was still too dark for me to see how big or deep the river was, and so I turned Courage upstream of the river and we followed it north.

When I had enough light to see, I saw that we'd been following a wide, gray-green river. When we came to a spot where I believed I could safely swim it and easily get Courage up the far bank, I stripped naked, stashed my clothes in the saddlebags, and Courage and I waded out into the water.

The river was slightly too deep for Courage to get across without swimming, and so my gear was all soaked when we reached the far bank. But I didn't much care. I didn't care about anything. I dressed into the wet clothes, and now I mounted Courage and rode west, up the hills and down the valleys and all the way through the tallgrass of the prairie. At the crest of each hill I looked out behind me for any evidence that I was still being pursued, but other than the wind blowing the grass the only movement I ever saw was the buffalo meandering from one hill to the next.

I had no appetite, and nothing to eat if I did. I was aimless and spent, and the only thing that motivated me to keep going was the threat that somewhere behind me a posse of Injuns was in pursuit.

I do not know how many days I continued on in such a manner. Maybe it was two days, or maybe it was a week. I suppose it could have been longer.

I alternated between walking and riding, sparing Courage as much as I could. I knew I was in Injun Territory, and I suspected I'd left the Cherokee lands behind, but I saw no one as I rode out across the empty plains. Just the bison and Courage kept me company.

I knew I was getting weak for want of food, but I was indifferent to my physical needs. I suppose a kind of deep sullenness had beset me at the murder of my wife. I was sad, lonesome, and I was not sure that anything could possibly lie ahead of me that would be worthwhile. I can't say that I wanted to die, because I was still fleeing my pursuers, but I can't much say that I wanted to live, neither.

I thought I was traveling west, but it's just as possible that I was ambling north. Near the conclusion of my lonesome journey, I crossed what must have been the Arkansas River and rode on another half day, and at that point I'd gone as far as I could go.

In a great flat space with nothing but green grass and herds of bison for as far as the eye could see, I tumbled down out of Courage's saddle, too weak to stand, too heartsick to care.

***

It was some time the next morning when a man knelt over me, softly slapping my face to wake me up.

"Jackson Speed?" he asked me. "Is that you?"

Weenonaw had gotten everyone in the family to call me by the Injun name she'd given me, and so it had been months since I'd heard a person address me by my proper name. I suppose the shock of hearing someone out in the prairie call me by my name is what snapped me out of my stupor, and I focused my eyes on the man kneeling over me.

"Aye," I said. "I am Jackson Speed. But who are ye that you would know that?"

The leathered Injun face staring at me with concern broke into a smile, and he said to me, "Do you not recognize your friend Jesse

Chisholm?"

It had not been until after our wedding that Weenonaw had christened me "Unega Galagina." As such, I'd been introduced to Jesse Chisholm as Jackson Speed, and not with my Cherokee name.

"But what are you doing here?" Chisholm asked. "You are filthy, boy. What has happened to you?"

"They killed my wife, Jesse," I said.

Chisholm stood up and began calling to people I could not see in a language I could not understand, and I was too weak to care much, and so I slipped back into unconsciousness.

***

Later that day I was lying on a pallet of blankets under a tent made of stretched buffalo hide and a Mexican boy was seated beside me and feeding me a warm soup of meat and vegetable broth.

"This is one of my adopted sons," Jesse said. "Let him feed you and get your strength back. And tell me what has happened to the niece of my friend Stand Watie."

I took some of the broth, and as I started to feel better, I told Jesse Chisholm everything that had transpired since Weenonaw and I had left Fayetteville. He did not interrupt me nor question me, and he merely nodded understanding as I told my story. I paused periodically while the Mexican boy fed me with the wooden spoon.

At the end of my story, Jesse shook his head sadly.

"I have tried to negotiate peace between the Old Settlers and the John Ross faction. It is a sad and useless war they fight, and it has cost you the life of your most beautiful wife. No wonder you are heart sick, Lieutenant Speed."

Jesse stood up and left me and the Mexican boy in the tent, and I continued to eat until the bowl was empty, and then I went to sleep on the bed of furs.

In the morning, I felt stronger and was up and moving. When I came out of the tent, I saw that Chisholm had half a dozen wagons loaded with goods. He explained to me that he was transporting the goods north to the various trading posts he owned.

"I am going to Fort Leavenworth where the white man's army is, and you may stay with them. When you are ready, you can make your way from Fort Leavenworth back to Stand Watie," Jesse told me.

"I ain't going back there," I said. I'd not really considered anything up until that moment, but I knew whatever I did, I was resolved that I'd had enough of Injun Territory. Without Weenonaw there warn't reason for me to stay in this place. And without considering any other options, I announced, "I will go back to Georgia where my family is."

Jesse nodded thoughtfully. "Yes, I do not blame you. I will write a letter to Stand Watie so that he will know what has happened to his niece and her husband."

So for the next two weeks, I was with Jesse Chisholm, his adopted Mexican children, and a couple of other hired on Injuns, as we took supplies up what would one day be known as the Chisholm Trail to some of Jesse's trading posts, eventually coming to Fort Leavenworth in Kansas. I helped them drive the ox teams that pulled the wagons, helped them ford rivers and round up cattle and repair wagon wheels, and I generally learned how to make myself useful as part of a wagon train. Some of it I knew already to do, having ridden security for the supply trains in Mexico, but the Texas Rangers never much helped with things like mending a broken axle or repairing a wheel. We just sat astride our horses looking ornery while the teamsters did the labor.

The daily chores kept my mind from the events that had transpired on the Neosho River, but at night when I bedded down, I was haunted by the memory of my murdered wife.

Cherokee Cock had sent me into Injun Territory to ease my soul, and for a time his advice had been successful. But now I was worse than I'd been when I'd left out of Mexico. With each passing day, I found I was longing more and more for a return to Georgia.

Eliza, that gorgeous woman with her bright red hair, was but a faded memory. I found it hard to even imagine her in my mind, what she looked like. Though I'd been married to Eliza considerably longer, I'd spent more time with Weenonaw than I had with Eliza. But back east I had a wife, and I found what I needed more than anything now was to be back home with her. I suppose by forcing Eliza into my mind, I was forcing Weenonaw out.

Fort Leavenworth could not get to me fast enough. When Jesse Chisholm called for a halt in the afternoons, I wanted to push on another mile or two. And in the mornings, the other hands were never able to break down the camp fast enough to suit me.

In eight days we came to the first of Chisholm's trading posts where we dropped a wagon's worth of supplies. In ten days we came to the second where we left another wagon. In twelve days, or maybe fourteen, we arrived at Fort Leavenworth where Jesse had established a trading post in the small settlement outside the fort.

Fort Leavenworth was typical of the western forts of the day – a sprawling campus with large parade grounds, barracks, officers' quarters, stables, cook houses and all sorts of other buildings, including a large hospital. The fort overlooked the Missouri River, and in a few months it would be the jumping off point for so many tens of thousands of men who would go west to seek fortune in the gold fields of California. But now, Fort Leavenworth was a relatively quiet place with only dragoons drilling outside the walls of the fort.

Of course Chisholm knew many of the officers at Fort Leavenworth, and after he saw to unloading another wagon at the trading post, Jesse took me to the fort where he introduced me as a hero from the war in Mexico to a major who was seated in a rocking chair on the porch of the officer's quarters. Chisholm didn't linger after making the introduction.

"I've got to be on my way," Jesse says to us. "Major, I'm going to leave young Lieutenant Speed here with you in the hopes that you can help him make his way back home to Georgia."

"I'll be glad to help the boy," the major said.

"Thank'ee Mister Chisholm," I said. "I appreciate all ye've done for me these past several days. I'd be grateful, too, if ye'd send that letter on to Stand Watie. I intend to write to him meself, but I do not know how long it will take me to find the words."

Old Jesse Chisholm nodded gravely and shook my hand. "I wish you luck, Lieutenant Speed. I will write to my friend Stand Watie. If our paths do not meet again in this world, I hope to see you reunited with your beautiful wife in the next."

I didn't say it to Jesse Chisholm who had not sniffed me out as a bigamist, but the thought went through my mind that I hoped to be reunited with my beautiful wife in this world. T'other one, though, not the dead one.

And with that, Jesse Chisholm left me on the porch of the officers' quarters at Fort Leavenworth, and my time living among the Cherokee came to an end.

"So, Lieutenant Speed, are you here to resume your career in the army?" the major asked me.

"I was always in the militia in Mexico," I was quick to point out, not wanting the major to think I was absconded from the army. "I was with the Georgia and Mississippi militias and then rode with the Texas Rangers."

The major, who had not bothered to stand up and was engaged all the while in whittling a stick, looked up at me from under the brim of his hat. "Rode with the Texas Rangers, huh?" he said. "You'd probably make it as a dragoon, then. We're a bit more formal in our training, but if you can ride and shoot well enough to serve with the Rangers, you could make a decent career in the army."

He was an ancient man with gray hair and strong build. In his uniform, even relaxed and whittling a stick, he looked like a typical sort of serious military man, but there was a twinkle in his eye that reminded me of an older Ben McCulloch, my former captain in the Texas Rangers. The old major also smelled a bit of whiskey, and I had to wonder if he was drunk even though it was not yet suppertime.

"I think I'm done with military life, sir," I said. "I'm sorry, Major – I guess I didn't catch your name."

"Major Nathan Boone," says he. "Have a seat, Lieutenant. I'll tell you about the time I was trapping along the Grand River with Matthias Vanbibber and a band of Osage stole all our horses and furs."

As it turned out, Major Nathan Boone was thrilled to have a new pair of ears to listen to his stories, and he had stories by score. [18]

You'll know him better as the youngest son of Daniel Boone, the pioneer who opened up Kentucky and fought Injuns all through the wilderness, and Major Boone had plenty of stories of his father to share as well. Over the next few days, I would spend most of my time with Major Boone – he was never engaged in much of the army work due to his age – and so he mostly rocked on the porch of the officers' quarters, whittled sticks, and sipped on whiskey. And with me present to hear his stories, he did a fair amount of reminiscing.

A steamer was due up from St. Louis in a few days, and I intended to buy passage for myself and my horse on that steamer and get at least as far east as the Mississippi. My intention was to be back in Georgia before autumn and at that point resume my marriage to Eliza.

In the meantime, I'd become the unofficial attendant to Major Boone, breakfasting with him, whittling sticks with him, sipping whiskey with him, partnering with him in card games, and – most of all – listening to stories of his explorations of the prairie and his days as an Injun fighter.

Boone had spent time at Fort Gibson down in Injun Territory, near Tahlequah, and knew both Stand Watie and John Ross, so he took a particular interest in hearing of my experiences of living with Watie.

"Three years ago, back in '45, I was at Evansville, Arkansas, with three companies of dragoons attempting to maintain the peace among the Cherokee," Boone recalled. "My primary goal at the time was to prevent your friend Stand Watie from raising an army large enough to threaten John Ross's government. I am sorry to learn they have still not yet settled their differences, though I am not particularly surprised. Stand Watie is as obstinate a man as I've ever met, and he never can see his own actions as stemming from anything other than good intentions. Likewise, the actions of his enemies are only ever deliberate slights against him."

Now, two hundred miles away and not enamored of his niece, I could see how Major Boone's assessment of my uncle-in-law was pretty accurate, and I nodded my agreement.

"And John Ross surrounds himself with people who will commit murder for him," Major Boone said.

"Aye, he does," I agreed, and in my mind I saw Weenonaw's limp body on the bank of the Neosho River.

Mostly Boone was full of stories that concluded with a punchline, and he reveled in telling the tales. Injuns out on the prairie who stole horses, or soldiers who accidentally shot themselves through carelessness or drunkenness. He talked some of hunting with his famous father, and by the time night fell, he was always deep in the drink and had to be helped to bed.

I gathered that the younger officers at Fort Leavenworth had heard his anecdotes enough that the stories no longer held much interest to them, and they all seemed quite pleased to have someone around for a few days who could take off of them the burden of having to listen to the old soldier. But I didn't mind much. It was good having a white man for company after having lived so long with the Injuns, and Major Boone's constant rambling prevented me from having to talk about or think too much about poor Weenonaw.

Two or three days after I arrived at Fort Leavenworth, Major Boone and I ventured over to the bluff overlooking the Missouri river and occupied ourselves in watching a wagon train ferry across the river. There were nearly two dozen wagons in the train and it included a herd of cattle, a team of oxen for each wagon and dozens of horses. Ferrying the river was an all-day adventure, and we occupied several hours in watching them. The group were pioneers bound for California where they intended to establish farms.

By then, of course, the Treaty of Guadalupe Hidalgo had been signed and the war was over. California was now a territory of the United States and would soon be a state, but word of the treaty had not yet reached Fort Leavenworth and neither we nor the settlers were aware of how things stood there. [19]

The group was led by a man named Abner Jamieson, a farmer from Indiana who told us he was compelled to go west because of the Manifest Destiny of the United States. "We shall inhabit this land from sea to sea," he assured us.

There were several families who were going along with him, all from Indiana and Illinois. A year before, a similar group had gone west, but the story of the terrible Donner Party was not yet enough known to deter similar emigrants from striking out west. [20]

Jamieson was enthralled with Major Boone, being a fan of the novels about the major's famous father, and spent the afternoon and evening with us clamoring for stories of Daniel Boone.

At some point in the evening, Major Boone encouraged me to travel west with the Jamieson group. I'd not told Major Boone that I had a wife waiting for me in Georgia, and he insisted an adventure to California would be just the thing for a young man. Jamieson readily agreed and offered to hire me on as a teamster, but I declined. I'd made up my mind that I was going back to Eliza and Georgia.

The next morning at sunrise, Jamieson and his wagon train set out for California, and I supposed that would be the last I would see of them.

Later that same day a mule team came in from Fort Laramie, carrying mail from out west, and with it my life would take yet another dramatic turn.

The team had been traveling for weeks by that time, having come something like five hundred miles or more. They would stay at Fort Leavenworth for a week or so before making a return trip with the mail that had been waiting to go west. Typically, those men would have been ready for a meal, a bath, and a bed, but a lieutenant among the mail carriers came immediately to Major Boone to deliver a bit of news that would soon turn the world's eyes to California. [21]

As it happened, Major Boone was the highest ranking officer at the fort that afternoon, or at least the highest ranking officer the lieutenant could find. When the lieutenant found the major, the two of us were whittling sticks on the porch of the officers' quarters, and Major Boone was telling me about the time he and his father fled the Shawnee in a canoe on the Ohio River.

"Major," the lieutenant said, coming up the front steps of the officers' quarters and removing his hat. "I have information that I was told to deliver to the commander of Fort Leavenworth, but you're the ranking officer I'm able to locate."

Major Boone raised his eyebrows at me and frowned — clearly he was more interested in finishing his story for me than he was in hearing some news from Fort Laramie.

"Very well," Boone said. "Let's hear your news lieutenant."

The lieutenant frowned at me, clearly trying to decide if he should deliver his information in front of a civilian.

"I was told not to repeat this message except to the commander of Fort Leavenworth," the lieutenant said.

Major Boone sighed his frustration and said, "This is Lieutenant Speed, lately returned from Mexico. You may say what you need to say in his presence."

The lieutenant screwed up his face but must have decided his responsibility to his orders ended where Major Boone's began.

"Among the post we're carrying is a dispatch to President Polk," the lieutenant said, pausing so that Major Boone could digest the gravity of the mail containing a letter for the president. "It's a letter from California, sir."

"That's good to know, lieutenant," Major Boone said. "I appreciate you providing me with that information. I'm not sure why it is so vital that it must interrupt me and Lieutenant Speed escaping the Shawnee on the Ohio, but I am glad to know that California is keeping President Polk informed of the goings-on there."

The lieutenant wrung his hat in his hands and shifted from one foot to the next. He looked around at the parade grounds for the Shawnee, and seeing none, he asked, "Escaping the Shawnee, sir?"

"I was just telling Lieutenant Speed about the time my father and I fled from the Shawnee in a canoe," Major Boone explained.

"Oh, I see," said the lieutenant, though I doubted he did. "That's not all, though, sir. I was told to share with you the contents of the letter."

"Ah, very well, then. And what are the contents of the letter?"

"Sir, they've discovered gold in California."

Major Boone chewed his lip for a moment. Then he said, "Gold, eh? How much of it?"

The lieutenant swallowed hard. "Sir, the word is that they are pulling nuggets out of the rivers at such a rate that hundreds of men a day are making a fortune."

Major Boone chewed his lip a while longer. "Is that right? Nuggets of gold?"

"Yes, sir," the lieutenant said. "I heard from one of our couriers that Colonel Mason, based in Yerba Buena, held in his hand a gold nugget bigger than a fist, and that was just one of dozens of nuggets discovered all on the same day." [22]

It was Major Boone's turn to swallow hard, and I could see behind the old gray eyes that he was thinking pretty hard on gold nuggets the size of a fist.

"Is that all?" he asked.

"They thought you would want to know, sir. When word reaches back East, sir, it might well cause a stampede of emigrants heading West."

"Thank you, lieutenant," Major Boone said. "Go and get yourself a meal and find a bed. You look like you could use a rest."

"Thank you, sir."

We watched the lieutenant straighten out his hat and fix it back on his head. He saluted and turned and went back down the steps. [23]

"That's an interesting turn of events," Major Boone said to me. "Gold nuggets the size of a fist. Men making fortunes."

"It's almost enough to make a man think twice about going back East," I said. "I almost wish now that I'd taken up Abner Jamieson on his offer to work his wagon train to California."

Major Boone nodded thoughtfully, as if he'd not heard me. I could tell his thoughts had shifted from the Shawnee on the Ohio River to the gold in California's rivers, and I suspect he was regretting that his age and health would prevent him from going to California hisself.

"If I were a young man, unfettered from the constraints of obligations, Lieutenant Speed, I believe I would go west to California and there seek my fortune." Major Boone looked hard at me for a moment. "Yes, if I were you, I'd be on my horse and riding west to catch up with Abner Jamieson and his wagon train, and I'd not say a word to any man among that train what it was that changed my mind."

***

All that afternoon I thought hard about Major Boone's advice. I thought about the prospects that awaited me back in Milledgeville, Georgia – running a store and maybe attending university, maybe becoming a lawyer and a politician. Those were all possible things, certainly, and enticing enough.

Now, I didn't know anything about gold at the time. I didn't know about panning a river or quartz veins or nuggets or dust, but I did know enough to know that a gold nugget the size of a fist was a thing worth finding, and the lieutenant said men by the hundreds were making a fortune in a day.

The only thing in Georgia that was even half as enticing as a fortune in gold had the prettiest red hair ye've ever seen and teats with cherry red tips, and I found that I could not make up my mind which was more compelling to me: – yellow gold or Eliza's milk-white skin and bright red nipples.

But by nightfall, I'd made up my mind what I would do, and I borrowed from Major Boone some paper, ink, and a feather quill, and that night before I went to sleep I wrote to Eliza the first letter I'd written to her since before I left Mexico.

My dearest Eliza,

I have so long pined for you in these days fighting

our country's war in Mexico. I am certain this letter finds you wondering what has become of your soldier husband, having heard nothing from me for many months.

From my last letters, you know that I was last with the Texas Rangers. I suffered an encounter with a couple of Mexican rancheros and that encounter left me wounded and convalescing for several weeks. When I was finally whole, I began a long journey home to you in Georgia, but my intentions to return home were interrupted when I found myself wintering in Indian Territory among the Cherokee. It is a long tale, better saved for when we are again together, but in the spring I accompanied an Indian trader to the army's Fort Leavenworth, where I am presently.

Though my most ardent desire is to return with all haste to your arms and to the bosom of my love, I am traveling not toward home but west to a place called Yerba Buena, in California, where I am led to believe a bountiful future awaits.

Eliza, they are pulling hundreds of nuggets of gold from the rivers in California, and I intend to go there and make my fortune. Having shed blood – my own and that belonging to a few fair Mexicans – in order that my country might obtain this territory of California, I believe that I am entitled to some share of the wealth contained there.

So I am traveling overland to Yerba Buena, California, to fetch us some gold. My ardent hope is that you will join me in California. I have been separated from you for so long, and I do not know how soon I will return to Milledgeville. So I am begging you, please –

however you can – come to me in California, and make your way there as fast as possible. It may be worthwhile to investigate passage by sea to California as it would be much faster than coming overland.

And my greatest hope is that you will make the fastest journey possible, as I do not know how long I can endure this terrible and prolonged absence from the woman who holds my heart.

Your loving husband,

Lt. Jackson Speed

P.S. Bring whatever digging implements and other conveniences you can from the store as I do not know what will be available in California. And bring a slave or two as we might employ them in digging up the gold I am sure we will find.

I sealed the letter and addressed it to Eliza.

I had no confidence the letter would arrive in Georgia. I had less confidence that she would act upon the plea contained within even if she ever received and read the letter.

I suppose it was the murder of my Cherokee wife that had me feeling so sentimental toward my first wife that I would even try to convince her to come and find me in California. I suspected that Eliza had probably long ago given me up for dead when she received no word from me month after month. I even wondered if perhaps she'd already remarried.

But on the chance that she was waiting for me, on the chance that she would receive the letter, and on the chance that she would actually come West, I decided it was worthwhile to at least try to reach her.

I had no idea what it would take to get to California by land or by sea, and I suppose in my mind I was thinking that maybe Eliza would arrive in California about the same time I did if she boarded a steamer to take her through the Gulf of Mexico. I'd read stories of ships rounding Cape Horn, but that was just a place name to me. I had little idea of where it was and even less an idea of how arduous a trip it might be.

The next morning, Major Boone assured me I would not regret my decision, and I set off to catch up to Abner Jamieson's wagon train.

CHAPTER 11

Undoubtedly, hundreds of thousands of words have been penned about the arduous journey from Kansas City to California. Countless men, both before and after me, left their lives along that trip. In my life I made the overland journey several times, both before and after the railroad made the trip a good bit easier and so much faster. And b'God I saw some of the worst of it on those various journeys: – terrible winters, vicious Injuns, thieves and backstabbers and gunslingers and hardships and obstacles placed in my way by nature and man alike.

But on that first overland trip to California it was a largely uneventful affair, strange as that may sound.

Some of the days were brutally hot out on the plains, and some of the nights were bitterly cold up in the mountains. River crossings were more than just a chore – they were an unholy burden. And there were days when Injuns of unknown tribes shadowed us on parallel ridges and gave us cause to fear not only that they would attempt to steal our livestock but also to fear for our safety.

But we never suffered attack from the tribes that haunted us, nor did they ever make off with enough of our livestock that we noticed.

Hot days were nothing to me having been encamped along the Rio Grande, and cold nights were eased by the application of blankets and fresh logs on a blazing fire.

Though Abner Jamieson's train consisted of plenty of children, there were also plenty of stout men who could carry supplies on their shoulders when the terrain made it necessary to unload the wagons to get them in and out of ravines or across rivers.

I'm not suggesting that my first overland trip was an easy affair, but I would neither say it was particularly difficult – especially considering some of the other overland trips I suffered through.

On good days of travel we made twenty-five miles in a day. On the typical day we did between fifteen and twenty. On some days, when the river crossings were difficult or the terrain too steep and rocky for loaded wagons, we camped at evening within sight of where we had camped the night before.

What Injuns we did encounter were peaceful enough, and two or three times they came into our camp to trade furs for whatever we were willing to give them. A few times they stole a cow or a horse, but never enough that we missed what beasts they took.

Abner Jamieson was a conservative man, and he brought with us twice what we would have needed to survive the trip. It made the chores of keeping up with the animals – a job that largely fell to me – more difficult because there were so many cows that would wander off. On crossings where the wagons had to be unloaded, we had so many water casks that the job was far more difficult and time consuming than it had to be. However, when we went twenty miles or more without seeing fresh water, our casks were never empty. You'll know that many a man died of thirst on the Overland Trail, but that was never a trouble for our party.

It is worth noting, I suppose, that Abner Jamieson's niece was on the trip. Her parents were both deceased, and Jamieson had adopted her and her four younger brothers. The boys ranged in age from eight to sixteen years, but the niece was my own age of eighteen. She and I struck up a friendship, and though she was plainer than the women I was accustomed to, I found that one hundred miles into the prairie with naught else but married women and young girls around, Willimenia Jamieson's homely looks had a certain appeal.

But Abner, who in addition to being a farmer was also a part time preacher, kept a pretty hawkish watch over his niece, and I never did have a proper opportunity with her.

I also briefly met the famed trapper and mountain man Jim Bridger that summer. [24] We camped for a couple of days at Fort Bridger, at the time nothing more than a walled trading post, where we took some time to rest and to graze the livestock. The man hisself was there at the fort and even advised Abner Jamieson that we should leave the Oregon Trail for a shorter route to the south, but fortunately our guide said he wasn't familiar with the recommended route and decided to keep on the Oregon Trail until we came to Fort Hall.

We didn't know it then, but it had been Bridger who advised the Donner Party to take the southern trail, and we know how that turned out for them. [25]

But Jim Bridger did turn useful for me. Bridger had a decent supply of goods at the trading post, and I bought from him a used carbine with a few balls and caps. The carbine was a Patent Arms model and an exact copy of my Paterson, except with a longer smoothbore barrel and a wooden stock. It took some getting used to, but I got reasonable accurate with it. I also bought from him a pick and a shovel, thinking those would be the implements with which I would find my fortune. My traveling companions did not know why I wanted a pick and shovel, but none of them cared enough to enquire. Stand Watie had paid me in Liberty silver dollars struck in New Orleans, and Bridger was glad to accept the coinage for his goods.

At the same time we were at Fort Bridger, there was a band of Snake Injuns encamped outside Bridger's trading post, and they were daily running horse races and gambling. As we were there for a couple of days, I decided to run Courage in one of their races.

The race was a straight dash of three hundred yards, and because this was the same sort of sport I'd gotten into with the Texas Rangers, I had some confidence that Courage could outpace any of them Injun horses. And so I put five dollars on the bet thinking I'd make back off them Injuns the money I'd spent on the carbine.

Jamieson's group were all cheering me on, and I was riding against a half dozen of the Snakes. Unlike my Cherokee in-laws, the Snakes looked the true image of a Western savage: – all dressed in skins and wearing necklaces of eagle talons and their long hair braided. But I thought about what Jesse Chisholm had told me, that these Plains Injuns was nothing more than a bunch of children who loved sport above anything, and I thought it would be nothing more than a good game. Even if things went poorly, the most it would cost me was five dollars.

Jim Bridger fired the gun that started the race, and right away Courage was out front of all them Injuns but one. One of them was neck-and-neck with us, so I got low on Courage's neck and called encouragement at him, and we started to gain some distance on the Injun.

That Snake brave was glancing at me, and as Courage got a horse length ahead of him, I glanced back at the Injun. When I did, I saw a murderous look on his face that scared the hell out of me. Now I don't know for sure if that Injun was just caught up in the moment of the race, or if he was seriously contemplating putting me in a grave if I beat him in a fair race, but I know that look on his face made me worry for my scalp.

At that moment, Courage bounded farther ahead. I'd now stretched my lead two horse lengths, and the winnings of the pot would surely be coming to me as we raced down upon the finish line. I was trying to calculate what those winnings would be and guessed it was something far less than the value I would put on my own scalp.

Whether Courage sensed my fear or simply had good judgement, just shy of the finish line the horse slid to a sudden stop, kicking up a massive cloud of dust and grass, and nearly tossing me from my saddle.

The Injun that had been keeping pace with us flew past and finished the race as the winner, though Courage had clearly shown hisself to be the better horse.

All the Injuns and the hangers-about at Fort Bridger roared with laughter at seeing me lose the race, and the Jamieson emigrants moaned their disappointment. I lost five silver dollars, but I counted it well spent if it saved me my scalp, and I rode away from the race convinced that I not only had the fastest horse on the prairie, but also the smartest one.

I returned to the rest of our group, and they mostly patted me on the back and told me I nearly had them Injuns beat. Some of them gave me some good-natured teasing about it.

"What happened, Jackson?" asked Slim, a boy a couple of years older than me who was another hired hand in our party. "Ye had them Injuns spitting your dust, and then ye pulled up."

Another hired hand, who I only knew as Brother, chimed in with Slim, "You wasn't skeered they was goin' to scalp ye if ye won, was ye?"

I laughed them off, but I could see there was some unrest among the Snakes. Anyone who watched the race knew I had the faster horse, and by all rights I should have won that race. It was plain to see that the man I'd nearly beat was taking some teasing from his friends, and he was getting angry over it. In a minute, he walked over to a half-breed who worked the trading post with Bridger and said something. He was so animated, waving his arms and pointing at me, that it was clear the man was in a huff. Bridger's half-breed nodded and held up soothing hands, but the up he comes over to me and says, "The rider over there, the one who won the race, he says you let him win and all the other braves are teasing him about it. He says he'll give you a chance to get back your money if you'll accept his challenge to a wrestling match."

"What?" I asked. "B'God the answer to that is 'no, sir.' He won the race, won the money, that's good enough for him. He doesn't also get the opportunity to beat hell out of me."

The half-breed, who could not have been more indifferent, went back to the Injuns and gave them my answer, and now they were all laughing and slapping the aggrieved rider on the back. Clearly, through my refusal to wrestle, his honor was restored.

I had no doubt, the mood he was in, that if I'd engaged in the wrestling match he'd have slipped a knife into my back.

Before we turned in for the night, Bridger hisself offered me a bit of advice. "You'll want to sleep with both eyes open if you want to keep that horse," he said to me. "Them Snakes'll come into your camp and take off with that horse if ye ain't careful."

That night Slim and Brother took turns with me keeping an eye on Courage, who we tied to one of the wagons instead of leaving him grazing in the corral with our other livestock.

When I rode out from Fort Leavenworth to join up with Jamieson's party, I had a concept that the wagon train would be a communal sort of group with every man helping every other and the entirety of the group sharing what they had. But I was sore mistaken.

For one thing, the families tended to divide themselves into separate groups within the camp, and every perceived offense seemed to deepen the rifts among them. So it was that if one group was angry with another group for some small thing, the second group could expect no assistance at river crossings or if a wagon broke a wheel. If a man needed a hammer and his neighbor had one, but was suffering from an injured pride, the hammer would only be offered at a fee. It wasn't like that when we first set out from Fort Leavenworth, but the longer along the trail we got, the more divided and petty were the people in the wagon train. Most of these petty insults and grudges happened among the married women, who whispered venom in their husband's ears, until half the relationships among the party were poisoned.

These squabbles even went down to the hired hands. If a family had a hand or two they'd hired on, those hands were loyal to that family and shared their hatred. But some of the hands were immune. Brother and Slim, like myself, were hired on by Jamieson, and our charge was to lend help along the wagon train wherever it was needed.

As such, I was fortunate that I was well liked by all the factions. I stayed out of the petty disputes. Not being tied by blood or wages to any of the primary families in the train made it easier on me and Jamieson's other hired hands to avoid the disputes.

For another thing, Jamieson paid me and the other hands a daily rate for our help with the train, but he charged me for every meal I ate and also made me rent from him the canvas tent and blanket I was using. He'd have required me to buy a fork and spoon from him, too, but I used my Bowie knife as a fork and also used it to whittle myself a spoon. I suspected that when we finally arrived in California I would discover that my meals and other sundry charges would come pretty close to matching exactly my daily pay. It turned out that I was right, too. For all those weeks of work, I walked away with just two dollars in pay. I did not bother complaining about it, for I was certain Jamieson would have a full accounting of every meal I'd eaten – and maybe even a few I didn't eat – that would confirm his math.

As it was, I was glad to have most of my earnings from my work for Stand Watie, half stashed in my saddlebags and t'other half in a pocketbook I kept always on my person.

After Fort Bridger we made our way to Fort Hall where we turned southwest, and below Fort Hall the Oregon Trail split off from the California Trail. We followed the Humboldt River and traveled through a desert, and even with Abner Jamieson's extra water we found our supplies dangerously low before we came to the Carson River.

In the Sierra Nevada we entered the hardest going we'd encountered. Even though it was mid-summer, the nights were so bitter cold that our water casks were topped with ice when we woke in the mornings. The trail was difficult going, and it seemed that every obstacle was a steep incline where wagons had to be worked over rocks. The livestock got bad about wandering in search of grass, and we were always an hour later leaving camp than we intended because time had to be spent to round up the cows.

At last we started coming down out of the Sierra Nevada, and as we came down into the valley, all along the way, we passed encampments full of men and mules near rivers and streams. We never stayed for any length of time whenever we encountered these camps – Abner Jamieson was leery of the men and determined it best to keep the women and children away from them. So the party as a whole did not discover what they were about, but I suspected, and I know now, that these were the first of the California gold miners, the Forty-Niners who arrived in California, or were already there, in '48.

In the valley below the Sierra Nevada we encamped outside a fort belonging to a man named John Sutter, a Dutchman who had established his fort a number of years prior, having obtained a land grant from the Mexican government. I'd not known it at the time, but it was at Sutter's mill that the first gold nugget was discovered. [26]

It was now early October. I'd spent more than four months traveling with Abner Jamieson's company and had not breathed a word of gold to any of them. But as we came into California, I lingered at every river and creek, watering Courage and looking at the river beds for anything yellow.

At Sutter's Fort we heard for the first time that the United States had won the war in Mexico and that we were now in U.S. territory. Abner Jamieson and the other men of his company celebrated the news, having come to California to live out their belief that the United States was destined to control the land from sea to sea.

I expected, too, that we would at any point encounter rumors of gold. It surprised me that we heard no mention of gold neither at Fort Bridger nor at Fort Hall nor at any of the other small trading posts along the way. Major Boone had advised me to keep the news of gold to myself on the journey, and I'd done that. I did not now want the others to learn of gold until I'd determined how to go about staking a claim.

As we made camp outside the fort, John Sutter hisself came out to greet us, along with some of his people. I hung about close enough to hear Sutter's interview with Abner Jamieson, and my heart sank when Sutter asked Jamieson if we'd come for the gold fields. But Jamieson didn't press the issue. Instead he told Sutter his group had come to claim land and set up farms in the fertile central valley. Sutter seemed relieved to learn that Jamieson was interested in farming, and he did not mention any more about the gold.

I'd put Courage out to graze and finished up my chores for the wagon train, and I decided to walk up to the fort to see what I could learn. What I knew for sure was that people at the fort were aware of the gold, and so I hoped that without any of the other settlers from our wagon train around, I could learn how to go about finding myself a fortune.

The fort was a large, adobe-walled structure with a big, open gate. I noticed there were a couple of canons near the entrance, and I wondered if those were intended to be used on the Mexicans or the Indians or both. When I entered, I found a large house in the middle of the fort that served as a storehouse, and rooms lined the inner wall of the fort. On the grounds inside the fort I spotted a man in military uniform and saw that he was a lieutenant – he'd have been about ten years older than me at the time. Compared to me he was a small man, shorter than I was by a good bit and thin and wiry. He had red hair and a thick, red beard at the time. He was seated in a wooden chair with a book open on his lap, but he was watching a small herd of Indian children playing in the yard and was not reading.

"Hello, lieutenant," I said approaching him.

"You come in with that wagon train just now?" he asked.

"I did. Name's Jackson Speed," I said.

"My name is Sherman," he told me, shaking my hand. "William Tecumseh Sherman. My friends all call me 'Cump.' Where have you and your people come from?" [27]

"I'm from Georgia," I said. "Them folks on the wagon train, they mostly come from Indiana and Illinois. I met up with them at Fort Leavenworth."

"Leavenworth?" Sherman asked. "You in the army?"

"Not the regular army," I said. "I was with the Georgia militia in Mexico, then served for a while as a lieutenant with the Mississippi militia. Then I was with the Texas Rangers."

"Is that right?" Sherman asked. "You saw action in Mexico?"

"I did," I said. "I was at Monterrey with the Mississippians, then I did some scouting as a Ranger."

"Just last month we received word that the war was won," Sherman said. "Treaty was signed at Guadeloupe Hidalgo. United States government now has just about every square inch of land from here to Texas."

"I'd not heard. We left out of Leavenworth in late April and haven't had any news since then."

"What brings your party to California?"

"The party, it's led by Abner Jamieson, they've come here to farm," I said. "But I was hoping for more prosperous endeavors."

Sherman's eyes narrowed. "Ye've heard about the gold, then?"

"I have," I said. "Word came through while I was at Leavenworth that they were pulling gold out of the rivers every day. Fortunes are being made, is what they're saying."

Sherman shrugged. "It's true enough that they're finding vast quantities of gold, and it's going for ten dollars an ounce.[28] Some are doing better than others. I've just completed a second tour of the gold fields, and I am amazed at how rapidly the gold fever has brought great quantities of people to our rivers."

This was truly disheartening news. "Well, Cump, is there any gold left?"

Sherman laughed. "I suppose there is still some."

"Where would a man go if he wanted to find some of that gold?"

"You walk out the front of this fort and keep walking west until your feet get wet, that's the Rio de los Americanos – the American River. You can go upstream or downstream, and you keep walking until you see some black sand. When you see that black sand, you stick your pan in the water and scoop up some of it. You shake your pan a bit, and when all the gravel and sand and water is out, the yellow dust you've got left in the bottom – that's your gold."

"Is it so easy?" I asked.

"Well, I'll tell you, Jackson Speed, if it was so easy, I wouldn't be sitting here reading this book. I'd be out there in the river with a pan and a bag of gold dust. I suspect your best opportunities are to follow the river back up into the Sierra Nevada. The first discovery was made on the Rio de los Americanos about 40 miles east from here, not far from a place called Coloma.[29] But winter will be here soon – sooner in the mountains – and you'll be hard pressed to make it through the winter on your own."

"So, where do I get one of those pans from?" I asked.

Cump laughed at that, too. "I'll tell you what, for your service to our nation in our recent victory over the Mexicans, I'll lend you my pan."

Cump got up out of his seat and walked into one of the rooms along the wall of the fort. He emerged in a moment with a round, almost flat pan.

"I got this for fun so I could try my hand at panning a bit," he said. "If you make your fortune with it, I'll expect you to find me and pay me for the pan. If you don't make your fortune, come find me and maybe I'll have something you can do. Captain Sutter, the owner of the fort here, he and I are going into business starting a store to supply the miners, and maybe I could give you a job there. Or, if you're inclined, maybe we'll have need for a soldier."

"I have experience at both. Back in Georgia my wife's grandfather owned a store, and I worked for him before I went off to war. While there's a chance I'd return to being a merchant, I ain't going back to soldiering." It was a vow I would break.

Cump looked me over. "How old are you, son?" he asked.

"Eighteen," I told him.

He shook his head. "You're awfully young to have fought in a war and been married," he said.

I nodded my agreement. "You don't know the half of it."

CHAPTER 12

Jamieson's wagon train stayed encamped at Sutter's Fort for a couple of weeks, during which time they all soon learned of the gold. We also heard the horror stories of the wagon train that came through the Sierra Nevada the previous winter and resorted to cannibalism to survive. With Sherman's warning about wintering in the Sierra Nevada ringing in my ears, and the horror stories of the Donner-Reed Party still fresh in the memories of the people at Sutter's Fort, I decided I was not going to chance going back up into the mountains during winter.

But there was time enough to ride out to the gold fields at Coloma and get my feet wet, stick my pan in the Rio de los Americanos, and see what I might be able to fetch from the river bottom. So I settled my account with Jamieson while he determined where best to take his wagons to start a career in digging in the soil and raising cattle, and decided that I would ride up to the gold fields. I was itching to move out pretty quick, too, as already some of the other hands from Jamieson's wagon train were thinking of doing the same.

Tecumseh Sherman, that red-haired devil who burned the South in '64, didn't have anything better to do for the next few days, so he offered to accompany me out to the gold fields, and I suppose it was a lucky thing for me that he did. He knew the route into the gold fields up to Coloma and Dry Diggins, [30] and he was known among the miners, having been to their camps with the military governor of the state a couple of times already.

Once we were away from Sutter's Fort, I discovered that the American River was teeming with men panning for gold. Mostly they slept on the ground under the stars and ate at cook tents where a meal went for exorbitant prices.

We made a leisurely ride east, back toward the Sierra Nevada, and generally following upstream the South Fork of the American River. I had with me my Bowie knife and Paterson from the war, the silver Stand Watie had paid me and a blanket Jesse Chisholm had given me for a bed roll, the shovel, pick, and carbine I'd bought from Bridger's Fort, and the pan Cump Sherman had donated to the cause, and I didn't have much of anything else. But I suppose I also carried with me a belief that in a day or two I'd have five hundred dollars in gold.

"In San Francisco, the town is virtually abandoned of all labor," Cump told me.

"San Francisco?" I asked.

"Yerba Buena," he said. "The town changed the name a year ago. It's now San Francisco. One of Sutter's men, building a saw mill about forty miles east of the fort on the American River, found the first gold while digging the trail-race for the mill. That was back in January. By early spring the word had spread down to San Francisco that there was gold discovered in the river, and every man-jack in the town with two good legs hiked it up toward the mountains."

"They've been panning the river all through the spring and summer, and are still at it. Up here in the river there's an island where three hundred Mormons are living and working the river from sunrise to sunset. In total, there are probably ten thousand men – Indians, Mexicans, Mormons, Negroes, Chinamen, and white men – digging up the river bed.

"The water of the river all flows out of the Sierra Nevada, and so even in the summer when it's hot like the blazes in the sun, the water is cold as ice. I'm not saying a man can't make a living in the river, but it seems a hell of a tough way to do it."

"A living?" I asked. "I came here to make a fortune."

Cump Sherman laughed. "Well, Jack Speed, I hope you do. I'd like to get paid for that pan. But hard truth is that most men are pulling out just enough gold to pay for their meals. Some aren't even doing that."

The ground through here was mostly dry dirt with some scattered timber, and the riverbed was in sight. Where we were at that moment, though the river flowed beside us, there were no prospectors.

"Why is no one mining here?" I asked.

"Most all of the land is United States government land, and Colonel Mason, the governor, has deemed it in the nation's interest to have the gold removed from the river, and so men can pan where they like. But along here, this is all territory claimed by Sutter, and he's not particularly enthusiastic about the prospecting. It's ruined his plans of Utopia." [31]

We rode on a ways farther and then Sherman led us down to the river bank.

"Want to try your hand at panning?"

"Here?" I asked. "What about Sutter?"

"He won't care about you dipping the pan in the water a couple of times."

So we dismounted, rolled up our pant legs and took off our shoes, and I followed Cump out into the riverbed. He was right about the water – it was so cold it hurt. He showed me how to scoop up some of the loose sand and gravel and swirl it around in my pan.

"The gold flakes are heavier than the pebbles and the sand," Cump explained. "The gold will settle in the pan as the water washes out the other debris. If there's gold you'll be left with little yellow flakes."

I scooped up the sand from the riverbed a number of times, and I fouled up the swirling motion my first few times. Tecumseh showed me how to do it again, and finally I started to get the knack of it. But we found no yellow flakes in the bottom of the pan.

Cump stepped out of the river and dried his feet and hands in the sun, but I kept at it, moving a few feet upstream, then a few more. And then I spotted black sand.

"Say, didn't you tell me to look for black sand?"

"That's right," Cump said.

I scooped the pan down into the black sand and carefully swirled the pan. Pebbles and sand swirled out with the water. I was slow and precise with it. I dipped the pan in the river to get more water and swirled again. And in the bottom of the pan, when everything else was swept away, I had a few small pieces of yellow flakes.

"I think I've got gold," I said.

I walked the pan up to the riverbank and showed it to Tecumseh. He ran his fingers over the flakes and picked one up. He put it up to his mouth and bit it, then examined it.

"I think you've found gold," he said, laughing. "Gold is a soft metal, so when you bite it you can bend it or your teeth will leave marks." He pointed to me how the flake was bent where he bit it.

And like that, I caught the gold fever. I spent another half hour at the black sand I'd found, scooping the pan in the riverbed and swirling it to find bits of gold in my pan. Tecumseh the whole time was watching me from the riverbank while the horses grazed on what grass they could find.

"We'd be get moving again, Jack," he told me eventually. "I'm sure you'd like to spend all afternoon making your fortune, but we should keep moving."

On the bank, I showed Sherman the gold I'd collected.

"That's more than half an ounce, would be my guess," he told me. "You've been at it for less than an hour and you've already made eight dollars."

I spent the next few days with Cump, riding from one gold camp to the next. In the camps we talked with the miners, who were all willing to show us their individual techniques for prospecting. In the bigger camps, they were using sluice boxes and rockers. In some camps the prospectors reported finding hundreds of dollars in gold, and in other camps they bemoaned months of back breaking labor to find barely enough to pay for supplies and meals, and they were worried about how they would survive the winter.

But none of the prospectors at any of the camps told us that they had found or seen a gold nugget as big as a fist. Not a one said he had made five hundred dollars in a month, much less a week.

One evening, as Cump and I lay on our blankets up on a knoll overlooking a camp down on the South Fork, with a blazing fire nearby to give us some heat through the night, I expressed to Sherman that I'd begun to feel a bit of discouragement.

"I'd heard they were pulling gold nuggets the size of a fist out of the river and that some people were making five hundred dollars in a week," I told him. "But talking to the prospectors in the camps, it sure doesn't seem that any of them are meeting with that sort of success."

"A lot of them came up into these hills thinking they'd make a fortune, and most of them are not," Tecumseh said. "That's why I'm planning to open up a store with Sutter rather than standing around in freezing cold water all day."

"I wrote my wife back in Georgia and told her to come out here because we could make a fortune," I said. "It seems like a damned fool thing to have done."

"Yep," Tecumseh said. "Probably shouldn't have done that."

CHAPTER 13

Already, miners who had spent most of the summer soaking wet while panning in the rivers and creeks were coming down out of the hills and planning to winter in the valley.

With no supplies to get me through a winter, I decided to ride back to Sutter's Fort with Sherman, and from there I joined a group of prospectors who were heading down to winter in Yerba Buena, or San Francisco as it was now called. [32]

Those men, whose names I never bothered to learn, had been panning since early spring, and they'd made decent sums. One of them had made six hundred dollars total. Another had made fifty dollars in a week several times over. The others had all made sums less than that, but still impressive enough. Twenty dollars in a week, two hundred dollars in a single month.

Their success, they told me, was in moving about. Some prospectors doggedly stayed in a single camp, convinced they'd selected well the spot that would make them a fortune, without ever finding any gold worth mentioning. But these men said if they did not find evidence of gold quickly they would move on.

"Digging for gold is a lot like women," one of them told me, with a grin on his face. "Never waste time on a dry hole."

By the time we reached the harbor where Yerba Buena was located, I felt like I'd received enough advice that I could go now into the mountains and in short order strike it rich, and I vacillated quite a bit whether I wanted to find a place in Yerba Buena to winter or try my luck in the hills before the first snows came. But it was now already November, and though these prospectors I was traveling with had renewed my optimism, I knew I could not survive a winter without supplies.

When at last we topped the ridge that overlooked the bay and the town of San Francisco, what we saw below us was a motley collection of clapboard buildings with a few permanent brick or adobe buildings. All along the hills surrounding the bayside town, canvas tents had been erected as permanent lodgings. Other than a couple of main streets and a square down near the water, there seemed to be no reason to the town. Buildings were tossed up in any old fashion so that adjacent buildings faced opposite directions.

From our vantage point, I could see the bay where there were already half a dozen abandoned ships – a problem that would soon get worse as ships' crews reached San Francisco, heard about the gold, and left their vessels to head up into the mountains [33] – but the hills around the bay largely obstructed my first view of the Pacific Ocean. Beyond the hills, what I could see of the ocean stretched out to the horizon, but it looked no different to me than the Gulf of Mexico.

As Tecumseh Sherman had told me, the town's labor had almost entirely disappeared. Construction projects had been left unfinished, the weekly newspaper had stopped printing, stores lacked clerks and restaurants had no cooks nor waiters.

Those who had not left to try to pan for gold had were concocting schemes to separate prospectors from the gold they found. Prices for everything were outrageous, and the only currency anyone would accept was gold. Stand Watie's silver dollars were nearly useless to me.

Already enough prospectors had come out of the mountains that there were no rooms for rent when I arrived in San Francisco. The miners I'd come into town with decided to pitch tents on a hillside and winter in their tents. They spent large sums of their gold to buy blankets and coats and boots. They invited me to come along with them, but I declined the offer.

Moffat & Co., an assaying business recently established to coin gold coming out of the rivers, was willing to trade ten dollars in silver coins for five dollar gold pieces, and in that manner I was able to get some currency that would be accepted by the merchants and tavern keepers. I did not trade out all of my silver from Watie, but the first real gold I got in California cost me double its value, which was disappointing to me.

I used a bit of the gold to put Courage in a livery. Any other livery anywhere else in the country would have cost twenty-five cents or less for a day, but in Gold Rush San Francisco in 1848, Courage's stay was going to cost me five dollars a week. I argued and pleaded with the stable owner, but the man was resolute that five dollars was the going rate. Wondering how a man with no gold could survive in a town with no rooms where everything was priced according to the excessive quantities of gold everyone seemed to have, I went to a saloon in hopes of finding a decent meal to help me think. The saloon nearest the livery was the Yerba Buena Saloon, a two-story, clapboard building with a painted sign below the windows on the second floor, and a wide covered porch in the front. On the inside, there were red velvet curtains at the windows, wooden tables and chairs on the board floor, and a large bar running along one wall from front to back. A large staircase at the back of the room led up to the second floor. I'd hoped to find a decent meal and maybe someone who could point me to a place where I could find a room, but instead, I found a whore who probably saved me from spending a winter of starvation.

Being still early in the day, the saloon was not overly crowded, and so I took a table and ordered a meal and a whiskey. I'd not been at the table long and was just getting into the food when a woman in a bright red dress asked if she could join me.

"You are a filthy mess," she said to me. "You look like you've been up in the gold fields for months."

I would guess she was in her mid-forties, certainly old enough to have been my mother. She was a hard looking woman with black hair that was fast turning gray. She had a square jaw and a nose that looked like it had been broken once or twice, both of which combined to give her face a mannish appearance. All the same, I suspected she'd have been striking if she was twenty years younger. Now she was a bit overweight, but her dress revealed a deep cavern between two large teats, and she was probably one of the more attractive women in San Francisco at the time. Conservatively, I would estimate there were probably thirty women in the town for every hundred men, and so even the homeliest of whores could make good wages.

"Yes ma'am," I said. "It's been a long while since I've had a decent meal indoors."

"Where are you from?" she asked.

"Georgia, ma'am," I said.

"I thought so," she said. "I knew a man from Alabama once, he always called me ma'am, too. So I knew right away you must be a Southerner."

"Yes, ma'am," I said.

"Did you do well in the gold fields?" she asked.

I was nervous about being swindled. Even in '48, before the city was overrun with thousands of drifters and ne'er do wells, San Francisco had a feel of a town where an unsuspecting man might easily become a victim of any number of crimes, and my natural cowardice had me more suspect in this town than I might normally have been most anywhere else. I was also toting my saddlebags around with me, and currently had them resting on the table, and any thief might well have guessed those saddlebags were full of gold.

"I haven't been in the territory long," I said. "I came in with a wagon train a while back and didn't spend much time in the river prospecting. I pulled out a bit of gold, but not enough to mention."

She made small talk with me for quite a while, asking me about myself. Mostly, I told everything pretty straight. I told her I had a wife back in Georgia and that I'd been in Mexico in the war. I kept expecting that she would make some sort of offer that would involve me trading whatever gold I might have for some service that she could undoubtedly perform. My expectation, looking at that red dress and her bountiful teats, was that she'd shortly be offering to get belly-to-belly with me at some rate significantly higher than what a slightly unattractive, forty-year-old woman would fetch in any other part of the world.

So you can imagine my surprise when, instead, she offered me a job.

"You never did tell me your name," she said, and so I introduced myself to her, and without even thinking I gave her my rank in the Mississippi Rifles, "Lieutenant Jackson Speed," I said.

"Well, Jack, my name is Josefina, but folks around here all know me as Lackawanna Jo. I own the Yerba Buena Saloon here, and the gambling floor above us, and I have a couple of other interests, besides," Lackawanna Jo told me. "As it happens, with a lot of the men coming down out of the mountains for the winter, I'm in need of some help around here, if you're looking for a job. I can't pay the wages you'd make doing other things, but what I can offer you is a room and two meals a day. In addition, I'd pay you seven dollars a week, which all told isn't too bad."

I wasn't sure what the work would be, but Lackawanna Jo was offering to take care of my three biggest concerns – where I would bed down, how I would afford to eat, and the five dollars a week I needed to keep Courage in the livery. If I didn't gamble or buy whores, I could keep two dollars a week to save for a tent and some other supplies to get me into the hills come spring.

"That sounds like a reasonable offer," I said. "I'd be glad to take the job."

Lackawanna Jo laughed pretty hard at me. "Don't you even want to know what the job is?"

"Well, I figured you would tell me," I said.

"Some of these miners are going to come into town flush with money, and they're going to cause trouble – getting drunk and getting into fights. I need a couple of big men, strong men, to watch over the place and make sure I don't have any trouble. I've got the saloon down here, but upstairs I've got a gambling floor with ten tables. In the back, too, I have a few rooms where I have some girls working for me. Do you know what I mean when I say that I've got some girls working for me?"

"I believe I do, yes, ma'am," says I, with a knowing wink.

"I like to keep the girls protected. I have three girls that work the back rooms. Two of them are Mexicans and one of them is an Indian girl. They're not particularly pretty girls, any of them. But to get men in the mood to pay for them, I have three women who work in the saloon and on the gambling floor, serving drinks and meals. They're all married women with husbands up prospecting in the mountains, and so it's strictly hands off with them.

"So what you'll be doing is keeping the peace in here. If fights break out from drunkenness in the saloon, you break up the fights. If someone accuses someone upstairs of cheating, you get them outside before they go to shooting at each other. And if any man lays a hand on one of the serving girls, you break his jaw.

"The best part about this job is we almost never have trouble, and the reason we almost never have trouble is because I keep a couple of big men around to keep the peace. Now, I don't want none of my customers beat up for being drunk or cheating at cards. Drunks and cheats just get escorted out before they cause trouble. Drunks are welcome back when they're sober, and cheats are welcome so long as they don't get caught. But if a man lays a hand on one of the serving girls, that's going too far. They're all decent, white women with husbands, and I won't have none of that here.

157

"I don't want you shooting no one, ever. I don't want to have the Yerba Buena Saloon to get the kind of reputation that keeps decent folk out. So if it's just a fight or a dispute over a card game, I don't want you beating up no one. You just send them out the door and let them know they're welcome back if they can behave. But if they touch the serving girls, you do whatever you think you have to.

"Now that you know what the job is, are you still interested, Jack?"

Well, keeping the peace wasn't the sort of job I was cut out for. Breaking up fights and stepping between gamblers who were bent on killing each other seemed like foolish behavior to me. But Lackawanna Jo made it out like the biggest part of my job would be standing around and looking mean, and that was something I could do. And if any real danger occurred, there was always another man working who could look after it.

"I sure would be interested, Miss Jo," I said.

As it turned out, Lackawanna Jo employed three other men to keep the peace, and the four of us shared one room with two beds, and the room was the fourth room on the hallway with the three whores, so during business hours we were constantly harassed with the grunts and moanings of prospectors who'd been so long away from woman flesh that they would grunt and moan over the three ugliest women I ever laid eyes on. But if they did their grunting and moaning with their eyes shut and imagined the serving girls, it probably wasn't so bad.

Among the other men I worked with were Little Wade, a man so large he made me feel small. He had bad joints and didn't move around well, but when he punched a man he punched hard. Little Wade was to be my bedmate, and so most of that winter I slept on a blanket on the floor, for there warn't room in the bed for the two of us. But I didn't mind the floor too much, as I kept reminding myself it was better than freezing to death in the hills.

The other two were brothers, Shane and Shannon McAllister, and they took turns tending the bar and working the floor. All three men were older than me. Little Wade had worked for Lackawanna Jo since she opened the saloon seven or eight years earlier. The McAllister brothers had recently been turned loose from the army after the cessation of the war. They intended to go eventually to the goldfields, but were saving for supplies. Jo had hired them on after her previous men – all but Wade – had gone off prospecting.

On my first day at work, Wade had encouraged me to establish a reputation in a hurry.

"If they're scared of you, they won't cause no trouble," he said. "If you get a reputation for being a mean sonuvabitch, people will know not to start trouble in here. That makes the decent folk feel safe to come here to gamble, and it makes the rough folk up to no good know that they need to go somewhere else to do it."

My first day or two at work there was not occasion to establish a reputation, but on the third day the perfect opportunity came up.

I'd already determined that any reputation establishing I was going to do would have to be with a man who warn't carrying a gun on his hip and who was drunk enough to be easily man-handled, or with a small man who was feeble enough that he wouldn't present a challenge. Anyone else who caused trouble would have to become the problem of Little Wade or the McAllister brothers.

My third day on the job, a man walked into the saloon who looked just the sort. He couldn't have been taller than five foot five, he was small framed and thin and looked like he hadn't had a hot meal in weeks. He was dirty as all hell and obviously had just come in from the hills.

On the job, I kept the Paterson on my hip, but because Lackawanna Jo didn't want any shooting in her saloon, I also stood in the saloon or on the gambling floor leaning against a pickaxe handle. The other boys thought it was silly to go so armed, claiming there was never trouble enough in the Yerba Buena Saloon that couldn't be handle with fists, but they didn't know my aversion to getting punched.

So this thin fellow, I would guess he was a few years older than me, he started drinking whiskey at the bar. He was paying in gold dust – another sure sign he was just off the goldfields, and Shane McAllister was using the scales to weigh his gold with each drink. Because he was so small framed, the boy didn't take long to start to get a little wobbly, and I kept my eye on him, waiting for the slightest transgression.

But he sat at the bar, quietly drinking and keeping to hisself, and I thought I was going to have to find a different mark. It was too bad, too, because the saloon was pretty full, and if I thrashed this man the word would spread quickly.

But then as he finished his last drink, and slid off his barstool, the man stumbled. I saw the whole thing, and I can assure you it was all an accident. He'd been sitting on the stool for at least two hours, he didn't know how wobbly his legs were after several whiskey drinks. But it was his bad luck that when he stumbled he reached out a hand to steady hisself, and when he did, he grabbled the right teat of one of the serving girls. By instinct alone, he gave it a squeeze, too, and I think that squeeze was his undoing, for the girl – the amply bosomed Susannah Thompson – let out a squeal of indignation and shrieked, "Hands off, you maggot!"

Everyone in the saloon heard her, but before she shrieked I was already on my way over.

The man was making a poor and drunken effort to apologize to the indignant Susannah Thompson when I swung the pickaxe handle like a club and smashed him in the back of the knee. The knee buckled, and he went down in a heap, shouting, "Bloody murder!"

But I warn't done.

"Keep them hands off the serving girls!" I shouted at him, and I bashed him in the gut with the end of the pickaxe handle. I was attempting to establish a reputation, don't ye know. The man was doubled up in pain – no whiskey he'd had was masking the beating he was taking.

Calm as ye please, I set my pickaxe handle down on the bar, and I bent over and picked him up bodily by the crotch of his britches and the collar of his shirt, and I carried him toward the door of the saloon. I was already a big, strong man in my youth, and I'd spent the previous summer lifting wagons and carrying casks of water over river crossings. Lifting this little man was no challenge to me.

I gave his head a good bang into the doorframe as I toted him through the door, and I tossed him into the street. A quarter of the saloon's patrons had followed me out and were lining the porch rails, and another quarter were jockeying for a view from the big front windows, so I didn't let up just because the man was now outside of my jurisdiction.

"We'll not be having your sort of perversion in the Yerba Buena," I told my crumpled victim as I stepped down off of the porch of the saloon. I grabbed him by the collar again and lifted his torso up off the street. I considered breaking his nose, but I suppose my better nature won over, and when I saw the look of terror on the man's face, I decided just to slap him a couple of times.

"You'll not be welcome back in here," I said. "Take your groping hands to some low class establishment."

When I walked back into the saloon, a few men cheered me for standing up for the virtue of a woman, and Susannah was in tears and telling any man who would listen how terrible an ordeal it had been for her to be so rudely violated by such a louse as that man.

My reputation was established. After that, everyone around the Yerba Buena Saloon began calling me "Pickaxe Jack," and Lackawanna Jo paid me an extra dollar that week.

I soon learned that everyone in San Francisco who had not gone to the hills looking for gold was almost exclusively employed in vice. When prospectors came down to have their dust made into coins, the whole town was there to relieve them of the coins. There warn't yet many whores, but Lackawanna Jo certainly didn't have a corner on the market. There was at least one other parlor house, and in tents here and there, prostitutes working on their own were doing a steady business. Some of the California Indians brought their wives down to the town and whored them out, and most of the others were Mexican women. None of them that I saw were worth paying for, but if ye've sent six months digging in a cold riverbed, any port in a storm will suffice, no matter if that port is fat or has a hairy mole on her upper lip.

If it wasn't whoring, then it was drinking. The Yerba Buena was one of the only saloons in a permanent structure, but by the end of my first month in town there were probably more than a dozen drinking houses set up in large canvas tents.

And if it wasn't whoring or drinking, then it was gambling. And everyone gambled. Prospectors, construction workers, bankers, business owners – they all gambled. It did not matter what social class or background or profession a person had, if they were in San Francisco, they were probably gambling.

And, of course, for a fair number of them, it was every bit of it – whoring, drinking, and gambling, because there was naught else to do.

But I managed to avoid the wicked behaviors. I didn't have enough gold to gamble or drink, and the whores that were available were enough to turn me celibate. I'd only ever been with beautiful women, Ashley Franks, the negro slave girl Bessie, Eliza, Marcelina de la Garza, and Weenonaw – four of the most beautiful specimens of womanhood that a man could find, and one middling looking negro girl that still surpassed nearly all the whores in San Francisco in the winter of '48-'49. I could not now see a time when I'd ever be so desperate for relief that any of the three whores in Lackawanna Jo's back rooms could entice me.

The serving girls were a different matter. They weren't any of them what you would call strictly beautiful, but by California standards they were right appealing. Miss Jo dressed them up in fine dresses that showed off their cleavage pretty well. She also made them wear coloring on their lips and cheeks which helped to enhance their faces a bit. Susannah, she was a plump thing, but she knew how to work her assets to good effect. Then there was Laura Leigh Smith, a brown haired girl with a pretty face and straight teeth but not a curve to be found on her stick figure. The other one was Hilde Wistergren, a Bavarian woman with blonde hair and blue eyes. Hilde was a happy medium between plump Susannah and the board-like Laura Leigh. But Hilde's husband was a big Bavarian who made regular trips in from the goldfields, and I was too scared of him to give her a try.

Laura Leigh's husband came back to San Francisco for the winter, but he'd become a drunk while working as a prospector and she was now supporting him and his habits. Both Laura Leigh and Hilde had rooms in a boarding house and husbands who frequently occupied their beds.

Susannah was my best bet if I was ever interested in getting my hands on some woman flesh – and I frequently was. For one, it was her honor I'd defended when I beat down that poor drunken fool who accidentally grabbed her teat, and for that alone she thought I was special. For another, Susannah's husband had gone off to the goldfields early in '48, back when word first spread that gold had been found, and no one had seen him nor heard from him since. Eight months without word from her husband, and Susannah was about ready to move on.

But Susannah was destitute when she came to work at the Yerba Buena, and Lackawanna Jo, taking pity on the girl, allowed Susannah to move into her own apartment. So Susannah and Miss Jo were roommates, which made it awkward. Lackawanna Jo took other people's marriage vows pretty serious, and Susannah was afraid she'd lose her job and her room and board if Jo found out about us. So the few times we were together, it had to be done in stolen opportunities.

My seven dollars a week didn't go far. The livery man got five dollars a week, and I was determined to save the other two dollars to buy supplies come spring. So I didn't drink or gamble. Because I worked late into the night, I slept late in the mornings. Most days I would eat one of my two meals a day when I woke up, and then I'd go over to the livery and take Courage out for a ride. Though it was terrible cold with deep snow up in the Sierra Nevada, down in San Francisco the climate was moderate and pleasant most all the time. I did use some of my wages from Stand Watie – converted to gold – to buy myself a new set of clothes and a warm coat, but I don't remember the temperature ever getting so cold that the coat wasn't enough to keep me comfortable, even on horseback.

So I'd ride Courage out through the hills for a couple of hours most days. It amazed me, as the weeks wore on, how many new tent sites would spring up from day to day, so that the city sprawled out for miles. Each time a few tents would appear in a cluster, that cluster of tents would soon grow to be its own little town. If twenty or thirty tents came up nearby each other, often with two or three prospectors sharing a tent, there would soon be a larger tent erected. That would be the tent that served as a meal house. Then there'd be another big tent, and this one would be the gambling house and saloon. Sometimes all three were under one tent. And once the bigger tents sprang up, like mushrooms smaller tents would appear around them over the next few days. A grouping of tents also would mean a corral would go up where horses and mules would be kept. Each of these clusters of tents became their own little towns.

Mostly I stayed to myself on these rides. The prospectors were a fun bunch, but they drank heavily and some of them were rougher than others. Everybody was suspicious of strangers – and in the tent towns on the hills, they were especially suspicious of strangers coming up from San Francisco because most of the prospectors – if they'd been around longer than a week – had already lost a fair amount of gold to cheats and swindlers from the city.

A couple of times I did run into some of the boys who'd worked with Abner Jamieson who, upon learning of the goldfields, abandoned Jamieson and his group and tried their hands at digging for gold. Most of them had fallen in with larger prospecting companies, having arrived too late in the year to obtain their own supplies. But when I was out during one of my rides, I spotted the two boys I'd been closest with on the wagon train – Slim and Brother – sharing a tent on the hillside, and I was glad to ride over and see them.

"Well, hello Jackson Speed," Brother greeted me. "I thought that looked like Courage coming up the hill. I'm glad to see you."

"Hey there, Brother," I said. "Howdy, Slim. Y'all been prospecting?"

I dismounted and left Courage to graze and took a seat on a log the boys had set up by their campfire.

"We heard about the gold up there at Sutter's fort," Brother told me. "We figured we'd try our hand at it and see if it was any better than farming."

Slim piped up, "Between us, we had just enough money to buy one pan, a mule, a pickaxe, and enough beans to get us through for a couple of weeks." It was a constant refrain there in California. Every conversation began, and often ended, with a discussion of how money didn't go far in buying supplies.

"How'd y'all do?" I asked.

"We got enough gold out the river to buy the tent and supplies to get us through the winter. We got some new coats, those blankets in the tent, and some victuals," Brother said.

I tried to count in my head. The tent was a good canvas tent. Coats didn't come cheap, and good thick blankets were the sort of thing only rich men could afford. They must have struck a pretty good claim, and done it in a short stretch.

"All that must've cost ye a fair bit," I said. "Y'all must've found a good hole to dig in."

"It took us a few days," Slim said. "It was tough to get the knack for it, and even tougher to get the right spot. But we kept going up into the hills until we were far away from the other prospectors, and we managed to get a good amount. What was it, Brother? Two hundred dollars?"

"That's about right. One hundred and eighty dollars. Ninety a piece."

"That's not bad. What did it take you, a month or so?"

Slim nodded his head. "Thereabouts. We got into the fort in October, and me and Brother was up in the goldfields from about mid-October to the first week of December. By then it was too cold to keep at it, so we came down here to sit out the winter."

"You going back in the spring?" I asked.

Brother surprised me when he shrugged his shoulders. "We ain't decided yet. The thing is, a man can get a good sum of money out of the river. But the cost to get at it is so high. Mules ain't cheap, and you have to have a couple of pack mules. This 'ere tent cost as much as a one room house with walls and a chimney back home. Everything costs so durn much that you end up spending all your gold just to get the supplies you need to go back and get more gold."

"We was just trying to figure if there was any way to get ahead with it," Slim said.

"Finding more gold," I said.

Brother nodded agreement. "That's the way I see it. We just have to find the right hole that got enough gold in it."

Slim chewed on his lip a while. "That's prob'ly right. Trouble is, ye ain't got no guarantees ye'll ever find the right hole."

"What you been doin', Jackson?" Brother asked. "We got to

California, and the next thing we knew you was gone."

"I went up into the hills, too, and spent a little bit of time panning," I told them. "But I decided to get a job in town and go up and be serious about it come spring. Like you boys was saying, the cost of supplies makes it tough."

"What job ye got?" Slim asked.

"I'm working in a saloon," I told them. "Keeping out the ne'er-do-wells."

Brother licked his lips. "Y'all got any girls in the saloon?"

"We've got some serving girls, but if ye lay a hand on them, I'll have to break your skull with a pickaxe handle," I told them. They both guffawed pretty good at that, but I think they gathered that I was serious.

"Ye got any girls ye can touch?" Slim asked.

"Some, but ye might want to get a good look at them in the daylight before ye spend any money," I advised.

Brother scrunched up his face. "That bad?"

"Pretty bad. Two Mexicans and an Indian, between 'em they've got six teats and three holes, so if that's all that matters ye're welcome to come down and pay the going rate. But I'd advise ye to do it in the dark."

Slim slapped his knee laughing, but Brother was thinking serious on it.

"I better get back down toward the town, but if y'all are going to be here a bit I'll stop by and see you again."

"Do that," Slim said. "We'll be here at least until mid-February."

"What's the name of yer saloon?" Brother asked.

"The Yerba Buena Saloon," I said, and I turned and pointed it out to them. "That two story building right there, down by the livery."

"I may come see ye," Brother said.

After leaving Slim and Brother I rode back down to the wharf, another frequent activity. Any time a new ship came in I would go down to the wharf and hang about for a while to see if I could spot Eliza arriving in California.

I did not know if she would come to San Francisco. For that matter, I did not even know if she'd ever received my letter. Nor did I know for sure how long it would take the letter to get to her if she did receive it. I figured it would take the letter three months to arrive in Milledgeville. I suspected, though I did not know, that it would probably take another three months for her to get out to California if she came by sea. Assuming she took a month to make the arrangements to come west, I figured the soonest I might see her would be November.

But November turned to December, and December was coming on to January, and pretty soon it got to be 1849 and Eliza was still not in San Francisco. And then I started to think that she might not come at all, though I prayed every day that I would see her coming off a ship at the wharf. My affair with Susannah was not so serious a thing that it could not be easily and quickly broken off if Eliza arrived. We were both married to other people, and we both understood that we'd have to end our once or twice a week meetings if either of our spouses ever appeared.

If Eliza did come, I was not sure how she would take to life in California. She was the daughter of a wealthy Georgia planter and the granddaughter of a wealthy store owner. She wasn't accustomed to the sort of hard labor it took to make a life out here, and there were no decent places for her to live. I couldn't imagine she'd take to sharing a room with Little Wade and the McAllister brothers.

But ever since Weenonaw's murder, I was sore missing Eliza.

Forgotten now were the days when I struggled to decide if I wanted a future with my Cherokee bride or if I wanted to return to Eliza's lovely pale skin and red hair. And even as I tried now, I could not imagine Eliza in my memory. When I thought about her and tried to remember what she looked like, her features were all distorted, and all I could remember for sure was that she was the prettiest girl I'd ever seen. And now I longed to see her again, to take in her beauty and to burn upon my brain every fine inch of her so that I would never again not remember her.

CHAPTER 14

In February of 1849, the boats started arriving in the bay from such far-flung places as the Sandwich Islands and China, and with them came more men bound for the goldfields. Up to that point, the men in the goldfields were already in California when news of the discovery began to spread. Towns emptied of inhabitants. Then people began to trickle in from Oregon and Mexico. But in early '49, the Gold Rush began in earnest. In those first couple of months of 1849, ships were bringing as many as a hundred or two hundred new people to the town every week. [34]

On my trips down to the wharf, I was amazed at the throngs of humanity daily coming off of boats.

Most used all the money they had just to arrive in San Francisco, and when they got there they found that prices for everything were at least twice what they would have paid back home. I was grateful that I had a warm, dry place to lay my head and that I knew where my next meal would come from.

The mass of immigrants meant that the city was rapidly growing, even as prospectors began to prepare to move back out to the goldfields. There warn't enough supplies, warn't enough food, warn't enough rooms, and as such, tempers began to run pretty hot in San Francisco during those first months of 1849. I found, too, that my reputation as Pickaxe Jack was unknown to too many of the newcomers who came into the Yerba Buena, drank too much and started trouble.

During those weeks of employment at the Yerba Buena, I got to know Lackawanna Jo pretty well. She'd come from Pennsylvania, having grown up the daughter of a farmer, and she had married a coal miner who dug coal in the valley of the Lackawanna River. An explosion at the mine had been the death of her husband. She had lived with her husband in a home owned by the mining company, and with her husband dead she was no longer welcome in the home. By that time her parents were also dead, the farm sold off, and Josefina found herself without a home and without a place to go. So she took what money she had and went west, first to Oregon and then to California, and she settled in Yerba Buena.

From others, I learned that Lackawanna Jo married an elderly Spaniard who had a good bit of wealth, and when he died she received the bulk of his estate. She converted that wealth into the Yerba Buena Saloon, and as best as I could tell she was probably the wealthiest citizen of San Francisco, or thereabouts. She had plenty of suitors, too. Half a dozen or more men, ranging in age from twenty to sixty, came frequently to the Yerba Buena to court her, but as best as I could tell they always left disappointed. At the Yerba Buena, Lackawanna Jo was royalty, and she was always in the saloon or on the gambling floor, laughing and having fun, and I doubted that any man would ever convince her to leave such a life.

As the town's population began to swell, Jo had a talk with me, Little Wade and the McAllister brothers.

"All these new people coming into town, most every one of them just passing through. And you mark my words, they are going to start trouble," she told us. "So I want you to be quick to put down any strangers that raise a voice. The regulars – we still give them the same treatment we always have. But when it comes to strangers, anyone cheating, cursing, or getting too drunk should be tossed out the door in as rough a manner as ye like. And give 'em worse if they touch one of the serving girls."

And so we did.

Little Wade and the McAllisters were quick to tell people to settle down, but Pickaxe Jack didn't bother to give out warnings. My style was to hit them from behind with the pickaxe handle. A warning could be met with a swinging fist, and my intention was to avoid getting punched or shot. But a pickaxe handle to the back of the knee would drop a man, and if he was big enough or looked like he might reach for his pistol, I'd bash him over the head from behind. As hard as I swung that club at some men's heads, it always surprised me that I never killed anyone or did them serious damage, but it's harder to really hurt a drunk man than you would think. Most of 'em, ye'd just bash their brains in and toss them into the street, and in a minute or two they'd be on their feet and stumbling to the next saloon.

When February turned to March, I decided it was time for me to head into the mountains. I'd talked to some of the folks who had been around long enough, and while they told me I could still expect to find treacherous rivers in the Sierra Nevada, the trails would likely be passable by the time I arrived there. So many new folks were arriving in California that I didn't want all the gold to be gone by the time I finally got started prospecting.

I put together a list of the supplies I would need – a mule and a tent, enough bacon and beans to keep me fed for a couple of months until I could hit some gold and make enough money to buy more, and a couple of good blankets if I could afford them. But when I counted up my earnings I discovered that even if I transferred all of Stand Watie's silver dollars into gold, there still wouldn't be enough to properly supply myself.

I was saving most all of the money I made at the Yerba Buena, but once Courage's five dollars a week had been subtracted, I discovered that my earnings for four months of work totaled out to around forty dollars, and that wouldn't buy me a decent pair of boots, much less a mule or a tent or anything else. And then I realized I was caught in the trap that over the next few years would turn so many prospectors who were seeking their fortune into hired men at the mines, hired bartenders, livery hands, journeymen and whatever other odd jobs there were to be had.

So many of these people arriving in California didn't have enough money to buy supplies, and so if they made it to the goldfields, it was to work for someone else for six dollars a day. And when a poor pair of boots cost thirty dollars and a good pair of boots cost five times that, no man could buy the supplies he needed to head into the hills. For a lot of them, that's what dragged them into the gambling houses – the lure of doubling their money in a night. It never happened, and they always started over from nothing.

But these were the troubles that confounded prospectors for years to come, and their troubles were not my troubles. My troubles were what concerned me.

Here it was, March, with those men who had come out of the hills now deciding it was time to think about returning and so many more coming into the bay by the boatload every week, and I didn't have money enough to get the supplies I would need. I was convinced that the same Providence that had spared me in Mexico had also sent me to seek a fortune in California, and I had only to get into those hills to claim my gold.

I rode out to see Slim and Brother and seek their advice.

"Yep, ye're in the same spot most o' the rest of us are in," Slim said, spitting at his campfire. "We ain't got money enough to buy supplies to return to the goldfields, and we can't get money until we get back into the goldfields."

"So what are y'all going to do?" I asked.

"We've been thinking on it," Brother said, "but we ain't come to no kind of conclusion yet. We could sell our mule, but then we'd be luggin' our own supplies up, and we're not sure we can do that. We've heard there's companies that'll hire you out at six dollars a day to work their claims, but then we're standing in a freezing cold river all day and anything we find belongs to someone else."

"But they'll feed us, and we can sell our mule and have that money, and if we earn some we will have enough money to buy supplies and set out on our own later in the year," Slim said.

"But supplies up by the river cost even more than they do here in San Francisco," Brother added.

The same conversation was being held over fires all through the hills around San Francisco, and the decision most of 'em reached was that they would start out for the goldfields without adequate supplies and hope for the best. For most of those men, life in the goldfields would be little different than life in the hills around San Francisco, and so they traded nothing for a hope at something. But for me, I at least had a warm, dry place where I could spend my nights, and, more importantly, I was eating passably well.

But I'd come to California for gold, not to beat up drunks in a saloon.

I could have sold Courage. For the price he'd have fetched I would have been able to buy two mules, a tent and a blanket. But I'd spent so long on the back of that horse, he'd been a good and smart companion, and I felt an attachment to him. I couldn't bear the thought of selling him to some miner who would work him to death.

Over the next few days I asked every prospector who came into the saloon what they intended to do, and most of them planned to either go up into the hills and hope they found gold soon enough to buy the supplies they needed, or they were going to find someone who would pay them a wage.

I could not blame those who were going with nothing more than a hope of discovering gold. In the town, everyone had gold. Either they had coins from the assay offices or they had a bag or two of gold dust. Every store and saloon and gambling house had scales for weighing out the gold dust, and most all of the scales were rigged for the benefit of the proprietor. But with so much gold all over the town, it was reasonable for everyone to expect to go into the hills and find at least enough gold to survive. And, of course, they all believed they would find more than that.

A week later I decided I would go to the goldfields, and I decided I would go with Slim and Brother. Whether they were going to work for someone else or go it on their own, I would accompany them into the hills. I rode out over the hills around the town and found them much emptied, even from a few days before. Now, rather than being dotted with tents and small corrals for mules and horses, I found most of the campsites abandoned. Left behind was all sorts of rubbish the men had decided they wouldn't need or didn't want to carry. Those prospectors who remained were scavenging the abandoned camps for anything they might find useful. Pots and pans, broken tent posts they intended to repair, broken tools – anything that might be repaired or cleaned and made useful again.

When I reached the spot where Brother and Slim had camped through the winter, I found their campsite was among those left empty. A prospector who'd been camped nearby, a fellow I'd seen any number of times when up visiting Slim and Brother, told me they'd left the day before.

"They said they was heading up to Dry Diggins," he said. "Said they would figure out which way to go when they were there, but they were out of gold and nearly out of food, and they figured if they didn't leave they'd never make it. You being on horseback, you can probably catch them up if you leave in the next couple of days. It'll take 'em a week to get to Dry Diggins, maybe more, and you can prob'ly catch them up without any trouble."

I rode back down to town and left Courage at the livery, and then I went to let Lackawanna Jo know that I'd be leaving.

"I ain't surprised," she said. "I knew you'd be going after gold sooner or later. Well, if ye get up there and ye find all the gold is gone, come on back and I'm sure I can find something for ye to do around here."

Jo gave me some jerky to take along, and optimistically donated to me a dozen buckskin bags that she told me she wanted me to fill with gold. "And when you've got all them bags filled, come give me one of 'em!"

At the livery, I convinced the man to sell me a pack mule for fifty dollars in Stand Watie's silver coins plus ten dollars in gold I'd earned at the Yerba Buena, which left me without much of anything to put on the mule's back. At most the mule warn't worth more than forty dollars, but he started out wanting seventy for it. I also convinced him to give me several lengths of worn and frayed rope he had lying about. I laid my saddlebags across the mule and used a bit of the rope to fashion a strap to hold the bags around him like a pack. Then I tied the shovel and pickaxe to the bags and put my blanket and clean clothes on the mule, tying everything down to the saddlebags. It looked ridiculous, but I didn't have naught else for supplies. My intention was that for all the mule lacked in carrying into the hills, he'd be loaded with gold on the return.

So that was how Pickaxe Jack left the Yerba Buena Saloon and ventured up into the goldfields in search of his fortune, with every man-jack along the way having a good laugh at his packless pack mule.

Most of the men leaving out of San Francisco to return to the goldfields had piled in together and taken wagons. Others paid to go up the river on boats hauled upstream by oxen. The path from San Francisco to Dry Diggins, the town known today as Placerville, was well worn, and I passed many men on foot on my way.

Coloma and Dry Diggins were already overrun with prospectors. Those who could find decent shelter for the winter had stayed in Coloma or Dry Diggins. Those who didn't had come to the hills around San Francisco where a tent and a campfire would be sufficient. The rivers were still swollen with snowmelt, but already men were starting to dig.

I asked around for Brother and Slim, but no one I encountered had heard of them. There were so many men working the river that I worried a man could have no hope to find any gold left.

A lot of the men around Dry Diggins had spent the winter there and had already been working the river for a couple of weeks. There seemed to be hundreds of them, digging in the river bottom, digging in the sand around the river, overturning rocks, working cradles and sluice boxes. Most of them worked in teams, planning to divide whatever they found, or worked for wages for enterprises formed back in San Francisco.

With so many men working the river down around Coloma and Dry Diggins, I decided if I was going to strike a fortune I needed to separate myself from the population of miners. So on Courage's back and with the mule's lead tied to my saddle, I started toward the distant mountains. My time with Cump Sherman the previous autumn had taught me a bit about prospecting, and so I was not entirely green, despite the look of my mule. But it would be a serious error to suggest that I had a good idea of what I was doing.

The first bit of California gold was discovered at the site where John Sutter was building a saw mill, and it was no surprise to me that he would want to mill lumber here. The landscape was covered up in enormous fir trees, nearly two hundred feet tall and perfectly straight. Pine and cedar trees also covered the valleys and hills, and I thought all those men looking for fortune in the river might do better to stop digging and start swinging an ax. In lumber they would find the fortune they were seeking. We were surrounded by some of the best timber I'd ever seen, and I'd come from Georgia all the way to California. As I picked my way along deer paths leading up into the mountains, I imagined myself finding enough gold to start a milling operation.

I caught myself daydreaming of setting up huge operations – mining, milling, construction. I thought I might strike a fortune and go back down to San Francisco and build hotels to house those hundreds of people arriving in town every week.

And I also imagined myself buying passage aboard a ship back to Georgia and arriving at home a rich man. In my daydreams, I saw Eliza waiting for me at our little home in Milledgeville, and the two of us coming back here to California to live on a huge ranch in the lush valley.

I had written Eliza from the Yerba Buena Saloon a couple of times, but I'd had no response from her. I doubted if the letters even had time to reach her in Milledgeville, and my true hope still was that she was not in Georgia but instead was bound for California. I suppose I was still suffering the loss of Weenonaw, but I was missing Eliza in a way I'd not missed her since I'd left for Mexico. I was thinking about her all the time, especially riding the trails into the mountains, and being out there on my own, I was feeling sore lonesome.

I rode for two days into the mountains. It was slow going through difficult terrain where I was often forced to dismount and lead horse and mule up steep slopes. I ate raspberries and some of the jerky Lackawanna Jo had given me. There wasn't much in the way of grass for Courage and the mule, and so I stopped any time I saw a clearing with grass where they could graze.

The river cut a deep gorge through the mountains, and the banks down to the river were usually very steep. Large boulders made it difficult to get near the river up here in the mountains, and the American River was narrower and ran faster than down in the valley near Dry Diggins and Sutter's Mill and Sutter's Fort.

The result was that few prospectors had come up this far, and that's what I was looking for. I was hunting virgin river, untouched by other miners, where the gold would be easier to find and more plentiful.

I suppose that I believed I had some kind of mystical prescience, and I was convinced that I was going to find a fortune in gold. That conviction did not make me different from the other miners standing in the freezing water who were all equally convinced they would strike a fortune. What separated me from the rest of 'em was that eventually I did. But at the time I was convinced that I would find my fortune higher up in the hills, away from the others.

After two days of picking my way along deer paths, I decided I was far enough removed from the other miners that it was time to try my luck. Also, I did not want to get so far removed from civilization that I could not go and get supplies when I did find gold. I still had no tent and spent my nights sleeping on my blanket with my coat over me and a fire blazing nearby. The days had warmed and the rain had let up, but the nights were still terrible cold in the hills.

There was not flat enough ground to sleep down by the river, and so I camped well up a hill overlooking the spot I'd picked to start prospecting. There was decent grazing for my small collection of livestock up at the campsite, and I fashioned a small corral with rope and broken branches, mostly to keep the mule from wandering too far off.

My first day at the spot, I took my pan and shovel down into the river and I dug at anything that looked like black sand and swirled it around in my pan. My first day on the river, all I discovered was a small mountain range of blisters forming up on my hands from constantly getting my hands wet in the freezing cold water and then working the shovel.

My second day on the river my toes were so numb from two days of standing in the cold water, that I was barely able to make the climb back up to my campsite.

My third day on the river, my back was sore, I could only painfully grasp the shovel with the blisters on my hands, and I was beginning to worry that I would lose my toes to the freezing water.

When I woke on the fourth morning, having still not pulled out the first bit of gold, I decided that there might be a good reason that there were no miners this far into the mountains. I concluded that I must have trekked beyond the goldfields.

A bit humbled, I decided to pack up my gear and move back closer to the valley. I'd wasted a week traveling too far into the mountains and finding no gold. I had this gnawing fear that all the gold would be gone before I could fill one of Lackawanna Jo's buckskin bags.

I came back down out of the mountains after a week, following the same deer paths that had brought me up there, and as I neared the valley and Dry Diggins but had still not yet encountered any miners, I decided to camp on a ridge overlooking a small creek that emptied into the American River. There was a bend in the river here, and there were boulders scattered along the bank and out into the river. The banks were steep, and the river was mostly inaccessible. I had to almost slide down the bank to even reach the river. After my first time scrambling to get back up the bank, I tied off a length of rope so that I had a way to both pull myself and drag gear back up the bank at the end of each day.

In my imagination, I could not envision other miners coming down to this spot.

I scouted along the bank, mostly walking through the river or crawling over boulders or gingerly stepping out across rocks.

I spotted a bit of black sand and I scooped my pan into the river, pulling up sand and rock. I swirled out the bigger debris, rinsing the pan with water. I swirled it more, allowing the sand to wash away. And as I swirled, I saw it – they describe it as a "flash," and sure enough it were. A bright yellow flash as the sand swirled around. There in my pan was a flake of gold no bigger than a toenail, but it was gold.

I worked that bit of river for a couple of days, and I found that the blisters warn't so bad, nor were the backaches, and the water warn't so cold, so long as I was retrieving gold from the riverbed.

The site was ideal. I had not seen nor heard evidence of other miners the whole time I was there. Big red fir trees lined the ridge, so that I had plenty of fuel for fires, and there was grass for grazing for Courage and the mule.

I built myself a small lean-to cabin with branches from the trees, and when the jerky was nearly all gone, I fished for trout in the river. Between the trout and some blackberries and raspberries I found not far away, I was able to gather enough food to keep myself full and strong.

For a week or longer I worked up and down the banks of the river, probably covering a mile in either direction. I was alone on that section of the river, and all the easy placer gold was mine for the taking. Some days I pulled out two or three ounces of gold without ever putting my shovel in the sand. I just scooped the loose stuff from the riverbed with my pan, swirled it around, and found gold.

If I'd had an ax, I'd have probably built myself a log cabin and stayed on that section of river for the rest of the season. Over the course of a week or more, I'd found something close to forty ounces of gold, most of it just sitting on top of the riverbed waiting for someone to come along and take it. Why, in a single week, I'd made more than five hundred dollars.

And I now understood how men went mad with gold fever and why they left everything to stand in the cold water flowing down out of the Sierra Nevada.

Sometime in mid-April, I was flipping over rocks on the river bank when a voice on a cliff above me said, "You're doing it all wrong."

I hadn't heard another human voice in weeks, and I was so startled that I dropped a good size rock on my freezing cold toes and hollered in pain.

I turned and looked at the far bank, and sitting up on a ledge was a man a good deal older than me, tall and lanky with his shirtsleeves and the legs of his britches rolled up. On his head he had a homemade leather hat like none I'd ever seen, but his clothes – other than that they were rolled at the ends – looked more appropriate for a gentleman farmer than a prospector. Above him, farther up the steep bank on the ridge, was a mule with a fully loaded pack.

"I've been watching you for half an hour now, boy, and you are doing it all wrong." He had to shout so that I could hear him over the noise of the river. He enunciated all his words in a thick Yankee accent, and the man couldn't have been more out of place.

"You've been watching me for half an hour?" I shouted back at him.

"You're probably standing right next to more gold than you've ever dreamed of, and you don't even know it."

"Huh?" I said.

"Have you a pick?" he asked.

I pointed to where my pick and shovel were on the bank.

"Do you see that rock there, that black one?" he asked. "And do you see that great big white stripe running through that rock? Take your pick and give that white stripe a solid hit."

"What do you know about it?" I asked.

"Now it makes no difference to me," the stranger shouted, "if you find gold or if you do not. I am simply offering you a suggestion as to how to go about finding gold. If you knew anything about the properties of gold, you would know that it attaches itself to quartz. If you want to find the big nuggets and the rich veins and not just the placer gold on the surface of the riverbed, you must break up the quartz."

I hesitated, certain he was putting me on and as soon as I hit the rock with the pick I'd be the butt of a joke. I looked around at the bank where the stranger was to see if there were others around that I'd not noticed. But there was no audience. If the old man was making fun of me, he was the only one going to be amused by it.

"Go on, now," he said. "We haven't got all day. Take a swing with the pickaxe there."

Reluctantly, I went and fetched the pick and walked back over to the big boulder he'd indicated. The thing was twice as tall as me and five feet around at its narrowest point. Running through the middle of the rock was a dirty-white streak of quartz. I tested the point of the pick, tapping it against the white vein. Small chunks of quartz came off.

I decided I'd give it a shot. I took careful aim and brought the point of the pickaxe down as hard as I could. Chips of the white rock smashed off, the axe handle shook like hell against my hands so that I dropped it. The old timer laughed pretty hard at that.

"Don't smash it! Chip it away!"

Frustrated and still fairly certain I was the butt of this stranger's joke, I picked up the pickaxe and started chipping at the white vein of quartz running through the rock. With a bit of force behind it, I was able to chip the quartz away in rocks the size of my fist or smaller. I chipped and chipped, digging a crevice into the rock where the vein of quartz ran. From time to time, the old man would shout at me to look at the rocks I was chipping away.

"Any gold in it?" he would ask.

"None," I would say.

I did this for fifteen or twenty minutes. It was hard labor, but I suppose no harder than digging sand out of the bottom of the river or off the bank. At last I had chipped deep into the quartz without any gold.

"Well, it isn't always there," the man said. "But if you want to find something other than a bag of dust – if you want real nuggets, underneath that quartz is where you look for it."

I was about to shout at the old man that he'd wasted my time and was lucky he was on the other side of the river where I could not easily get at him, but without being told, he got up from his perch, scrambled up the hillside to his mule, and started walking off.

Glad to be done with the stranger, I decided to give up for the day and checked the trotlines I'd run across the river. Each morning before I went to work with my pan, I'd run four lines to fish for my supper, and most days I managed to catch two or three fish to cook over my fire. This day I had two decent sized trout.

I cleaned the fish down by the river and toted them up the bank in a bag tied over my shoulder.

My daily routine was to use the hot coals of my campfire to get my fire going again, and once I had hot coals I put the fish fillets on a flat rock in the middle of my fire – I had no pans or pots, but I found that by building up the fire around the rock and laying the fillets of trout on the rock they could cook up and be pretty edible. Some nights I would crush blackberries over the trout fillets to give them a bit of a different flavor.

Because I'd packed so poorly for expedition into the goldfields, my gold pan also served as my plate in the evenings. I was looking forward to taking my diggings to a town and getting properly supplied, for I'd not had a meal in weeks that did not include bits of sand, no matter how much I rinsed my pan prior to a meal.

About the time I got ready to tuck into my supper, I heard the clatter of supplies banging against each other on a packed mule. I'd heard the same noise a thousand times in Mexico and on the trail from San Francisco to Dry Diggins. It was the telltale sound of the miners, and it was unmistakable.

I wasn't regular wearing my Paterson on my hip because I'd seen no people for so long, but I always made sure the holster with the Paterson was hanging on a nearby branch in case of bears or other animals. The Paterson was closer than the carbine at that particular moment, so I snatched the Paterson from its holster and waited until I could see the mule making the noise, I had a bad feeling, though that I already knew the man and the mule. I suspected the stranger who'd convinced me to take a swing at a rock had made his way across the river and back to my camp.

Eventually, I saw the stranger and his mule come out from behind a stand of cedar trees near my camp.

"There you are!" he said. "I didn't think I'd ever find you. Had to go a mile and a half upstream to find a place where I could cross the river with the mule and work my way back here. What's for supper?"

"I'm having trout," I told him. "Not sure what you're having."

I wanted him to not feel welcome. The buckskin bag I'd been keeping all my gold dust in was sitting just at the opening of the lean-to I'd built for myself. I put my eyes on it and wondered if I could get it hid before he spied it.

The fellow came right up into my camp and lashed his mule to a pine branch. From the pack on the mule he extracted a tin plate and a metal fork. He cocked his head and looked down his nose at my pan.

"I'll have some of that fish," he said. "What's that on it? A blackberry sauce?"

"Something like that," I said.

He looked around at the camp, at the lean-to, the corral I'd build for Courage and the mule. "This might be one of the poorest mining camps I've ever seen," he said, adjusting a big rock and taking a seat on it. He held his plate out toward me.

Using my knife, I scraped half of one fillet onto his plate, along with some of the smashed up blackberries.

"What's yer name, son?" the old timer asked.

"My name's Jackson Speed," I said. "Folks down in San Francisco call me Pickaxe Jack."

"I've never heard of you. How long you been prospecting in these hills?"

"A few weeks," I answered.

Though I did not ask, the old timer provided me with his own answer to his question, and then gave me a lecture on prospecting. "I've only recently come to California, myself," he said. "I am amazed, though, at the lack of knowledge among the men prospecting in the goldfields. On the boat to San Francisco, I availed myself of many journals and books so that I would know all about the processes and techniques of gold mining, and I learned about the metal itself. How can men expect to find a thing that they know nothing about? Take yourself, for example. Here you are, back bent, water up to your knees, sliding your pan into the sand, when all the while an enormous vein of quartz is within striking distance from you. You don't even know, do you, that gold attaches itself to quartz."

"Well, I heard you say it, but I've seen no evidence," I said.

"You have no idea what you're doing," the stranger said over a mouthful of trout.

"I'm doing just fine," I said.

Now he started laughing. "You have no tent," he said. Then he pointed at the morsel of fish on the tip of my knife. "You have no fork!"

He looked around my camp, and I saw his eyes fix on the bag of gold dust in the lean-to. The Paterson was sitting beside me in the dirt, so I snatched it up in a hurry.

"You'll keep your hands off that bag," I said, clutching the Paterson but not pointing it directly at him.

"Oh, put that thing away," he said. "I am not interested in your gold. I have more than that poor little bag on the mule."

I set the Paterson back down, but I looked at him pretty hard to make certain he knew I'd shoot him if he went for the gold. I could see he had an old musket on the mule, but I didn't see that he was armed with anything more than a knife and fork on his person.

"So what are ye here for?" I asked.

"Supper!" the old timer said. "Fish is good. I like it with the blackberry sauce. You're not a bad cook for your lack of pan. What did you say your name is?"

"Jackson Speed," I said.

"Well, Mister Speed, slide some more of that fish onto my plate," he said, holding the plate out to me again. "My name is Obadiah Bush."
35

When we were done with our supper Obadiah took his pack off his mule as if he intended to stay.

"No sense in going farther tonight," says he.

Without asking, he put his mule into my makeshift corral with Courage and my mule, and then he went to work on his pack. He took out a canvas tent. He had not posts for the tent, but instead tied a rope between two trees and tossed half the tent over the rope, then he used more rope to pull out the sides. He raked up a pile of pine straw to make hisself a bed and draped a couple of blankets over the pile, and he still had a spare blanket to put over himself.

I noticed among his pack he had pots and pans, a small sluice box and other instruments for finding gold. He had at least another suit of clothes, a spare pair of boots, and a dozen bags similar to my buckskin bags that all looked full. If they were indeed full of gold, the old man could have bought half of California.

I slept that night with my Paterson beside me and my bag of gold stuffed down the leg of my trousers. It was a fitful sleep anyway, I kept waking up with a start, worried that Obadiah was going to shoot me in my sleep. I had no evidence that the bags of gold he had didn't come from miners he'd shot dead. But as best as I knew, he never rose during the night.

The sun was already casting light into the valley when I finally woke the next morning. I'd slept much later than I typically did, I suppose because I'd slept so poorly through the night. When I woke, I smelled food cooking.

"I do not know how you get any gold at all from that river, sleeping as late as you do," Obadiah said to me as I began to stir. He was leaned over the campfire with a skillet over the fire in one hand and a wooden spatula in the other. "I purchased some bacon when I was down in Dry Diggins, and some beans, so I figured we'd have a breakfast of beans and bacon to get us started."

And just like that, Obadiah Bush became my prospecting partner – whether I wanted one or not.

CHAPTER 15

After breakfast, we scrambled down the bank to the river. Obadiah took his chisel and hammer, a pan and a shovel. He strapped a sluice box onto my back, and I toted my shovel, pick and pan. He was sprightly and strong for his age.

Obadiah showed me how to use the hammer and chisel to chip away at the quartz veins we found in rocks, assuring me that was where I would find gold worth mining for – not placer gold to be panned out of riverbeds or dug from sandy banks, but real gold deposits where thousands of dollars could be crushed from the quartz. We spent the day chipping away at quartz with his hammer and chisel and my pick, but we found no quartz gold in any of the rocks we chipped at.

The next day we panned the river together, and he helped me find the best spots. He showed me how to dump shovelfuls of sand and rock down into the sluice box and how to pick through it for gold flakes. We flipped over rocks and small boulders and in the course of that we found a couple of decent sized nuggets of gold.

We walked up and down the river from camp, going as much as a couple of miles along the river, trying different spots. We found a creek and we panned and dug a ways up the creek.

We ate the fish I caught for dinner and for breakfast we ate Obadiah's bacon and beans.

I learned that he was a schoolmaster from New York, and he talked the whole time as if he was still standing at the front of a classroom. It took him every bit of three weeks to remember my name and he seldom showed any curiosity about my opinion on any subject. But I was not offended by his lack of interest in me, because with his help I was finding gold faster than I had done before his arrival.

When he learned that I was from Georgia, he issued lecture after lecture against slavery, but I told him I didn't have any slaves and so he didn't seem to hold it against me. Nevertheless, the lectures were never ceasing. At times, but seldom, he talked to me about his wife and children back home in New York, but mostly I was just his classroom of one. Whether he was talking about the metallurgy of gold or slavery or government or history, Obadiah Bush forever was assaulting me with orations that must have been oft-repeated to his pupils. But he seemed to have an innate knack for understanding where to find the gold.

After several weeks of panning and digging all along the river within a couple of miles of our campsite, Obadiah finally announced to me that we were wasting our time.

"We're still just getting surface gold," he said to me. "This is the gold that over thousands of years has washed down the river. If we're going to strike a big claim, the kind worth digging for, we'll have to find a vein."

I'd filled a bag and a half with gold flakes and gold dust. I was certain I had more than a thousand dollars in gold, and I didn't have any complaints about that. But it wasn't the sort of fortune I was hoping for. And neither, it seemed, was it sufficient to appease Teacher Bush. Obadiah was intent on finding the veins that would lead to fist-sized nuggets.

So after a couple days more of panning and digging along the banks of the river where we were, we decided to abandon our spot and go to town to seek supplies, and from there go to look for a better claim. We loaded all the supplies on my mule; I rode Courage, and Obadiah rode his mule.

We went quite a ways down the river without seeing a soul, but eventually we began passing mining camps where dozens of miners congregated. As we rode past during the day, the camps were mostly empty as miners worked the river and nearby creeks. No minute of daylight was wasted around camp. At the larger camps, we found tents set up with cookhouses, and a couple of times we stopped for a meal. The food was poor – pork and beans was the most common meal served in these makeshift cookhouses – and it was priced to keep the miners hungry or the cooks rich. At one cookhouse we paid twelve dollars each for a plate, and at another we paid twenty dollars – the extra price added because the meal was cooked by a woman. I'd not seen a woman in weeks, and so I sought her out to give her my compliments and see if she might like to sneak off into the woods, but when I found her I discovered she was at least seventy-years-old, out-weighed me by forty pounds and was the ugliest Injun woman I'd ever seen. Her face looked as if it she'd got it too near a cook fire, and when it set ablaze someone had beat the flames out with a shovel. I skipped offering the invitation to the woods and instead suggested that the beans could cook a bit longer and the pork could be improved with some blackberry sauce.

Within eight miles of Dry Diggins, there were three thousand men if there was one, and maybe there was twice that many by the time you got up among the small creeks. When Obadiah Bush and I arrived at Dry Diggins, you'd have thought it was a European capital for all the activity. Thousands of people had turned up in Dry Diggins. Even in the short time since I'd come through, the town had grown significantly, and everywhere there were hastily constructed canvas shelters that served as saloons or eating houses or stores. Every man-jack who could walk and talk was selling something, and most everyone who was selling something was trying to swindle folks out of their gold.

It was sometime in late spring when Obadiah Bush and I came into Dry Diggins, and just then was the prime time of the year to be heading into the goldfields. As such, only a few miners were in town – those just coming in from the port at San Francisco or those, like Obadiah and me, who had already been into the hills and gulches and were making a run for fresh supplies.

We were walking along the main road through town, Obadiah pulling his mule and me walking Courage with my mule tied to Courage's saddle horn.

"Well if that ain't a thing," says I, spying a handcrafted wooden sign hanging above a large store recently erected from timbers and white canvas.

"What's a thing?" Obadiah asks.

"The store there, it's called 'Brooks' Dry Goods and Hard Ware,'" I said, pointing to the sign.

"Indeed it is," said Obadiah, not seeing the significance.

"That's the name of the store my wife's grandfather had back in Georgia," I said.

"Oh yes," Obadiah said. "The store you ran prior to leaving for the war in Mexico." It caught me off guard that he remembered, for I never did think he paid that much attention to me whenever I said something of myself.

"Well, it's probably as good a place as any to buy supplies," I said. "Maybe it will be good luck to us."

So I tied Courage off to the post out front, and Obadiah and I walked in through the open door.

The store was similar in construction to thousands of other structures that would be erected in boomtowns from the Mississippi to the Pacific over the next thirty or forty years. Large support timbers were erected at the corners and along the sides, and boards were nailed to those timbers up to about five feet high to give the building some solid walls. Sheets of white canvas were stretched over a few rafters to give some height to the structure. It was the sort of building that could be erected in a couple of days so that the shop owner would lose no time in getting to business, but a poorly placed ember would turn the tinder structure into a fiery death trap in seconds. But these sorts of structures – used for cookhouses, saloons, and shops – were convenient for towns that would cease to exist in a few months when the gold was all dug up.

There were two dozen men in the store picking over its contents, most of which were just piled or stacked on the dirt floor. Though the store could not have even existed two months previous, it did not have much in the way of inventory, and I suspected Old Man Brooks – Eliza's grandfather – would have been sore disappointed to see a shop bearing his name looking so meager.

What I did notice right away was that there were a fair number of rockers or cradles, what some of the miners used to sift sand.

Obadiah had noticed them, too. "We should buy one of them rockers," he said.

There were only half a dozen standing to one side of the store, and a number of miners were standing around bickering with a boy I assumed to be a clerk over the price. I paid no attention to the clerk and figured I'd wait for the other miners to make their purchase before picking out a rocker.

In the meantime, I'd put together a list of supplies that I wanted, some of which would make digging easier and some of which would make life more comfortable. The supplies that would aid in the digging were my priority.

I found a bucket half full of chisels and selected two sturdy ones. I also found a solid mallet for hitting the chisels. I looked over the sluice boxes for sale, but those did not interest me in the way the cradles did. I also picked up a lantern and some oil, but the price for the oil was so unreasonable that I put back both items.

I did add to my collection a tin plate and a large tin coffee cup as well as a tin coffee pot and a cast iron skillet. These were simple things that would make camp life more endurable.

I saw no tents or sheets of canvas I could use to make a tent, which disappointed me greatly, but there were a few woolen blankets, and so I grabbed a couple of them.

Obadiah had been looking through perishables. He had a couple of bags of coffee. We'd agreed to split costs on those items we would both use, and the easiest way to do that with the perishables was to just buy two of everything.

"Five dollars," he said.

"Well, it's a steep price to pay, but I'll be happy to pay two dollars and fifty cents to have coffee for a while."

"Five dollars a bag," he said.

"What else do they have?" I asked.

"Some bacon, some dried beans, a little sugar, some sacks of flour and cornmeal. We should buy some of all of that and be prepared to stay at least three or four months in camp," Obadiah recommended.

By now the other miners who had been bickering over the cost of the cradles had bought two and were gone. I took the supplies I intended to buy over to a counter and stacked them up to free up my hands so that I could have a look for myself at the cradles. The clerk who'd been helping the other miners had taken their money and then walked out through the open flaps at the back of the store. I could see now that in the yard behind the store the boy was actually constructing the sluice boxes and cradles.

As I started over to look at the cradles for myself, a flash of the prettiest red hair I'd ever seen either side of the Mississippi caught my eye, and it wouldn't be stretching it a bit to say that the flash of red stirred me in places that the yellow flashes in my pan never did. B'God if it warn't a lovely, pale white woman topped with glorious locks of red hair who so reminded me of my Southern Belle that I nearly ran to her to snatch her up and give her a good and proper kiss.

She was standing with her back to me, so I'd still not had a good look at her, but I knew already I'd not be leaving Dry Diggins without seeing the rest of her.

From across the big tent Obadiah Bush called to me, "Jack Speed," says he, "would you like to have a tin of soap powder?"

Hearing my name, the woman looked up sharp, directly at me, and though I'd spent months trying to remember what she looked like, there was now no mistaking it. The red head standing outside the back of the store was my own Eliza, here in California, and my heart was so full I couldn't do naught but burst into tears as she ran into my arms.

CHAPTER 16

"Oh, Jackson!" Eliza said, her arms so tight around me, her lips against my neck, my cheeks, my chin, my lips. She kissed me all over my face. "I did not think I would ever find you!"

And we were both shedding tears like the Rio De Los Americanos pouring down out of the Sierra Nevada in March.

My arms were folded around her skinny little waist, pressing her hard up against my body, and I looked into her lovely green eyes. "I did not know if you would come," I said. "It has been so long."

I was still a young man back in those days and given to sentimentality, and I swore to God that now that Eliza was back in my arms I'd never have a stray eye for another pretty girl again.

She gave me a few more kisses on my face, never minding that those places not covered over with whiskers were plastered with dirt and dust, and then she leaned back, staying in my embrace, so that she could see me proper.

"Oh, Jack," she said, and though her eyes were full of tears she started to laugh. "Darling Jackson. You are a sight, aren't ye? Filthy and smelly, but I've never been so happy in all my life. I have so much to tell you!"

I started to say that I had so much to tell her, too, but then I thought about Marcilina de la Garza and Weenonaw, and I realized it would be better to hear her own stories first while I thought about what I could say and what parts would be better left out.

"And I want to hear every bit of it," I said. Feeling her pressed up against me, smelling her, looking into those lovely green eyes, what I really wanted to was to find a private spot, for we were beginning to draw a crowd of onlookers. Obadiah had taken a keen interest, and the clerk in the yard out back had come into the tent and was watching us. It was only then that I realized that the clerk was Eliza's younger brother Johnny.

Eliza pushed her face into my chest, still clutching tight to me. "When I received your letter, I was overcome with joy," she said. "I had thought you were dead it had been so long since I had heard from you. And that you were in Kansas was such a shock! Granddaddy said I was a fool, but I determined immediately that I would come to California to join you here."

"You're a damn good girl, Eliza," says I. "A fine wife, ye are."

Even with her face buried in my chest, she proceeded to give me chapter and verse on her doings over the past few months, and I was immediately reminded that she could prattle on as well as any woman living. "And I did just like you said in your letter – I brought every tool and utensil I could think of for digging and prospecting, and all the conveniences a body might need for roughing it on the frontier. And then I thought, if we will need these things, maybe others will also need these things. And Granddaddy was ever so proud of the way I was thinking about it, and so he sent me with enough supplies to open the store here. And Johnny came to build these boxes and rocking cradles and to help me with the store. And I brought Jimbo to help you dig gold, like you asked, but so far all he's done is help work our store."

Jimbo was one of Eliza's grandfather's slaves, and he got through life by doing as he was told and never giving any answer but a "yaz sah," and so I liked him pretty well. He'd worked with me quite a bit at the store back in Milledgeville, and I knew his back was strong enough to shovel mountains of dirt out of a river.

"Ye've done real good, Eliza," I said.

"Oh, Jack," she said, and a shrewd tone slipped into her voice. "I've done better than that. Every day a hundred prospectors come into our store and spend no less than fifty dollars in gold. I've marked the prices up so much on everything, and still they just buy, buy, buy. Granddaddy promised to send us regular shipments of inventory, but if we don't get some soon we'll be sold out.

"We arrived in San Francisco late in February, and Johnny and I immediately made our way up here to Dry Diggins. Of course no one much was here, and no one we encountered had heard of you, and I feared I might never find you. But we built the store here and opened for business in less than a week, and almost immediately the miners started showing up – and I swear to you, Jack, there's not five men in ten in these goldfields who hasn't bought half or all of their supplies from us."

"Did you come by sea, then?" I asked.

"We did. We took a boat from Savannah to Panama," she said. "Then it was a hellish journey up a river and through a jungle to reach the Pacific Ocean, and we boarded another boat in Panama City to come to California." Conspiratorially, Eliza whispered, "Poor Johnny got a terrible case of dysentery in the Panamanian jungle." [36]

At that point, Eliza seemed to have had enough of me. She gently, but surely, pushed herself out of my embrace. "Jack, I've got some tins of soap powder over there, and also some tooth powder and some toothbrushes. Why don't you go and collect some of those things and go out back and have yourself a wash. I'll see about some supper."

I pointed to the supplies I'd stacked over on the counter. "I'll need those things," I said. "And what Obadiah over there has."

"I'll have Jimbo come collect all of it," Eliza said. "Come on now, and let's get you cleaned up so I can tolerate to be around you."

I got the soap powder and the toothbrush and tooth powder, and Eliza found a good razor, and she led me out back.

The yard was a cluttered mess of tools and scraps and boards and cradles already under production. In the coming years, young Johnny would turn his skills at woodworking into a profitable business for, him and me both. He had a knack for building, particularly with wood, and made some of the finest mahogany furniture ye ever did see. He built the furniture and I arranged to have it shipped to New York, Boston, Philadelphia, and even on to Europe, and we made a good business out of it. But for the moment, he was making some of the finest cradles ever to shake California gold from California sand.

"Johnny, you go and mind the store," Eliza said to him. "Jimbo you go and collect Mars Jack's supplies and stow them in my cabin."

"Then go with that old man in there and see to my horse and our two mules," I said. "Unload the packs somewhere where they'll be safe and put the animals in the yard back here."

"Yaz sah, Mars Jack," Jimbo said. "Sho is good to see you again, Mars Jack. I know Miss Eliza has been frettin' o'er ye fo goin' on three year now."

If you're going to have slaves, Jimbo was the kind to have. He worked as hard as ye asked him to and never talked back. If he spoke behind your back, you never heard a whisper of it. And he doted on my wife, as did all of her grandfather's slaves. Except Bessie, the large buxomed hussy I'd been getting belly-to-belly with before getting engaged to Eliza. Bessie was a jealous and vindictive woman, and a few beatings would have served her well.

But Jimbo's words rang in my mind. "Three years? Has it been so long?" I asked Eliza.

"Almost, yes. You left in the summer of '46, Jack. We've been apart for much more of our marriage than we ever were together."

I felt some pangs of remorse, I don't mind admitting it. Not much good had happened to me in the intervening years, and the only reason I'd ever left in the first place was because a cuckolded husband was seeking to kill me, so I ran all the way to Mexico to escape him. I never imagined when I boarded that train with the Jasper Greens that I would be three years separated from my wife and home.

Dry Diggins at the time was not more than a few dozen buildings of varying permanency situated down in a hollow among the rolling hills. All around were the tall straight firs and pines that littered the California landscape. There was a main road leading through the center of town, but the structures were all haphazard in arrangement so that there were any number of little alleyways, and a couple of times the main road through the center of town was forced to make a hard turn, for a building had been erected right in the center of where the road might properly have run.

Many of the buildings were simple log cabins, others resembled Eliza's store with stretched canvas roofs and plank board walls. A few others were more permanent, constructed of good timber, some with rock walls and glass windows and proper roofing.

Eliza and Johnny had picked a spot to build their store with a small stream running beside it, so they had fresh water. Beyond the yard, they had constructed two small buildings. One was storage for the store, and the other served as Eliza's home. Jimbo was sleeping inside a tent in the yard, and Johnny was sleeping inside the store each night to protect the goods inside.

With the soap powder in one hand and a tin bucket in the other and a big towel draped over Eliza's shoulder, we walked together down to the stream. We were out of sight of the town, and so I stripped out of my clothes, sat on a rock in the middle of the stream, and washed myself in the freezing cold water. Eliza laughed at my consternation each time I filled the tin bucket and dumped the icy stream water down over my head, but I could tell she was enjoying watching me.

Oh, aye, three years away from Ol' Jackie Speed had only increased her appetite, which suited me fine.

"I don't suppose you have a change of clothes, do you?" she asked me.

"I do not," I said.

"Well, you just keep scrubbing yourself with that soap, and I'll go and fetch some of Johnny's clothes."

I did as I was told, and it didn't feel too bad, despite the cold, to scrub away weeks of dirt. I thoroughly enjoyed brushing my teeth, which I was afraid had developed a permanent layer of scuz. I'd chewed some sticks up in the hills, but I didn't think I'd properly brushed my teeth in two months.

Soon Eliza returned with some britches and a shirt, and I saw, too, that she had a razor.

"Let's get your face looking proper," she said. And so I stood with my feet in the stream while she stood on the bank and shaved the whiskers off my cheeks. "I believe I'm going to leave this tuft of whiskers on your chin," she said. "It makes you look dashing."

At last, satisfied that her husband was sufficiently cleaned and shaved, she allowed me out of the stream and gave me the towel to dry myself.

I put on Johnny's britches, but they were too short for me and looked absurd. The shirt was big on him so that it fit me well enough, but where I was tall and broad in the shoulders, Johnny was shorter and wiry.

"There now," Eliza said, examining me. "You don't look half bad, Jack."

Her eyes were soft and full of love as she looked at me.

"I am happy to be reunited with you," I said to her.

"I am happy, too, Jack," she said, and now she slid into another embrace, pushing her face into my chest, and I could feel her taking deep breaths to smell me.

Supper consisted of bacon and eggs with dried fruit, but the real treat was sweet corn bread like I'd not had since leaving Georgia. Victuals in Dry Diggins were no more plentiful nor varied than they were in any of the mining camps, and just as expensive. Eliza and Johnny were making money enough to afford to eat better than any of the miners, but the variety of food simply did not exist. Almost everything available was what could be brought up from San Francisco.

I was still in San Francisco when Eliza and Johnny came ashore from Panama. They spent a couple of days in the city attempting to locate me, but they'd never come into the Yerba Buena Saloon. Unable to find me, they had assumed I was up in the goldfields, and so they set off east. They hired three wagons to bring all their supplies up.

They went first to Coloma, and then came to Dry Diggins. When they arrived here, the town was overrun with miners coming up from San Francisco but not yet able to get into the swollen river. And with so many miners in town, they concluded this was the spot where they should establish the store. Johnny and Jimbo did all the construction, and Eliza started selling supplies even before the store was fully erected.

I told them how I had wintered in San Francisco and gone into the hills as soon as I could.

Though I had a bag and a half full of gold dust I'd dug out of the American River, it was no comparison to the gold Johnny and Eliza were digging out of their store.

Obadiah was uncharacteristically quiet throughout most of supper, and I assumed he had simply met his match and could not out-talk my red-headed bride. But the fact was, something was gnawing on old Obadiah Bush.

Eliza was just in the process of offering me a fourth piece of cornbread when Obadiah cleared his throat loudly. "So, Jack, I suppose first thing in the morning we'll be going back into the gold fields?"

I'd not given a thought to what the morrow would bring, nor had I considered how Eliza might feel about it.

"Well," says I slowly, looking from Obadiah to Eliza. "I suppose that is why I am here." I watched Eliza to see what response she might have, but she was only looking intently at me. "So I guess in the morning we probably should go back up into the hills. I mean, we came to town only to get supplies, really."

I kept my eyes on Eliza, but her face was stony and gave nothing away. And then she smiled at me. "Not tomorrow, Jack," she said. "You and Obadiah should stay here for a day or two while I help Johnny get situated. And once he's prepared to take over the store, we'll go prospecting. It will only be a day or two."

I looked to Obadiah to see how he might respond, and I could see he wasn't happy at all.

"You said 'we' will go prospecting. You intend on going with us?" he asked Eliza.

"Well, of course," Eliza said.

"I am not convinced that panning for gold is an appropriate activity for a young woman. There are all sorts of dangers along the river – bear and Indians, for example. And the other miners. Some number of these men are most unsavory."

"I've been apart from my husband for nearly three years. Now that I have him back, I'm not likely to turn loose of him again so soon. Surely I can swirl water in a pan as well as anyone. And as far as the dangers are concerned, Mister Obadiah, I'll not fear anything so long as Jack Speed is nearby. You do know, don't you, that he's recently come from the War in Mexico where he acquitted himself quite bravely and earned a reputation? Why, he was the principle hero of the charge on Monterrey."

I swelled with pride to hear Eliza speak of me in such a way, indifferent as to whether or not there was any truth in it. "The Hero of El Teneria, they called me," I added. Besides, I'd been the better part of two months in the hills of the Sierra Nevada, and I'd not seen a bear.

Obadiah grunted, but he seemed to think better of arguing.

"That's all well and good," he said, "however, I must protest about the use of enforced labor. Your slave will not be going with us and forced to work on my behalf."

Eliza laughed. Surely she'd cottoned on that Obadiah was a Yankee – his atrocious accent gave that away – but she probably did not realize he was also a strict abolitionist. Eliza, of course, would have never met an abolitionist prior to this and might not have even understood what one was.

"Well, Jimbo ain't being enforced," Eliza said. "I asked him before we came to California if he wanted to come dig gold with Mars Jackson, and he was quite excited about the prospect. He worked for Jackson back in Milledgeville, and he thinks very fondly on Mister Speed."

"Be that as it may," Obadiah said, "he is still a man in bondage, unpaid for his labor and disallowed from coming and going as he pleases. And I'll not be a party to the usage of him when there is no proper compensation."

"Oh, Lawd," Eliza exclaimed. In the most sympathetic tone she could muster, as if addressing a simpleton, she added, "Mister Obadiah, bless your heart, Jimbo's a slave. He don't get paid for working."

"That is my point, exactly," Obadiah said.

"Well, then why don't you pay him a wage for his labor?" Eliza offered.

I decided at this point to intervene. Obadiah didn't know Eliza, but I knew well enough that her porcelain complexion and lovely visage were a mere pretense to hide a fiery temper that could erupt at any moment.

"I'll tell you what," says I. "That ain't a bad idea a'tall. Why don't you and I go in half and pay Ol' Jimbo a wage. We can pay him a dollar or two a day. You know as well as I do, Obadiah, that we can use the help. He's here, so it would be foolish not put him to work. And because you're an abolitionist, and I understand your feelings on that, I'll be glad to acquiesce to your sentiments on the issue by paying Jimbo. Would that be all right?"

I smiled and nodded at Obadiah, urging him to accept the offer, and he reluctantly agreed. Eliza rolled her eyes as if it was the most absurd notion she'd ever heard. And I suppose for her it probably was. Paying a slave was as silly an idea to Eliza as knitting socks for cats.

I never did have any feelings on slavery one way or another. I thought it was a damned shame so much humanity was wasted over the issue during the war, and I never did care for the numbers of times some Yankee bastard or Johnny Reb took a shot at me all because some damn negroes were in bondage. But I certainly was never an abolitionist, nor did I ever own any slaves – other than those I inherited through my marriage to Eliza. The fact is, when it came to slavery, I never cared much about any of it other than being glad that I warn't one. There were times, certainly, when I found it useful to have a slave to do a job for me and didn't have to pay him, but I also found that I got a better job done if I was paying a man a wage to do it. And some slaves, no matter how much you whipped, could not stop themselves from sass and back talk, and the consternation of abiding their tongues was often more expensive than handing a man a couple of dollars to do a job properly.

Of course, I never had a need to have any cotton or rice picked, and those were jobs too big to be paying out wages to have done. So I suppose if I'd owned a plantation – or grown up on one, as Eliza had – that I'd have taken a different attitude toward it. You'll notice, when Lincoln abolished slavery, there never were any more plantations.

Though I'd managed to avoid a confrontation between Obadiah

and Eliza, an icy silence remained through the rest of supper.

The sun was not yet set when we finished up our meal. Obadiah announced that he was going down to the saloon to get a drink, and Johnny said he was going to work on the cradles for a bit. He lit several lanterns and hung them in the yard so that he and Jimbo could continue to work even after dark.

I suggested to Eliza that we take a walk in the twilight.

Along the path leading south out of Dry Diggins there were more than a hundred tents and lean-tos erected by miners preparing to venture into the goldfields. I understood why Obadiah wanted to get a jump on them. There would be more in Coloma and all through the valley coming up from San Francisco. If we did not soon get out and stake a good claim, there might not be good claims left to stake.

We walked out beyond the miners' tents, Eliza with both hands wrapped around my arm and her head leaning into my shoulder in a way that felt so comfortable to me. So many of them miners we passed knew Eliza by name and called out to her that I developed a bit of jealousy.

"Hello Miss Eliza!" they called to her.

"Did you find your beau, or did you find a new beau?" one damned fool called to her.

Eliza just smiled and waved and laughed as they called out and made their damned jokes.

"You haven't been too familiar with these fellows, have ye?" I asked her.

"Oh, Jackson," she said, slapping my arm playfully and smiling all the while, "of course I have not, and shame on you for suggesting such a thing. But they all come into the store, and I've asked half the men in California if they knew where I might find you. I suspect your name is better known in California than even back home in Milledgeville."

Unless her temper was flared, Eliza couldn't have a conversation with a man where she did not present herself as flirtatious.

"Come to think of it, though, a few fair number of 'em have offered to marry me if ye turned out to be dead somewhere."

"I'll bet they did," I said, perturbed at the notion.

We wandered aimlessly up a hill and through the trees. A cool breeze was blowing, and the birds were all chirping, and it felt so good to be reunited with my wife that I didn't give much thought to where we were going or how far we had gone. The woods were dark, but neither of us cared much as we strolled along.

Eliza asked me all about the journey from Leavenworth, and I told her of the enormous mountains and the hellish deserts and the long, seemingly endless, flat plains. She seemed to think the two weeks she spent in a jungle in Panama, first in a long canoe and then on the back of a mule, were probably worse than the six months in a wagon train, but I wasn't convinced.

I suppose we'd wandered a mile from town, maybe a bit more, when we came upon another campsite, this one tucked in a clearing well away from the main road.

A large bonfire was burning in the middle of the camp, and there must have been upwards of two dozen men, all drinking whiskey from bottles and having a raucous good time. Someone in the group was strumming a guitar and singing, and I was fairly certain the song was in Spanish.

Perhaps it was having just come from fighting Mexicans, but as we neared them and I realized all of the men were Mexican, my natural tendency to avoid trouble made me stop.

"We might be well advised to not approach this camp," I suggested. "Let's turn around and start back to Dry Diggins before night is fully upon us and we can't see a thing.

Even Eliza, who seldom saw trouble before it was upon her, agreed that we should not wander any closer to camp.

But it was too late.

One of the men from the camp was staggering through the woods, looking for a tree onto which he intended to relieve himself, when he caught sight of us.

"Hola, amigos!" he yelled loudly. Then, opening his drunken eyes a little wider, he said, "Chica!"

I didn't like the looks of him a bit as he started stumbling toward us, and I clutched my fist around the Paterson on my hip.

"Now you just hold your horses there, hombre," I said, and I slid the Paterson a ways out of its holster.

"Chica!" the drunken fool yelled, and I thought there was a sudden quiet coming from the camp. He took two more steps toward us, and his fat, drunken face was full of lust. His eyes were only on Eliza, so I took a step between him and her so that he would have to look at me, and I snatched the Paterson the rest of the way from its holster. I was nervous as hell, but I felt the best way to back down a drunken Mexican was with the threat to put him down. He stopped where he was, but I could tell he was trying to decide whether or not I was really going to shoot him or if he should keep coming at Eliza.

"Maybe we should go, Jackson," Eliza whispered at me.

"I'm not sure I want to turn my back on him," I said.

"More of them are coming from the camp," Eliza said.

I glanced toward the camp, and sure enough, shadows seemed to be coming straight out of the bonfire and into the woods.

"If I tell ye to run, ye've got to run as fast as you can," I said. "Get back to the road and run back to Dry Diggins. Don't stop running. Can you do that?"

"I can," Eliza assured me, and I believed she probably could.

I counted only four or five shadows coming through the woods at us. The rest of the Mexicans in the camp were uninterested, drinking and laughing as they were. And about then, the guitar strumming resumed.

I waited a few more moments, allowing them to get closer. If it came to it that I was going to have to shoot some of them, I wanted them close enough that I could be sure of hitting them.

"What is going on here Ho-zay?" one of the Mexicans asked as he neared us.

"Y'all just stop right there," I said, and I lifted the Paterson up a bit so they could see it easier.

"Whoa! Amigo! There is no need for that," the one coming toward us said. "We are all friends here."

"Chica," José repeated, and I didn't care a bit for his tone of voice, and he started toward us again.

I took a hard look at the other Mexicans who had joined us in the woods, and though it was dark I could not see that any of them were armed.

Though my belly rumbles with fear and a cold sweat will break out on my forehead, I have found at times that a bold front was the best way to deal with a situation. When I found myself accosted by one of Eliza's suitors before we were married, I punched him in the nose when he wasn't expecting it. That sort of thing – sudden and unexpected violence – tends to have the effect of at least buying you a bit of time in which you can run away. And sometimes a big, strong front is enough to back 'em down entirely and ye don't even need to run.

I cocked back the hammer on the Paterson and aimed it up at José's head. My intention was to splatter his damned brains over the other Mexicans and let them decide if they wanted to keep taking steps toward me. My guess was that they would not.

As I cocked the hammer, the trigger of the Paterson dropped down. [37] I didn't hesitate, in one motion I slid my index finger down onto the trigger and pulled it back. The Paterson exploded in a burst of noise and flame, and the ball smacked a tree about a foot away from José's head.

All those damned Mexicans in the woods jumped and hollered, and I could see a bunch of them down by the campfire jump up, too. José was too drunk to know he'd nearly been shot in the face, and he just stood their grinning and swaying.

"Whoa!" the leader of the Mexicans said, putting both hands up in a gesture of surrender, though he was grinning like hell as if he'd enjoyed the event. "There is no need, amigo, we are all friends here." He turned his head and looked at one of the other men. "Go and get José and take him back to camp before he gets his fool head shot away."

I kept the Paterson on those boys fetching José, and when they had him and were dragging him away, I pointed the Paterson at the leader who'd been talking.

"Look here, now," I told him, "my wife and I were just enjoying an evening stroll. We ain't come here looking for trouble. Y'all go on back to yer camp there and we'll be on about our way."

The Mexican was still grinning. He still had his hands open, palms-out, and raised up in the air. "There is no need to be afraid, amigo. No one here will hurt you."

Now Eliza stepped out from behind me. I don't know if she was emboldened by the shooting of the Paterson or if she'd just been biding her time. But the damned woman had an answer pretty quick for the Mexican, and she didn't seem to care much that we were well outnumbered and I only had four chambers left loaded.

"I'll tell ye right now that my husband is not afraid of you and your little band of rascals," Eliza said. "He dealt with plenty of men just like you at Monterrey, and he's not afraid one bit to deal with you, too."

The Mexican dropped the grin and dropped his hands, too. "Monterrey?" he asked. "So you were a soldier in the war against my people?"

"Lieutenant Jackson Speed," Eliza said. "Not just some soldier. An officer."

I wished like hell she would stop talking.

"Lieutenant?" the Mexican said. He made me nervous as hell. His easy manner, his good English, something about his bearing even there in the dark — he reminded me of all the rancheros I ever saw in Mexico during the war. These rancheros were men of wealth, typically of Spanish descent, and they were some vicious, brutal bastards. It was a couple of these rancheros who nearly dragged me to my death behind their horses.

"Well, lieutenant, my name is Joaquin Murrieta. Have you heard of me?"

My stomach was in my throat at this point, and I found it hard to speak. I'd been steady enough until the man dropped his hands, even with the Paterson still pointing at him. He was too confident, being an unarmed man with a revolver aimed at his chest, and his confidence scared me.

And now he was giving me his name and asking if I'd ever heard of him. I've known dangerous men in my time. Why, didn't Billy Bonney look me in the eye and say to me, "I've heard of you Jack Speed. Heard all about ye. My name's Will Bonney, but people call me Billy the Kid. Ye ever heard of me?"

Dangerous men like to have a reputation, and they want to know if you know that reputation before they shoot ye in the gut. I learned that the answer was always, "Why, yes indeed, I've heard all about what a dangerous and vicious killer you are, and I would kindly ask that ye not kill me." That's what they want to hear. It makes them feel good to know they're known. But I was still young enough, and had not yet met enough dangerous men in my life, to know the proper way to answer Joaquin Murrieta.

"Sorry," I said. "Never have heard of ye."

Murrieta laughed, and on cue the other men with him all gave a laugh, too.

"Well, you will hear of me, Lieutenant Speed. I assure you of that."

To prove he wasn't scared and that he was in control, Joaquin Murrieta took a step toward me.

"Now, lieutenant, if you would like to leave these woods alive with your wife, I suggest you leave now."

I didn't need to be told twice. Still keeping the Paterson on him, I took Eliza by the elbow with my other hand and started walking slowly backwards.

"You're not going to let him talk to you like that, are ye?" Eliza asked, even as I pulled her back through the woods and away from Joaquin Murrieta.

"Yes, Eliza, my love," I said. "I think today it's best if we let him talk to me like that. There must be two dozen men at that campfire, and even if I shoot and kill as many of them as I possibly can, that's only going to be four of them. Which leaves me trying to take on a score of them with just fisticuffs. It somehow don't seem advisable."

Even Eliza, with her temper riled like it was, saw the wisdom in flight, and so she turned and started walking through the woods ahead of me while I continued to slowly back up and keep Joaquin Murrieta and his men in my sight.

At last, satisfied that they would not be giving pursuit, I turned and caught up with Eliza, and briskly we walked through the dark woods until we came out on a hillside overlooking the road back to Dry Diggins.

Now that we were well away, Eliza turned to me and said, "Those men were despicable brutes. This is our country now, and they should learn proper manners."

"I wouldn't argue with you," I said, "but when there's two dozen banditos and one of me, it might not be the right time to teach them those manners."

"Hmph," Eliza said derisively. "I don't doubt you could have dealt with them. Drunken bullies is all they were."

"Maybe," says I. "At any rate, them Mexicans ain't what's on my mind now."

It had grown so dark that I could no longer see her well, but I could tell by the tone of her voice that she was smiling. "Is that right, Lieutenant? And so tell, me, what is on your mind now?"

"Well," says I, "I've missed ye something awful, Eliza. It's hard on a man to go so long without seeing his wife, and now that I've seen ye again, I'm a bit eager to get your belly pressed up against my belly, don't ye know."

"Oh my," Eliza said, but I could tell she was still smiling. "Perhaps we should walk faster, then."

We double timed it back to Dry Diggins, and not because of the Mexican banditos somewhere in the woods behind us.

When we arrived at the store we found it all closed up with young Johnny inside. He had a lantern lit and was reading by the light. Big Jim was snoring in his tent in the yard, and Courage and the two mules were likewise in the yard now. Obadiah Bush had also pitched his tent in the yard.

Eliza and I went silent as we could through the yard and back to the little hut she called home.

We lit a lantern when we got inside.

It wasn't much. A stuffed mattress on a bed frame Johnny had likely made in the yard, a hand-hewn table and chair, a large trunk where she kept her personals, a bed pan and a washstand with a porcelain bowl and pitcher. All of the furniture except the trunk looked like Johnny had built it in his spare time.

"It's a bed for one, I'm afraid," Eliza said.

"Aye, that'll be sufficient. I expect we'll be snuggled up pretty tight anyway."

I hung the lantern from a nail in one of the support timbers. It had been so long since I'd seen her undressed.

"Take your clothes off," I said to her, and Eliza didn't have to be told twice.

The dress she was wearing was like nothing she'd have worn back home, but a simple calico dress of cotton. She slid it off over her head and laid it down on the top of her trunk. She then unlaced her underthings and stepped out of them.

Though the sun had turned her chest and neck and arms a bit red, the rest of her was a lovely pale, except for that shock of red. And on her pert teats, two cherry red nipples that had been the stuff of my dreams at Camp Belknap.

"Oh, aye," I said. "That's a sight I've not seen for far too long. Spin around for me. Let me have a good look at ye. Not quite so fast. Do it again, but slower this time. And stop covering yourself with your arms. Ye've got naught to be ashamed of. Oh, stunning."

I took in every inch of her, and I burned the image on my brain. Having struggled to remember what she looked like for so long, I now wanted to never forget again. And do ye know, I can close my eyes now – all these years later – and I can see her in that little hut with its canvas top there in California, spinning for me – once too fast, a second time because I asked her to go more slowly, and a third time because she saw how much I liked it. Aye, I can see it now, all these years later, when I shut my eyes and try to remember.

"Have you missed me, Jack?"

"I have."

She giggled. "I can see that ye have, Jackie Speed."

I took her up in my arms, lifting her from her feet, and I kissed her roughly. Even as I held her up, she started stripping her brother's shirt off me, but it wasn't going well, so I set her down and we damn near tore the clothes to get them off.

I dragged her down to the bed with me, and we kissed and touched each other hungrily, making up for all those lost months. I attacked her greedily, as if I'd not been with another woman since I'd last seen her, and she came at me with the same enthusiasm. I briefly wondered if it had been nearly three years since she'd touched a man or if, like me, she'd found comfort where she was. But then I let go of that line of thinking pretty quick. I figured if I went off to kill Mexicans and marry an Injun, then I didn't have much right to wonder what she'd been up to.

I'd gotten one of those cherry red nipples pinched between my thumb and forefinger, and I was rolling it to make her squeal, and I wondered if we were keeping Jimbo and Obadiah awake, when quite suddenly we were not the ones making the most noise in Dry Diggins that night.

From outside, and not far away, we heard a terrible racket of what was clearly pistol shots, and it sounded like it was coming from the store. It must have been four for five shots in rapid succession, and then a few more.

215

"What is that?" Eliza said, her voice full of alarm. She sat up, brushed my hands away from her glorious teats, and cocked her ear when we heard another three or four shots.

"Someone's shooting their pistols," I said.

"It sounds like it's coming from the store," Eliza said. I couldn't argue with her. It was damned close. "Oh, Jack! You must go and make certain Johnny is okay!"

"Eliza," I said, giving a look down between my legs. "I ain't really in a position to go wandering around outside."

"Just put on your britches and go and see what's happening!"

A couple of more shots went off, and I decided there was no point in arguing.

I slid on Johnny's trousers that were too short, pulled on his shirt and strapped my Paterson onto my hip. I'd not reloaded it, and the thought went through my mind that I only had four chambers loaded. I looked around among my belongings – piled by Jimbo into one corner – and found my sheathed carbine. I pulled it out of its leather sheath and checked the chambers to be sure it was fully loaded.

"I'll be back," I said.

I came out of the cabin to find Jimbo and Obadiah both coming out of their tents and pulling on their own clothes. I hurried through the back flaps of the store where Johnny had fallen asleep with the lantern still glowing. He was awake now, but still on his blankets.

"What is that?" he asked me.

Now we heard it again, but it was farther away, going into the town proper.

"Drunken fools, I reckon," I said.

Obadiah and Jimbo joined us in the store, and a moment later Eliza came running in. She'd put on a dress, but she still looked quite a bit disheveled.

"Should we go and see what's happening?" Johnny asked.

"Not I," said Obadiah. "If it does not concern me, I do not intend to get involved. This sort of behavior is why I do not hang about in the miner camps."

I looked at Eliza. Frankly, I was eager to get back to business in her hut. We heard more shots, another four or five.

"I'm going out there," Johnny said, and he didn't hesitate neither, marching right out the front tent flaps.

"Jack, don't you let my baby brother go alone!"

I sighed heavily. "Jimbo, you stay with Miss Eliza and don't let anyone come in here and bother her." I followed Johnny out of the front flap of the store.

We jogged along the street, which was now filling with townspeople coming out to find out who was shooting and why. When we got near the center of town, we could see them – half a dozen mounted men, each of them with a revolver in his hand, randomly firing shots. As we got nearer, where the lanterns in the buildings cast enough light that we could see, I saw that the men firing the revolvers were all Mexicans, and I was fairly certain one of them was my friend from the woods, José.

A large crowd had gathered along the street, and miners from the tents along the road were running into town behind us.

The Mexicans were riding in circles, firing random shots into the air, yelling and laughing, all of them drunk as they could be.

"Well ain't you goin' to do something?" a man beside me asked.

"Me?" I said, incredulous that he should suggest this was somehow my responsibility.

217

"Yer totin' them guns!" he said. "Shoot them bastard Mexicans!"

I was even more appalled when I realized there were others around us who were taking up his call.

"Yeah, drop one of 'em and they'll stop this nonsense," someone said.

"Shoot 'em!" someone else encouraged.

Johnny looked at with a mixture of horror and fascination, wondering if I would do it.

To my consternation, some damn fool gave my shoulder a push and I stumbled out in front of the mob.

The Mexicans had not noticed me, standing twenty yards away from them as they rode in circles and fired into the air, but a fair number of people in the crowd had seen me. I was standing there in britches too short for me, a loose shirt, no boots, a carbine in my fist and a Paterson strapped to my hip. I suppose the crowd had every right to assume I'd come to save them from these half dozen drunken Mexicans. And now they started cheering for me and hollering at me to shoot back.

My intention was to quickly step back into the crowd before the Mexicans saw me. And I was just about to, when I took a look and realized that the Mexicans were now just cocking back their hammers and firing on empty chambers. They'd shot themselves all out. With the commotion of the yelling crowd and everyone's ears ringing from all the shooting, I suppose no one else even realized that the Mexicans had emptied their pistolas.

Realizing there would be no return fire, I raised up the carbine, took aim at fat José, reasoning that I could not miss him. I cocked back the hammer of the carbine and pulled the trigger.

The carbine spit flame and smoke, and I had to crane my neck to see what damage I'd wrought.

I'd been aiming for his torso, hoping to knock him down off the horse, but the shot went high and wide and instead hit his revolver, smashing the thing out of his hand.

All the same, the shock made the drunken José fall out of his saddle as if I'd fired the ball straight into his chest. Even as drunk as he was, he howled in pain for the splintered revolver in his hand had done him a terrible injury.

Half the Mexicans sobered up right now, realized right away they were about to be in a hell of a mess, and they skedaddled the way they'd come, pushing through the crowd, sliding down a side street, and hightailing it out of town as fast as they could go.

But José and the remaining two were not so lucky. By now the mob had realized what I'd realized – the Mexicans were shooting empty chambers. The crowd rushed forward, dragging the other two Mexicans out of their saddles. And dozens of the men of Dry Diggins set upon José and his two friends, punching and stomping boomtown justice into them.

Inevitably, someone yelled, "Hang 'em!" because you can only stomp and punch justice into someone for so long. Eventually boomtown justice demands that necks get stretched.

"Hang 'em!" the mob took up the call, and it took only moments for someone to produce several long ropes.

"I've no desire to stay and watch," I said to Johnny.

"No," Johnny said. "I guess I don't either."

I didn't have any sympathy for José, and my only regret was that the good people of Dry Diggins did not hang all six of them Mexicans. They deserved nothing less for interrupting what was promising to be one of the best nights I'd spent since I'd seen Weenonaw killed in Indian Territory.

"That was a hell of a shot," some man said, slapping me on the shoulder. "You shot that pistola right out of his hand!" I ignored the man, not wanting to point out that I'd been aiming for the widest part of the man, and I started back toward the store with Johnny following close behind.

When we returned to the store, Eliza and Jimbo were still in the store. Eliza was full of questions, so we told her what had happened. I did not realize it, but Johnny was awestruck. Just like all the others who'd seen it, Johnny thought I purposefully shot that pistola out of José's hand.

"They were riding in circles through the middle of town, shooting into the air," Johnny told Eliza. "The street was crowded with curious watchers, but no one was willing to do anything. Finally, someone suggested to Jackson that he should return fire. So Jack stepped out in front of the entire crowd so that it was just him, facing down these crazed Mexicans.

"Cool as you please, Jack raises up his carbine, cocks the hammer back and – bam! – just like that, he shoots the pistol out of one of their hands! He shot the pistol! What were you Jack, 15 yards away?"

"Maybe twenty," says I.

"It was an amazing shot," Johnny said. "Truly amazing. I ain't never seen shooting like it before. And when Jack shot the pistol out of his hand, the Mexican fell right off his horse. That's when the rest of the crowd rushed forward and apprehended three of them."

"What about the other three?" Eliza asked.

"They rode off," Johnny said.

Eliza curled her mouth in disgust. "Well, Jackson, ye should've shot them, too, for interrupting us."

Aye, she was a girl after my own heart.

"Interrupting you?" Johnny asked.

"Our sleep, boy," I said. "Something I am eager to get back to."

"Yeah, I'll be plumb tuckered tomorrow," Johnny said.

We helped Johnny close up the flaps of the tent and watched Jimbo go back to his tent.

I'll say it didn't take long before Eliza and I resumed where we had left off.

She was a fine woman, as exceptionally proportioned as a woman could be, and I'd seldom found a pleasure to equal it when I had my belly pressed against her belly.

And when we were both satiated and lying in each other's arms, Eliza said to me, "You can't possibly be serious about paying Jimbo."

CHAPTER 17

The next day another hundred miners came up from San Francisco, and the dozens of them who'd been camped along the road broke camp and started toward the goldfields, some to find a hole to dig, some to find a man to pay them to dig a hole.

"It's like this almost every day," Eliza told me. "Scores of new miners come into town, buy up supplies, and the ones from the previous day start for the goldfields."

The new miners were greeted by the sight of three Mexicans hanging by the necks in three trees at the edge of town, and that was the end of Dry Diggins. The town would spend the next year of its existence known as Hangtown. A year or so later, the women and church-going folks of the town would petition to change the name, and Hangtown would become Placerville, but for now Dry Diggins would bear the ominous moniker of Hangtown. I never did hear of a mob hanging anyone else at Hangtown, so it was probably appropriate that they change the name, but I can vouch that during the year that Dry Diggins was Hangtown and before it was Placerville, folks arriving to town after dark did so in a quiet and respectful manner. [39]

More important than the new miners, at least as far as Eliza was concerned, was the arrival of a fresh inventory of supplies. Her grandfather had arranged shipment to San Francisco, and Eliza and Johnny had arranged in advance that any supplies that came in for them would be delivered up to Dry Diggins. The fresh supplies included more tools, tents, blankets, raw lumber, bags of flour and other foodstuffs. There was also a letter from Eliza's grandfather, Old Man Brooks, who informed us that since her departure the news of gold was spreading all over the East Coast, and every man under the age of sixty was giving thought to traveling out to California.

"By the end of summer, California will be overrun with prospectors," Obadiah said grumpily. "If we do not strike a rich claim between now and then, we'll be unlikely to ever do so."

On our ride back into Dry Diggins to fetch supplies, we had followed the river much of the way, and there were a couple of spots – as yet untouched by miners – that Obadiah thought looked promising. He was eager to get back to the river to get to those spots before they were overrun. As such, he assisted in the unloading of the wagons with Johnny's fresh inventory.

The delivery of supplies also meant that Eliza and I would have a tent and a couple of extra blankets.

Eliza also arranged to hire a couple of boys to come into the store to help Johnny so that he would not have to do everything hisself. His cradles and sluice boxes were making good money at the store, and Johnny's value was not in clerking or stocking inventory.

Early the next morning, before the sun was up, Obadiah, Jimbo and I packed the mules, and we were on the trail before just about everyone.

Eliza rode Courage while Obadiah, Jimbo, and I walked and led the two mules, both of them now properly laden. It reminded me of the work I'd done in Mexico as a teamster before that damned Jeff Davis had me charging into Fort Teneria. I'd not cared much for being a teamster in Mexico, and it wasn't any more enjoyable now.

Obadiah and I had taken two days to ride in from our previous camp, but our intention was to get to the spot where he wanted to start digging in one day. It was nearer to town than our previous spot, but still well beyond where any of the other miners were prospecting.

I didn't argue with Obadiah. Before coming to California, he'd gathered up books about metallurgy, specifically related to gold, and he had devoured these books on ship. He had studied everything he could find about the subject of gold, and he seemed better informed than any other miner I'd encountered – all of whom knew to scour the black sand deposits but seemed to know not much else about finding gold. The placer gold was plentiful enough that a man could at least earn his living with a pan. But Obadiah was intent on doing better than that. He wanted the nuggets and the veins of gold that he knew went deep into the earth, and he was convinced that finding those veins meant finding the quartz in the rock.

We'd done well enough at our first site that I trusted Obadiah to make me a wealthy man.

We passed by Chile Bar, which by that time was full of what seemed to be at least a thousand Chilean miners, and from there we continued east, roughly following the path of the river. We were short of our destination by nightfall, and so we left the worn path we'd been walking and hiked a way into the trees to find a spot to camp. With so many people coming into the wilderness with nothing but the shirt on their back, it made us nervous to camp too close to the road where we might fall victim to thieves, or worse.

In the morning, we rose early, made a breakfast and broke camp. Just as we were loading up the mules, we heard a terrible commotion along the path below us. We were not in sight of the path, so I drew out my Paterson and went to see what was making the noise. It sounded, honestly, like cavalry regiment, and I suppose it was.

When I got near enough to see, I counted more than two dozen horsemen riding east. They looked to me to be Mexican, though from the distance and through the trees I could not be certain. They did not, though, have mules or packs to suggest they were going into the hills to seek gold – at least not the gold to be got from the river. No, if these men were seeking gold, it was the gold they would get at the end of their pistolas.

"We'll want to let them get well ahead of us," I said to Obadiah

224

after reporting what I'd seen. He nodded his agreement, but was well perturbed that we would be delayed further.

"For what it's worth, they'll not be working those spots you're interested in," I said to him.

So we delayed the start of our trip for another hour, and then decided to resume the journey, believing the riders were well ahead of us.

I was not sure, but I feared it was Joaquin Murrieta and his gang of banditos.

We were far enough into the hills that the American River flowed through a deep gulch, with steep banks on either side, so as we followed the path we could not see the river. Periodically, Obadiah would wander down the hillside to lay eyes on the river to determine how close we might be to the spot he was seeking.

After walking all morning, at last Obadiah came running up the hill to us.

"It's down here!" he called. "Go no farther! I have found the spot!"

We left Jimbo with the mules and the horse, and Eliza and I walked with Obadiah down to the place he'd found.

It was a terrible location.

The river ran deep and narrow between two sheer banks of stone. The banks, cut away by the river over the course of centuries, were twenty feet straight up on both sides. Even the descent to the banks was steep and would make for a troublesome climb up and down. As we approached the banks, Eliza and I had to grab hold of trees to keep from losing our footing and sliding down.

"But it's impossible," Eliza said. "How will we even get down to the river?"

"We will find a way," Obadiah said. And then he pointed out some of the rocks on the far bank. "Look at those wide veins of quartz," he said. "There, under that quartz, we will find the gold that will make the trouble worthwhile. This is the spot where we will dig."

"But how will we even get over to those rocks?" Eliza asked. "The river is running too fast. It is too deep."

I looked downstream. Not far from where we stood the river took a hard turn, and there the rocky bank was a sheer cliff thirty feet high. And Eliza was correct – the current would sweep us off our feet. It would be impossible to move from one bank to the other.

I looked upstream, and I saw something hopeful. Fifty yards upstream of us, a deer was standing on a rock against the bank, dipping its face in between a couple of rocks to get a drink from the river.

It was hard to see, because the banks were either sheer rock or covered in thick growth of trees, but I could make out a gentle slope on the same side of the river where we were. There had to be a path there that the deer had followed. At the same spot, the river rushed over and in between rocks, and I believed I could follow a trail of rock that would allow us to ford the river, so long as it did not rise another foot or more.

I pointed to the deer. "That's our spot," I said. "Y'all go back up to Jimbo and the animals, and I'll work my way over there and find the path. I'll meet you back up on the road."

It was rough going among the trees and the steep hillside, but eventually – working from tree to tree to keep from losing my foothold – I got to the spot where the ground leveled out into something more manageable. There was nowhere flat enough to build a camp, but I was able to easily walk all the way down to the river. Once there, I tested the ford, and it was no problem to step over the rushing water and move from rock to rock to get to the far bank. A few of the footfalls were on submerged rock, but I managed to keep my balance even when I was standing in the water. I was sure with a stick to help keep balance, we could all easily make our way from one bank to the other. And from there, it was tricky in places, but it would be easy enough to get down to the rocks where we'd seen the wide quartz veins.

Delighted at my success, I hurried back over the rocks and up the bank. It was a long walk back up the hill to the road, and I was exhausted and out of breath by the time I finally reached the road and found Eliza, Obadiah and Jimbo.

"We'll have to make camp somewhere up here," I said. "But we can get to the river, and across to the far bank. So let's find a spot for camp and in the morning we can get to prospecting."

We went farther up the hill to get away from the path, and we managed to find a decent spot, secluded from anyone stumbling upon us. We set up our tents, cut down some trees, collected firewood to last us at least a few days, and constructed a small corral to keep the mules.

The next morning, we got started on the river.

We found a few spots where the river did not rush between rocks with such a current and where it was not so deep, and I spent some time teaching Eliza to pan the sandy bottom. Jimbo, Obadiah and I, meanwhile, went to work busting quartz veins with chisels and hammers and pickaxes. At times we would pan or dig the sandy banks.

On those days when we did not find gold early, Jimbo and I would go to panning through the afternoon. But not Obadiah. He was convinced that we would find the gold under the quartz, and he wasted little time on panning.

The placer gold was rich all through the area we worked. Whether in the pans or the cradle, every day we took out flakes as big as a thumb nail and filled bags with gold dust.

But the quartz gold continued to elude us.

Jimbo became adept at busting the quartz rock, and he didn't care much that it was fruitless labor because Obadiah was paying him to do it.

Life in the camp wasn't too terrible, and I've no doubt that most nights Jimbo and Obadiah found it difficult to sleep for the noise Eliza and I made in our tent. We ate fairly well at first, but after a few weeks our supplies began to run thin. And though we'd pulled a fair amount of gold from the river banks, we'd not made half as much in the way of a fortune as Eliza was sure her brother Johnny was doing back at the store. I suspected she was correct.

We moved upstream a ways and then back downstream, searching for quartz that would yield gold, but our efforts proved unsuccessful. Obadiah grew frustrated, and Eliza was getting irritable. The sun beat down on us day after day, and even with her big straw hat offering some protection, her exposed skin was getting pink with burns. The novelty of the adventure of prospecting for gold wore off. Her elation at being reunited with me diminished. Her patience with the hardships of camping beside a California river grew thin.

I suppose it was late in June sometime, or perhaps early in July, and our supplies were disappearing, we'd not struck enough gold to call our endeavors a success, and the back of Eliza's neck was so burned she could not comfortably turn her head to look from one side to the next. At supper – nothing more than a couple of strips of bacon and some thin cornbread – Eliza gave vent to her aggravation. Obadiah is what set her off.

"The reason I am an abolitionist," he was saying conversationally, answering a question no one had asked, "is because the idea of owning another man and keeping him in bondage cannot be reconciled with Christian morals. Can a Christian man truly believe that God intends for him to forcibly use the labor of black men? Does God see the Negro race as nothing more than a beast of burden, like a pack mule or a horse?"

About every two or three days, Obadiah would provide us a lecture on the ills of slavery. I do not know if he did it simply to rile Eliza, or if he sincerely hoped he might change her mind on the subject. I chose to ignore him, and was grateful that Eliza endured the lectures without argument. Whatever Jimbo might have thought of Obadiah's preaching, he was smart enough not to say a thing about it in front of Miss Eliza.

"Oh, damn it all to hell," Eliza shrieked.

Obadiah shut his trap, and old Jimbo went to grinning. I suppose, like me, Jimbo knew it was only a matter of time before Obadiah's sermonizing would be more than Eliza could take.

"I beg your pardon?" Obadiah said.

"Mister Obadiah," Eliza said, "have you once heard Jimbo make a complaint about his life or his treatment? He's well cared for – he has food and shelter, he ain't whipped, and if he gets sick is he expected to pay for his own doctoring? My grandfather goes to great expense to keep Jimbo healthy and happy. Ain't that right, Jimbo?"

Jimbo, who never did argue with Old Man Brooks nor with Eliza – regardless of whether or not he agreed – said simply, "Yes ma'am, Miss Eliza. You and your grandfather always do make sure I gets fed and has a place to sleeps."

I wasn't sure if he was grinning because he was excited to see what Eliza would do with Obadiah or if he was grinning because Obadiah had finally gotten Eliza angry enough to have a fit. Either way, Jimbo kept on smiling.

"So you see, Mister Obadiah, slaves are well cared for. And without them, you would not have those cotton shirts you wear. It's fine for a man who makes his living lecturing children in a school house to talk of Christian morals, but if you ain't never tried to have a cotton plantation, well then I guess you don't know nothing about what ye're talking about. You don't know the labor it takes to pick that cotton, and the price that allows you to wear a cotton undershirt is possible only because of the slaves who pick the cotton."

Having grown up on a cotton plantation, I could not believe that Eliza had not seen things that made her wonder for herself about the

morals of beating a man half to death or breaking up a family –
separating mother from child because drought had made for a poor
cotton harvest and the plantation owner had to sell off some slaves to
pay debts. But those who were raised on a plantation never did allow
such seditious thoughts to turn into speech or argument. These ideas –
if spread – could unravel the fabric of the South. Or worse, they could
lead to a slave revolt.

I was already thinking that too many more nights around a
campfire with Obadiah, and we'd have to beat hell out of Jimbo once
we were back in Georgia to keep him from spreading any ideas.

I had no interest in listening to any more.

"Tarnation," I said, standing up. "We ain't got enough cornmeal to
have more'n two more meals. And the bacon is running out. And I don't
want to go back to just eating fish all the time. Tomorrow, Obadiah, you
and Jimbo take the mules and head on back to town. Go and see Johnny
Brooks at the store and get us supplies to last us another couple of
months. Cornmeal and flour, a hundred pounds of bacon. We need
more coffee beans and sugar, too. Beans and whatever else Johnny's
got that will keep. Take the gold we've gotten and pay him for the
supplies, and give him the rest and have him keep it safe for us. Having
all these bags of gold in camp makes me nervous as hell when we're all
down at the river. Why, someone stumbles on our campsite in the
middle of the day and we might never see any of this gold again. And if
Johnny's got any horses, buy three of them so we can move faster if we
decide to move to a different hole. We've dug money enough out of the
river to afford some horses."

Obadiah, who couldn't stand to be told what to do, offered a
protest. "Perhaps you and Eliza should return to the store," he started.

"Naw, I've done thought about it. Me and Eliza can pan for gold
and break rocks. It'd be best if you and Jimbo go."

My real reason for not wanting to go was that I didn't care for the thought of walking all that way. If I went with Eliza, she'd ride Courage and I would have to walk. I could go by myself, but I'd grown comfortable having Eliza beside me every night, and I wasn't interested in giving that up – even for a few days.

"Now, Eliza and I are going to go for a walk before it gets too dark. So if you need to do anything to be ready to leave in the morning, do it now."

I held a hand out for Eliza and helped her out of her camp chair. Before we left camp, I grabbed the carbine and my Paterson. We'd not seen a bear yet, but we'd seen plenty of signs of bear, and I was always nervous any time we fried up bacon that they would come searching for the source of the smell.

We walked out away from camp, over a ridge and down a hill. I knew there was a creek not terribly far from our camp. I'd been to the spot where the stream emptied into the American River and found quite a bit of placer gold in the sand deposited there. We usually pulled water we needed out of the American River, but the walk up the hill was so steep in places that sometimes Jimbo went and fetched river from the stream. He'd told me the stream was farther from camp than the American River, but the walk was easier. I'd never been far enough from camp to get to the stream, but I wanted to get Eliza out of camp before she or Obadiah said something that might break up our little group.

When we finally came to the stream, it was a narrow thing running down big drops and in between giant boulders. There among the trees, with the little waterfalls, it was a very picturesque scene.

"It's quite pretty over here," Eliza said. "I can't believe we've never been over here before."

"Aye, it's delightful," I said.

We walked to the bank of the stream and together climbed down beside its little waterfall to the muddy bank below.

"Oh!" Eliza exclaimed, and she squatted down onto her knees beside the bank and plunged her hand into the water. When she pulled it back out, there was a nugget of gold the size of my thumb sitting in the palm of her hand.

She handed it to me, and I was stunned by the weight of it. "That's heavy," I said.

I examined the gold carefully, and I realized some portion of it was attached to quartz. Most of the nugget was gold, but one side of it was clearly quartz rock.

Immediately I started looking around, and I realized the rock all around us was full of a white quartz.

"Stand back," I said to Eliza.

She took several steps down the bank away from me, and I aimed the carbine at a vein of red quartz. I cocked back the hammer and pulled the trigger. The carbine spit fire and shot a ball of lead into the quartz.

"Jackson!" Eliza yelled as little bits of quartz exploded from the vein and rained down over our heads.

I grabbed up a rock about the size of my fist and started pounding away at the cracked quartz. Chunks of quartz began to break off, and as they did, I saw that there were thick yellow lines running all through the quartz. It was so easy to see the gold, thick inside every chunk of quartz I chipped away.

I hammered and hammered with the rock, and now every time a piece of quartz dropped off into the water, Eliza snatched it out to hold up and examine. And each time, she exclaimed at the metallic yellow running all through the quartz.

In minutes, we were holding more weight in gold than we could pan in a day, but it was all inside the quartz.

I realized, too, that the vein of quartz ran deep into the earth.

"Look at how deep it runs," I said to Eliza. "Look at it! This is it, Eliza! We've found the veta madre!" [40]

"Jack Speed, we're covered in gold! B'God get yerself in me now! Ravage me you beautiful man!"

And so I did, right there in the sandy creek, with nuggets of gold all around us, we made love in the cool water like a couple smitten teenagers who snuck off to the creek together.

We didn't have proper tools to keep working at the quartz, and it was starting to get dark. I didn't want to get lost out in the woods. I packed mud into the vein of quartz where I'd chipped it away, and I buried the quartz nuggets in the soft bank.

"We'll come back for this when Obadiah and Jimbo have left," I told Eliza.

"Are you not going to tell Obadiah about it?" she asked.

The thought had crossed my mind. I'd found it. He'd had nothing to do with it. But it was a fleeting thought only.

"No, I'll tell him. When he gets back from town. If I tell him now, he'll never leave tomorrow. He'll want to come here and bust up this rock. But I think we could do for a few days without his lectures, and so I don't want to tell him until he gets back."

CHAPTER 18

Obadiah and Jimbo were gone ten days. They'd been gone so long, I began to worry they'd not find their way back, or worse, they'd been robbed of the gold and killed.

In the intervening days, Eliza and I went down to the stream every day with picks and shovels, pans and chisels and hammers. Eliza panned the stream and came up with enormous deposits of placer gold. And I swung the pick and hammered the chisel and generally beat hell out of the quartz vein, and then I beat more hell out of the quartz rocks, and Eliza collected the smashings in tin buckets. She'd wash out the buckets in Cump Sherman's gold pan and collect the gold into bags. But there was more quartz than I could smash on my own, and so some of what we collected were the quartz rocks still loaded with gold.

I had no idea how much gold we were getting, but we were starting to estimate it in pounds rather than ounces. Most of the gold was running through each of the small quartz rocks, but sometimes we would knock loose whole nuggets of gold, some of the size of a thumb, others the size of a fist. We even found veins of gold that were two to three inches wide.

The delay for Obadiah and Jimbo had been that Johnny was not at the store when they arrived. He'd left his clerks in charge and gone to San Francisco. He was again nearly out of supplies at the store, and he'd gone to replenish his inventory.

"Prices for everything in San Francisco were so high, but he said he had no choice but to either pay the prices or close the store until more inventory arrived," Obadiah explained. "So we waited for Johnny to come back up from San Francisco, and that's what took us so long."

Nevertheless, they'd bought a third mule and three horses. The horses were fair, but not good mounts. They were older and didn't have much quickness in them.

"Well, I've got something to show you," I told Obadiah. I went into the tent and fetched a bag of the gold-lined quartz rocks.

Obadiah emptied it on the ground beside the campfire. Silently, he picked up rock after rock and examined them individually. He looked at a score of rocks, slowly turning them in his fingers.

"This quartz has gold all in it," he said quietly.

"It is an enormous vein of quartz," I said. "And it is slap full of gold."

"There is more?" Obadiah asked. He was almost breathless.

"We've been digging it the whole time you've been gone. Smashing away the quartz. Picking up the chunks of rocks. And we've found some big nuggets attached the quartz. I've got more gold nuggets than I have bags to fit it in," I said. "And there seems to be no end to the gold we've been digging out."

"Inside the quartz?" he said. He felt the full measure of his vindication.

"Inside the quartz," I said.

"Wha-hoo!" Obadiah shouted. "Take me to it!"

"It's nearly dark," I said. "Tomorrow. It's not going anywhere."

With Jimbo and Obadiah to help, we busted deeper into the quartz, following the vein up the rock. And then we discovered that the slab of quartz we were digging into went deep into the hillside itself, and we started shoveling the dirt away to expose the slab. If ye look in the books, they'll tell you that George McKnight's discovery on Gold Hill was the first big hardrock mining operation in the California Gold Rush, but it ain't so. We were digging quartz out of the earth a full year before George McKnight ever lifted his frying pan. [41]

For weeks we chipped away at the quartz and smashed quartz rocks and separated gold from quartz. And we dug into the hillside to get at it. We set Jimbo to work at the bottom of the slab to dig a race to reroute the stream so that we could dig into the bedrock. Even Eliza was working every day with a pickaxe so that she raised enormous blisters on her hands. And with the summer sun blazing down on us, the work was brutally hot. Worse, we were pulling gold out by the pound, but at the rate we were moving it could be years before we got all the gold out. And it still had to be smashed out of the quartz and the quartz washed away. Our job was bigger than anything we could do on our own. We would all die of old age before we collected all the gold there.

By this time we had moved the camp down to the claim, so we were no longer walking a mile or more back to camp every afternoon. Often we stopped during the heat of the afternoon to eat and rest, and then we worked by lantern late into the evening.

One afternoon, while we were resting after a morning of work, Obadiah brought up the problem we faced.

"We need to hire a company," Obadiah said. "We need men working this claim. It will take us years to dig out all this gold and get it separated from the quartz. I'll be dead before I spend the first bit of gold."

"We agreed to keep the claim quiet," I said.

"Yes. And we should keep it quiet. But we've got to have help with it all the same. We need to build a stamp mill to crush the quartz and channel the river into an enormous sluice box to wash the quartz away. Your wife's brother. Maybe he could help. Maybe he has met some men in town. Men we can trust to keep quiet – if such a man still exists in California. Because the other thing we have to worry about is claim jumpers. If word gets out about what we've found here, or if someone stumbles upon us, we have to worry about defending the claim."

"So what do you suggest we do?"

"You and Eliza ride back to town. Talk to Johnny, see if you can find a few hands to work the claim. See if you can have Johnny register the claim for us in San Francisco. Perhaps if it is done there instead of in Coloma or Dry Diggins –"

"Hangtown," I said.

"Yes, Hangtown. If he registers the claim in San Francisco, then maybe there is less chance that people will hear about it – at least not people who might know where to find us. And while you're in town, see if you can bring back some hands. With the gold we're pulling from this claim, we can easily pay a dozen men for a year. And it might take that long to get all this gold. Maybe longer. This quartz might run so deep that it takes us ten years."

We worked into the evening some, and the next day Eliza and I saddled up Courage and one of the other horses and rode into town. Leaving the mules behind, and with both of us mounted, we made Hangtown before night. On the way, we noted that the mining camps were much farther along the river now than when we'd last come through, and there were more miners than ever before. And when we arrived in Hangtown, we found that there were even more miners in town. They were arriving from the East by the overland route now, as well as in ships coming from all over the world.

Eliza spent the next day at the store with Johnny, explaining to him why we needed him to go to San Francisco to register our claim. Johnny was making monthly trips to San Francisco, anyway. He was going to buy supplies and check for further shipments from their grandfather. I didn't tell Eliza, but I suspected he also probably had a girl in San Francisco he was going to see. Johnny was only a year or so younger than me, which would have put him at eighteen. I know if it was me, the reason I would go to San Francisco once a month would be to find a filly, even if I had to pay her for her time and trouble. I was the last person to judge him for going to town to meet a girl. I just hoped she didn't give him any lasting reminders of their time together.

The biggest camps at that time were between Coloma and Hangtown, and so while Eliza was with Johnny, I rode out to the mining camps, following the river, and looking for Brother and Slim. I was nervous to hire complete strangers to work our claim. They could just as easily gut us in our sleep and take the claim for themselves as they could take a day's wages for digging gold for another man. Having come cross country with Brother and Slim, I believed I could not only count on them not to shoot me in my sleep but to also help me defend the claim if it came to that.

I rode right through the camps and down to the banks where the men were working. I didn't stop anywhere, but I asked men all along the river if they knew Brother and Slim. I'd been all morning riding through camps when finally someone called out an affirmative response.

"I know Brother and Slim," a man said. "They spent the winter on the hill overlooking San Francisco, right?"

"That's right," I said. "Came here last year on a wagon train."

The man was knee deep in the American River with a shovel in his hand. He pushed the blade of the shovel into the sand and leaned against the handle. "Sure. Brother and Slim."

"Do you know where they are?" I asked.

"They hired on with a company working the river about a mile downstream from here," the man said.

"Thank'ee," I said, and spurred Courage on down the river.

I did not have to ask for them again. As I rode along beside the river – which seemed to be one continuous mining camp all the way from Hangtown to Coloma – I heard someone calling out.

"Jack! Jack Speed!"

I looked out across the mining operations to see who was calling my name, and there on the far bank, waving his hat, I could see Slim calling to me. And there, near him, I saw Brother, too.

"Slim!" I called back. "I've been looking for ye! Come on over here and have a chat with me. You and Brother, both!"

Down here the river was wide and shallow enough that they were able to wade through it without trouble. Both men came up to the bank where I was standing.

"How much are they paying you boys?" I asked.

"You looking for work?" Slim asked.

"How much?" I asked.

"We're making fifteen dollars a day plus meals," Brother told me.

"The meals any good?" I asked.

"Fair to middling," Slim said.

"Is that enough for y'all to get by? I mean, are you doing what ye came out here to do?"

Slim laughed. "We'd still rather be digging for ourselves, but unless we found gold in a hurry, we couldn't afford to do it."

Brother said, "You looking for work?"

"No, I'm actually looking to hire you to come work for me," I said. "I could afford to pay you thirty dollars a day, and I can feed you."

Slim's eyes narrowed.

"You find a good hole?"

I looked around and saw that the miners nearby were paying attention. I slid down out of my saddle and walked Courage away from the river, and Slim and Brother followed me.

When we were a safe distance from eavesdropping ears, I said to them, "Boys, the truth of it is I've got a claim that's producing real well. I need hands to work it. People I can trust. A couple of boys who will drop their shovels and pick up rifles if they have to. You're about the only people out here I know and trust."

I reached into one of my saddlebags and pulled out a bag filled with some of the bigger nuggets we'd gotten from the quartz. I handed it over to Slim and he took a look inside. The bag had about five pounds of gold in it and was worth more than fourteen hundred dollars.

"That ain't just placer gold," Slim said, his voice no more than a whisper. He held the bag for Brother to see. Brother let out a soft whistle. He reached his hand inside and pulled out a couple of the nuggets, running his fingers over them.

"That's about an afternoon of work in that bag, boys," I said. "My claim is real good. You boys come work for me, and when we're done pulling gold out of my hole, I'll give you a share of it. I'll make you rich."

Slim looked at Brother, and Brother just kept on looking at the gold in the bag.

"What do ye think?" Slim said.

"Well, of course we're going to go," Brother said. "Just let us go cash out here."

"Don't say a word to nobody," I said. "I'd rather not have to defend the claim if I can help it."

"Right," Slim said. "We won't tell nobody."

"Not a word," Brother agreed.

"When you're done here, come out to Hangtown. Ye've been there?"

"Sure," Brother said.

"Out on the main road through town there's a store called Brooks' Hard Ware. Y'all come out there this afternoon. I'll be there waiting for you. And don't tell nobody where you're going. If word gets out the river could fill up with folks looking to jump our claim."

It was the first time I'd negotiated from a position of wealth, and it felt good to hire these boys and promise them that they'd be wealthy men. The thirty dollars a day I'd promised them was outrageous for a day's wage, but I had enough gold in that bag to pay them for the next forty days. And I was pulling at least that much gold out of our claim every week. In an easy day of working, I could make five hundred dollars without Slim and Brother.

Now that I had some ability to toss money around, I found I liked doing it pretty well.

I left Slim and Brother to finish out their business and make their own way to Hangtown. Even though they'd promised not to say a word about where they were leaving to, I still worried that some of the other miners in their company had taken notice and would follow them.

It didn't take me long to get back to Hangtown now that I wasn't riding through the camps looking for someone. When I got there, I asked Johnny to get me supplies together for Slim and Brother.

"Do you have any rifles or pistols?"

"I have a few muskets I picked up in San Francisco the last time I was there," Johnny said. "I can sell them for a lot, though. A hundred dollars for a musket and fifty for a bag of lead balls. Gunpowder ain't cheap, neither."

"Figure it all up. I want both of them to have two muskets a piece. What about livestock? Is there anywhere here I can buy a mule or a horse?"

Johnny laughed. "There ain't any horses in town for sale any more, but there's a feller selling pack mules."

"Well, take this bag of gold and go buy a team of four mules. I'll make Slim and Brother bring the mules up. We're going to need a lot of supplies – food and another cradle, a sluice box. Slim and Brother have their own tent, but we might as well get them another tent so they don't have to share one. I want these boys to feel like they're living high on the hog. I want them indebted to us. If they think we're treating them well, they'll be less likely to steal from us."

I had expected that by now the store's profits would have slowed, and I wondered if Johnny might consider coming up to the claim and working with us. But it was still a race to see if Johnny was going to make more money or if we would. Of course, the arrangement between Eliza and Johnny was that a quarter of the profit from the store was Eliza's, a quarter went to Johnny, and half went to Old Man Brooks. So having Johnny at the store was still making me money, and Johnny seemed much happier making cradles and sluice boxes than he would have been swinging a pickaxe.

While Johnny went off in search of mules, I went off in search of miners.

With Slim and Brother working for me, I felt confident now about hiring a couple of strangers. I wasn't going to buy them guns, but I didn't mind buying them tents and tools. I also needed to hire on a cook. I was going to have nine or ten people in camp, and I'd need someone to feed all of them.

I walked out to the tents where the miners who had just arrived were camped, and I found what I was looking for easy enough. In the woods not far off the road I spotted a poorly made lean-to shelter, and I walked over to it. Seated around a campfire were three Injun boys and a squaw.

"Y'all got any English?" I asked them.

None of the boys were over sixteen. The girl was older, but not by much. Maybe she was about Johnny's age. She was the one who stood up and answered me. "We all speak English," she said.

"What tribe?" I asked, as if I knew anything about the local Injuns. They were all round-faced like the Western tribes, and so I knew they weren't Cherokee.

"Our people are Ochecame," she said.

"Where'd you learn English?"

"Our parents worked at Sutter's Fort," she said.

"These are your brothers, then?" I asked.

"They are," she said.

"Where are they now, your parents?"

"Our father is at Sutter's Fort still, but our mother died. Our father sent us out to find work."

"Digging for gold?"

"We can dig for gold," she said. "We have been here for a week, and no one has hired us."

"Can you cook?" I asked her.

"I can," she said. "I worked in the kitchen at Sutter's Fort."

"I'll pay each of you ten dollars a day," I said. "Will you work for that?"

"We will," she said.

"Then come on with me." I looked at the boys, who had not said anything. "Do y'all speak English or not?"

"We do," one of the boys said.

"Y'all understand you'll be digging gold. I'll expect you to work hard. I'll feed you and give you tools and a tent to sleep in, but you've got to work hard."

"They will work hard," the sister said.

"Get your things and come along," I said.

These Injuns were no more likely than Brother and Slim to shoot me in my sleep. If there was trouble, they'd probably run, but I wasn't sure that I'd stick around if there was trouble, so I couldn't blame them if they ran.

By nightfall, Slim and Brother and the four Injuns were all camped in the back yard of the store. I'd tried to put all four of the Injuns into one tent, seeing as how they were siblings, but Eliza insisted it wasn't proper for the girl to sleep with her brothers, and so I ended up having to buy two tents for the Indians. Johnny had found us three decent mules, and we had supplies enough to feed our small company for at least a couple of months and provide them with the tools they needed to get the gold out of the ground.

In the morning, I helped Slim and Brother pack the mules. The Indian boys all gathered around, but they weren't much use at loading packs. With the mules toting our supplies, I sent Slim and Brother ahead with the mules and the Injuns. I told them the route to follow and promised that Eliza and I would catch them up before nightfall. I wanted to give them a big enough head start that Eliza and I wouldn't have to go too slow. I also wanted to talk to Johnny.

"When the time comes for us to bring our gold down out of the hills, it's going to be a lot of gold," I told him. "Hundreds of pounds of gold. There's not a man working this river who wouldn't shoot us dead for a handful of what we'll have. It's going to be damned dangerous when we bring that gold out. So the next time you're in San Francisco, you need to see about getting some guns. Good guns. A carbine like mine, some revolvers like the one I carry. And we're going to need at least a couple of wagons, too."

"Can you get wagons up to your camp?" Johnny asked me.

"No, but we can make a few trips with the mules and bring the gold here quietly. We can stow it here, but when we take it down to San Francisco, we'll need to take it all in one trip. So over the next few weeks, I need you to see about getting a couple of wagons and getting some guns."

"I can do that," Johnny said. "You're smart to be thinking like that. You know there's been some killings at some of the mining camps. They say there is a Mexican bandito who is killing prospectors and stealing their gold." Johnny squinched up his face in thought. "What's his name? I can't recollect, but I've heard about him."

"A Mexican?" I asked.

"That's right. A downright vicious fellow, too. Starts with a J, but it's pronounced like a W. Wakeem someone."

"Joaquin?" I asked. "Joaquin Murrieta?"

"That's it!" Johnny said. "You've already heard of him?"

"Heard of him?" I said. "Johnny, I've met him."

"Well, you don't want to meet him again," Johnny said. "They say most folks who meet him don't live to talk about it."

"Well, you keep your ears open here in town," I said. "If you hear people talking about our claim, you need to try to warn us."

California was a damned dangerous place in 1849, and I had discovered a huge pile of the thing that was making it so dangerous. I wanted to be prepared when I brought my huge pile of gold out of the hills.

CHAPTER 19

We were not far out from Chile Bar when we saw a dozen riders coming down the road toward us. I didn't give them a thought as they approached us. Eliza and I walked our horses off the side of the road to give them plenty of room to pass. I didn't even look at them as they went past. But then I heard one of them pull up on his reins and wheel his horse, and I turned to look. As the lead man turned his horse around toward us, the others all reined in and did likewise. I realized, looking at them then, that it was a band of Mexicans, and the man in the lead looked frightfully like Joaquin Murrieta, the bandito we'd encountered in the woods and the one who'd been making a name for hisself my killing prospectors.

"Lieutenant Jackson Speed!" Murrieta said, grinning ear to ear.

We were within sight of the river, but it was still a hundred yards away. Down in the river men were working, but none of them paid any attention to what was happening on the road. We'd not yet caught up to Slim and Brother, so it was just me and Eliza and Joaquin Murrieta and his men.

I didn't respond to Murrieta, but I dropped my hand down to the grip of my Paterson. "If I have to shoot this revolver, you ride like hell," I said to Eliza.

"Lieutenant Speed, who was at Monterrey fighting my people," Joaquin Murrieta said. "I have been looking for you, mi amigo. The night we met, my friend José and two more of my friends were murdered in town. And I wanted to ask you if you knew anything about that."

I gulped hard. My mouth was dry from the trail, and I was finding it damned difficult to speak.

"I don't know anything about that," I said.

"I thought it was very strange," Joaquin Murrieta mused, "that the very same night that my friend José offended you and you drew your gun on him, he was also murdered. Do you not find that peculiar?"

"Like I said, I don't know anything about it. And now my wife and I will be on our way."

"Are you taking a woman to the goldfields?" Joaquin Murrieta asked. "The goldfields are a dangerous place, mi amigo. Perhaps your woman would prefer to go back to town. My friends and I will escort her!"

Joaquin Murrieta thought that sounded like a great joke, and he began to laugh. All his bandito friends also laughed at his joke.

I had five shots in the Paterson and five more in the carbine, assuming I could get it out before they overtook me. If every shot told, I could kill ten of them. But that would leave me two or three more to deal with – they were all skipping and dancing around on the horses, and it was tough to count them and know for sure. But making every shot hit its mark before they could get to me would be no easy task. I figured the best I could probably do was shoot a couple of them.

"She'll be fine riding with me," I said.

Joaquin Murrieta obviously thought he was quite a handsome man with his thin moustache and chin whiskers shaved into a triangle and long, curly, black hair. He grinned at me and said, "Perhaps we should ask the lady her opinion. Perhaps you do not speak for her, mi amigo. Would you care to ride back to town in the company of myself and my men?"

"I'll be riding with my husband," Eliza said, the words sounding like ice. "And you would be well advised not to anger him."

Joaquin and his men all laughed at that, too. I prayed to God that Eliza would keep her mouth shut and not say anything else.

"Have you found yourself some California gold, Lieutenant Speed?" Murrieta said. His tone was full of derision, and the smirk on his face made him seem dangerous. "Are you striking it rich?"

"We're just out for a ride," I said.

Joaquin Murrieta sat his horse quietly for a moment, staring intently at me and chewing on his bottom lip. At last he said, "The gold here belongs to me and to my people, Lieutenant Speed. You gringos are trespassing on stolen land. I will see you again."

Now Murrieta snapped his reins, wheeled his horse, and rode off hard back toward Hangtown, and his men followed his lead. I watched them ride away over a ridge and out of sight.

"Let's hurry and catch up to Slim and Brother," I said to Eliza.

We pushed the horses on a little faster as long as there was a road, which was not long. When the road diminished into a path, we had to take it slower so that we did not run into low hanging branches. All the same, we soon caught up with Slim and Brother and the rest of our small company.

I didn't mention anything to them about Murrieta and his band. I didn't want them to be skittish about going so far away from the other goldfields.

We stopped late in the afternoon and camped off the road in a large clearing on the top of a hill. We collected firewood, unloaded the beasts, and put up our tents. We put the Indian girl, who had the Christian name Mary, to work cooking up some victuals. I had Eliza watch her to make certain she knew what she was doing. I was a bit skeptical that she'd be a decent cook, but I figured we could teach her well enough to cook camp food.

Brother and Slim and I were walking along the clearing, looking out over the expanse of rolling hills, gulches and craggy cliffs.

"How long before we get to the claim?" Brother asked.

"Early afternoon tomorrow we'll be there," I said.

From where we stood, we could see the gulch where the American River ran down below the road, but we could not see the river itself.

"Say," Slim said. "Jack, I don't mean to sound worrisome, but you don't think them Injuns told anyone we were going into the hills for a rich claim, do you?"

"I don't, Slim. I found them at their camp and they came directly to the store with me. Unless they snuck out at night – and I don't believe they did – they never had opportunity."

"Huh," Slim said. He took off his hat and ran a hand through his hair. I waited for him to say something more, but he did not.

"Slim, why do ye ask?" I said.

"Well," Slim said, holding his hat out to block the setting sun on the horizon. "Some while ago, on the trail, I looked back when we were up on a hill, and it looked to me like two men were following us down the trail. They were mounted, and so I expected they'd pass us by. But they never did. And now, I believe I can see where they've camped down below us."

I was immediately alarmed at this news, and not because I was worried about claim jumpers. My first thought was Joaquin Murrieta's promise to meet me again.

I looked down into the valley below us but at first saw no sign of anyone camping. While our hilltop was cleared of trees, the valley below us was thick with the tall pines. But then I saw movement and realized there were two horses. I could not see any men, but the horses were unmistakable.

"Maybe we ought to go down there and see what they're about," Brother suggested.

If they were Joaquin Murrieta's men, I had no desire to poke that bear. But I also did not want them to follow us to the camp. My fear was that I was going to have to kill these men, and I didn't know if Slim and Brother would be willing for thirty dollars a day to commit murder with me.

"No," I said to Brother. "I ain't sure that's the smart thing to do. But in the morning, when we set out, if they're still following us, I'll have a plan to deal with them."

We broke camp and were on our way before the sun was up the next morning. It was slow going picking our way along the path without good light, and even if we'd managed to break camp and get away unnoticed, I knew we would not get so far that our pursuers could not catch us easily enough.

By noon we reached the top of a ridge that was within a couple of miles of our camp. At the top of the ridge I looked back down the path and was disappointed, but not surprised, to see our pursuers were still with us.

I dismounted and told Slim to go on ahead to the camp with the Injuns and the mules. I directed him how to find it. "If you keep on along this deer path, you'll come to a creek. When you get to the creek, follow it south, and just before it meets the South Fork of the American River, you'll come to the camp. Obadiah is the older white man, and Jimbo is the black man. Just tell them you're the hands I hired."

"You and your wife are going to try to lead them men off away from the camp?" Slim asked.

"We are," I said. "If these men are who I believe they are, it's me they're following. I'd rather Eliza go on with you, but I think if they see me alone they will know I'm trying to lead them the wrong way."

Slim nodded thoughtfully. "I have an idea, Jack," he said. "Why don't you let Eliza go on foot. Have her lead Brother and the others down to the camp. I'll take her horse and put on her hat. They ain't close enough to us that they would notice it was a man in a woman's hat. That away, we can lead them off in the wrong direction, and maybe if we find the right spot we stop among the trees or bushes somewhere, let them come up to us, and we ambush 'em."

"Ambush 'em?" I asked. "You mean commit murder?"

Slim shrugged his shoulders and nodded ominously.

"Eliza," I said, calling to her. "I want you to lead Brother and the Injuns down to the camp on foot. Let Slim here have your hat and horse."

If Eliza understood what we had in mind, I could not say, but she readily gave up her horse and hat and led Brother and the Injuns along the path through the woods that would take them to our campsite. Slim, meanwhile, slid a shovel out of one of the packs on one of the mules and strapped it to the saddle on Eliza's horse.

Up on the high ridge the recent months without much rain and the hot sun had burned off most of the vegetation, and so we were riding into the open without any cover. We took the horses at a pretty good clip, riding fast for two reasons – we didn't want Joaquin Murrieta's men to get a good look at Slim and realize he was not Eliza, nor did we want them to have time to think about whether to follow Brother, Eliza and the Injuns.

When we were well along the dirt path, I risked a quick look over my shoulder to be sure our pursuers had taken the bait, and it appeared they had. I could see dust rising on the trail behind us.

The ridge ran for quite a way. The path basically ran along the crest of a long mountain, and on the slope to our left, the western slope, it was heavily vegetated with long stands of big trees. The right side, though, the steeper slope, was barren for a ways down. But ahead we could see where the elevation of the ridge dropped, and there the slope was not so harsh and the trees covered both sides.

"Up here would be a good place to do it, if we're going to," Slim said.

"Aye," I said. We urged the horses forward, and when we got to the cover of the trees and undergrowth, we wheeled off the path.

Slim had a loaded musket, and I had both the Paterson and the carbine. We quickly led the horses down the slope some and behind some blackberry bushes that would block them from view from the path, and then Slim and I moved closer up to the path and hid behind a couple of wide trees.

"It would be good if we could make our first shots tell," I said to him.

We waited several minutes before we heard the men coming along the path. Their horses were coming on pretty hard. They'd lost sight of us and were hurrying to try to catch us up. I knew it would be no easy thing to shoot two riders moving at speed.

I peered out from around the tree where I was hiding and raised up the carbine to my shoulder. I cocked back the hammer and waited, breathing easy so that my aim would be true.

"I'll take the first one," I whispered to Slim. "You shoot the second one." Slim nodded and raised up his musket.

Now they came into sight, moving pretty quick and never seeing either me nor Slim. I followed the first one with the barrel of the carbine, matching his speed until I was confident of the shot. I pulled the trigger and the gun exploded to spit out its load.

As if he'd been caught on a line, the first rider jerked back and fell off his horse when the ball hit him square in the chest. I was already cocking back the hammer on the carbine in case Slim missed when his musket exploded its shot. The second rider fell just as the first one had.

"Got him!" Slim hollered, well pleased with himself.

We rushed forward and found both men choking on their last breaths, their chests both opened up where the big lead balls had struck them.

For all the men I've seen shot to death, I never could get accustomed to seeing a man die. It wasn't that I felt any remorse for them or sorrow, but a man choking and spluttering and gasping his last breaths is a pitiful sight. With whatever realization he has left in his dying moments, you can see on his face the regret for all the decisions that led him to this moment. How many boys in Abe Lincoln's war did I watch as they died, and every one of them had a moment when they recalled that day they enlisted — so full of hope that they might be a hero for their country — and every one of them, recalling that day, regretted it in their final moment.

Now these two Mexican bastards were regretting the day they'd decided to ride with Joaquin Murrieta.

As distasteful as it was to me to look at them, I did study them and knew for certain they'd been with Murrieta when Eliza and I had encountered him the previous day.

"Need to get them buried," Slim said. "We should bury their saddles with them. I'll take their guns and anything else they have that's useful, and we can take the horses. But people might recognize their saddles."

I got Slim's shovel and walked down to where we'd tied up our horses.

"Think this is far enough off the path?" I asked.

"Probably," Slim said, craning his neck to see how far down I'd gone.

I didn't care much for the labor of digging a grave for the two Mexicans, but it meant that Slim was stuck with the labor of dragging their bodies down to the grave. Digging the hole was harder work, but if

I didn't like watching a man die, I also preferred not to muck around with his body too much if I could help it.

So I dug the hole deep enough that if we got rain anytime soon the bodies wouldn't wash out and be exposed. Meanwhile, Slim rounded up the two horses, took the weapons and whatever else he could find that he wanted off the bodies, and then he dragged the bodies one at a time down to their final resting place. When he slid the bodies in, and tossed the saddles after them, I filled in the dirt back on top of them. Together, we rolled a couple of fallen tree trunks, small ones, over on top of the grave to keep coyotes from digging them up.

We didn't say much as we rode back down to the camp, leading the horses of the two men we'd just murdered. I didn't have any remorse about it, and Slim didn't seem too bothered, either. We just didn't talk about it. When the Mississippi Rifles stormed Fort Teneria in Monterrey, Mexican soldiers were fleeing out the back of the fort. We chased them down and used our Bowie knives to stab them in the back before they could get away. It was brutal murder, and I didn't feel any remorse about that, either. In my mind, the two things were basically the same. That's not to say I took any pleasure in it, other than the knowledge that in both situations – back in Monterrey and now in California – I'd ruthlessly killed men so that they would not later have the opportunity to kill me.

When we arrived at camp, no one asked where we'd got horses and revolvers from or what had happened to the men who'd pursued us.

CHAPTER 20

Slim and Brother and the Injuns we'd hired were all good workers. I was worried about the Injuns, with them being just children, but they didn't complain, and what they lacked in strength they made up for in willingness.

Mary was a poor cook to begin with. Her food was bland. But Eliza helped her some, and Obadiah, who was a pretty good hand at cooking on a campfire, helped her more. Eventually, the victuals improved. And life in our campsite was pretty happy.

I knew for sure that both Brother and Slim were pocketing gold nuggets here and there, and I was fairly certain the Injuns were, too, but there was so much of the stuff that I never could get upset about it. And the deeper we dug into the hillside, the more gold we found within the quartz.

Obadiah directed us in the construction of a rough stamp to crush the quartz, and we used sluice boxes to wash the quartz away and collect the gold. Some of it came out in dust and some in flakes, but we were also getting some good sized nuggets, too.

Brother and Slim and the oldest Injun boy dug into the hillside and brought out the quartz rock. Jimbo busted up the rock with our stamp machine, and Eliza directed the younger Injun boys who used the cradle and the sluice box to wash away the quartz and collect the gold.

Gold Hill Mine was credited as being the first coyote mine in California, but the truth was we were mining for quartz gold in a hillside a full year before George McKnight. And McKnight had the advantage of knowing what he was doing and how to do it. Most of what we did was based solely on Obadiah Bush's ingenuity.

Everyone at the camp had their jobs, which left me and Obadiah free to dig a little, smash rock a little, wash rock a little and keep prospecting. Obadiah was convinced that if we'd found so much gold in one spot there would be other gold deposits nearby. So he and I constructed small dams along the creek to divert the water, and we dug into the muddy creek bed in several places until we did, in fact, find more deposits.

We worked like this sun up to sun down – and even by lantern light well after dark. Every day we were pulling from the earth gold worth hundreds of dollars. It was during these days in 1849 that I made a fortune. Though I continue to this day to own a company that prospects and digs gold, silver, and copper in California, Nevada, New Mexico, and even up to Colorado, the profits from it are small. Too many claims come to nothing, and when my engineers do find precious metals, it costs too much to get it out of the ground. If my company managers were worth anything, they'd have moved the entire operation to Alaska back in '96.

My decision in the spring of 1848 to go to California made me a wealthy man, no doubt, but it very nearly proved to be the death of me.

Close to two months of working like this, and Eliza and I decided to ride back to Hangtown. We loaded three mules with burlap sacks full of gold – it was easily ninety thousand dollars in gold, more money than most men ever saw in a lifetime. We hid the sacks with blankets, but all the same it made me nervous to have so much gold. And so I gave Eliza one of the revolvers we took off of the Mexicans. I took some interest in watching as she hiked up her skirt and strapped the holster to her thigh on the outside of her bloomers so she could keep it secreted under her skirt. There was something right pretty about seeing her strap the leather holster over her white, lace-edged bloomers.

We set out in the morning before the sun was up. My intention was to make the ride in one day, even with the mules slowing us down. I wasn't going to get caught having to camp along the road with three mules, each one toting a hundred pounds of gold.

We weren't two miles from our camp when we encountered miners working the American River. This was the closest we'd ever seen them to our claim.

"They'll be on top of us in a week or two," I said to Eliza. "They're spreading farther out from the towns, farther up into the hills."

"Can we protect our claim?" Eliza asked.

"That's a good question," I told her.

At that time, miners in the goldfields were making their own rules and their own laws. Once there was a large group of prospectors around us no one would attempt to jump the claim. The worry was that before other prospectors showed up, the first company or group to stumble upon us, might try to take the claim.

We pushed the mules about as hard as they would go, and even so we rode into Hangtown with the sun already below the hills to the west. When we arrived at the store, we found it nearly empty of supplies.

Johnny was there alone, he no longer had any clerks working for him because there wasn't enough inventory in the place to make help necessary. I led the horses and the mules to the back yard, and Johnny went with me.

"I've been down to San Francisco, but there's nothing to buy there at a price that I could resell it," Johnny told us. "I've had no new shipments from Granddaddy, and my inventory here is nearly all gone. You cannot imagine the hundreds of prospectors who have come through here in the last month. They've bought up nearly everything I have. I don't even have any raw lumber to make more boxes or cradles."

"It's just as well, Johnny," I said to him. "We're going to have other chores for you soon enough. We've hit pay dirt, and it's time to start bringing it out of the mountains."

As I spoke, I was untying the pack from one of the mules. With a flourish, I flung off the blanket covering the sacks of gold.

"One hundred pounds of gold," I said. "Or thereabouts. I ain't never been great at math, Johnny, but I reckon that one hundred pounds of gold, at the going rate of about twenty dollars an ounce, is worth something close to thirty-two thousand dollars. And I've got two more bags just like that one."

With his eyes wide, Johnny came over and took one of the burlap sacks off the mule. I was delighted to see how much trouble he had managing its weight.

"Heavy, ain't it?" I said.

"It is," Johnny said, dropping the sack onto the ground. He untied it at the top and looked inside, holding a lantern close so he could see better. "Jack, it's a fortune."

"And that's not half of what we've already dug out of the ground and have back at our campsite," I said. "Johnny, were you able to get a wagon?"

"I have a wagon," he said. "I don't have any beasts to pull it, but I did buy a wagon."

"We can hitch it to the mules," I said. "We're going to need you to come up with the wagon, and we need to start getting this gold back to San Francisco."

We unloaded and mules and put the sacks of gold in the cabin Johnny had built for storage for inventory. It worked fine, because the cabin was empty except for the bags and sacks of gold dust Johnny had earned at the store.

What Johnny did have that I'd not had in many, many months, was steak. Real beef, not jerky, and I was thrilled to have it.

"I sure have been worried about y'all up there in the hills," Johnny confessed as we ate. "Every prospector that comes to town who's been in the goldfields has stories of the banditos. They've ridden into mining camps and killed every man they could find. In some of the small villages, Joaquin Murrieta and his men have ridden in and killed men and even raped the women. This bandit Murrieta, he's been as far south as Los Angeles and two days later he's raided mining camps as far north as the Yuba River. It's impossible the distances he covers, but he seems to be everywhere."

"Thieves!" Eliza said.

"He's not stealing gold, at least not much of it. They seem more intent on just killing folks," Johnny said. "At one camp, some folks rode in and found thirty men all shot to death, but there were bags of gold just sitting out in plain view. It didn't look like he'd stole any of it. He just went there to kill folks."

"That doesn't make sense," I said. "Just killing folks for the sake of killing folks? Surely he's stealing gold, too."

"Some folks say some white men killed his wife, and so he kills to avenge her. Others say he's still fighting the war. Either way, it seems to be revenge and not gold that he's after."

You see, even then the rumors about Joaquin Murrieta were rampant and romanticized, so can ye blame Yellowbird for the fiction he wrote?

"They say the army is coming up next month to try to track him down," Johnny said.

"Well, if he's really riding from Los Angeles to the Yuba River in two days, the army will be hard pressed to catch him," I said. Of course, I knew no such feat had taken place. But if he'd truly murdered thirty men in a camp, it made me nervous as hell about my gold being

259

protected by just seven men.

"We'd be wise to get that gold out of the hill as quick as we can and get out of these hills," I said. "Johnny, can you hire any men to help you move the gold down to San Francisco?"

"Sure," Johnny said. "Those boys that I had working for me as clerks. I could put a musket in each of their hands."

"I think it's time you do that," I said. "Load up the gold we brought down out of the hills and the gold ye've earned here at the store, and take it into San Francisco. What's the name of that assay office there?"

"Moffat," Johnny said. "I've seen some of their coins." [42]

"Start having it made into bars and coins," I said.

Though we had months or maybe even years of work still to do, and much more gold to get at, I was already beginning to imagine leaving California. We needed the gold melted into bars and coins that could travel. As soon as I was confident there was nothing more in California to add to my fortune, I wanted to find myself on a ship back east. I wanted away from here as soon as could be. The reason was simple, I'd suddenly grown nervous about the banditos killing folks in California.

Johnny's news of Joaquin Murrieta gave me a bad feeling. Even if I didn't believe half of it, even if I didn't believe that Murrieta and his banditos were responsible for killing 30 men – if it was just half that number, it was still more people than we had in our camp. If Joaquin and his men were to ride in to our camp, guns blazing, I didn't wonder whether he'd be able to kill all of us. Didn't Johnny say the banditos were looking for secluded camps? And wasn't our camp secluded by design?

And Joaquin Murrieta certainly had cause to come riding into our camp with pistolas spitting hellfire. I'd murdered two of his men and helped with the lynching of three others.

Though it was the first time in weeks I'd managed to get into a real bed that offered much comfort at all, I had a terrible night's sleep. I dreamt that I was back at Monterrey, storming the walls at El Teneria. But instead of finding a regiment of frightened Mexicans running out the back of the fort, I found Joaquin Murrieta and his banditos. In his hands, Joaquin Murrieta held the saddles that belonged to the two men Slim and I had shot, and the banditos had Slim and Brother, with nooses tied around their necks, and another one was holding a noose with no one in it. And Obadiah, sitting on a wagon full of gold, pointed at the empty noose and said, "This one is for you, Jack. It is not what you sought in California, but it is what you found." And then Eliza was there, standing next to me, and she whispered in my ear: "You'd better run, Jack Speed."

In the morning Johnny said he would sell what was left of the inventory at the store at some sort of reduced rate – still more than he could get for the same things back in Milledgeville, but less than he'd been selling supplies for.

"I should be cleaned out in a week," he said. "I'll sell the store, or tear it down if I cannot sell it, and I'll take this first load of gold to San Francisco. It will probably take me the better part of a month to sell off the store, take the wagon to San Francisco and get back out here. And when I do get back, I'll come straight to the claim to get the next wagon load of gold."

I drew Johnny a map that would help him know how to find us when he came back up into the foothills of the Sierra Nevada to join us.

The day was hot, and we got a late start, and so we were already resigned to sleeping under the stars that night and arriving back at camp the next day. Because we were not in a hurry, and because I felt safer about being near crowds of people, we rode out through the goldfields, staying close to the miners.

While none of the prospectors were overt or rude, Eliza elicited a fair number of lustful looks from miners who'd not seen a decent looking woman in weeks or months. I suppose it was because of Eliza, but any time we stopped and dismounted, we got a fair number of folks to come up out of the river and chat with us.

I asked them how they were doing, asked about their techniques.

Most of the folks we talked to were still on their own or in small groups. Most of them were just panning or digging in small holes. In the coming months, many more prospectors would adopt Obadiah's techniques of damming the river, or diverting it, and digging into the exposed riverbed down to the bedrock. In a year or two, most of the prospecting would be done by men working for companies – many financed by wealthy Easterners who never did come to California but still got a share of the California gold.

Now, too, more and more of the men we encountered had come to California in overland wagon trains and had not been here longer than a few weeks. Unlike those of us with calloused hands, their hands were raw with blisters, and they were still wondering where to find more than a handful of placer gold. As we chatted with them, they all remarked on the prices of things and how unprepared they were for that. They had to find gold just to buy their supper, and most of them complained they weren't even finding enough to eat more than every other day.

It was odd to me, having been in California almost a year now, to feel like an old timer talking to greenhorns.

To stay near the prospectors, we followed the river and did not stay with the road or paths we usually took. But as we got farther up into the hills, the steep banks forced us away from the river in places. Here, where the river narrowed and the banks were more difficult, we found large pockets where there were no prospectors. But all the big sandbars were still overrun with miners.

I did not explain to Eliza why I was interested in staying near the mining camps. I didn't want her to worry, and even more I did not want

262

her to know that I was scared of encountering Joaquin Murrieta. But these miners, the ones in more secluded locations, they were the ones I was most interested in talking to.

"Have y'all had trouble with banditos?" I asked these men when we were able to ride down close to the river and chat with them.

They all said they'd heard stories of Murrieta – most actually named him – but no one we encountered had actually seen him. Except for one man.

"I came in overland, and as our wagon train came over the mountains, some of us went off prospecting there," he told us. "We spent a couple of weeks panning in the rivers, but it was all stone bottom and we weren't finding much of nothing worthwhile. For a couple of days I went off with another boy looking for deer or rabbit or anything to shoot for dinner, and when we came back, we found in our camp a score of men, all Mexicans. We didn't go into camp. Instead, we stayed up among the rocks and watched them. They were picking through the supplies. The other four men with us, they was all dead – murdered."

"And you know it was Murrieta?" I asked.

"There was one man, obviously the leader. He had long hair, a trimmed beard and moustache. We could hear them calling him 'Joaquin.' We left the camp and made our way back out to the trail, and we took up with the next wagon train that came through. When we got down to Hangtown, we reported it and described the man. Everyone there said it must have been Joaquin Murrieta."

His description was close enough, and I didn't doubt that it was Murrieta. It gave me no comfort to have confirmation that Murrieta and his banditos had actually raided a camp of prospectors and killed the men they found there.

Others had stories. One prospector claimed that Murrieta and his men had ridden onto a ranch south of the goldfields. They had killed the ranchero and some of his hands and kidnapped the man's wife and two daughters. Another said Murrieta and the banditos had ridden into a camp, stolen bags of gold dust and kidnapped the Injun women who were cooks at that camp. Another told us Murrieta had gone into San Francisco itself and kidnapped all the whores from a bordello.

If the stories all put together could be believed, Joaquin Murrieta and his men had killed more than a thousand prospectors and kidnapped upwards of two hundred women of all sorts whom he was now holding prisoner as concubines and cooks. I concluded that the stories could not all be believed, but I feared there was enough truth in at least some of them.

As we rode between camps along a path away from the river, Eliza at last said, "Jackson, why are you asking all these men about Joaquin Murrieta?"

"I'm asking them lots of questions," I told her, which was true enough. I asked about any big claims they'd heard of, I asked about their mining techniques, I asked every miner we encountered where they were from and how long they'd been out west.

"Yes," Eliza said thoughtfully, "but you're asking lots of different questions. The only question you've asked every one of them is about Joaquin Murrieta."

"Well, the truth is, I'm worried about the stories we've been hearing," I said. "I didn't like this man none too much when we met him, and we've encountered him twice now. I'd just like to know what to expect if we meet him again."

Eliza glanced down at the Paterson on my hip. "Jack, if half of what we've been told about this man Joaquin Murrieta is true, you'd best plan to use that straight away if we meet him again."

CHAPTER 21

We ate supper at a miner's camp and then rode a ways into the woods to unroll our blankets and sleep under the stars. We were well secluded and away from the road, and I took full advantage of the opportunity to be alone with Eliza.

Ever since we'd found the gold, though, Eliza was as insatiable as I was meself. She'd certainly had cause in three years of marriage to have some concerns about her choice of husbands. Not long after we were married I'd disappeared to fight in Mexico and then more than two years later, out of the blue, I summoned her to join me in California to dig for gold. She'd be forgiven if she wondered what sort of husband I was going to make. But now that we'd found gold, and enough of it to live well for the rest of our lives, Eliza seemed to have some trust in me and the future I was going to make for her.

I'll admit, it was doing me good, too, to have Eliza showering me with affection. I'll not say I'd forgotten Weenonaw, but Eliza's presence was a balm that soothed the sorrow I'd felt watching my Cherokee bride gunned down.

With the sun coming up, Eliza and I rose and got our day started. We didn't bother cooking any kind of breakfast and just ate some jerky and biscuits. I rolled up our blankets and saddled the horses, and I watched as Eliza strapped the revolver to her thigh.

"Is that comfortable?" I asked her. "Doesn't it chafe a bit?"

"The bloomers keep down the chafing some," Eliza said. "It's not particularly comfortable, especially when I'm riding, but if the time comes that I need this revolver, I'll decide that the chafing wasn't so bad."

"Well, you're a good girl to endure the discomfort, and we'll hope it's all for nothing."

"It's been quite a bit of discomfort out here, Jackson," Eliza said, fingering the raw callouses on her palms. "I suppose I never expected to work so hard in all my life. My shoulders, arms, and thighs are all sore as can be, sunburned neck, rough and calloused hands. And now chafing on my thigh."

Still, even as she said it, Eliza smiled at me.

"I didn't mean for it to be so hard on ye," I said. "I just couldn't stand to be without ye any longer. I knew, I just had a feeling when I first heard about the gold here, that I could come here and strike a fortune. But I couldn't bear to do it if I didn't have hope that ye'd be joining me here. We'd been too long separated."

Eliza slid herself up into the saddle of her horse, and I hefted myself up onto Courage.

"When I received your letter, I was so relieved to know you were still alive. For months I thought you were dead. But it crushed my heart, Jack, when I read that you were coming to California. It was the wrong way," she said. "I needed you to come home, come back to me in Milledgeville, and it seemed you were going to the other side of the world. And when I read that you wanted me to join you here, I resolved that it did not matter what the hardships were – whether it was the sea travel, or the travel through Panama, or the impossibility of finding you in this territory, or even the blisters, the sore muscles, the burning sun or the chafing – I resolved that I would endure anything to be with my husband."

I gave her a grin and a wink, the kind I usually reserved for the ladies I was trying to woo.

"Like I said, you're good girl, Eliza, and ye make me a fine wife."

We picked our way back out to the road and continued our journey up into the hills toward our campsite.

We'd not been far along the road when I heard coming from behind us a thunderous noise, and as I wheeled about to see what it was, I realized that more than a dozen riders were coming down on us, and before I could draw out the Paterson or put my heels in Courage's side, they were riding up around us, a couple of them getting in between Eliza and me, and one rider was right beside me, leaning over and putting his hand on the stock of my carbine so that I could not snatch it from its scabbard.

What I noticed first was that the man leaning beside me stank like the devil. He was a fat and an unfair burden on his horse, his beard looked like a thousand wires going off in a thousand directions of their own choosing, and what parts of his face were uncovered by whiskers were plastered with dried dirt and dust.

And then I heard the smooth voice of Joaquin Murrieta. "Amigo! How lucky I am to have crossed paths with you again, Lieutenant Speed."

I looked up and saw his smiling face, hands spread wide as he held his balance in the saddle with his legs. His gesture and words, even the tone of his voice, all presented a façade of friendliness. But I knew it was only a façade. There was venom flowing beneath that surface.

"Lieutenant Speed, I have a question for you," Murrieta said. "Can you explain to me why it is that every time you and I meet, I lose some of my men?"

I swallowed hard and tried my best to sound perplexed. "I'm sure I have no idea what you are talking about."

Murrieta's smile only grew wider. "I think that is not true, mi amigo. But I will refresh your memory. The first night we met, in the woods, do you remember?"

"Sure," I said. "Your friend José was a little drunk."

"And later that night, José and two more of my men rode into town, and the next time I saw them, they were hanging by their necks from a tree in the town square," Murrieta said. "And the last time I saw you, with your lovely wife, was out on the road. Two of my men split off from the rest of our group that day. And we have never seen those men again."

"I sure am sorry for your troubles," I said. "But that ain't got nothing to do with me. I didn't hang them men, and I don't know anything about the men who split off from your group. Now, Señor Murrieta, if you would be so kind as to ask your men to move, we would like to be on our way."

Joaquin Murrieta's smile dropped and he sat his horse, which now stopped dancing. He was looking back and forth between me and Eliza. I could tell he was thinking about what to do with us.

"Take his guns," Murrieta said, and before I could move the smelly, fat bastard beside me had slid the Paterson out of my holster. He then took the carbine. "You and your wife will ride with us, Lieutenant Speed. And if you attempt to get away, we will just simply kill both of you."

Murrieta wheeled his horse off the roadway and into the tall trees. The fat Mexican pressed his horse into Courage to move us, and I nodded my head at Eliza so that she would go without a fight.

They rode us out through the woods for quite a ways, and then we were out on a ridge overlooking a deep gulch. We rode the lip of the ridge until it dropped down into a grassy valley, but the grass was nearly all dead from lack of rain. We were riding generally to the northeast. We forded a small creek running through the valley, and soon enough the valley turned into rolling hills, and we were riding along beside the steep cliffs of a mountain. We came to another creek and followed it north, riding for several miles along the bank of the creek.

No one spoke. We rode pretty hard without stopping or walking the horses, and the sun traversed the sky as we went.

It was coming on to late afternoon when at last we turned away from the creek, rode over a big ridge and then followed a rocky, switchback path down into a deep and narrow gulch, and when we reached the bottom of the gulch we at last came to a halt. There before us were a half dozen roughly constructed log cabins, and waiting outside were another half dozen or more of Murrieta's men.

"Take them down off their horses and tie them up over by the tree," Murrieta said to his men, and he went directly into one of the cabins while a couple of his men took the saddle off his horse.

Night was coming fast, and down in the gulch the sun was already well below the horizon. It was difficult to see. There was a dry creek bed running through the bottom of the gulch, and a few scattered California pines ran the length of the gulch. The cabins had been built in a clearing – I presumed Murrieta and his men had made the clearing by felling the trees they used to build the cabins. On either side of the gulch there were steep, barren hillsides, rocky and dusty with enormous boulders jutting out from the hillsides.

Murrieta's men treated us roughly, pushing us over the rocky terrain to one of the tall pine trees, and there they lashed our wrists and ankles and pushed us onto the ground at the base of the tree. The fat Mexican who'd taken my guns sat down on a boulder not far from us and watched us. The others all tended to their horses and then took the saddles off Courage and Eliza's horse.

With our hands bound in front and our ankles tied together, we sat down on the rocky ground under a tall pine. I was finding it hard to catch my breath. Bound and abducted by banditos – it had not been this bad for me since that day in Mexico when a couple of rancheros lassoed me and tried to drag me to my death. Not even when them Injuns were chasing me and killed Weenonaw. At least then I was on the run and not captured and bound like this. In my fear, I prayed to God that Marcilina de la Garza would step out of one of Joaquin Murrieta's log cabins and commence to shooting these Mexican bastards that had kidnapped us. That seemed an impossible salvation, though.

"What are we going to do?" Eliza whispered at me.

I was too scared to think. The whole day, throughout the ride up to Murrieta's hideout, I had looked for any opportunity to try to escape. But all I could think of was watching John Ross's men shoot down Weenonaw on that riverbank. The image flashed through my mind over and over. I could not bear to now watch Murrieta and his men kill Eliza. Nor could I bear to imagine what they intended to do to me.

I'd been in enough tight spots – even at that point in my life – and I was certain sure that if some opportunity came along I would be able to seize it and escape. And once away, I believed there was no way Joaquin Murrieta and his men would be able to recapture me.

But I could not see how I would also get Eliza out with me. It was one thing for me to make a mad scramble to safety on my own, but I could not think up an opportunity that would allow me to get Eliza safely away as well.

"I do not know," I said. "I am thinking."

Especially now, tied and exhausted, I racked my brain to try to decide what I would do if I had an opportunity to run. Would I stay with Eliza and endure whatever fate Joaquin Murrieta could design for us, or would I run and save myself?

"Can we have our blankets?" I asked the fat Mexican watching us, but he ignored me and did not answer.

It was a terrible night. We were high enough up in the Sierra Nevada that the night was chilly, and that was made worse because our clothes were soaked with sweat from the ride in the scorching sun. We were hungry, having eaten almost nothing for breakfast, and we'd had nothing all day. The Mexicans had a half dozen women or so – a couple of them were Mexican, a couple Indians and at least one white woman – who cooked up some supper over an open flame. The food smelled decent enough, but they offered us none of it. The ground was too rocky for us to find any comfort in lying down. I leaned back with my back and head on the ground and told Eliza to lay against me so that maybe she could get some sleep, but if she slept it was for nothing more than short spells when exhaustion forced her to nod off. But her discomfort was quick to wake her back up.

When Eliza was not lying against me, I tried to work the knots on the rope tied around my wrists, but there was nothing I could do to get them loose, and my efforts seemed to only make the knot chew deeper into my flesh.

I expected when the sun came up that Joaquin Murrieta would announce his plans for us, or kill us, or whatever he had in mind. But all through the morning he ignored us. Murrieta and his men spent most of the day talking near the campfire. Several of the men rode off during the afternoon but came back a while later with water, I assumed they got it from the creek we'd ridden along. They poured some of the water into a trough for the horses and the rest they drank or used to cook. They did not offer us any water, nor did they waste any of it on a bath for themselves, no matter how desperately they needed it.

I listened whenever I could to our abductors. They spoke mostly in Spanish, and they talked so fast that I could only understand the smallest amount of what they said. I did learn that some of the others, four of them as it turned out, all also bore the first name Joaquin, and so they called them all by their first and last names. Joaquin Murrieta. Joaquin Botellier. Joaquin Carrillo. Joaquin Ocomorenia. Joaquin Valenzuela. I now understood, too, why some of the prospectors who told us about the banditos referred to them as "The Five Joaquins." I also understood how the Bandito Joaquin could be in Los Angeles one day and up on the Feather River the next. There were five of them riding across California, marauding and causing mischief, which made it much easier for one man to be in five places at once. [43]

The fat Mexican stood guard over us most of the day, and I learned that his name was Manuel Garcia. Later he would adopt a new moniker that most folks would know him by.

Though there were five Joaquins, there was no doubt which one was in charge.

At one point during the day one of the others, I believe it was Joaquin Ocomorenia, lit a cigar and began puffing away on it. Soon, Joaquin Murrieta appeared from inside one of the log cabins. The two of them began arguing, and from what I could gather, Joaquin Murrieta was livid that Ocomorenia was smoking on of Murrieta's cigars. They both shouted at each other, and then a minute later Joaquin Murrieta knocked the other Joaquin to the ground with a punch to the throat. When Ocomorenia was on the ground, gasping for air, Joaquin Murrieta sat on top of him and bashed him in the face with his fists. Then Murrieta drew out a knife and used it to cut the lobe off of one of Joaquin Ocomorenia's ears. The other Joaquin squealed with pain and begged for mercy, but none of the other men offered him any assistance.

Joaquin Murrieta was the unchallenged master of these banditos, and he ruled them with brutality.

When he was finished carving up Ocomorenia's ear, he snatched up one of the Indian women who served as a cook and he dragged her by the hair into one of the log cabins. With a lump in my throat, I wondered if that was the fate in store for Eliza. And if it was, I wondered if I might steal away while Murrieta was so occupied.

The banditos of the Five Joaquins all laughed and joked as the woman screamed and begged to be left alone, and her screams did not subside until after Joaquin Murrieta left the cabin. And this is the man that Yellowbird turned into a romantic hero.

Joaquin Ocomorenia, meanwhile, wrapped a bandage around his head to stop the bleeding from his ear, but he never raised an objection or complaint with Murrieta.

I did not know what Joaquin Murrieta intended for me, or for Eliza, but I could guess that it would be frightfully unpleasant.

I suppose it was just boredom later in the day that made me start kicking away the loose gravel of the dry creek bed. Maybe it was habit after months of shoveling sand and swirling it around in a pan. Regardless of what made me do it, I started digging my heels into the dirt and kicking it around. It was not that I expected to find anything worthwhile in Murrieta's hidden camp, but there was nothing else to do.

And then I saw a flash of yellow as I kicked over some fresh dirt. I leaned forward to get a better look at it, and I was sure it was a tiny nugget of gold. I kicked my heels in a little deeper, pushed the dirt around, and I was certain that I saw another flash of gold. I looked around and realized that some of the nearby boulders had streaks of quartz running through them.

Was it possible, I wondered, that Joaquin Murrieta and his banditos were sitting on top of pay dirt and had no idea?

The more I kicked at the dirt with my heels, the more convinced I was that there was gold all in that dry creek bed.

I realized that I had not completely given up on any hope of escape when I caught myself kicking the dirt and rocks back into place with the thought that if I got out of this trouble I might find my way back here and do some digging.

Late in the afternoon, while there was still light, some of them took turns shooting at clay pots they stacked on a boulder.

But they never talked to us. They never offered us food nor water. None of the Joaquins. Not Manuel Garcia who watched over us with a musket in his hand and my Paterson in his belt.

Exhaustion had overtaken us both, and Eliza and I fell in and out of sleep through the next night. But we were so hungry, so thirsty and so cold that neither of us ever slept for long.

We did not talk much, either. There was nothing to say. I cannot speak for Eliza, but I was too frightened for conversation. If I said anything at all, through a dry throat, I whispered to Eliza to keep hoping. "There might yet be an opportunity for escape," I told her.

"I know, Jack, that you faced many tribulations in the war," Eliza said. "I trust you to know what's best to do and to get us out of this alive."

Well, that was misplaced trust if ever trust was misplaced, but I didn't bother disabusing her of the notion.

I thought of the Texas Rangers I'd been with in Mexico – Ben McCulloch, Big Jim, and Cherokee Cock. How would they have dealt with this situation? Ignorant bravery was the conclusion I reached. They would demand Joaquin Murrieta do his worst or turn them loose, and surely they would be shot dead for their demands.

I wondered how Stand Watie would respond to this terrible situation. Probably not differently from McCulloch or Cockrell.

In the early morning of our second day as hostages of the bandito Joaquin Murrieta, still long before the sun came up, Eliza whispered to me, "Jack, are you asleep?"

"I am not," I whispered back. Our throats were both dry, and our whispers hoarse.

"In one of your letters, when you were still in Mexico, you told me that you rode into Santa Anna's camp with the Texas Rangers."

"That's right," I said. "I did do that."

"Jack, I thought Santa Anna was the Mexican general."

"He was," I said.

"Then why did you ride into his camp?"

I told Eliza all about our midnight reconnaissance ride to Encarnacion, the ranch where Santa Anna's army was encamped. I told her about riding through the pickets, our mad dash through the camp, knocking over tents and kicking down stacked arms. I told her about counting the campfires – and even exhausted, starving and scared as I was, I took credit for Ben McCulloch's arithmetic. And then I told her about our dash to safety.

"How many were there?" she asked me.

"How many what?"

"Campfires," Eliza said. "How many did you count?"

"Oh, I don't have any idea. I cannot remember now."

"That's too bad," Eliza said. "Do you think they are going to kill us?"

I thought they were going to do a good bit worse than that to Eliza, but I didn't want to tell her what I thought.

"They might," I said.

"Do you think we can get away?" Eliza asked.

By this time I did not think we could get away. I was exhausted and weak, and I thought that even if Joaquin Murrieta cut the ropes binding me and told me I had an hour to run before he would pursue, I would not make it more than a hundred yards from the camp. But I also did not want to tell Eliza that.

"We might," I said.

"I hope we do," Eliza said. "This is not what I wanted to have happen. But if I must die, Jack, I'm not afraid to die with you."

I suppose she was attempting to express affection and demonstrate to me that she was also brave, but it was that sort of foolish notion that left so many husbands and wives dead from the

Mississippi to the Pacific back in those days. Over and over back then, husbands and wives settling or traveling would together face down a band of murderous Injuns or a gang of thieves, all raping and killing and taking whatever they wanted out on the prairies or high in the mountains, and the only thing it ever got those husbands and wives was two graves dug side by side.

Had I ever homesteaded out on the prairie, ye can bet for sure that if I saw the dust trail of a dozen braves billowing over the distant landscape, I'd have been astride my horse and fleeing to higher ground before my wife had time to ask if we were having visitors for supper.

***

I was asleep when dawn broke, and I did not wake up when Murrieta's banditos started to stir. So I was asleep when Joaquin Murrieta kicked me in the head to wake me up. He had not kicked me hard, so the pain was not so bad as the shock of being awake. My wrists and ankles burned where the ropes had rubbed them raw. My mouth was dry from lack of water, and I felt weak from no food. I was stiff and sore, too, from sleeping on a pile of rocks. Eliza was already awake and sitting up.

"Tell me Lieutenant Speed," Murrieta said when my eyes were open, "your country won the war against my country. The United States has taken vast territories from the Mexican people. But I want to know from you, from an officer of the United States army who fought against my people, today, sitting here in my camp, do you feel like you won a great victory over the people of Mexico? Do you feel like you are the victor?"

"We could use some water," I said. "And some food."

Murrieta leaned down toward me and slapped me across the face with the back of his hand. I saw stars when he hit me, and my jaw felt like it was no longer in the right spot.

"When I ask you a question, lieutenant, I expect you to answer it.

Do you feel victorious?"

"Not particularly," I muttered.

Murrieta leaned back and laughed, and some of his men who were watching all laughed with him. I doubted if many of them spoke English or understood what we were saying.

"I have been looking at your wife," Murrieta said. "I believe I will take her as my own wife. I believe she will find I am a much better husband to her than you are. Do you like to know that I intend to take your wife as my own?"

"You'll not!" Eliza said, though her voice was hoarse. "I already have a husband, and I'll not be taking another."

"Oh, but you'll soon not have a husband, and when your husband is dead you will want a husband who can protect you," Murrieta said.

I mustered up whatever courage I had, which was not much, and faced Murrieta like Ben McCulloch would.

"Why not just kill me?" I said. "Why leave us tied here?"

Murrieta nodded as if he was glad I asked the question. "Before I kill you, I want you to know, Lieutenant Speed, what it feels like to be conquered. If you are to eat, you must beg me for food. If you are to drink, you must beg me for water. Because you are conquered. You are not victorious. Do you understand? I am victorious over you!"

"The army is coming for you," I said. "Ye've raided too many camps, killed too many men. When we were in Hangtown two days ago, or maybe it was three days ago, they were talking about it. I imagine it'll be Cump Sherman who leads a cavalry regiment up into these mountains to find you. Maybe they're already up here, closing in on you now."

Joaquin Murrieta looked at me to see if there was evidence that I was lying. For just a moment, I saw his confidence disappear. The thought of a cavalry regiment in the mountains seeking him out seemed to make him nervous. And because I provided a name of the man leading the cavalry, it gave some weight to my words. Of course, I had no idea if what I was saying was true, but neither did Murrieta, and it rattled him. So I pressed the issue.

"If they find us as your prisoners, especially a white woman, they'll slaughter you and all your men. Any survivors will be hung from that tree over there," I said, nodding toward a nearby pine.

Murrieta even looked over at the tree.

"Yes, sir," I continued. For a second time, I gave him the name of the only army man in California I knew, hoping that naming an officer would lend credibility to what I was saying. "Lieutenant Tecumseh Sherman and the cavalry. They'll be on you soon enough. Why, Cump Sherman loves chasing down banditos better than any other army work."

Murrieta kicked me in the head again, though this time the pain came from the force of the kick and not from the surprise of it. I reeled and fell over with lights dancing in front of my eyes and a ringing in my ear.

Murrieta walked back over to his men. The day before I had counted them. There were nineteen men in the camp, including Murrieta hisself and the other four Joaquins. Murrieta talked to his men in Spanish, and though I'd picked up a little of the language while living with Marcilina de la Garza, they spoke too fast for me to catch everything they said. Though I got the gist of it – Murrieta was telling some of his men to ride back to Hangtown and see if the army was really forming up to come look for them.

In a moment, eight of the men saddled their horses and rode out of the canyon, up the switchback trail and out of view. As they rode off, one of the other men brought us a couple of plates of stew and a canteen of water.

With our wrists tied, all we could do was hold the plates to our faces and eat the stew like dogs. At first, Eliza refused to eat.

"Keep up your strength," I told her. "If there is a chance to run, we've got to be strong enough to do it."

Reluctantly, she ate the food off the plate, and we shared the water.

When we had some of our strength back, I said to Eliza, "Do you think you can loosen this rope on my wrists?"

"Maybe," she said. "Slide over closer to me."

Eliza took a sharp rock in her hands and went to carving on the ropes. It was slow going, but thread by thread she was chewing through the rope. I kept a watch on the Mexicans to make sure none of them were paying any attention to us.

With eight of Murrieta's men riding to Hangtown, I decided our chance was going to have to come soon. I doubted that the odds would ever get better than eleven to one. If I was going to run, I needed to do it soon while those eight men were out of the camp.

An hour or so later, with Eliza still cutting at the rope, I watched as the fat Mexican, Manuel Garcia, led Courage out of the corral. He'd put my saddle on my horse, and was now going to try to ride Courage. I noted, too, that he still had my Paterson tucked in his belt, and the carbine was back in its scabbard strapped to my saddle. The fat bastard had taken possession of all my belongings. I felt thankful that my britches were too small to get around his belly.

The fat Manuel Garcia took Courage by the reins and tried to step into the stirrup, but Courage – smart horse that he was – had calculated Manuel Garcia's girth and wasn't having none of that on his back. Courage danced in circles, keeping the fat Mexican from getting a foot into the stirrup. Garcia cussed the horse and jerked on the reins, and finally Courage held still.

"I've almost got it," Eliza whispered, and just then I felt the tension on my wrist break as the rope gave way. My hands were free.

I reached down to my feet and picked at the knot tying my ankles together. It was tough to do, I was nearly panicked. My heart was thumping so fast in my chest for fear that one of the banditos would see that my wrists were loose.

Just as the fat Mexican hefted himself up into my saddle on my horse, the knot gave way and I was able to slide an end of the rope out of the knot. Now I was pulling both ends of the rope back out of the knot, and in a moment I would be free.

The fat Mexican rested his weight down into the saddle, and at that moment Courage reared, kicking his forelegs out high into the air as he stood up tall on his hind legs.

Manuel Garcia, arms flapping in the air like a fat, flightless bird, slid off the back of my horse and landed roughly on his back, the air all knocked out of him.

I was weak and sore, and as I pushed myself to my feet, I found that my legs and feet were nearly worthless, but absolute, sheer terror spurred me on. Without a word to Eliza, who had just helped me secure my freedom from those ropes, I ran as fast as I could manage right toward Courage.

Planting a foot on Manuel Garcia's fat face, I launched myself toward Courage, grabbing hold of the saddle horn and dragging myself onto his back.

Already, before I'd managed to drag myself into the saddle, Courage was breaking into a full run, heading directly toward the switchback path. It's a fact that I was always a good horseman, and I never did yet see a horse I couldn't make useful when it came time to run from trouble, but Courage always seemed to sense before I gave a command which way to go when a chase was on. And sometimes he knew better than me.

All hell was breaking loose behind me as I struggled to grab hold of the reins. I could hear Murrieta's banditos shouting up a terrible commotion, and as Courage maneuvered through the first switchback on the trail leading out of the gulch, I heard a shot as one of them fired a musket at us. I buried my head into Courage's mane, and prayed that the horse had legs to get us up the trail and out of that canyon before they got off another shot. And my prayers were answered as Courage dashed from one switchback to the next, taking the trail at a speed that was neither safe for me nor him. But his ankles didn't turn, and I didn't fall out of the saddle, and lickety-split we were reaching the ridge above and racing toward the creek in the long valley.

I did not look back. I knew that I could not bear it if I looked back in time to see them shoot Eliza, if that's what they chose to do. It made me sick to think that I had abandoned her, but there was nothing else for it. The opportunity for which I had prayed had presented itself, and I would have been a fool to not take advantage of it. It was not my fault that the opportunity had only been for one of us and not for both of us.

We rode hard for the creek, and when we got to it, I turned Courage to jump it. I'd seen on the other side of the creek that there were trees where we might disappear from sight. I knew it would not take the banditos long to follow, and I did not want to get caught out in the open valley where they could see me and have it be a race all the way to Hangtown.

Once we were in among the trees, I pulled Courage to a stop. I drew out the carbine to be sure it was still loaded, and then I dismounted. Hiding among the trees, I watched the ridge and waited for the banditos who I was sure would be coming after me.

It took them longer to give chase than I expected. I suppose they had to devise a plan and saddle up their horses, but I would have thought they would be chasing me almost immediately. I suppose it was as much as half an hour after I made my escape that I watched as five riders came up over the ridge and raced down to the creek. They followed the creek through the valley the same way we had approached Murrieta's hideout two days before. I watched them ride down the valley until they were out of sight.

I could not believe my luck. I was convinced that Joaquin Murrieta was going to murder me in that damned gulch and bury me in the dry creek bed. The fact that I was free and on the run was nothing short of a miracle. And now I had been blessed a second time, as my pursuers rode off for Hangtown, while I watched them go, hidden in the woods.

I got back in the saddle, and instead of following the valley to the southwest to go back toward Hangtown and the goldfields, I decided to turn north – the opposite direction from the way the posse chasing me had gone – and try to find my way back to civilization in that direction.

I figured once I was back to safety I could find the army and tell them how to find Murrieta's camp. And maybe they would find Eliza still alive.

CHAPTER 22

It was a thin wood I was riding through, and I was scared to death that the pursuers Murrieta had sent after me would turn back and find me. Hiding among these trees was getting more difficult as the woods got thinner the farther I went.

Courage and I picked our way slowly among the trees. I supposed we could have gone quicker, but Courage seemed reluctant to take every step. And I was reluctant to hurry him along.

I've mourned a fair few people in my life, but I never did feel the necessity to risk my own life to save someone else's. I always reckoned that as sorrowful as another man – or woman's – death might have been to me, suffering the grief was a far sight better than getting killed meself.

As such, the feelings of regret that were troubling me were foreign and unfamiliar to me. But that's what was keeping me from running as fast as I should have. I was feeling remorse over abandoning Eliza behind. And with each step that Courage took, I felt all the worse about it.

There weren't but six of them left in the camp, I told myself. And I'm not a bad shot with the carbine. I thought about maybe sneaking back up to the canyon, positioning myself behind one of the boulders, and picking off Murrieta's banditos one at a time. I had five shots in the carbine. I reasoned that if I shot three or four of them, maybe the others would run.

I considered, too, that maybe I could sneak into the canyon after dark, untie Eliza and sneak her out.

At the least, I told myself, I could sneak back into the canyon and just see for myself what was happening. Maybe there would be another opportunity that would present itself, an opportunity to get Eliza out of there.

But I told myself, too, that most likely Murrieta had already shot and killed Eliza in a fit of rage over my escape, and going back would only endanger myself unnecessarily.

Even as Courage continued to go north, I told myself that Ben McCulloch or Cherokee Cock or Stand Watie would go back for their wives. None of those men would leave a woman to a brute like Joaquin Murrieta. They would, at least, go back and know for sure.

I could sneak into the canyon and if there was no opportunity to get Eliza out, I could always leave and continue to flee north and hope to send Cump Sherman and the cavalry to save her. And if she was already dead, if Murrieta had killed her because I had gone on escape, I could at least tell Sherman where to take his cavalry to exact my revenge.

At length, after going back and forth in my mind, I convinced myself that it would be no thing to at least sneak into the canyon, position myself above the gulch behind a boulder, and see for myself whether or not there was an opportunity to rescue my wife, even if it went against every natural tendency I possessed.

"All right, damn ye," I said to the horse, as if it was his idea, "let's go back and see if we can rescue Eliza."

At the word, with no other prompting from me, Courage wheeled around and began a quick trot through the trees, retracing our path quite a bit faster than we'd been going. It was almost as if he understood me and had just been waiting for the command. But then, Courage was often uncanny like that.

Before we got to the canyon, I led Courage out of the woods and back across the creek, and then up to ridge that would eventually overlook the canyon. I had a good view of the valley and could see none of Murrieta's banditos riding through the valley. The men he'd sent after me had expected I would flee the way I'd come to the camp, the way that was familiar to me, and I imagined they were probably going at a full run back toward Hangtown. Meanwhile, I was coming back toward the camp from the opposite direction.

The ridge I was traveling along now broke into two big ridges, one that dropped south to the east and the other dropped south to the west, and a big canyon formed between the two ridges. I realized that this canyon was where Murrieta's camp was located.

I pulled Courage to a halt and studied the lay of the land. This eastern ridge, it was the one I'd ridden over on the switchback trail, and it was where I initially thought I would approach Murrieta's camp from.

But the eastern ridge was rocky and barren, and my approach would have to be slow and careful. The eastern ridge, too, would be the one where the afternoon sun would shine down upon me and make me easy to see as I tried to move along the ridge.

The western ridge was heavily wooded at the top. The steep slope into the canyon was equally barren and rocky, but the trees at the top of the ridge were thick and would conceal me as I neared the camp. And anyone down in the canyon looking up at the western ridge would have the afternoon sun in their eyes, and that might also help to conceal my approach. I also believed they would never expect me to make my return on the western slope, if they even expected that I would return at all.

Courage and I trotted over to the western ridge and up to the top of it where we could ride through the woods and not have to worry about being seen. It was not long before I found myself overlooking the camp with the log cabins, the dry creek bed and what remained of Joaquin Murrieta's banditos.

I lashed Courage's reins to a branch and slid the carbine out of its scabbard.

My plan had worked well. Coming out of the woods and slowly creeping down to the first big boulder overlooking Murrieta's camp, I knew that no one in the canyon would be able to easily see me with the afternoon sun coming down behind me. Unless I stood tall on the ridge and made a silhouette against the sky, I was convinced they would not see me up on the slope of the canyon.

Positioned behind a big boulder, I was able to peer around it and have a good view of the camp.

Unbelievably, I could see that Eliza was still down near the dry creek bed where I had left her. I thought surely if they had not killed her they would have at least moved her, but she was still in the same spot. I could even see the ropes that had bound my wrists and ankles still on the ground beside her.

Manuel Garcia, the fat Mexican who had tried to ride Courage, was standing near the cabins with my Paterson still tucked in his belt and a musket in his hands. Joaquin Murrieta was there, too, engaged in conversation with Garcia. Murrieta was in a rage. He was very animated as he spoke, driving one hand into the other to emphasize his words, pacing back and forth before Garcia, and pointing first one way and then another. I did not know if he was still raging over my escape, but I took some satisfaction in believing that he was.

From my vantage point I could see Joaquin Murrieta and Manuel Garcia. A different Mexican was now guarding Eliza. So that was three of them I could see. By my count, there should be three more banditos down in the canyon, but I did not immediately see them. They might have been in the cabins, or maybe they were standing guard on the hillside. I did not think they had been sent away because there were still several horses in the corral.

The women who cooked the meals were engaged at a water trough behind the cabins where they were washing clothes. I could see all seven of them.

I was not close enough to shoot Garcia and Joaquin Murrieta, but from where I was sure I could easily shoot the Mexican standing over Eliza. I could shoot him and take a wild shot at Murrieta and Garcia, maybe force them into a cabin. But Eliza could not get up and run, and I was not about to chase down into that canyon and try to get her out.

And even if I did somehow manage to get her, I still had no way to escape Murrieta. Both of us on Courage would slow us down. Murrieta would easily catch us. Eliza would need a horse or we had no prayer of getting away.

From behind the boulder I weighed my options, and everything seemed to suggest I had made a mistake in coming back. I had made good my escape. I had lost the posse – sent them in the wrong direction entirely. All I'd had to do was keep riding until I found civilization. But foolishly I had returned to the danger.

The Mexican guarding Eliza was paying no attention to her. He was standing nearby, but he was watching Murrieta and Garcia. Murrieta was still full of rage, shouting at Garcia. He would pace back and forth, turn and shout some more.

I could not think of any way that I could rescue Eliza. The only possible hope I had of trying to get her out of there would be after dark, and it would require me to sneak into the gulch, steal a horse, tackle and saddle, cut her loose and ride out without alerting Murrieta or any of his men. And all this, I knew, would be impossible.

I crouched behind the boulder, knowing there was no hope that I could do anything here for Eliza. There was still the chance that I could ride out, find Lieutenant Sherman or someone with the army, and send back help. Murrieta had not yet killed her, maybe it was possible that the cavalry could find her before he did.

I decided then that I would crawl back up the canyon slope, gather up Courage and make my dash for safety. I had qualms about abandoning my wife for a second time in one day, but I saw nothing else for it.

And that's when a commotion on the opposite canyon slope caught my attention. It was over at the top of the ridge on the switchback trail. I looked around my boulder and saw that the riders who'd been sent to chase me down were now returning. Five men were coming over the top of the ridge and riding down into the canyon along the switchback trail.

I watched below me as Joaquin Murrieta and Manuel Garcia stopped their talking and stepped out away from the cabin so that they could look up the trail to see who was returning. I could almost see Murrieta's mind working as he counted the riders. And with only five horsemen riding down the trail, Murrieta knew they had failed to find me.

He stomped away from the cabin toward the base of the trail, which was not terribly far from where Eliza was. Manuel Garcia followed Murrieta.

As the riders reached the bottom of the gulch, they dismounted, and before they could offer excuses or explanations, Joaquin Murrieta set about them in a rage – a continuation of what he'd been giving to Manuel Garcia.

Somewhere in the camp there were still three banditos I'd not yet seen. Below me now the numbers I knew about had grown from three to eight. But Murrieta and Garcia both had walked into easy range. I could hit them, or damn near, from where I was.

And there, just a few steps from Eliza, were five horses, recently unburdened from their riders who had all dismounted. If she were not tied, now might be the opportunity simply because she would have a horse on which to make her escape.

I wondered if I should try something reckless and foolish. Just below my perch there was another large boulder. I laid flat on the ground and slid myself down toward it. I was closer now. I was certain I could hit at least one target from here, if not two, before the men could scatter. But I still had no way to get Eliza on one of those horses.

Thinking of her, I glanced away from Murietta, still raging at his men, and looked at Eliza. She made an odd sight, sitting there among those shouting Mexicans, all forgotten and forlorn. But she was working like the devil at something. It was hard for me to see from the angle I was at because the big pine tree was in the way. So I shifted to the other side of the boulder and looked around to see if it gave me a better angle. And indeed it did! I could see that Eliza – with her captors paying no attention to her, was picking at her ropes with something pressed between her hands. I could not be certain, but it looked to me like she had her sharpened rock and was cutting loose her bonds.

I prayed that she would hurry. Now was the time. If I saw that rope snap, I knew I could drop one or two of the banditos. And maybe I could scatter the others. And maybe it would buy her enough time to get mounted.

It would mean a chase, for sure, but with renewed hope that Eliza might escape, I believed we could out pace Murietta and his men.

I pulled the hammer of the carbine back to half-cock and waited.

One of the banditos who'd been sent after me was now shouting his excuses at Murrieta, but Joaquin grabbed the man and shook him by the shoulders, shouting in his face. They were shouting Spanish at each other, so I couldn't understand everything, but Joaquin was saying he'd told them not to come back without me.

And then I saw the movement I'd been waiting for. Eliza's hands suddenly parted – the rope had snapped. And now she was pulling against the knot on her ankles, and I could see her desperation, I knew her fear that she get her ankles free before anyone saw that she'd broken the bonds on her wrists.

I slowly, as silently as I could, thumbed back the hammer on the carbine all the way.

"Come on, Eliza," I whispered to myself. "Faster, girl. Faster."

Now her hands were working frantically. She'd loosed the first end of the rope.

I looked back to the Mexicans to be sure none of them took a glance at her.

Others of the men who'd ridden after me were now shouting back at Murrieta, and that fat bastard Garcia had stepped in and was yelling back at them.

And that's when all hell broke loose. So many things happened at once.

The Mexican who'd been standing guard over Eliza had been a spectator of the shouting match this whole time, but just now he started to turn to look down at his charge.

Without giving thought to the consequences, I took aim with the carbine to shoot him down before he could do anything to stop Eliza. She'd not yet gotten the rope around her ankles completely untied.

But before I pulled the trigger on the carbine, one of Joaquin Murrieta's banditos decided he'd had enough with getting yelled at, and he drew out a big knife and lunged for Murrieta.

Garcia, seeing the man coming with the knife, drew his revolver and gut-shot the bandito.

Eliza's guard turned back quick to see who'd been shot, but when Garcia's revolver went off, I pulled my own trigger, and the Mexican who'd been guarding Eliza went down in a heap with a great big hole opened up in his back.

I cocked back the hammer on the carbine to bring up the next cylinder. Murrieta, Garcia, and the other four banditos – not including the one who'd been gut shot – all started looking around to see where my shot had come from. They were all snatching out their pistolas.

It was all happening in half-seconds. Garcia and Murrieta were both obscured from my view because of the pine tree. I did not have a sure shot at either of them. Two of the other banditos were half-hidden behind their horses. But the other two presented easy targets.

The men down in the canyon were looking at both slopes. They had no idea where I'd shot from.

I aimed carefully and fired my second shot with the carbine. I hit one of the banditos in the leg. He dropped his gun and began to holler, limping away on one foot and screaming, "Asesinado! Asesinado!"

I glanced at Eliza and in a half-second wondered what foolishness had got into her head. She was still seated on the ground, but she was snatching up her skirt and exposing her legs. And then I remembered: – the revolver under her dress! I watched as Eliza slid it from its holster, cocked back the hammer and pointed it in the general direction of the Mexicans.

I took aim again and fired the carbine just as Eliza shot.

Two shots at once must have been enough to convince Joaquin Murrieta and his banditos that they needed to seek shelter. All of them who were still standing jumped into a run, making for the log cabins.

"Eliza!" I shouted. "The horses! Get on one of those horses and come now!"

Eliza fired another wild shot at the fleeing Mexicans, but that was the only delay. She ran over to the horses and took one by the reins. She swung herself quickly into the saddle, and then had the presence of mind to round up the other horses and chase them toward the switchback trail.

The banditos had run to the first log cabin, and I now took a long shot at the cabin. Whether my shot hit the cabin or not, I did not know, but it was enough to keep Murrieta or the others from opening the door.

Unlike Murrieta and his men, Eliza had found me up on the slope. Astride the horse, she was now at the foot of the switchback trail. The other four horses, all riderless, were dashing up the trail.

"There's no trail on that side!" Eliza shouted to me.

"Go!" I said. "Get to the ridge and turn that way!" I pointed generally north. "These two ridges meet a few miles from here. I'll meet you!"

Now I ran, as best I could up the steep slope of the canyon, to where Courage was tied. He was antsy after hearing the gunfire, dancing around. I untied him and got into the saddle, and as quick as he could, Courage was racing along through the trees. I had to duck low to dodge a few low branches, but most of the California pines were tall with all the branches up near the tops.

I did not know if we had seconds or minutes of a head start on Murrieta and his gang. I was sure they would be after us with a plan to commit murder. I did not know if they had heard what I'd shouted, about Eliza riding to the north. My gut was turning summersaults, and my heart was pounding in my throat. I was full of fear, imagining all the ways Murrieta would catch us before we could reach safety.

CHAPTER 23

"The other horses followed me," Eliza said, riding up to the spot where the two ridges came together. I'd out-paced her to this point, and it had been a nervous few minutes waiting for her until she rode into view. Behind her were three horses without riders. I was not sure what had happened to the fourth.

By way of explanation for her train of horses, Eliza said, "When I rode out on this one, the other horses were already running up the trail — I suppose they were frightened from all the shooting. I reached the top of the ridge, and the horses all just sort of followed me."

It was a small miracle, really. Any pursuit Murrieta and the others might have offered would now be delayed. The only horses in camp that were saddled and ready to go were with us. Murrieta and his gang of banditos would have to take the time to saddle other horses. Easily, it could give us a half hour lead on Murrieta. If we were lucky, there would not be enough saddles or tackle, maybe not even enough good horses, and Murrieta would be forced to leave some portion of his gang behind.

Perhaps more importantly, the horses that followed Eliza were also toting weaponry. All four of the horses had muskets on their saddles, and a quick look through the saddle bags revealed they were also carrying balls and powder. If it came to a shooting match, at least I was better armed now. My plan, though, was to not allow the thing to reach that point.

"We should not linger," I said.

With no riders to tell them different, the other horses kept following, which suited me fine. It meant we could ride pretty hard and switch mounts, and now we rode hard. It was already getting dark, but I believed we had to keep moving.

Eliza was exhausted, and it was only fear that was pushing me on. We both needed to eat and sleep. But I knew somewhere behind us Joaquin Murrieta was pursuing.

So we pressed on through the darkness. I dismounted and walked ahead while Eliza rode. We were in a forest of California pines and firs and cypress trees that seemed to go on forever, and with the sun down we could not move quickly for fear of braining ourselves on a low branch or getting turned around and lost in the woods. So I walked ahead, leading Courage, with Eliza and the other horses all following.

At length we stopped, tied up the horses and relieved them of their saddles, and we slept for what remained of the night on a bed of dirt and pine needles.

We slept later than we should have. Even so, when I woke up I took the time to reload the carbine and Eliza's revolver. I checked the saddle bags on the horses for any food. There were canteens with water, which was a godsend, but we had nothing to eat.

I gently shook Eliza awake. "We need to keep moving," I said to her. "Eliza, darling, we've got to keep moving."

She opened her eyes and smiled when she saw me. "Oh, Jack. Thank you for coming back for me. When you ran and got on Courage, I thought I was doomed. I could not believe you had left me there. I feared you had ridden back to Hangtown to try to rise up a posse to come and rescue me, and I worried you would be too late to save me. Joaquin Murrieta was in such a state! He yelled and cursed and stomped his feet, and I thought surely he would shoot me dead. But Jack, you're my hero, you came back for me."

I kissed her forehead. "I would never leave you," I said. "I just had to find the right moment to get you out of there."

I helped her to her feet, and she wrapped her arms around me. I held her close for a moment, but I was eager to be on our way. "We should go now," I said.

"Surely they'll never find us in this forest," Eliza said.

"We've been following a deer path," I said. "If they found the path and they stuck to it, they will still be behind us. We cannot waste any time."

I could see that Eliza was exhausted. And we were both hungry. I would have liked to have found some blackberries, but it was too late in the season for blackberries anyway.

Mostly we'd gone through a valley, but now we were coming to a mountain ridge and we were going to have to go over it. We rode the horses, but we could not move fast. Even along the trail, we hit steep sections where it was difficult for the horses to climb, and at times we were both forced to dismount and walk. It was exhausting and worse than that we were moving too slow.

I did not know much of anything about California beyond what I'd seen for myself – the layout of the countryside or the rivers or anything. I knew the Sierra Nevada were to the east, the Pacific Ocean to the west, Oregon to the north and the South Fork of the American River ran between Coloma and Hangtown. I'd heard other miners talk of the Feather River and knew it was somewhere to the north of Hangtown and Coloma. I assumed, therefore, that we would eventually come to the Feather River and be able to follow it until we found a mining camp. Now, with a map in front of me, I know better where we were. We'd come to a small river known now as Pilot Creek, though at the time I suppose it had no name. We were near the South Fork of the Rubicon River, not far from where it meets up with the Middle Fork of the American River.

But at the time, as we descended into a valley and saw a small river below us, I believed we had come across the Feather River. It was midafternoon by now, with the sun already moving over our left shoulders.

"If we follow this river to the west, we will eventually come into mining camps," I said. "That's where we'll find safety."

So we followed Pilot Creek, believing it was the Feather River that, in fact, came nowhere near where we were.

Being in a valley the way we were made me nervous. It was possible that Murrieta might see us from a high ridge and be able to trail us and we would never know he was there. But there was a thick canopy from the trees overhead, and my hope was that we would remain hidden from above.

After an hour or so of following the creek, we dismounted and watered the horses and let them graze on what they could find. While we were dismounted like this, I kept the carbine in my hands and my eyes on the ridges behind us.

"Can we be sure that Murrieta has not followed us?" Eliza said, putting a hand on my shoulder.

"I think we would be fools to believe he has not," I said. "We must be prepared that any moment he could come riding up behind us. We've got to hope that we soon come to a mining camp. Maybe before dark. I don't want to spend another night out here on our own."

I didn't say it to Eliza, but at that moment I was prepared to abandon California. I'd leave the gold to Obadiah, Brother, Slim, Johnny Brooks – hell, I'd even leave the gold to Jimbo. I just wanted to be out of that wretched country and as far away from Joaquin Murrieta as it was possible to get.

When the horses were watered and had eaten the little available to them, we mounted up on fresh horses and set out, following the creek again.

We pushed on like this through the afternoon, and it was coming onto dark when we came upon a large sandbar, and on the sandbar we saw half a dozen men working with shovels. I was relieved to see they were white men and not Mexicans or Indians or Chinamen.

"Y'all boys finding any thing?" I asked, announcing our presence.

The men looked up, a good bit startled to have us ride up like that, and I think they'd have been less friendly if Eliza had not been with me.

"Howdy," one of them said. He watched us as we rode closer to him and down onto the sandbar where he and the others were working. "I sure didn't expect to see a man and woman come riding up like this."

"No, I reckon not," I said. "We on the Feather River here?"

The men all gave each other queer looks, and their spokesman said, "Naw. This ain't the Feather River. This here is just a creek, a tributary to the Rubicon River."

I tried to place the Rubicon River in my understanding of California, but it served no purpose because I had not at that point ever heard of it.

"How long y'all been here?" I asked.

"We've been working this hole about two months," the man said, and I could tell by the look on his face that he remained perplexed as to our existence.

"Diggings any good?" I asked.

"We've done all right," he said. "Say, where are you coming from with a woman with you?"

"Oh," I said, acting astonished that he should be surprised by us. "My name's Lieutenant Jackson Speed, and this is my wife Miss Eliza Speed. The fact is, we was prospecting over on the South Fork of the American River when we were abducted by some banditos. We recently escaped from them, and we are now trying to make our way back toward Hangtown."

The man squished his face up, deep in thought. He took his hat off his head and scratched at his hair. With his other hand, he rubbed the whiskers on his cheeks. He pushed the hat back down on his head.

"I ain't real clear where Hangtown's at," he said.

"Little mining town over near the South Fork of the American River," says I. "Was known for a bit as Dry Diggins."

Now the man's eyes lit up. "Oh, sure, Dry Diggins. We come through there a few months back, before we set off to try digging up here. You're a long way from home."

Now one of the other prospectors who'd been listening to our conversation stepped toward us. "Did you say you was abducted by banditos?" the man asked.

"That's right," says I. As evidence, I held out my wrists that were still cut all to hell from the ropes Murrieta tied me with.

"How come?" the man asked.

"Well, I suppose because they're banditos and that's the sort of thing banditos do," I said.

The man nodded thoughtfully. "I guess that makes sense. Did you catch the name of any of them?"

I hesitated before answering. Joaquin Murrieta's name was infamous among the prospectors, even all the way back to 1849. I didn't want to scare these fellows and have them run us out of their camp. But my calculations were of no use.

"It was the bandito Joaquin Murrieta!" Eliza said. I shot Eliza a look, hoping that she understood that I wanted her to keep quiet. She did not understand my look.

"Tarnation," the second man said. "And where's he at now?"

"We're concerned he might be tracking us," Eliza said. I pursed my lips as if they were buttoned shut and tried to get Eliza to button her own, but it was no use. "We may only be a few hours ahead of him!"

Now a third prospector from the group walked up, having listened to our conversation. "Ain't that the feller we heard about back in the other camps. Ain't he the one shooting up miners and stealing their gold?"

"It sure is," the second one said.

Before the thing got too sideways, I decided to press our issue.

"Look here, boys," says I. "This fellow, whether he's the real Joaquin Murrieta or not, whether he's really following us up or not, none of that really matters. My wife and I need food. We've not eaten a decent meal for a couple of days or more. And we need help. We need to sleep. We need protection."

The three men looked at each other. I noticed the others had abandoned their pans and pickaxes and shovels and were also listening.

"We ain't got a lot extra," the first spokesman of the group said. "We can feed you a little bit, seeing as how you've had some trouble. And if you want to spend the night here, I suppose that's okay. But we're not positioned to offer you anything more than that. Come morning, ye'll have to ride on. We don't need your troubles to become our troubles."

The men all quit their digging for the day and took us to their camp. There we unsaddled our horses while they cooked up some supper. It was just pork and beans, but Eliza and I were both famished and ate with gusto.

The men were generous enough to allow us the use of a tent and blankets, and we both slept soundly through the night. At my encouragement, the men took turns keeping watch through the night.

Come morning, they cooked up a breakfast of bacon, eggs, and cornbread. It wasn't bad at all, and it went a long way toward helping us get back our strength.

The group's spokesman, though, came to me as we were finishing our breakfast and made it clear that we would have to be on our way.

"You follow this creek downstream," he said. "Eventually, maybe eight or ten miles, you'll come to the spot where this creek empties into the Rubicon River. That's the South Fork of the Rubicon. Another mile down river, and the Rubicon meets the Middle Fork of the American River. You keep following that, and it's probably two days – not more than three – to Dry Diggins."

"Are there more mining camps below you here?" I asked.

"We're pretty secluded here," he said. "When you get to the Middle Fork of the American River you won't be far from some good size mining camps, but you'll go quite a ways before you get to them."

"We sure are grateful that y'all gave us a place to sleep and some food," I told the miners. "I suppose now we'd best be on our way. We need to get to where we can find the army and send them to Joaquin Murrieta's hideout."

I was nervous about being out on our own in the wilderness, but we could not stay indefinitely with these miners. They'd made it pretty plain they wanted us gone after breakfast, which was fine with me. I wasn't convinced these men were even capable of offering us any protection if Murrieta and the other banditos showed up.

I walked over to get the horses ready to leave but had only just picked up Courage's saddle when a shot rang out and then echoed off the canyon wall on the opposite side of the river.

I don't know why, but at first I thought nothing of it. I suppose I just thought it was one of the miners shooting at game. But then Eliza screamed, and I looked back to the campfire where she was still sitting with some of the prospectors, and I saw that one of the men at the campfire had fallen to the ground, clutching his belly.

And in an instant, I saw coming through the woods eight or ten men. They were all on foot, but I recognized them as banditos of the gang the Five Joaquins.

I dropped Courage's saddle but grabbed the carbine out of its sheath.

In the campsite, all hell was breaking loose. The prospectors, with one of their own gunned down, were rising to defend themselves. The Five Joaquins, seeking to murder me and Eliza, weren't likely to let these prospectors stand in their way. Using knives and pistolas, the Five Joaquins were making short work of the prospectors who were armed with axes and shovels.

"Eliza!" I shouted. "Hurry to me!"

Eliza had been rooted to the spot when the violence erupted suddenly around her. But hearing me, she jumped up from the campfire and began to run into the woods where I was standing with the carbine in my hands.

One of the banditos spotted Eliza and set off after her at a run, and he was quickly closing the distance on her. He was bound to reach her before she reached me, and there were no prospectors between the two of them to slow his pursuit.

I raised the carbine and took careful aim. It was a tight shot, for I was going to have to shoot past Eliza to hit the man running behind her. I'd spent a fair amount of my youth with my uncle shooting at squirrel and rabbits and deer, and shooting came naturally for me. So I was confident when I pulled back the trigger and the powder exploded. Through the smoke I could see Eliza still running toward me, and the bandito was collapsing to the ground. I wasn't sure that it was a mortal wound, but it had done what was necessary to put him down.

I scanned the campsite. The banditos were all engaged in the fight. The prospectors were rapidly losing the battle. Eliza grabbed up one of the saddles, but I took her by the wrist and pulled her away.

"There's no time for that," I said. "We're on foot now!"

We turned and fled through the woods. There was no path to follow – none that we saw, anyway – and so we just ran away from the sounds of the fight behind us. The river cut a deep canyon, and the terrain was terrible for flight. Under our feet were loose rocks and sandy dirt, and branches from the tall fir and pines were constantly interrupting our progress. But we just kept running without looking back.

Exhaustion was overcoming us when Eliza stumbled on some loose rock and fell to the ground. She cut her hands and elbows on rocks as she tried to catch herself.

While she was on the ground, I grabbed my Bowie knife in my fist and cut away her skirt at about the knees so that she could run easier in it. Only now, for the first time, did I take the opportunity to look behind us to see if Murrieta was giving chase.

"I don't see anyone," Eliza said.

"Nor do I. We've got to keep going, though. They found us at the miners' camp. They'll find us again."

"All those men are dead, aren't they?" Eliza asked.

"I imagine so," I said. "If any of them survive, it won't be for a lack of trying on Murrieta's part. The same is true with us. We should keep moving."

Eliza was still on the ground. Her hands were cut and bloody and she was breathing hard. "I don't know if I can keep going, Jack," she said.

"There's no choice," I said. "If they catch us, they will murder me and do a good bit worse to you." I did not tell her that if she did not get up and start moving I was going to leave her there. But I'd already made my mind up on that account.

I pulled Eliza to her feet. Ahead of us the canyon became rockier and steeper with some sheer drops over granite outcroppings down to the river. We needed to get above this terrain.

"Up the hill," I said. "Get to the top of the ridge. We should keep the river in sight, but we've got to get to higher ground." I pointed a way so that she would still be advancing away from the camp, but up the hill at the same time. "Just go that way, higher than those outcroppings there ahead of us. Keep going to the top of the ridge. I'll follow behind you."

With the carbine up, I scanned the woods behind us, searching for any pursuers. I did not know how far we had come, but I could hear nothing more from the fighting at the camp. Either the Five Joaquin banditos had done in the miners or we had gone so far that we could no longer hear the fighting.

I could see no one behind us. I looked forward and saw that Eliza was nearing the top of the ridge and was up above the rocky outcroppings that dropped down to the river.

A squirrel or a bird or some animal made a noise, and I looked back behind me, my heart in my throat as I expected to see some number of the Five Joaquins behind me. But there was nothing there. I had the stock of the carbine in my shoulder and was looking down the barrel through the woods. It was hard to breathe, and the sweat was running down my face and stinging my eyes. I took a deep breath. I just wanted to be someplace safe, surrounded by Cump Sherman and every soldier California could muster.

I was growing despondent over our situation. We'd been abducted in broad daylight, bound and held in the wilderness by this gang of roving banditos, threatened, terrorized and chased.

"This is a God forsaken place," I said to myself.

I took one last look through the woods but saw nothing. I found it impossible to believe that Joaquin Murrieta had given up his pursuit, but none of them were behind us. So now I turned and started to catch up to Eliza. I reached the top of the ridge and looked out through the trees, but I could see nothing of Eliza. I turned and looked behind me and back down the hill. There was still no sign of anyone pursuing us. But now I could also find no sign of Eliza ahead of me.

I ran along the ridge, keeping the river in sight, but I could not find Eliza. Several times I stopped and looked around – down by the river, through the woods, along the ridge – but I could not find her. I didn't understand how she had gotten so far in front of me. At last, I saw movement through the trees down near the river, and I was sure it was Eliza. It would do no use to call to her. There were rapids on the river nearby, and the rush of the water was loud even up on the ridge. And I could not take the chance that Murrieta or any of the banditos would be close enough to hear me. So I started down the slope toward the river to try to catch up to Eliza.

Down below me I could see that the river as it dropped over three very large falls over enormous granite rocks. The falls resembled giant stair steps. Each drop created a large pool in the rock before the next drop. It was a beautiful spot in the river with the steep slopes on either bank, and those slopes combined with the tall fir and pine trees to create a lovely and secluded spot. It would have been a beautiful spot for a picnic, maybe a swim in the river, if we weren't being chased by murderous banditos.

There was not a lot of water running through the river, so the river made a pleasant, easy slide over the rocks. Below the three big drops, there were a few smaller drops where the water pooled below each one until the river finally continued along its way.

As I descended the slope, I was looking at the water fall and not paying enough attention to anything else. So I didn't see Joaquin Murrieta until he stepped out from behind the trunk of the big pine tree and punched me so hard in the face that I dropped the carbine and fell backwards on the ground.

CHAPTER 24

Manuel Garcia stepped out from behind another tree with my Paterson revolver in his fist and a grin on his fat face.

"We caught you, amigo," Garcia said. "And your woman, too."

Joaquin Murrieta bent over and picked up the carbine. "You shot my men with this gun," he said.

Now two more of Joaquin Murrieta's men approached us from down near the river, and they had Eliza with them, pushing her roughly forward.

"I should have killed you by now," Joaquin Murrieta said. "I wanted to draw this out, for the fun of it, and watch you suffer as my people have suffered. But I should have just killed you."

The other two banditos reached us and held Eliza between them.

"Before you die, Lieutenant Speed, I want you to know that your wife will be going back with us. I have decided to make her my own wife. She will be much happier with me than she has been with you, because I will beat her and rape her every day until she learns to be happy with me."

All the fight was gone from Eliza. I might have expected her to protest or insult, but she had nothing to say. I was certain she felt as hopeless as I did.

I've been in more tight spots than I ever cared to find myself in, and there in California by that pleasant waterfall with Joaquin Murrieta standing over me and Manuel Garcia pointing my Paterson at me – that was as tight as any of them.

"I have gold!" I said. Buying my life was the only thing I could think to do.

"I do not care about gold," Murrieta said. "I have all I need. And I take all that I want."

"It's more than ye'll get in any mining camp," I said. "Tens of thousands of dollars in gold. I can take you to it."

Joaquin Murrieta spat on the ground beside me. "All I want from you, Lieutenant Speed, is revenge for my people."

The smile dropped from his face as he surveyed me. "I have chased you far through the wilderness. The chase is over. The rabbit is caught. I am done with you."

Murrieta turned and walked toward Eliza and the other two men. As he passed by Manuel Garcia he said, "Shoot this dog."

I was still flat on my back. Garcia smiled and walked close to me. He was going to put the Paterson right in my face and shoot. I rolled slightly on my side so he could not see what I was doing, and I slid the Bowie knife from its sheath on my belt.

"Amigo," Garcia said. "This is for our people in Monterrey."

He leaned forward, pointing the Paterson so close to my face that I could smell the metal of the gun. Garcia cocked the hammer of the revolver, and I watched as the trigger dropped. I decided to strike before he could get his finger to the trigger. Just as he reached forward with this finger, I swiped at the revolver with the Bowie knife.

The knife was sharpened to a better edge than I realized. Garcia let out a scream as the knife sliced through his three fingers on the grip just above the knuckles. The Paterson clattered to the ground, and Garcia's three fat fingers looked like bloody sausages laying out my chest. Revulsion at the three severed fingers made me jump, and the fingers dropped down into the dirt.

Garcia was still hollering, he was clutching his wounded hand in his other hand and dancing around, blood pouring out of the stumps on his hand.

As I sprang to my feet, Joaquin Murrieta was spinning to face us, the carbine in his hand. Garcia was between me and Murrieta, so I shoved the fat Mexican bastard toward Murrieta, and the three of us went down in a heap, tumbling a few yards down the steep slope.

When we came to a stop, the three of us were spread out across the ground. The carbine was beside me. Murrieta was the first to get to his feet, and there was no time to bring the gun up to shoot him. I grabbed the carbine by the barrel as I got my feet below me, and I one-handed swung it like a club, catching Murrieta in the face. He reeled and stumbled back, and I had time to flip the gun around and draw back the hammer with my thumb.

I intended to shoot Murrieta, but Eliza screamed at me. I spun in her direction and saw that one of the men who'd been holding her was coming at me with a knife. I didn't raise the carbine to aim, I just held it level with my hip and waited until the man was nearly atop me, and I squeezed the trigger. He took the full impact of the ball in the gut, and it doubled him over and spun him sideways, and he toppled onto the ground and tumbled down the slope toward the river below.

Manuel Garcia was getting to his feet, and I was feeling some confidence now that the banditos were bleeding and dying at my hands. I again turned the rifle, taking it by the barrel, and I jabbed it as hard as I could to hit Garcia in the face. But I missed his face and caught him in his fat neck, and the effect was just as good. With blood spewing from his fingers, he now fell to his knees, gasping and coughing and hacking to try to get a breath.

I flipped the rifle again and pointed the barrel down the hill at Murrieta. I felt exhilarated. I had a sudden image of myself as some sort of Viking or Crusader from days of yore, standing on the hillside vanquishing my foes. The closest thing I'd ever known to it was that day at Fort Teneria when the Mexicans had seen me standing on the ramparts and they had fled out the back, and me and a hundred Mississippians had jumped down into that mass of humanity and started stabbing them in the backs as they tried to run.

I've seen it in other men countless times. The blood lust was up and they knew neither fear nor mercy. Most of the time ye see it happen, the man striking down his opponents is damn close to death hisself because all it takes is one lucky swipe with a saber or one lucky shot from a rifle and the vanquisher becomes the vanquished. But today, all the luck was with me.

I fired the carbine at Murrieta, and the ball cut a ravine across the side of his face. So much blood poured from his cheek that I thought I'd killed him.

Garcia was staggered and offered no threat. That left only the other man who had Eliza. I now turned to him and cocked the hammer on the carbine. There were two full chambers by my count.

The man was of two minds, and I could see it on his face. He had a revolver in one fist and was clinging to Eliza's shirt sleeve with the other. But he was debating if he should turn and run or if he should stand and fight. I looked down the barrel of the carbine at him and nodded my head like he should flee.

"Go on and get!" I yelled at him. "Vamonos!" It was a poor translation, but he caught my meaning. Believing I intended to let him escape with his life, he turned loose of Eliza and started to run back up the hill. I squeezed the trigger and watched as the ball caught him in the back. He fell down and rolled some ways back down the slope.

By my count, the only one still left alive was Garcia, and I decided it was time to dispatch him. I cocked back the hammer on the carbine and turned back down the slope. Garcia was still whimpering over the lost fingers and gagging over the carbine butt to the throat. He was on his hands and knees. I raised up the carbine but failed to shoot Garcia.

Joaquin Murrieta was not nearly as dead as I thought, and he now tackled me to the ground. When he hit me, I fired the carbine but the ball shot well wide of its target.

Again I was flat on my back, but now Murrieta was straddling me, and he was pummeling me with punches. I put my arms up to protect my face as the fists came at me.

Vicious and dangerous as he was, Joaquin Murrieta was a smaller man than me, shorter by almost half a foot and slighter by fifteen or twenty pounds. And maybe he was a deadly bandito and murderer, but he was locked in a fight to the death with Jackie Speed, and coward I may be, I've come up against plenty of vicious murderers in my time, and I've yet to find one who was able to beat me when it was a struggle to the death. Joaquin Murrieta was no better than any of the rest of 'em.

I reached up and grabbed him by the throat and bucked him off at the same time. He was light enough that I easily toppled him over.

But now Murrieta was reaching for the carbine.

"Jack Speed!"

Eliza was yelling at me, but I was too frightened to take my eyes of Murrieta. His hand was on the carbine.

"Jackson Speed! Catch!"

Now I looked and I saw that she was tossing to me my Paterson from where Manuel Garcia had dropped it when I sliced off his fingers.

I reached out and snatched the revolver out of the air, and I was already cocking back the hammer with my thumb when Murrieta fired the carbine.

The ball passed by my face so close that I heard it snap and felt the wind from it as the ball pierced the air. My bowels dissolved to liquid, and I fired the Paterson solely from fear. It wasn't a bad shot, though.

Murrieta doubled as the ball punched him in the gut. He staggered backwards and dropped to a knee. I thought, at last, I'd ended our nightmare. But Joaquin Murrieta was not the sort of nightmare that easily quit. He drew out a knife from his belt, struggled to his feet, and started at me again.

This time I pointed the Paterson and took careful aim. I shot him in the gut a second time, and now he fell on his face.

I got to my own feet and walked over to where Joaquin Murrieta was coughing up blood in his final death throes.

How many hundreds of boys did I watch run up a hill on some battlefield in Virginia, Pennsylvania, Tennessee or Georgia only to catch a ball of lead in the belly? It happened to all of them who were gut shot. They knew they were dying and all the fight was out of them. They had enough time as they choked on their own blood to consider the poor choices they'd made that led them to this moment. Some of them wanted their mamas or their sweethearts. Some of them prayed and others cried. All of them just wanted to live, but they knew they would not.

Joaquin Murrieta wanted water. "Agua," he said, spitting blood. I was standing over him, and I wasn't sure he could see me. "Por favor. Water."

I put the barrel of the Paterson up to his bloody lips, and he stuck out his tongue as if it was a canteen I was putting up to his mouth. I cocked back the hammer of the Paterson, pointed it at his eye and pulled the trigger. Then I kicked his body so that he slid the rest of the way down the slope, dropped over the granite rocks and down into the river below. There was just enough of a current to carry the body the short ways to the first water fall. Grotesquely, Joaquin Murrieta's body slid over the water fall and splashed into the pool below. The current carried him to the next drop, and his body slid over that fall. I watched as his body went over the third and fourth fall, and then he got hung up among the rocks and the current didn't carry him any farther.

CHAPTER 25

While I was killing off Joaquin Murrieta, Manuel Garcia was fleeing through the woods.

You'll know, if you ever read Yellowbird's fiction, that Garcia became known as Three-Fingered Jack (it amused me to know he was named for the fingers I took and not the two he kept) and he continued to terrorize miners and hapless travelers in California for many years. The Five Joaquins, excepting one, continued to rape, murder and pillage across the California goldfields for the next few years. They all used the name Joaquin Murrieta because it was easier for them to steal a dead man's reputation than it was to make one of their own, and it when it comes to outlawry, the most important weapon ye can have is your reputation. And, I suspect, there were probably plenty of others who never rode with the Five Joaquins who likewise adopted Murrieta's name and reputation for theirselves.

In '53, I think it was, the state — for the gold-heavy California was already a state — decided it could stand no more of Joaquin Murrieta's raping, murdering, and pillaging, and so it put a five-thousand dollar bounty on him.

Former Texas Ranger Harry Love put together a posse and went off and killed some Mexican and put his head in a jar of alcohol. Likewise, Harry killed Manuel Garcia, and he put Garcia's hand in the jar as well.

I had occasion on one of my return trips to California to view the head for myself, because it had been set on a shelf behind the bar in the Gold Nugget Saloon. If ye've ever seen a head that's marinated in alcohol for 20 years or so, ye'll know it doesn't preserve too well. I twisted and turned the jar and peered at it for quite a while, before I finally discovered the truth. I don't doubt that Harry Love collected the head of a California bandito, nor do I doubt that it was the head of Joaquin. I also do not doubt that the Joaquin in question deserved to be shot dead and his head taken for a prize. But, of course, it never was the real Joaquin Murrieta, who at that time was still long-dead at the bottom of a canyon with two balls of lead in his gut and one in his eye.

But I did come to recognize the head in the jar of alcohol, and I did it when I discovered the head was missing an earlobe. Why, it was my old friend Joaquin Ocomorenia's head in that jar! Hadn't I seen for meself when Joaquin Murrieta cut that lobe off his ear?

The Five Joaquins were all a bunch of damned, dangerous ruffians, and the world was better without any of them.

There is little else to tell of my first visit to California that would be of much interest.

With Joaquin Murrieta dead, Eliza and I made our way back to the mining camp. There we found that all the prospectors had been killed, along with a couple of Joaquin Murrieta's banditos, who looked as if they'd been bashed to death with shovels.

I saw no point in leaving the prospectors' gold or livestock unattended, so I went through all of their tents and gathered up everything that looked valuable, including several bags of placer gold. Eliza helped me to pack everything onto the mules that belonged to the prospectors, and then we saddled our horses and rode down river until we at last came to a mining camp of some size. We told them there what we had endured, and they fed us and sheltered us for a couple of days while we got back our strength. But no vigilante posse was formed up to chase surviving banditos because the prospectors at that camp had recently struck a pretty good hole, and everyone was eager to keep digging rather than chase Mexican outlaws through the hills and forests.

So we kept on riding all the way back to Coloma, and there at last we found Tecumseh Sherman. Cump was eager for something to do, and so he put together a posse of half a dozen mounted infantrymen and more than a score of hired guns who were willing to ride out of the goldfields for a few days if the U.S. Government was willing to pay them for it.

You might expect that I'd have been a bit nervous about returning to the hills in search of Murrieta's hideout, knowing it could still be occupied by as many as four Joaquins, and the truth is under any other circumstances I'd have just drawn Cump Sherman a map and wished him luck. But I'd kicked my heels into the dirt of that dry creek bed, and I was certain sure the spot was full of gold.

So while Cump Sherman was hiring up a posse, I was hiring up my own band of men. I even used the gold I'd taken from the prospectors' camp to buy my men some mules to ride out on.

If ever there was a motley organization to take up a march, we were the very picture of it.

At the front was Cump Sherman and his mounted privates of the United States Army. Behind them were the rough men who made up the posse that Sherman raised in Coloma. Most of them were miners who'd struck out and were happy to earn a wage.

Behind the posse came me and Eliza, with four Chinamen, eight local Injuns and two Chileans who'd had a falling out with their brethren at Chile Bar. The Chinamen were all armed only with picks and shovels, but I'd bought muskets for the Injuns and given the two Chileans two pistolas each that we'd taken off the dead banditos.

Even with the soldiers and the posse and my own team of armed prospectors, I was a bit nervous about returning to the dry creek bed where Joaquin Murrieta and his men had made their hideout. I was all but certain what remained of the Five Joaquins would have abandoned their hideout, but even so, riding into the known hideout of a gang of Mexican banditos was as unnatural to me as using a gaggle of rattlesnakes for a game of pick-a-stick.

But I was certain sure that dry creek bed was full of gold.

And so it was.

Over the next few months, pausing only on the coldest days of the winter, my Chinamen and Injuns dug deep into the dry creek bed and the sides of the gulch, and every day that they dug they found more gold. At the time, it was the deepest mine in California, and probably still ranks among the best producing.

By the time winter hit, Johnny Brooks, Brother, Slim, Obadiah, Jimbo and the rest of our band from our original strike had moved to the dry creek bed. In the spring of 1850 we hired hands to work our original claim, which didn't get pinched out for another year.

It was in the spring of 1850 when I decided that it was time to leave California. I'd been down in Hangtown, now named Placerville, when I heard about an uprising among the Pomo Injuns where two ranchers were killed. The talk in town was that the U.S. Army Dragoons were going after the Pomo, and everyone was hoping it would be a massacre. Which it was. [44]

Eliza had already been hinting that she wanted to return to Georgia.

Our mining operation had grown so large that we now had a grist mill and a sawmill, and Johnny had directed the construction of dozens of log cabins, a cookhouse, a saloon, and a company store, and we had quite a nice little village at the mine, Eliza was homesick for civilization.

"What is the good of all this gold if we are out here in the wilderness where the gold can't purchase anything?" she said. And it wasn't something she noted in passing. It was becoming a daily refrain.

So when it seemed that California would shortly be pitched into a full-blown Indian War, I decided it was time to take Eliza home.

By this time, Obadiah and I had formed up the Speedy Bush Exploration and Extraction Company with papers registered in San Francisco. Slim and Brother were hired on as our superintendents, and we'd already staked out other claims near the Dry Bed Mine.

Convinced that my holdings were in good hands – for I trusted Slim and Brother as if they were family – I agreed that it was time to go back east. Johnny Brooks decided to go with us, as well. So we purchased passage aboard a ship to take us around the Horn and back east to Savannah.

You'll know that my company did well. Through the 1850s, Slim and Brother, working on my payroll, opened mining operations all through the Sierra Nevada foothills. We had mines along the rivers, on the sides of canyons, in dried up riverbeds. They started mining operations in northern California. When the gold became harder to find by the 1860s, Slim and Brother managed to diversify my business by opening silver and copper mines in Nevada and New Mexico, and I made a second fortune in silver.

Not that Slim and Brother didn't get rich in the process, too. In truth, they probably skimmed enough off the top that they managed to make a bigger fortune than I ever saw, but I never had complaints about the way they handled my business out in California. Slim had his own interests – he opened a hotel in San Francisco and had a ranch in the valley.

Brother served in the California legislature and ran unsuccessfully for governor. He got fat and died of a heart attack back in '88. He was with two prostitutes in one of the rooms in Slim's hotel.

All things considered, the three of us did pretty well considering we started for California as hired hands on Abner Jamieson's wagon train.

Obadiah Bush did not fare as well as the rest of us.

In '51, Obadiah sailed for home with a trunk full of gold and a contract that said he and I were partners in our company. But Obadiah died on the ship and was buried at sea. For a few years I expected to hear from his family. I figured they'd be looking for his share of the company, but I never did hear from them. Eventually I had a lawyer draw up some new incorporation papers that left out any mention of Obadiah Bush, though I kept his name in the company's name.

I don't know what happened to the trunk full of gold that Obadiah was taking back to New York, but I suspect the ship's captain ensured that it never arrived home. Which is just as well, for Obadiah's family undoubtedly would have spent the lot of it on abolitionist nonsense.

When Eliza, Johnny and I decided to go back east, Jimbo asked me if we'd leave him in California. By that time he was acting as a foreman in the mines, and he told me he liked pretty well being able to boss around the Chinamen. I didn't grant him his freedom, as such, but without informing Eliza, I did put him on the company payroll. And Jimbo spent the remainder of his life earning wages and beating the hell out of Chinamen who didn't work hard enough.

I returned to California a number of times in my life, especially after 1869. [45] I always found it to be a dangerous place full of rough and bad men, but it wasn't so different from other places I've been – even on the civilized East Coast. Why, I've been assaulted and nearly murdered in Baltimore and New York, Savannah and Charleston, Chicago, St. Louis, and Dallas, and a dozen other towns from New Haven to New Mexico. And that doesn't even include all the times during the war that some Yankee bastard or Rebel sonuvabitch tried to put me in a grave.

So I can't say too much bad about California, after all. Besides, had it not been for the gold in California, I might have turned out to be a politician. I'd have still been rich, of course, but I would have had trouble looking myself in a mirror.

EPILOGUE

In September of 1863, at the Battle of Chickamauga, that damned Hoosier John Wilder [45] shot me in the shoulder with one of his Spencer rifles and damn near killed me. I suppose it was a blessing, though, because it put me out of most of the rest of the war. I went first to a hospital in Atlanta, and then I went home to convalesce.

But when I arrived home to Milledgeville, I learned that my home was no longer there. In '62 – at the height of the war – Eliza packed all our belongings into some wagons and traveled about forty miles north where she paid in cash for a beautiful home not far from the town square.

So broken though I was by John Wilder's bullet, I traveled from Milledgeville to Madison where I was finally able to being my convalescing.

What prompted this particular event of imbecility was that Eliza had come across a copy of White's Statistics of Georgia which promised of Madison, "in point of intelligence, refinement, and hospitality, this town acknowledges no superior." [46]

Milledgeville, as the state capital, had become foul and depressing during the war, she told me, and she could no longer bear to live there. We were familiar already with Madison, a quaint and beautiful little town and the place where my parents lived when I was born, and so we knew it was a lovely place. But when White's confirmed Eliza's suspicions that Madison was so much superior to Milledgeville, she decided to move.

"But you don't move in the middle of a war," I tried to explain to her.

She explained to me that the previous owner of the home had been shot dead in the war and his family was no longer able to afford the place, and Eliza was able to buy this mansion, its gardens – which occupied a full block – and carriage house, for about half its actual value. Even better, the family accepted Confederate currency, so Eliza didn't have to pay them in gold. In truth, it was like we bought the house for nothing. She even managed to rent our home to a prominent state senator, who paid his rent in silver because Eliza refused to accept Confederate bills.

So I could not argue with her business acumen. The home is a lovely place, and we have forever enjoyed living here.

When my old friend Cump Sherman burned Atlanta, I read about it in the newspaper from the rocking chair on my front porch in Madison.

Around the third week of November, the local Home Guard came round the house, pounding upon the door and demanding that I join them north of town to face the Yankee army.

When I came out of the house I was confronted by three men. Two of them were so ancient I was fairly certain they'd ridden in Phinizey's Dragoons with my old man at Clarke's Fort back around 1801. The first was toting a smoothbore musket. The second had an 1808 blunderbuss, of all the most ridiculous things. The third man was not even a man, but a boy of about 10 years old, and I swear to my Maker, he was carrying a bent cavalry sword with which he intended to fight off the entire Yankee army.

"Colonel Speed," the man with the blunderbuss addressed me. "We have come to demand that you take up your duty and ride with us to face the invading force."

"The three of you are going to face the Yankees?" I asked.

"We have an artillery crew manning a cannon in a field north of town and about forty other men who are already assembling there with the artillery," he said.

"You're the only one with any real army experience who can help," the boy spoke up. "And ye out-rank the captain of the home guard."

It was true, Jeff Davis hisself made me a colonel, but what these ragtag elements of the Southern Army did not know was that I was a major in the Union Army, so I even outranked myself.

"I'm convalescing," I told them, and I started to shut the door. But the old man with the musket pushed the barrel of the musket up against the door and kept it open. He was surprising strong.

"I seen you two days ago lift up one of your little children, toss him into the air and catch him," the old man said. "I ain't saying you wasn't shot, but I am saying you're well enough to ride north of town with us."

I sighed heavily and told them to stand their ground while I got dressed.

I put on my gray, wool overcoat – the one with the hole in the shoulder and the blood stains – and my gray britches. I saddled up one of the horses in the stable, and I rode north while my three companions rode in a wagon drawn by two mules.

When I arrived at the farm north of town where the defenders of Madison were collecting, I found that my regiment was all just as poor as my honor guard. Old men and boys was all the Confederacy had left to offer to the Union guns.

The rolling hills north of town were all well cleared and being farmed before the war. Now those farms were mostly abandoned while the men who owned and worked them were off being killed in Virginia. But the cleared fields gave us an open view when the Yanks approached from the northwest.

I already had a plan in mind. I did not know if I would be successful, but the truth was I had as much interest in defending Madison as did the rest of our Home Guard, and I was willing to give it a try. I did not believe that I would be shot, or I'd have not done it.

"Y'all load up that cannon," I ordered. "Every man see to it that his rifle is loaded and primed. Or his blunderbuss. I am riding out to parley with the enemy."

I tied a white flag to the end of my father's saber, the one he'd used when he'd been in the dragoons, and holding the flag aloft, I rode out across the fields toward the advancing Union army.

I rode three-quarters of the way to the Union line and saw that a small band of men were riding out to meet me. I hoped – I was counting on it – that whatever general was in charge would be someone I knew personally.

And indeed, it was.

"Howdy, Cump," I said in as friendly a way as I could when my friend from California rode up to me, surrounded by – of all things – Alabama cavalry. The First Alabama Cavalry of the Union Army consisted of Southern boys from Alabama who'd stayed loyal to the Union, and the regiment had the honor of riding escort for the commanding general.

Sherman took a long look at me, and finally his devil face split into a grin. "Jack Speed," he said. "I see ye ain't a lieutenant any more."

"Colonel," I said. "At least, in one army."

Sherman looked at the blood stain on my shoulder.

"Wounded?" he asked.

"Up at Chickamauga," I told him.

"Well, I'm glad ye ain't killed. So what can I do for you today, Jack?"

"Here's the thing, Cump," says I. "I've got an army of about 40 old men and boys back there. We've got a cannon and a blunderbuss, and I'm afraid we're pretty committed to defending the town of Madison."

Sherman looked out over the hillside.

"A blunderbuss?" he asked me.

"Looks to be from about the turn of the century," I said.

"Say, Jackson," Cump says. "You made quite a bit in your diggings out in California, didn't ye?"

If it was a bribe he was looking for, I'd be willing to pay quite a bit to spare my new home.

"I did okay, Cump."

Cump spat in the dirt. "We're going to ride together for a minute, boys," he said to the Alabamians riding escort, and he led me off at a walk away from his escort. I figured he was about to name his price.

"The thing that's bothering me, Jack, is you went out to California and made a great big fortune digging gold, but ye never did make things right with me."

"I understand what ye're saying, Cump," says I. "Name your price, and I'll tell you if I can meet it."

Cump scratched his chin thoughtfully. "I figure it at about twenty dollars," Cump said. "But I ain't going to take Confederate bills."

I thought I'd misheard him.

"Twenty dollars?" I asked.

Cump was grinning. "That's right. About twenty dollars. When I loaned you that pan for prospecting back at Sutter's Fort, I told ye you could pay me for it if you found any gold. Well, Jack, you found the gold, but ye never did pay me for it."

Back then I was in the habit of always carrying a few gold coins on me, so I reached into my pocket and came out with two twenty dollar gold coins.

"Take them both," I said to Sherman. "I figure I must owe ye some interest."

Sherman took them.

"What do you want me to do about your army?" he asked.

"I guess what I'd really like is for you to just go around the town. You can cut out to the east here, through those fields, and pass by the town entirely."

Sherman scratched his chin thoughtfully again.

"If ye can't do that — if ye feel like ye have to put on a show — then I'd appreciate it if you'd fire a few shots well short and see if that won't scare them off. At least the boys. If the old men want to get killed, that's no concern of mine. But the boys are pretty young."

This was before Sherman's army got to Andersonville. If they'd made it to the prison and seen how the South was treating P.O.W.'s, I suspect Sherman's answer would have been different. [47]

"It's good to see you again, Jack. This war is almost over, now. It looks likely you and I both will survive it, and I'm glad for that. Listen here, you make sure none of those old men fire off their blunderbusses, and that cannon stays silent, and we'll take these fields east of town and go around Madison. But if any of them do anything foolish — if they take a shot at us — I'll be obliged to engage your Home Guard. Is that fair?"

I shook his hand. Thank the Lord Eliza had not been present to see me shake his hand! Though he spared Madison, Sherman's treatment of Atlanta and the rest of our state made him forever the most hated man in Eliza's heart. Ever since '64, if I wanted to rile her, all I had to do was say his name.

That was how I saved the town of Madison from destruction. It cost me two gold coins, but I thought it was money well spent if it spared my house and my belongings. Over the years all sorts of foolish rumors were spread. Some said the mayor of Madison was a longtime friend of Sherman's. Others claimed our state representative had a brother who was a roommate of Sherman's at West Point.

I did not doubt that both the mayor and the state representative liberally spread those rumors themselves, but there never was no truth in anything a politician said.

No sir, Madison was spared because Ol' Jackie Speed struck it rich in California using Cump Sherman's gold pan. [48]

the end

FOOTNOTES

[1] Joaquin Murrieta was a legendary bandito in California during the early days of the California Gold Rush. Of Mexican descent, Murrieta was known as the "Robin Hood of El Dorado." Depending on the source, Murrieta was acting in revenge for a raped and murdered lover or fighting against the United States government that had recently annexed California at the end of the Mexican-American War. Often cast as a romantic anti-hero, it is nearly impossible to untangle Murrieta the bandit from Murrieta's romantic legend. Speed refers to "Yellowbird's mythology." Yellowbird was the Cherokee name of John Rollin Ridge, the nephew of the Cherokee tribal chief and Confederate general Stand Watie. Ridge was a newspaper writer and poet. In "The Life and Adventures of Joaquin Murieta," Ridge penned one of the earliest Cherokee novels and was the first to romanticize Murieta.

[2] It is often difficult to pinpoint exactly when Speed wrote each volume of his memoirs, but we have a hint here that this particular memoir was written after 1907. Speed notes that Oklahoma was Indian Territory at the time of the events he describes but says that at the time of the writing of this memoir it was a state. Oklahoma achieved statehood in November 1907.

[3] The Preston Trail actually began in Austin, Texas, north of San Antonio, and traveled north to Preston, Texas, at the Red River, but the road from San Antonio to Austin would have been well-worn at the time.

[4] Alexander Cockrell and his wife Sarah Cockrell were among the most important of the founders of the city of Dallas. Speed accurately reports that Alexander Cockrell had lived among the Cherokee Indians in Indian Territory for a number of years, working as a slave catcher for Cherokee Chieftain John Ross. He served briefly as a Texas Ranger under Ben McCulloch in the Mexican-American War, but in September of 1847 he married Sarah Horton. Their union produced five children before Alexander was killed in 1858. During their short marriage, though, Alexander and Sarah acquired property, ran the ferry over the Trinity River, built a sawmill, and manufactured bricks. After Alexander's death, Sarah Horton Cockrell continued to be one of the most important figures in the city's early days. She ran three hotels and operated a toll bridge over the Trinity River. It is no exaggeration to say that Sarah Horton Cockrell was among the most successful pioneer women in the 1800s, and the couple's contribution to the founding of Dallas is immense.

[5] Speed accurately describes the events of Alexander Cockrell's untimely demise. He had loaned $200 to a city marshal who, instead of paying back the loan, killed Cockrell by shooting him in the back.

[6] Standhope Watie (1806-1871) was a chief among the Cherokee and the head of one faction of the Cherokee nation. Prior to the forced removal of the Cherokee from Georgia in the early 1830s, Watie's father and uncle had signed an agreement with the United States government to sell Cherokee land in North Georgia and Tennessee and move the tribe to Oklahoma. But another faction of the tribe, led by John Ross, opposed the treaty and refused to leave until the United State army

forced them onto what is now known as the Trail of Tears. The feud between the two factions of the tribe continued in Oklahoma and resulted in numerous assassinations and attempted assassinations – including several attempts on Watie's life. During the American Civil War, Watie and his faction sided with the Confederacy, and Watie became a general in the Confederate army. In fact, Watie was the last Confederate general to surrender at the end of the war.

[7] Speed's recollections of the events surrounding his involvement in the Mexican-American War are recounted in the first book of his memoirs, Jackson Speed: The Hero of El Teneria.

[8] Speed's tales from the Mexican-American war account favorably with the historical record. In fact, General Zachary Taylor did ask Ben McCulloch to scout Santa Anna's forces at the Encarnacion hacienda, and McCulloch and fewer than twenty Texas Rangers rode through Santa Anna's camp at night and were able to determine Santa Anna's strength. And Taylor was able to beat Santa Anna soon after at the battle of Buena Vista.

[9] As brief as it is, Speed's recounting of the Ross-Watie feud is correct. The feud lasted well into the 1860s with assassinations committed by both sides. During the Civil War, Watie's faction of the tribe sided with the Confederacy while Ross's faction sided with the Union. Watie's plantation was burned by Ross sympathizers during the war, and Watie also burned Ross's home. After the war, Watie rose to prominence among the Cherokee people and replaced Ross as the tribe's principal chief.

[10] Bigamy was not outlawed by the United States federal government until 1862, and even then those laws were not widely enforced. Some states may have had laws against bigamy prior to 1862, but one can

certainly understand why Speed would not have wanted his first wife, Eliza Speed, to find out about his second bride, Weenonaw Speed.

[11] Koo-wees-gu-wee was John Ross's Cherokee name.

[12] Rose Cottage was the name of John Ross's plantation at Park Hill, a small community near the Cherokee capital of Tahlequah. Rose Hill was some 60 miles south of Stand Watie's Spavinaw River plantation.

[13] Jesse Chisholm (1806-1868) was a contemporary of Stand Watie, and in the 1840s he was already an important man in Indian Territory. He served as an interpreter for the United States government not just among the Cherokee but also among other plains tribes. He owned several trading posts in Texas, Indian Territory, and all the way up into Kansas. Though today he is most famous for the cattle trail that bore his name, Chisholm never drove cattle along the Chisholm Trail, and neither did cowboys drive cattle along the trail during his time. Instead, Chisholm used the trail to cart goods to his trading posts.

[14] There is no accurate count available for the number of children Jesse Chisholm rescued, but throughout his travels and dealings with the Plains Tribes, he frequently found children who had been kidnapped, usually from Mexican homes. Chisholm would take the children, sometimes paying for them, and try to locate and return them to their families. When he could not locate family, he would adopt the children as his own. The Comanche, in particular, knew they could sell kidnapped children to Chisholm.

[15] Speed never makes the exact connection between Weenonaw and Stand Watie, but her decision to name him Galagina offers interesting possibilities. Stand Watie had an older brother who used the name Elias

Boudinot. Boudinot was a newspaper editor for the Cherokee Phoenix and a prominent leader in the Cherokee Nation. Like Watie, Boudinot favored voluntary removal, which put him at odds with John Ross. The Ross faction assassinated Boudinot outside his Oklahoma home in 1839 and on the same day also assassinated his cousin and uncle, John and Major Ridge. It is part of the historical record that John Ridge was Yellowbird's father, but no sources point to the identity of Weenonaw. However, Watie's older brother, Elias Boudinot, at birth was named Galagina Uwatie. It is pure speculation on the part of the editor, but perhaps Weenonaw was one of Boudinot's six children, and she has named Jackson Speed after her assassinated father.

[16] Coming through Lee Town and passing by Elkhorn Tavern, Speed was in the vicinity of interesting American history, even if he did not realize it. As noted, this was the site of the Battle of Elkhorn Tavern, in which his uncle-in-law, Stand Watie, and his former commander in the Texas Rangers, Ben McCulloch, would both serve as Confederate generals. McCulloch was killed March 2, 1862, during the Battle of Elkhorn Tavern (or the Battle of Pea Ridge). The Trail of Tears also passed directly in front of the Elkhorn Tavern. The Tavern still stands today, preserved as part of the Pea Ridge National Military Park. The site of Lee Town is all abandoned and there is no evidence remaining of the town, which was abandoned shortly after the Civil War.

[17] Possibly this is the attorney, judge and politician Jonas M. Tebbetts who was an important figure in the early history of Fayetteville and a pro-Union Southerner during the Civil War. When Union forces entered the city in February of 1862, Tebbetts volunteered his home to serve as headquarters to the Union army. The Union forces withdrew from the city ahead of the Confederate army led by Ben McCulloch. When McCulloch entered the city, he had Tebbetts arrested and sentenced to death. But McCulloch was then killed at the Battle of Pea Ridge, and Tebbetts was released from prison. He fled to Missouri to live the remainder of the war and then returned to Fayetteville. Born in 1820, Tebbetts would survive his 1862 death sentence and live until 1913.

[18] Nearly 70-years-old when Jackson Speed arrived at Fort Leavenworth, Major Nathan Boone – the youngest son of the famed explorer and pioneer Daniel Boone – was on the verge of retirement in the spring of 1848. He would return to his Missouri home in September on sick leave, and though he would not officially retire for a couple of years (and be promoted to Colonel in that time), Boone would not return to Fort Leavenworth or the army. Speed's description of Major Boone corresponds with other accounts of him in later life at Fort Leavenworth. Junior officers noted that he drank heavily and often retold stories they'd already heard many times. But the old Army Ranger certainly had stories to tell. Boone served in a local militia or the army at various times throughout the first half of the 1800s. He journeyed from Kentucky to Missouri with his famous father and homesteaded in Missouri while it was still a Spanish territory. He was in the Blackhawk War and led an expedition into the plains of modern-day Oklahoma. He had also been in charge of three companies the army sent to the Cherokee nation a few years prior to this where he mediated and for a time brought a halt to the feud between Stand Watie and John Ross.

[19] The Treaty of Guadalupe Hidalgo was the official peace treaty ending the Mexican-American War. It was signed in February, 1848, but news of the treaty traveled slowly.

[20] It might seem odd that the tale of the Donner Party, which even now haunts each successive generation with the terrible idea of cannibalism, would have been largely unknown in 1848. In May of 1846 the Donner-Reed Party set out to go to California. They were delayed by one mishap after another, and they were stranded in the high Sierra Nevada in the winter of 1846-47. Their plight was well known to settlers in California and along the Oregon Trail, but news traveled so slowly at the time that the fate of the Donner-Reed Party was largely unknown east of the Mississippi by the spring of 1848.

[21] The actual distance from Fort Laramie to Fort Leavenworth is closer to 630 miles.

[22] Yerba Buena was the Spanish settlement that would become San Francisco. Colonel Richard Barnes Mason was the military governor of California in 1848, based not in Yerba Buena but in Monterey, California.

[23] The identity of the lieutenant, and his claim to be in possession of a letter for President Polk from Col. Mason, the military governor of California, creates a mystery. William Tecumseh Sherman, the famed Union general, in 1848 was a lieutenant acting as aide to Col. Mason. Sherman left a very detailed account of how Mason first learned of the discovery of gold and a tour Mason and Sherman made of the gold fields in the summer of 1848. It was not until after that tour, in the fall of 1848, that Sherman penned for Col. Mason a letter to be delivered to President Polk announcing the discovery of gold. That letter was sent with Lieutenant Lucian Loeser, not overland, but by sea, and it was sent well after Speed was at Fort Leavenworth. Certainly by the spring of 1848 word was beginning to get out of California that gold had been discovered. By summer of 1848, gold seekers were already coming into California from as far away as Oregon and even the Sandwich Islands. But Speed's recollection seems to be clear that he encountered a lieutenant carrying a letter on behalf of Col. Mason for the president. Undoubtedly the lieutenant had knowledge of the gold discovery and probably was told to pass that information along when he got back east. But Speed's recollection does not coincide with Sherman's description of events. What is most troubling about Speed's account is that the timeline does not seem to work. Gold was discovered in California on January 24 of 1848. As noted, it was months before any official confirmation of the discovery happened. Even if a messenger had left immediately upon the discovery (unlikely as that would have put the messenger attempting to cross the Sierra Nevada in the winter months), the fastest overland journey at the time still took the better part of four

months. Speed is not exactly clear about when he was at Fort Leavenworth, but it must have been late April or very early in May. It seems, therefore, impossible that the messenger bore any official notification for the president about the discovery of gold. And it also strains credulity that the lieutenant could have had any word at all about the discovery of gold. Nevertheless, based on everything that follows, one must conclude that Speed is accurate, at least, that an army lieutenant bore some information about the gold discovery, official or not.

[24] Jim Bridger (1804-1881) was among the first and most famous of the early mountain men. He was a famous storyteller, earning a reputation for spinning humorous yarns. In 1842 he established a fur trading post in present-day Wyoming that became Fort Bridger, a stop on the Oregon Trail on the Green River. There are a number of towns and other places (including a mountain range) named for the famous guide.

[25] In 1846, Jim Bridger advised the Donner Party that they would be safe to take a shorter route to California, and that advice proved to be fatal. The Donner Party was trapped in the Sierra Nevada in winter, and members of the Donner Party resorted to cannibalism to survive the winter.

[26] John Sutter was actually born in Germany and raised in Switzerland. He was an early California pioneer who came to California via Hawaii. Sutter established a virtual fiefdom at his fort near the convergence of the Sacramento and American rivers, and there he welcomed Mexicans, Indians and whites, alike. He employed many Indians, some who worked for him willingly and others who were coerced. One of Sutter's employees, James W. Marshall, while constructing a mill at the present-day site of Coloma, California, discovered gold in the American River, leading to the 1849 California Gold Rush. Sutter was also responsible for surveying and establishing the City of Sacramento at the site of his fort

in the Central Valley.

[27] William Tecumseh Sherman is best known for his role in the American Civil War as the Union General who burned Georgia on the famous "March to the Sea." But his military career began, like many other Civil War generals, during the Mexican-American War. Sherman did not see action during the war. Instead, he was in California where he worked directly under the military governor of California, Col. William B. Mason. Sherman's memoirs serve as an excellent source for a first-hand account of the early days of the Gold Rush. As Speed notes, Sherman's friends called him by his middle name and a shortened version of his middle name, "Cump."

[28] Perhaps it is accurate that in 1848, when Speed first arrived in California, gold was going for $10 an ounce, but at its height in 1849, gold was going for more than $20 an ounce. In general, the price around San Francisco through 1849 was around $18 an ounce.

[29] Sutter's Fort was located at the site of present-day Sacramento, and the mill Sutter was building was near the town of Coloma, about 40 miles east of Sacramento.

[30] The town of Dry Diggings began as one of the first boom towns of the California Gold Rush. Over the next few years, many such towns were destined to disappear just as fast as they popped up, but Dry Diggings persevered. Known initially as "Old Dry Diggings" and named for the practice of digging dry dirt and moving it by the cartload to running water to separate the gold from the dirt, Dry Diggings a year later became known by its new name, Hangtown, after three men were hanged there. By 1850, though, the local Temperance League and some of the local church organizations, sought a more respectable name, and Hangtown became Placerville. Placerville remains today a thriving

community.

[31] John Sutter's name is irrevocably tied in history to the California Gold Rush, but the discovery of gold at Sutter's mill ruined him. Sutter intended to build in the California valley a utopian, communal society. But his hands at the fort mostly left him to go into the goldfields.

[32] As a Mexican city, the port of San Francisco was known as Yerba Buena. In August of 1846, roughly a month after U.S. expeditionary forces invaded and took control of most of California during the Mexican-American War, Lt. Washington Bartlett was given temporary command of Yerba Buena. In January of 1847, Lt. Bartlett issued an order changing the name of Yerba Buena to San Francisco.

[33] Abandoned ships in San Francisco Bay proved to be an ongoing problem for the next several years. The bay was littered with dozens of ships. In 1849, some number of ships, including the Niantic, were intentionally run aground when their crews deserted them, and were turned into hotels. Abandoned ships in the bay became such a problem in 1850 and 1851, that ships entering the harbor sometimes had to wait days to be able to unload cargo.

[34] By the last six months of 1849, 1,000 people a week were arriving in San Francisco by ship. The town's population was counted at 812 in 1848, with 70 percent being men and the other 30 percent being women or children. Estimates of San Francisco's population at the end of 1849 put the number at 25,000.

[35] While there is no way to be certain, all the clues that Speed relates suggest that the Obadiah Bush he met on the South Fork of the American River was the ancestor of both the 41st and 43rd United States

presidents. A direct ancestor of the presidents, Obadiah Bush was born in 1797 in New York. He worked as a schoolmaster and was an active member of the American Anti-Slavery Society. Bush petitioned the New York legislature to secede from the Union to protest slavery. Bush fathered seven sons. Though few details are available regarding Bush's adventures in California, it was believed that he had done well enough in the Gold Rush to settle in California. In 1851 he was bound on a ship back to New York, presumably to settle affairs there and collect his family to bring them to California, when he died aboard ship and was given a sea burial.

[36] In the mid-1800s, the fastest way for a prospector to get from the East Coast to California was by ship through the Caribbean Sea to Panama. There, travelers would disembark and by canoe they would travel up the Chagres River. Then they had to travel by mule or horse through the jungle to Panama City where they would board a ship for California. The journey took roughly three months, but many died from cholera or yellow fever. The overland journey at this point typically to four to six months. The alternative sea route took travelers around Cape Horn at the southern tip of South America. Large waves and frigid temperatures could make the journey unpleasant, but of the three possible routes to California, this was the safest. The trip around the Horn could take up to eight months.

[37] The Colt Paterson was among the earliest of the pistols with a revolving cylinder. There was no trigger guard on the gun, and the trigger folded up into the frame of the pistol. A mechanism released the trigger when the hammer was cocked.

[38] Camp Belknap was the staging ground on the Rio Grande for the expeditionary force under General Taylor that would invade Mexico.

[39] While Speed provides details otherwise lost to history, his account of the events in Dry Diggings that resulted in the name change are largely corroborated by other sources. Most sources only note that three men rode into town shooting and creating a general ruckus. Some sources claim the three hangings were the result of two separate instances and occurred on at least two separate nights. But in general, all sources agree that three men – whether together or separately – who were probably all intoxicated, rode into town in the middle of the night shooting into the air. The men were hung in the town square for their drunken and disorderly behavior, and the town's name was briefly changed to Hangtown.

[40] "Veta madre" translates to "mother lode." Veta Madre was the name given to a 7-mile long silver vein discovered in the 1500s in modern-day Mexico, and the term was common in Mexican mining. So many of the prospectors in California during the Gold Rush were Mexican that sure the phrase "mother lode" originated from this. Though the exact location of Speed's large discovery is unknown, the location descriptions in his memoirs suggest it was somewhere in present-day El Dorado County, which likely did make it part of the famous California Mother Lode.

[41] In October of 1850, George McKnight (sometimes known as George Knight) saw an outcropping of quartz and noticed gold veins running through the white quartz. Using a cast-iron skillet, McKnight bashed away at the quartz and discovered a gold vein 4-inches wide. McKnight named the site "Gold Hill" and his claim was the Gold Hill Mine, and over the course of seven years, McKnight and his company would dig $4 million worth of gold out of Gold Hill Mine.

[42] Moffatt & Company was among the first private smelting and coining operations in San Francisco and enjoyed a good reputation as assayers. The company initially minted rectangular gold ingots ranging in price

from about $10 up to more than $200, but eventually the office began minting coins rather than ingots.

[43] There were in fact four other Joaquins riding with Joaquin Murrieta in 1849, and the gang was known as The Five Joaquins. They are accused of any number of crimes from cattle rustling to murder. John Rollin Ridge (Yellow Bird) was the author of the first fictionalized account of the banditos, "The Life and Adventures of Joaquin Murieta." Numerous other fictionalized accounts of Joaquin Murrieta would be given over the years, and his legend grew so that he was often called "The Mexican Robin Hood." Some have credited Joaquin Murrieta as being the inspiration for Zorro.

[44] In 1849, Pomo Indians enslaved and cruelly treated by two white California ranchers rose up and killed both ranchers, Andrew Kelsey and Charles Stone. In response to the murders, United States dragoons in 1850 caught the Pomo Indians and killed scores of them. Estimates put the dead at as few as 60 to as many as 400. Most of those killed were old men, women, and children, as the younger men of the tribe were off hunting when the dragoons struck.

[45] Colonel John Wilder was the commander of Indiana's mounted infantry known as the Lightning Brigade. Wilder personally fronted the money to equip the brigade with new Spencer Repeating Rifles. The 7-shot repeating rifles, operated with a lever action, gave the Lightning Brigade such superior firepower that Confederates who came up against them often thought they were facing numbers significantly greater. At Chickamauga, Wilder and the Lightning Brigade used their superior fire power to protect the Union retreat.

[46] "Statistics of the State of Georgia" was a book published in 1855 by George White and contained various facts about the cities and counties

throughout the state.

[47] Andersonville (officially, Camp Sumter) was the notorious prison in Southwest Georgia where Union Prisoners of War were held. Conditions at Andersonville were terrible. The prison was overcrowded and unsanitary. Prisoners lacked sufficient water and food. Of the 45,000 prisoners believed to have been held at Andersonville, some 13,000 died – mostly from scurvy and dysentery. When the Union army under Sherman liberated Andersonville, Union soldiers took a dim view of showing any mercy to the South.

[48] Many legends have grown up about why Sherman spared Madison in his March to Savannah, and Speed accurately – or nearly accurately – provides a couple of them. Another legend is that Sherman spared Madison because he found the town to be so lovely that he could not burn it. As he often does in his memoirs, Speed sheds light on yet another historical mystery in his explanation of why Sherman spared Madison.

Titles by Robert R. Peecher Jr.

Jackson Speed: The Hero of El Teneria
  Volume I of the Jackson Speed Memoirs
Jackson Speed and the Blood Tubs
  Volume II of the Jackson Speed Memoirs
Jackson Speed on the Orange Turnpike
  Volume III of the Jackson Speed Memoirs
Jackson Speed at the High Tide
  Volume IV of the Jackson Speed Memoirs
Jackson Speed and the Fugitive Slaves
  Volume V of the Jackson Speed Memoirs
Jackson Speed In the Rush
  Volume VI of the Jackson Speed Memoirs

Also by Robert Peecher:

**Four Things My Wife Hates About Mornings
  & Other Collected Stories**

Iron Curling Ale

Praise for Jackson Speed

"Great fun! … A picaresque romp through the Mexican American War."
   – Arthur Wayne Glowka, author of "The Texiad"

"Robert Peecher has a fine sense of balance, weighing farce against carnage in a uniquely entertaining style that is a delight to read. As in the two previous volumes, the reader is dared to disbelieve Speed is fictional while presented with a convincing forgery that he is not, wrapped in details famous and obscure about the intrigue and horrors of the American Civil War.."
   - Christopher Botkin, author of "Water Music"

"Robert Peecher has done great work with Jackson Speed."
   - Readers' Favorite

"Peecher's humorous style builds a character of questionable integrity that the reader grows to like."

"The history is true and the fiction is fun."

"The quick and engaging dialogue pulled me in from the first couple of sentences, and the compelling, well-paced style in which the action scenes were written kept me always eager to see what would happen next. Jackson Speed was fun to explore as a character; his voice is playful and a bit mysterious as he invites the reader into his memories."

"I found this book difficult to put down as I wanted to quickly find out what would happen next to our not so loveable antihero."
   - Amazon Reader Reviews

Follow the author and get updates on the next Jackson Speed novel:
ROBERTPEECHER.COM

Made in the USA
Monee, IL
25 May 2020

31830143R00193